# Praise For Karen Hancock's Novels:

## The Light of Eidon

Karen Hancock has a gift for creating believable characters on harrowing spiritual quests. This adventure takes place in an imagined history that is sometimes eerie and foreign, sometimes startlingly familiar, but always thought-provoking. Plainly, this is the first book in a major new series.

—Kathy Tyers, author of the FIREBIRD Trilogy

Karen Hancock fits that small niche reserved for today's finest novelists as she implants solid truth into words with which I can identify, words that fascinate and cut to the heart. *The Light of Eidon* is far more than a novel of fantasy or allegory—it is a word picture of the ancient struggle between Light and darkness.

—Hannah Alexander, author of *Urgent Care* and *The Crystal Cavern*

## Arena

"Hancock's intense debut is an excellent . . . contribution to the genre. . . . If this book is any indication, the future should be bright for this promising novelist."

—*Publisher's Weekly*

"Good contemporary Christian allegory is rare, but this first-time novelist delivers an engrossing, well-paced contribution to the genre. . . . The genuinely enthralling mix of adventure, romance, and vivid imagery fused with spirtual symbolism invites readers to lose themselves in Hancock's imaginary world."

—*Christianity Today*

"In evangelical fiction's best science fiction of the year, Hancock works out a progression of faith by trial somewhat like *Pilgrim's Progress.* But she departs from the conventions of allegory to draw her characters in depth, and the flora and fauna of her arid alien landscape are carefully thought through."

—*Booklist* Top Ten Christian Novels 2002

"A classic in the making for the modern era . . ."

—*Library Journal*

# Books by Karen Hancock

*Arena*

LEGENDS OF THE GUARDIAN-KING
*The Light of Eidon*

03C

LEGENDS OF THE GUARDIAN-KING

KAREN HANCOCK

# THE LIGHT OF EIDON

BETHANYHOUSE
MINNEAPOLIS, MINNESOTA

*The Light of Eidon*


Cover illustration by Bill Graff/Peter Glöege
Cover design by Lookout Design Group, Inc.



Published by Bethany House Publishers
11400 Hampshire Avenue South
Bloomington, Minnesota 55438
www.bethanyhouse.com

Bethany House Publishers is a Division of
Baker Book House Company, Grand Rapids, Michigan.

Printed in the United States of America

**Library of Congress Cataloging-in-Publication Data**

Hancock, Karen.
The light of Eidon / by Karen Hancock.
p. cm. — (Legends of the guardian-king)
ISBN 0-7642-2794-7 (pbk.)
I. Title. II. Series: Hancock, Karen. Legends of the guardian-king.
PS3608.A698L54 2003
813'.6—dc21 2003002568

KAREN HANCOCK graduated in 1975 from the University of Arizona with bachelor's degrees in Biology and Wildlife Biology. Along with writing, she is a semi-professional watercolorist and has exhibited her work in a number of national juried shows. She, her husband, and their son, whom Karen home-schooled for eight years, reside in Arizona.

For discussion and further information, Karen invites you to visit her Web site at *www.kmhancock.com*.

# ACKNOWLEDGMENTS

Every good gift comes from above.

I consider it an awesome gift that the Lord has seen fit to put this book into print, and I know that apart from Him, it never could have happened. Whatever talent, ability, time, energy, training, and insights I might have used to produce it have all come from Him. Part of that provision has been the many people He has used to help me along the way, both in the writing and in making a way for it to be published. Thank you . . .

First and foremost, to Robert B. Thieme Jr., under whose ministry I studied when this book was begun, and to Robert R. McLaughlin, under whose ministry I study now. Their faithful study and teaching of the Word of God have produced the lifeblood of my spiritual growth and enabled the function of my gift. Apart from the inculcation of the Word of God, I'd have given up long ago and would have little to say.

Second, to my husband, Stuart, who started the whole thing rolling with his suggestion that I write a book, who supported me all along the way, and who has given me the precious gift of time in which to write.

To my dear friends, Nancy Belt, Donna Henley, and Kelli Nolan, whose unswerving devotion to our Lord and His Word have been a refreshment and encouragement more times than I can count. I stand in awe to have been blessed with friends like you.

To Kathy Tyers, who has traveled this writing road with me from the beginning. Your gifts of encouragement, comradeship, and critical evaluation have been invaluable—to say nothing of the doors you have opened for me!

To Steve Laube, for courage, commitment, and vision. And to Karen

Schurrer, for insightful editing and an unwaveringly gracious attitude. You have both been a joy to work with.

Thanks to all the folks at Bethany House: Carol, Steve, Dave, Brett, Teresa, Jeanne, Alison, Joel, and the many others who are part of the team. I am amazed by and deeply grateful for all the work you do.

Thanks to Brandilyn Collins, Karlene Price, and Randi Durham for your gracious efforts in getting the word out on *Arena*; and to all the others who have given away copies and urged their friends to read it. You are the best marketers in the world.

Special thanks to the many readers who send me letters or e-mails. Your kind words, prayers, and encouragement are priceless.

And, finally, to those who have helped me with this book along the way, both knowingly and unknowingly, from critiquing to encouragement to agenting to advising to providing example: Wanda June Alexander, Donna Joy Boxerman, Liz Danforth, Deanna Durbin, Suzanne Farris, Roberta Gellis, Robert Herder, Dean Koontz, Adele Leone, Jeanette Ratzlaff, Linda Smith, Mike Stackpole, Edward Willett. Thank you. It's been a long road, and I have not forgotten your kindnesses.

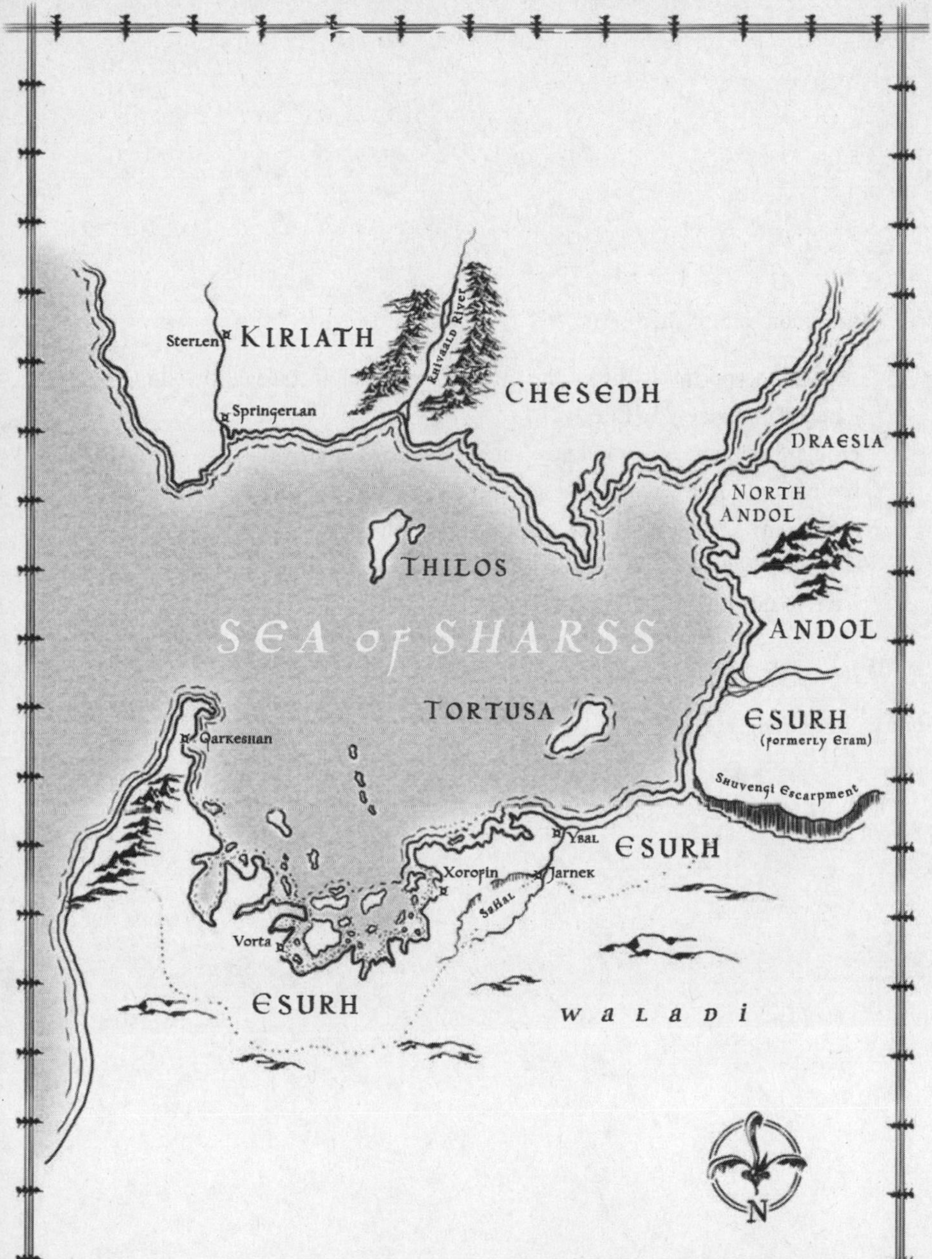
Sterlen
KIRIATH
Khivaald River
Springerlan
CHESEDH
DRAESIA
NORTH
ANDOL
THILOS
SEA of SHARSS
ANDOL
TORTUSA
ESURH
(formerly Eram)
Qarkeshan
Shuvengi Escarpment
Ybal
ESURH
Xorofin
Jarnek
Sahal
Vorta
ESURH
WALADI
N

And Eidon said to them,

"I will grant you my Light by the blood of my Son, and it will dwell in your hearts and give you Life.
Through my Light will you know me.
Through my Light will I shield and bless you.
Through my Light will you stand against the Shadow.
Reach out, therefore, and close your hand upon it, that you may be made alive, and My Power become yours."

—From the *Second Word of Revelation*
*Scroll of Amicus*

# GUARDIANS
OF THE
# HOLY FLAMES

PART ONE

# CHAPTER 1

"Why do we serve the Flames?"

"To ward the realm from Shadow."

"Why must we guard our purity?"

"To keep the Flames strong and bright."

They sat cross-legged on the barge cabin's single, narrow bunk, facing each other—Novice and discipler—their voices alternating in a steady rhythm of question and answer that had gone unbroken for nearly an hour. Since the noon prayer service they had been reviewing the six codices of the First Guardian Station, codices Eldrin must know tomorrow for the final test of his novitiate. He had long since learned them so well he could answer without hesitation, but he didn't mind the repetition. Right now it was just the sort of superficial mental occupation he needed to keep his thoughts off . . . other things.

"What is the source of the Shadow?" asked his discipler, one bony, ink-stained finger pressed to the page of the open catechism in his lap.

"The arrogance of Moroq conceived it," Eldrin replied. "The passions of the flesh sustain it."

"Who is Moroq?"

"The dark son of Eidon and Lord Ruler of the rhu'ema. The Adversary. No man can stand against him, save One."

"And that One is?"

"Eidon, Lord of Light, Creator of All, Defender of Man. Soon may he come, and swift be his judgment."

The rhythm ended, and the silence that filled the void after it made Eldrin's ears ring. He noticed the heat again, the sweat trickling down his chest beneath his wool tunic, the stifling mantle of his long, unbound hair weighing on his back. A fitful breeze danced through the high, open portal in the bulkhead, carrying the river's dank odor and a disharmonious chorus of voices from the crowds on its bank. Thunder rumbled out of the distance.

Anxiety, held at bay by the long recitation, came oozing back. Soon they would be docking, disembarking, and marching up to the temple to begin the long ritual that would end with his initiation as a Guardian of the Holy Flames. Or not, if things went badly.

His discipler, Brother Belmir, smiled at him over small, round spectacles. "Flawless, as usual. Shall we do another?"

"I defer to your judgment, Brother." Eldrin uncrossed his legs and recrossed them in opposite order, wincing as feeling tingled back.

"We'll do a random selection, then." Belmir leafed through the catechism, yellowed pages just brushing the slender gray braid that dangled over his shoulder. He was a small, birdlike man, all bones and angles, with a deeply lined face and shrewd gray eyes behind the spectacles. He wore the four gold cords of his station at his left wrist and, at his throat, the ruby amulet all Guardians were granted upon acceptance into the Holy Brotherhood of the Mataio.

Tomorrow Eldrin should receive an amulet of his own.

It was a day he had anticipated for eight long years; now the closer it got, the more uneasy he became. What if he walked up to the lip of the great bronze brazier tomorrow and the Flames rejected him?

From the beginning people said he would fail. He came from a family of soldiers and kings, not peacemakers—purveyors of death and destruction, not healing. As heads of state, as commanders of armies, even with their own hands, his antecedents had spilled the blood of thousands. How dared he presume Eidon might overlook that?

*"You can't renounce your blood, boy,"* Brother Cyril had rasped at him in the Watch library the night before they'd left for Springerlan. The words had cycled through his mind ever since, eroding his confidence. Was he unfit? Was it only the infamous Kalladorne will—and pride—that had brought him this far? Were his recent, unsettling dreams, and the growing uneasiness they birthed, Eidon's way of warning him off? Or were they simply products of

his own fear, a dread that he would fail even in this?

"Eldrin?"

Belmir had resumed the catechism and was waiting for an answer. Eldrin flushed. "I beg your pardon, Brother. Could you repeat the question?"

Belmir lifted a bushy brow, then softly closed the book and removed his glasses. "I think we'll stop with the codices for now. Why don't you tell me what's troubling you?"

The heat in Eldrin's face mounted. *Was I that obvious*? He stared at his worn leather satchel lying on the floor by the bunk and groped for words.

"I've been . . . thinking about the Test," he said finally.

"And?"

He made himself look at the older man. "Is it true that if I approach the Flames unworthily, I might—"

"Unworthily? Sweet fires aloft, Eldrin! Surely you don't believe yourself unworthy!" His eyes narrowed. "Is this what Cyril said to you in the library the night before we left?"

"How did you know about Brother Cyril?"

Belmir shook his head, ignoring the question. "I'm surprised at you, Eldrin. Cyril's been babbling that 'tainted blood' nonsense for years, and you've never given it a thought. Why now, all of a sudden?"

*Because in forty-eight hours I'm going to prove once and for all which of us is right?*

"He's probably realized how far his prediction was off," Belmir continued, "and hopes to scare you into quitting. I doubt he'll admit he's wrong even after you've embraced the Flames and received your Calling. He can be as stubborn as a rusty hinge."

"He said my House is cursed," Eldrin murmured. "That I'll go mad if I attempt the Flames."

Belmir frowned, and for a moment Eldrin expected another outburst on Cyril's many shortcomings. Then the stern look softened and the older man shook his head. "There is no curse, Eldrin. It's true there was antagonism between your family and the Mataio once, but that is decades past." He snorted softly. "If Eidon wanted you out, do you think you'd still be here? Believe me, I didn't make it easy for you. The injustice, the abuse, the unreasonable demands—you took it all. Never lost your temper, never refused an order, never gave up. You've amazed me, frankly. And I must say I've never had a Novice more prepared or more devoted to Eidon than you are. Don't doubt yourself, son. Truth be told—"

A thunder of footfalls followed by the appearance of a first-year Novice in the doorway interrupted him. "Brother Belmir! Haverallans have come from the Keep, asking for you and Brother Eldrin."

"Haverallans?" Belmir frowned at the boy, closing the book. "What could they want?"

*When did we dock?* Eldrin wondered. Had he been so engrossed in his problems he hadn't noticed?

Belmir set the heavy catechism aside and got up to lift their woolen mantles from the hook by the door, tossing Eldrin's into his lap. "Make sure you pull up the cowl. We'll have to cross the open deck, and there's sure to be a crowd."

"Aye, there's a crowd," the boy assured them. "Even before we entered the city, people were lining up along the riverbanks. They're on barges and rooftops and all the bridges. And the square is packed."

"Wonderful," Eldrin murmured, shrugging on the mantle as he followed Belmir into the passageway.

This was the last stop before trip's end some two leagues yet downriver. Here, at Springerlan's outer edge, they were to pick up the thirty-six attendants required for the coming Procession, four for each of the nine Initiates already on board.

All thirty-six were milling on deck as Eldrin and Belmir stepped into the bright afternoon sunlight and pressed toward the barge's stern cabin. Risking a glance shoreward, Eldrin saw that their vessel was one of many moored along the walled, railed riverbank. A crane clanked and squealed as it lifted a half-ton hogshead from a neighboring barge to shore. Those who manned the machine were not working at full capacity, hampered as much by their own curiosity as by the crowd that jammed the square beyond them.

With a sigh, Eldrin ducked his head. The notion of traveling unnoticed hadn't seemed unreasonable at first. Being two feet taller now and eight years older, and with his blond hair grown to his waist, he looked nothing like the boy he'd been. Nor the soldier-prince his family would've made him. After years of being out of the public eye, who was likely to recognize him?

Apparently anyone who'd ever laid eyes on his now deceased father, King Meren, or any of the other Kalladornes—which seemed to be everyone. In every city along the river a crowd had awaited him or had gathered soon after his arrival to gawk and whisper in his wake. Not simply idlers, but farmers, merchants, craftsmen, their wives and children—people with other things to do. Yet they turned out in ever increasing numbers the closer he got to Springerlan, as if they regarded him as someone important—when he hadn't even been that as a prince.

The barge's stern cabin, considerably larger than Eldrin's sleeping cubicle, was cool and dimly lit. Four men awaited them, dark silhouettes against the pale light sneaking in around curtained windows.

Eldrin stopped just inside the door as Belmir crossed the room and bowed. "Glory to Eidon, and praise," he murmured.

"May his Flames burn forever," one of the strangers intoned. His voice was rich and musical, the kind of voice you took notice of.

They conferred quietly, and as Eldrin's eyes adjusted he examined the newcomers with interest. One was tall and blond and garbed in the brown habit of a Novice Initiate, though he was much older than the norm for that station; the other three wore the pale mantles and long, thick pigtails of full Guardians. Only by their rank cords could one discern their exalted status as members of the Order of St. Haverall, the most elite in all the Mataio.

The conversation ended. Sighing resignedly, Belmir turned to Eldrin. "I'm afraid you won't be participating in the Procession," he said.

Eldrin wondered if he had heard right.

"The High Father feels you'll be safer entering the city anonymously," his discipler added.

*Safer? Safer from what?*

Belmir gestured at the other men. "Brother Rhiad and his companions will escort you."

*How can I not participate in the Procession? It's part of the ritual. This is unheard of. . . .*

But the High Father's mandates carried the weight of a command from Eidon himself—so clearly, Eldrin had little choice.

He glanced unhappily at the one Belmir called Rhiad. A handsome man, his sharp features were softened by large brown eyes fringed with thick lashes. Silver-threaded black hair fell in a fat braid to his waist, and he wore more cords of rank than Eldrin could casually count. Seven or eight at least.

The Haverallan addressed him gravely. "Springerlan is in turmoil right now—warring factions, riots, worker uprisings. It's been like this for weeks. The river sectors have always been the worst for that, as you must know, and the Procession cuts right through them. Granted, the king's men are out in force today, but given the size of the crowds and the rumors concerning the political significance of your return . . . well, we thought it better to be discreet."

*Political significance of my return? What is going on?*

Rhiad did not elaborate. Instead he held out a gray mantle similar to what he and his Guardian companions wore. As Eldrin shrugged off his own mantle and replaced it with the gray one, the holy man continued. "We'll have to pass through the crowd to reach our coach. Make sure you keep your head down." He paused to study Eldrin intently, then added, "If anything does go wrong, you must do precisely as I command. No questions, no hesitation. Can you do that?"

Eldrin nodded.

Rhiad pulled up his cowl, his face disappearing into its depths. His companions did likewise, and the three of them herded Eldrin back out to the bright afternoon. The fourth man—the too-old Novice—stayed behind.

As they stepped onto the gangplank Eldrin had his first clear look at the square. Somber-tunicked commoners stood shoulder to shoulder, staring at the barge. Others hung out windows or clung to the warehouse roofs. He saw no women or children among them.

Thunder rumbled again, drawing his eye to the anvil of clouds now boiling over the escarpment rising beyond the city. It would rain before the afternoon ended. Not a good omen for the Procession.

Rhiad led him over the gangplank and onto the brick-paved bank. Bodies jostled around him, resisting his passage. The air hung thick and close. Forgotten feelings of claustrophobia welled in him, and he breathed a prayer for deliverance. Rhiad shoved ahead, calling for people to stand aside. Eldrin followed resolutely, staring at the Guardian's heels. Then a red-haired man lurched into the space between them, colliding with Eldrin and knocking him off balance. In the moment of recovery, Eldrin found himself staring down into a pair of shrewd brown eyes. They flicked across his features, then returned to meet his own eyes with a significance that told him he had been recognized.

Alarmed, Eldrin averted his face and pressed by the stranger, lengthening his stride to catch up with his guide as he braced for the cry that would betray his presence.

*His Light will be my protection. . . .*

Five steps. Ten. Twenty. Thunder growled again from over the escarpment. And still the cry did not go up. A stolen glance revealed they were nearly across the square. Could it be the man hadn't recognized him after all?

And then, ringing clearly over the muttering crowd, a voice cried, "There he is!"

Eldrin flinched, sick with dread, awaiting the worst. The man went on. "There on the bow. At the back of the group. It's Prince Abramm!"

Bewilderment gave way to sudden comprehension—the too-old blond "Novice" had come as a stand-in.

Other voices answered the first.

"No, it can't be. . . ."

"It is, I tell you. Look how tall he is."

Eldrin plunged forward, wobbly-kneed.

More voices lifted around him, confirming or contesting the identification as people pointed and elbowed each other. He was nearly to the coach when someone yelled, "Go back to your Watch, pigeon! So long as Eidon lives, *you'll* never touch the throne!"

Eldrin's step faltered. He looked around—in vain—for the speaker, then remembered himself and ducked his head. The crowd appeared as startled at the outburst as he was; dockworker and sightseer alike seemed held in a web of silent astonishment. Then a rumbling arose from the front ranks, resolving into cheering voices: "Hail Abramm! Hail Abramm!"

The rear of a dark, windowless coach loomed ahead. Rhiad made straight for its open side door and swung up into the cab. As Eldrin scrambled awkwardly after him, he risked a glance back at the barge, now in clear line of sight. Sure enough, the blond "Novice" stood on the foredeck with the other Initiates.

As Eldrin's momentum carried him into the coach his eye caught briefly on something else—a sight that burned in his brain even after he had slid to the far side of the thinly padded bench. The red-haired man who had bumped into him had climbed one of the nearby hogsheads and from that perch intently watched the holy men.

There could be no question of recognition.

The other Guardians climbed into the cab, one at Eldrin's side, one at Rhiad's. The door shut with a click. Rhiad knocked on the partition behind him, and the coach lurched into motion. The crowd's cries swelled to a roar, but whether angry or celebratory, Eldrin could not tell.

The coach moved slowly at first. A dim light poured through high, horizontal side slits, illumining the blank, tense faces of his companions. No one spoke.

Eldrin stared at the wooden partition behind Rhiad, reeling with the knowledge that something significant had just occurred, and he had not the faintest idea what it was.

*"You'll never touch the throne."*

It made no sense. Even if he had not renounced his titles, he was born fifth in the line of succession—no doubt further now, since his four older brothers must have sired sons in the last eight years. He owned no land, possessed no seat on the governing Table of Lords, and stood to inherit not one copper of his father's wealth. To make anything of his life, he'd been expected to enter the military and progress through the ranks. But he'd been an inept swordsman and disinclined to pursue a life of violence. Instead he'd followed the call to higher things, choosing religious orders.

His family had been aghast, mortified that one of their own should ally himself with the pacifist Holy Brethren. His father had disinherited him, an irrational form of punishment to be sure: How did you disinherit someone who stood to inherit nothing in the first place? It did, however, remove him from the line of succession. Perhaps that had been the king's true intent, though it seemed a paranoid one.

In less than two days now, Eldrin would seal his decision, progressing from the lowliest rank of Novice Initiate to the merely lowly rank of Initiate Brother. With seven holy stations yet to attain, he would still be a nobody and certainly no political threat to anyone.

As the coach gained speed, his companions relaxed, and soon Eldrin grew aware of Rhiad's appraisal, the cool, dispassionate gaze making him increasingly uncomfortable. He tried to ignore it, glad when the holy man finally spoke.

"Seeing you now, I understand what the fuss is about. You're not as brawny as your brothers, but it's obvious you're a Kalladorne. Excuse me—*were* a Kalladorne."

Since it was not Eldrin's place to make idle comments to or ask questions of his superiors, he said nothing.

The coach bumped, rumbling over a rough section of cobbles.

"Not that it matters, of course," Rhiad went on. "It's just that most folks believed you only entered the Mataio because there was nothing better for you outside. Now that that's changed, well, they get ideas."

"What do—" Eldrin choked off the impertinent question and stared into his lap. "Forgive me, Brother."

Inside he writhed with incomprehension, curiosity, frustration.

"No one's told you, have they?" Rhiad sounded surprised. "I suppose you had no need to know."

Eldrin looked up.

"About your father? Your brothers?"

"My father is dead." A cold nausea dropped into the pit of his stomach. *Surely they would have told me if my brothers had died, too.* But the starkly worded message that had brought him the news of his sire's passing had given no details. It had come at the start of his second year, totally unexpected, for his father had been a strong man in the prime of life. There was no mention of how he died, or where, the lack of detail making it all the more surreal.

Thereafter he'd received little word from home and the matter was forgotten, crowded out by the realities of life in the Watch. The few letters he did receive were all censored, of course. It was the duty of the Watch elders to protect him from distraction so he could concentrate on Eidon.

"Aarol died in the same incident as your father," Rhiad told him. "Elian followed three years later, Stefan six months after that."

*Aarol? Elian? Stefan? All dead?* Eldrin had never been close to his brothers, but the news stunned him all the same.

"For the last two and a half years, your brother Raynen has been king. And he is, as yet, childless. So you see"—Rhiad smiled briefly—"you are but a heartbeat from the throne."

Abruptly the coach slowed, stuttering over the bricks as it slued to one side and stopped. The Guardians sat forward, exchanging uneasy glances. A panel slid open in the wall behind Rhiad.

"We've got rioting ahead, Brothers," the driver said. Only his lips showed through the window.

Rhiad twisted to face the lips. "Can we go around?"

"We'll have to backtrack a ways. Uh-oh. Looks like they've seen us."

"Have we passed Ridge Street yet?" Rhiad asked.

"We're at the intersection now."

The Guardians looked at one another again, their concern escalating.

"Do you think it's staged?" one of them asked.

"Of course it is," Rhiad said softly. And then to the driver, "Get us out of here. Now. Go back to the wharf if need be."

Turning around was a tricky procedure—backing, going forward, backing again. They waited out the maneuvers in tense silence, flinching at the sudden cries that preceded a flurry of thumps against the side and top of the cab. More cries, more thumps, a scream of pain, another of rage. The coach finished its turning and started forward, only to stop again. A din of furious screaming rushed around them, accompanied by the crash of breaking glass and more thuds on the cab walls. It began to rock back and forth, gaining arc with every cycle.

"We'll be trapped in here," the Haverallan to Eldrin's left murmured.

Rhiad nodded. "As soon as it goes over, we'll open the door. Eldrin, stay with me. Do exactly as I say."

Eldrin nodded, heart pounding. He still had no idea what was happening—or why—but he knew it wasn't good. The coach reached the end of an arc and rocked back violently, to teeter on the edge of falling. The cascade of sound outside intensified; more hands thumped along the cab's wall, pushing it over with a crash. Eldrin's seatmate pinned him to the wall, which was now the floor. As they struggled free of each other, daylight speared the dark interior, and the other three Guardians scrambled out the door.

Eldrin was pulled up and shoved over the lip of the opening. He slid upright off the cab's edge to stand behind Rhiad. The three guards who had accompanied the coach had formed a wall against the mob, brandishing long, gleaming swords at men armed with clubs and rocks. Shielding Eldrin with his own body, Rhiad edged along the side of the fallen coach. A tomato hit the side of Eldrin's head, and then the swords were overcome by the sheer force of the crowd, bodies forcing the guards back in hand-to-hand struggle.

Rhiad shoved Eldrin sideways, then threw something small and white at the feet of the ruffians surging around the swordsmen. A column of lemon-colored smoke erupted from the cobbles where it hit, and the front-runners collapsed in apparent swoon a heartbeat later. As their companions recoiled in astonishment and alarm, Rhiad grabbed Eldrin and dashed for an alleyway looming between the brick buildings on the side away from the mob.

Seeing their prey escaping, the mob surged forward again. Another egg plumed yellow smoke, and three more men dropped. Eldrin inhaled a whiff of sulfur, and a wave of wooziness washed over him. Rhiad jerked him onward. He caught a glimpse of the Guardian's amulet flaring red with Eidon's protective light, saw men leaping toward the alleyway to cut off their escape—and then inexplicably slowing and stopping well short of the opening, staring at Rhiad as if they were enspelled.

A chill of awe rushed up Eldrin's spine.

*His Light will be my protection. . . .*

They were going to make it!

Then a rock bounced off the back of Rhiad's head, collapsing him to his knees, and the frozen men surged forward again, blocking off the alleyway. As Eldrin stepped to the Guardian's side, something slammed into the back of his own shoulder. He staggered forward, the rush of pain stealing his breath and loosing a sudden, furious aggression.

A rod struck him across the back, the new pain stoking the fire. Before he knew what he was doing, he'd grabbed the weapon on the second downswing, twisted it from his attacker's hands, and cocked it back, ready to swing. Only to find himself looking into a ring of shocked and frozen faces.

Their shock became his own.

*I will touch no weapon of warfare. His Light will be my protection.*

Horrified, he dropped the club. *Holy Eidon, what have I done?*

His tormentors leapt forward in a tide of stinking, filthy bodies; hands punched him, jerked him, shoved him. The furious clamor of their voices assaulted his ears. Nearby a horseman pressed his mount in Eldrin's direction, beating the rioters off with his quirt.

Then something crashed into the side of Eldrin's head and the world spun. His ears rang, his knees collapsed, and white light exploded in his brain, enveloping him as the ground flew up to jar the wind from him. Sucking air, he struggled to hands and knees, fighting to stay conscious. His hair slid forward around his face and arms like a veil, hot blood flowing down the side of his neck and dripping onto the cobbles. Bands of fire wrapped his chest as he braced for more blows.

Instead hard hands dug into his shoulders and closed round his legs, lifting him upward as someone stuffed a rag in his mouth. He struggled to breathe past the obstruction and the smothering veil of his own hair, seeking vainly to free himself as the light in his brain flared, burning everything away.

## CHAPTER

# 2

Eldrin awoke as a deafening crack of thunder rolled across the city, rattling windows and shingles. He lay on his side, wrists bound behind him and pressed between his back and a cold stone wall. Wet cobbles dug into his shoulder and head, and the pungence of smoke and damp wool was all but suffocating. His head pounded rhythms of outrage; beneath that pulsed various lesser aches from shoulder, back, and ribs.

He stared at the backs of his eyelids, breathing slowly, trying to move his awareness past the symphony of pain to his surroundings.

Where was he? What had happened? Had they left him for dead?

A faint rhythmic clicking answered the unvoiced questions.

He cracked his eyelids.

Stone walls soared around him, reaching up to narrow clerestories that let in the dim light of an afternoon darkened by storm. Bales of cream-colored wool stacked ten high filled the main space and formed the fourth wall of the ten-foot pocket in which he lay, clearly the back end of some Southdock warehouse. A veil of smoke hung in the air.

Two men crouched near the base of the stacked bales, gambling at kadfli, the gold-tipped black wands clicking softly as they were tossed onto the cobbles. The men bent to study the fall, murmuring over the results. Then one of them laughed and scooped up the wands with a scab-covered arm to begin another round.

Outside thunder rumbled again and raindrops briefly spattered the roof.

From this vantage Eldrin could not see his captors' faces. They were rough, working-class men clad in dirty homespun tunics and britches. Their hair was long and tangled, their beards unkempt. Sheathed short-blades dangled at their belts beside scarred coin pouches, the latter hanging in empty folds.

Not far from them a rat emerged from a pile of loose wool and stopped to watch them, its whiskered nose working, eyes shining like ebony stickpins. When they ignored it, it scurried forward, keeping to the shadows along the wall until it left Eldrin's field of sight.

One of his captors loosed a crow of victory, recapturing Eldrin's attention. As the other man leaned back in apparent disgust, light flashed off something on his chest, and Eldrin stared, slowly going cold with recognition. It was a golden shield, fused into the man's flesh by the power of no man. The mark was an indelible visible sign of the evil to which its bearer had sold his soul, the mark of those called Terstans.

Servants of the Adversary, Terstans hated the Flames above all else. If they had their way, there would be no Flames, no Brotherhood, no Mataio at all. They blasphemed the tenets of Holy Writ, ridiculed the work of the Guardians, and scoffed at the power of the Flames to protect. Only their own power, they claimed, would save Kiriath.

But all their power did was drive them mad, corrupt their bodies, and eventually kill them.

These two already sported the telltale boils on arms and faces, and even from where he lay, Eldrin saw the ring of white curd encircling the irises of the man facing him. Eventually that curd would fill his eye sockets; his spine would twist and bend; his hands would stiffen into claws. Then his organs would fail, passing his suffering soul straight to the arms of his Master in Torments.

Though this was the closest Eldrin had ever come to these servants of evil, he had long been warned of their guile, their perversity, their tenacious antagonism to the truth. Terstans had been a blight to the realm for centuries. Some Mataians considered them the cause of all Kiriath's troubles, wanted them cast out—even killed—if they wouldn't renounce their heresy. Of all the sects in Springerlan, the Terstans had most reason to fear Eldrin.

*"Your brothers are dead . . . you stand but a heartbeat from the throne."*

Wearing the crown, he could easily revoke the laws protecting freedom of faith and see the Terstans destroyed or driven from the realm. No wonder they'd kidnapped him. He was surprised they hadn't killed him. Did they hope to convert him? To ensnare him in their evil and brand their mark upon his chest against his will?

He shut his eyes, shuddering. *His Light will be my refuge.*

*Click, click.*

*Please, my Lord Eidon. You know my heart. I only want to serve you, however that may be.*

*Even,* he asked himself grimly, *if it's to give your life for your faith?*

He shuddered again, praying he would find the will to endure if it came to that.

A faint, frantic *scritch-scritch-scritch* erupted from somewhere beyond the top of his head. Fluffs of wool floated out into his field of vision. The rat again. It paused in its rustlings as thunder rumbled and the rain spatter increased. Then a flurry of tiny clicks raced toward Eldrin, and the creature burst into sight, inches from his face. It stopped to sniff and lick a dark bloodstain on the cobbles. His blood.

The rodent drew closer, eyes bright, whiskers quivering. Fat, gray, smelling of sewage, it seemed bigger close up. Its nose touched his brow, his eye; a delicate paw rested on his nose.

With a cry of revulsion Eldrin lurched backward, slamming his head into the wall behind him. Stars wheeled past his vision as across the floor the Terstans' heads swiveled round.

"He's awake," one muttered.

The other started toward him, and the rat scurried away. In a moment the two men stood over him. Both had the curd in their eyes. Eldrin watched them warily, expecting to be kicked or spat upon.

"Guess he's gonna make it," the older one said in a deep, time-roughened voice.

"He doesn't *look* dangerous," the younger one commented.

"Looks mean nothing, Jafeth," his companion said. He had a bulbous nose and piglike eyes. "This skinny idiot could bring down the whole realm."

Jafeth shifted uncomfortably. "Do you suppose they're still looking for him?"

"Aye, they're lookin'."

"If they find us, I mean, with him and all—"

"They willna find us." The bigger man headed back for the bales.

"They'll kill us if they do, won't they?"

"They willna find us."

"But—"

"It's the *storm*, Jafeth!" the older man cried sharply. "By the Words, think! The birds want to go to ground. Even if they force 'em, the wind and rain will make 'em nearly useless. All they have right now is human legs and eyes. And thousands of places to search. They willna find us."

A blinding flash attended by a wall-shaking crack punctuated his claim. Then the heavens opened in earnest and the roar of a violent downpour obliterated all other sound. Rain pounded the roof, gusted against the windows, and smacked the streets outside. The Terstans paused, apparently to appreciate its intensity, then returned to their game.

Eldrin lay still, sick with dread. He did not know what all the talk of birds meant—probably nothing; all Terstans were mad—but he did know the man was right about the number of potential hiding places in Southdock and the limitations of human legs. It could be hours, even days, before he was found.

The storm continued for some time, lightning and thunder rolling back and forth across the wide valley in which the royal city of Springerlan sprawled. Eldrin's hands went to sleep first, then his arms. His neck ached like fury, but when he tried to sit up to ease it, he found himself unable, could only lie in his own blood and misery and pray. *His Light will be my refuge. His name will be my joy.*

Eventually the celestial fireworks ended and the rain eased. Jafeth disappeared into the growing darkness and soon returned with a lantern, a loaf of bread, and a jug. The lantern he hung from a rod jammed between the bales of wood. The food and drink he shared with his companion.

Far off across the bay, the cannon at Kildar Fortress boomed, signaling day's end. By now Eldrin had added a powerful thirst to his list of discomforts and, ironically, the desperate need to relieve himself. He had been squirming and trying not to moan for some minutes when the older Terstan suddenly looked round at him, glaring. "What's the matter with you?"

In a rasping voice, Eldrin explained his need.

The Terstan glowered at him for a long time, Jafeth watching warily. Then he grunted and picked up the jug. " 'Fraid you'll have to wet yourself, highness," he sneered. He considered a moment, then started to chuckle. The jug gurgled as he lifted it and took a long swig.

Watching him drink was torture. Eldrin swallowed on a raw throat and closed his eyes. A sudden crash followed by a rumble of footfalls and jingling metal jerked them open again, in time to see his two guards spring to their feet. A moment later three men burst from the dark aisle between wool bales and wall, rapiers drawn. Eldrin's captors sprang to cut them off.

"Meridon!" the older one grated.

"What have you done with him?!" the lead swordsman—apparently Meridon—demanded. "If you've killed him, so help me—"

"We're no murderers," the big Terstan protested. "If anythin' we saved his life."

"After putting it in danger to begin with!" Meridon, rapier still drawn, peered around the Terstan's shoulder, and Eldrin got another shock. It was the red-haired man he'd seen at the wharf.

"So what do you intend to do with him now that you have him?" Meridon asked.

"Sell him, o' course."

A moment of silence followed. Meridon's voice, when it came, sounded strangled. "By the Words, man! He's the king's brother!"

"He's the Mataio's pawn. And do na say you wouldn't be happy if he disappeared."

"It'd be a death sentence."

Finally Eldrin grasped what they intended and the shock overwhelmed his poor bladder, a warm dampness permeating the front of his robe. He was not to be converted but rather sold to Thilosian slavers and borne across the sea to the lands of the south.

"He's too skinny for the Games," the Terstan said. "And he can read and write. He'll sell as a scribe right off. That's na so bad a life."

"Assuming they don't guess who he really is," Meridon said grimly.

"How would they guess?"

"One look at his face and it's obvious."

"To a Kiriathan maybe, but how many Thilosians know Kiriathan royalty?"

"Their queen is a Kalladorne," Meridon pointed out. "They'd get top price from the Esurhites for him." He paused. "Do you have any idea what *they* would do with a prince of Kalladorne blood? Especially one as weak as he?"

Eldrin shut his eyes again, choking on his terror. *Sweet Elspeth, have mercy! Lord Eidon, please, not that!*

The Terstan said nothing.

"You know I can't let you do this," Meridon said softly. "Make it easy for me, and I'll tell the king you got away."

Trembling, seized with a deep nausea, Eldrin listened and prayed and went limp with relief when the Terstan sighed and apparently gave in. He heard a receding shuffle, and when he looked again only Meridon and his two companions remained. The men sheathed their rapiers and Meridon stepped to Eldrin's side, bending over him and slicing through the bonds on his wrists with his dagger. Then strong hands gripped his shoulders, lifting him up to a sitting position.

"Rest easy, my lord," his rescuer said as Eldrin's world kaleidoscoped around him. "It'll pass."

When at last Eldrin dared open his eyes, the first thing he saw was the bloody river that soaked the left side of his tunic. He touched his ear and stared at the blood on his fingertips.

"Scalp wounds bleed like fury," Meridon said. "Seem worse than they are."

Eldrin blinked up at him. He was definitely the man from the dock, though he appeared younger than Eldrin had first thought him. Freckles spattered his upturned nose, and wide brown eyes might have imparted a look of scampish innocence were they not so cold and hard.

He wore the short-cropped hair of a rank-and-file soldier, and in addition to the sheathed rapier, a shorter blade hilted with the golden likeness of a ram's head was scabbarded at his right hip. The hand resting on its hilt was callused and webbed with the scars of constant sword work. His leather jerkin was likewise scored from longtime abuse and stained now with fresh blood.

"Captain Trap Meridon, at your service, my lord," Meridon said coolly. "With the King's Guard."

*King's Guard? No wonder the Terstan had given in.*

"You were at the dock."

Meridon eased back on one booted heel, resting a hand on the opposite upraised knee. His expression was stony, his eyes like flint. "We figured they'd take you off early. So did the others, apparently."

"The Terstans, you mean?"

Meridon nodded.

Eldrin fingered the cut again. "I don't understand," he said finally. "I've been disowned. I'm out of the succession. Even if I hadn't renounced it all, I'm still ineligible."

Meridon's eyes hooded. "The Table of Lords voted six months ago to restore your inheritance."

Eldrin stared at him, nausea clawing once more at his gut. Blood pounded a tympani in his ears. The iron bands were back on his chest.

"You didn't know," Meridon said.

Eldrin shook his head. "I only learned about my brothers this afternoon." *"You had no need to know."* He swallowed. "Well, it changes nothing. Once I have touched the Flames and taken my vows, I will return to Haverall's Watch, and that will be the end of it."

Meridon raised a mocking red brow. "I doubt very much you will return to Haverall's Watch, my lord." He exchanged a glance with his dark-bearded companions. "Forgive my bluntness, Your Highness, but the measure to reinstate you was sponsored by lords of *Mataian* persuasion. They pushed it through the Table with the High Father's blessing. Don't tell me you aren't destined for more than meditations in a distant Watch tower."

He held up a hand, stopping Eldrin's indignant protest.

"Think, my lord Abramm," he said forcefully, no longer bothering to hide his impatience. "Do you not find it significant that your father and all the brothers between you and the Crown save one have died? And that, only since *you* joined the Mataio?"

Gooseflesh crawled up the backs of Eldrin's arms. "What are you saying, Captain?"

"That your kinsmen were murdered, my lord. And Raynen will follow, once you take your final vows."

Eldrin looked away from Meridon's piercing gaze, glanced uneasily at the other men, then at the bales of dirty wool. The rat had returned, watching warily from within the shadow.

"You'll be granted special dispensation to rule," Meridon went on. "The Guardian-King who will deliver the realm from evil. There's already talk of it, and at the rate Beltha'adi is expanding his empire down south, it won't be long before the realm may well *need* a deliverer."

Eldrin stared at the soldier in spite of himself, part of him incensed, deriding the notion, another part held in horrified abeyance. It was possible. The High Father had the power to grant such dispensation. And everyone knew that the ancient, allegedly immortal Lord Beltha'adi and his soldiers of the Black Moon served the Adversary—steadily expanding his kingdom of darkness and tyranny with their might. But it went against all he believed in, all he had built his life upon these last eight years.

"I seek only to serve Eidon," he said. "I don't want to be king."

Again that mocking brow came up. "Not even if the High Father told you it was Eidon's will?"

Eldrin did not answer. That would never come to pass. He could accomplish far more in Eidon's service as a full Guardian, nurturing and protecting his Flames in the Keep, than he could playing politics on the throne. "What are you going to do with me?"

"What do you *want* me to do with you, my lord?"

"Bring me to the Keep."

"Very well." Meridon stood and offered him a hand, his eyes still cold.

Eldrin almost refused his help, but rising turned out to be harder than he expected. Reluctantly he grasped the man's hand, the palm hard and rough, the grip steel-strong. Meridon hauled him to his feet. The world swam briefly, then settled.

Eldrin loosed a breath and straightened the tunic around his bony frame, cringing with distaste and mortification as he recalled how the garment had come to be so wet.

"This way, my lord."

"Captain, I am not your 'lord.' My name is Eldrin now."

Meridon regarded him stonily, then turned away with a snort. He headed toward the dark aisle, only to stop and fling his dirk into the shadowed corner behind them. A screech pierced the building's heavy silence as in the corner the rat squirmed out its life, impaled by the captain's blade.

Meridon walked over to it, removed the dirk, wiped it on his britches, then continued wordlessly on his way.

Eldrin swallowed, trailing his guide more reluctantly than ever.

Meridon brought him to the Avenue of the Keep without incident, stepping out a mere twenty feet from the Keep's tall wrought-iron gates. "Here you are, my lord. I recommend you not venture into Southdock after this. You might not be so fortunate next time."

"If I ever go there again, it will be too soon," Eldrin assured him. "Thank you for your help."

The soldier bowed, his sword scabbard jingling. "Good night, Your Highness."

"One thing more, Captain—"

Half turned, Meridon glanced back.

"If you honestly believe those things you told me," Eldrin said, "why didn't you let them sell me to the slavers? From your standpoint it would seem the practical thing to do."

Meridon's dark eyes narrowed. "Because you are the king's brother. And because he still has hope you will change your mind." He hesitated; then that mocking brow came up and he added, "If it is truly Eidon you seek, my lord, you are looking in the wrong place." He bowed again and walked into the night.

Eldrin watched him go, at first in shock, then in rising anger. Looking in the wrong place? How dare he! Did he think being captain of the King's Guard gave him leave to spout blasphemies?

Thunder growled as another gust of sprinkles spattered the already wet cobbles. Drawing a deep breath to calm himself, Eldrin turned back toward the Keep looming on the hill above him, the white square forms of its library and dormitory flanking the gleaming, gold-plated dome of the Holy Sanctum. The dome's mullioned glass pinnacle glowed redly against the dark sky, revealing the everlasting light of the Sacred Flames within.

*Looking in the wrong place indeed! And where else would I look, Captain Meridon? Shall I ask the Terstans?*

He frowned as a sudden notion occurred to him—Meridon had spared the kidnappers, had been almost solicitous to them, when he should've killed them or at the least arrested them for having threatened a member of the royal family. Moreover the kidnappers had clearly known him better than would be expected of a pair of Southdock ruffians. And hadn't the one said that Meridon would be as happy as they to see Eldrin gone? He thought of the man's hard eyes, the cold distaste in his manner, the clear communication that he did not like Eldrin or anything that Eldrin represented. *"If it is truly Eidon that you seek, my lord, you are looking in the wrong place."*

Was it possible that Meridon was. . . ? No. Raynen would never allow a man so openly allied with the Evil One to command his own guard.

A gust of wind whipped around him, lifting his hair over his shoulders and piercing the thin weave of his tunic. Shivering, he hurried up the sidewalk toward the Keep's iron gates.

Inside he was welcomed with open arms, Rhiad and his men having returned after a fruitless search to gather a larger force. Belmir was there as well, and Eldrin learned he was not the only Initiate to have had a bad day. As feared, the Procession had been disrupted by rioting and somehow a fire had gotten started. The flames and smoke had sent half the Initiates scurrying for the Keep, while the other half retreated to the safety of the barge. The storm had put out the fire and doused the riot, but the ceremony was in a shambles.

Bathed and wearing a fresh tunic, Eldrin was with Belmir in one of the private chapels recounting what had happened—and confessing his many sins—when Rhiad burst in upon them, trailed by his two shadows and demanding to know if it was really Captain Meridon who had rescued him.

Annoyed in spite of himself, Eldrin breathed out a long breath and said that it was. "Or at least that's who he claimed to be."

A simple description convinced Rhiad the man was indeed Meridon, and the three Guardians exchanged grim glances.

"Saints, they're getting subtle," one of them murmured.

"You know this Meridon?" Belmir asked.

Rhiad grimaced. "Captain of the King's Guard? Who doesn't?" He looked at Eldrin. "Meridon's as much a Terstan as the men he rescued you from—if it *was* a rescue."

"You're saying it was staged?" Belmir asked.

"Of course it was staged. Meridon probably wanted to get to him alone." He turned to Eldrin again. "I'll wager he filled your ear with all manner of crazy stories, too—about your family being murdered and the High Father wanting the Crown?"

Eldrin stared up at him in surprise.

Rhiad chuckled. "Yes, I see he did. That tale's been around for years." He shook his head. "The evidence doesn't support the theory, though. There are no suspects, nothing to indicate anything but that the deaths were accidental. And your father and Aarol were most certainly not murdered by a man. Their mauling is well documented."

"Then how can they claim—?"

He shrugged. "They're all mad. And they lie as easily as they speak."

"I don't understand," Eldrin said. "Why would my brother make a Terstan the captain of his own guard?"

Rhiad lifted a dark brow. "Because your brother is a Terstan himself." He smiled at Eldrin's unveiled shock. "Don't tell anyone, though. He still believes it's a secret."

CHAPTER

# 3

Eldrin jerked awake and back to the reality of the cold stone beneath his knees, the draft at his back, the flickering oil lamp on the stand before him. Heart drumming, he groped at his chest, shuddering with relief when his fingers slid over smooth skin. There was no shieldmark. It was only a nightmare.

He sagged back onto his heels, wincing at the painful tingling in his legs. Afterimages roiled in his mind: his hands reaching into flames, a searing flash of red, an overpowering sense of evil that seized him and burned a Terstan's shield of heresy onto his chest before he could pull away.

Eldrin swallowed hard, stroking the thin, hairless skin over his breastbone as the images faded into the familiar reality of the Penitent Cell's stone walls. He had confessed his fear and anger to Belmir last night, his discipler transferring the sins to the *aergon* for judgment. Once laden with sin, the hand-long consecrated oak slats were then cast into the great Flames and consumed. His penance was a night's worth of prayer, meditation, and praise in one of the solitary cells surrounding the Great Sanctum.

The lamp guttered, the yellow droplet of flame perched precariously on its lip. In the distance, the university clock tolled: one, two, three, four. Outside, up under the eaves, pigeons rustled and cooed, and the faint tang of the sea drifted down to him.

This was not the first time he had dreamed of the Flames finding him unworthy, especially of late, but it was by far the worst. To have dreamed they made him a Terstan? It was an unthinkable, hideous blasphemy and deeply shaming. No truly worthy Initiate would conjure such a heresy, even in his sleep.

And certainly yesterday's events revealed serious flaws in his character. When he'd grabbed that rod from his assailant he'd had every intention of hurting someone, eagerly feeding the power of Eidon's enemy with his own malicious passions.

It was reprehensible, disgusting. It was also a typical Kalladorne reaction.

He shuddered, nauseated with the conviction that despite what Belmir said, he didn't have what it took to be a true Guardian after all. That that was why he was the only Initiate Eidon had not yet touched in meditations. Because he was unworthy and always would be.

He closed his eyes, feeling a sudden tightness in his chest. The thought of living past the death of his dream was unbearable.

*Oh, Lord Eidon, you above all others must know my desire is genuine. Please,* please *let me know you.*

He had wanted this for eighteen years, remembering the day the desire had been kindled within him as if it were yesterday. He'd been playing with his sister, Carissa, in the garden. Hot and tired, he'd flopped onto the grass beside their nurse and stared at the sky.

"Is Eidon behind those clouds?" he had asked the nurse.

She hadn't known but thought perhaps he was.

"Well, then," Abramm persisted, "how can he be in the Flames, too?"

"He is everywhere," the nurse said, returning to her needlework. "And anyway, it's Tersius, his Son, who's in the Flames, not Eidon himself."

Abramm had asked more questions, but mostly the nurse did not know the answers and, more important, did not care. When she began to speak irritably, he asked no more and addressed the clouds instead. *Are you up there, Lord Eidon? Nurse says you can hear my thoughts. If you can, well, I'm pleased to meet you, sir.* He had waited a bit and sighed with resignation when no response came. He was only three, and clearly Lord Eidon, like Abramm's own father, was much too busy and important to speak to little boys. Perhaps when he was older . . .

Years later Abramm's mother, a devout Mataian, had invited young Brother Saeral to come to the palace as spiritual instructor for her children, and from the start Abramm had considered him a personal savior sent by Eidon himself. A weak and sickly child, more given to scholarship than athletics, Abramm was the unhappy exception in a family where physical prowess was the measuring stick of worth. The more disappointing he became as a soldier-prince, the more he was drawn to Brother Saeral and the spiritual comforts he offered. Bright and eager, the young prince excelled in theology, learning verses and doctrines effortlessly. While his siblings tried every imaginable ploy to avoid religious edification, Abramm memorized much of the First Word of Revelation and scatterings of the Second.

Finally, at the age of thirteen, grieving over the unexpected death of his mother and faced with the prospect of entering Barracks to begin the military training traditional for a Kalladorne prince, Abramm defied tradition by renouncing his titles and entering the Guardian Novitiate instead. His family erupted in a storm of outrage, but he would not be swayed.

He could still recall the feel of the razor sliding over his skull in the initiation ritual on that first day, stripping away his blond locks in a visible sign of all he had given up: his clothing, his pleasures, his noble titles—all that had made up his former life. Delighted to exchange Prince Abramm for Eldrin, he'd felt a fierce, hot joy in his chest, and never had he been so certain he had made the right choice.

During the next eight years, secluded in Haverall's Watch, he labored diligently to conform to Eidon's standards, careful to observe every commandment, accepting the injustices and harsh disciplines with equanimity, knowing the pride of royal blood required extra effort to deflate. Sometimes he even inflicted the disciplines upon himself, for only he knew how flawed he really was, and he wanted desperately to be found acceptable, to find at last that which would satisfy the thirst that had driven him since he was three.

Until a week ago he had been confident he would find it.

Then the doubts began.

*Not everyone is suited to this life.*

*There is no shame in changing one's mind.*

*One cannot help the blood one is born with, but one must recognize reality when one sees it.*

The thoughts spawned a fear that he would always be unworthy, no matter how hard he worked. Yet the desire to know Eidon remained, and had not his teachers assured him such desires were planted by Eidon himself, the call upon those who would be his servants?

Perhaps his dream had been only a warning that he hadn't worked hard enough to purge himself of the extra measure of Kalladorne pride.

A tenuous hope brightened. At dawn, when his penance period ended, he would go before the Flames to fast and pray and meditate until the final veil of corruption was stripped from his soul, and he would not leave until it was done.

The final hour passed with agonizing slowness, but at last the morning bells rang and he was free. Pulling his ragged Initiate's mantle from its hook, he headed straight for the Great Sanctum.

Not having seen the place in the eight years of serving his novitiate, he was unprepared for its jaw-dropping size, the massive bowl seeming wider, deeper, and more magnificent than he recalled. Concentric descending levels encircled a central tiered dais of white marble. In the midst of this lay the Well of Flames, crimson tongues licking upward in the darkness.

Formed when Eidon's son, Tersius, had given himself over to death and transformation outside Xorofin almost a thousand years ago, the Flames required no oil, no wood, no fuel at all save the sacrifices and purity of the Guardians sworn to keep them. Though they could not cook a meal nor warm a weary traveler, they remained Kiriath's most valuable asset, guarding her borders against the evil that continually sought egress.

Since Moroq and his rhu'ema could not function in the presence of Eidon's Light, it was the Adversary's intent to wrap the world in arcane shadow. For centuries a permanent fog had covered the southern deserts, and even now his servants—men in the form of the great Esurhite armies of the Black Moon—were slowly spreading it into the lands east of the Sea of Sharss and northward toward Kiriath. Without her Guardians to keep the Flames alive, Kiriath would be swallowed up like the others, no matter how great her army or her king.

Removing his sandals at the door, Eldrin descended into the silence. The aura of the Flames' ancient power rippled across his flesh with an eerie sense of awareness, as if the eye of Eidon himself watched him as he approached.

At the lowest level he knelt behind the guardrail of the white marble moat and gazed into the living, leaping fingers of flame, five strides away and towering above him. Scarlet, russet, and crimson danced around deeper tones of purple and royal blue, a never-ending metamorphosis of shape and line and color that snared the eye and drew the mind into their depths. *"The depths,"* said the Second Word, *"of Eidon himself."*

"Your Light is my refuge," Eldrin murmured. "Your Words are my sustenance. Your Name is my joy. . . ."

"Eldrin?"

The voice startled him, then pierced his heart in a flood of memories. He leapt up to face the man who had come up beside him—and faltered in uncertainty. Dressed in the standard linen robe and mantle of any mid-level, rank-and-file Guardian, the man wore no ornamentation save the softly glowing amulet at his throat. Nothing indicated exalted rank; the usual wrist cords were missing altogether. His cowl hung in limp folds around his shoulders, baring a head of silver hair and a wrinkled, pleasant face.

"It *is* you!" the man cried, smiling broadly. Again the voice struck chords of memory, and the smile finally confirmed them.

"Master Saeral?" Eldrin breathed, delighted, wonderstruck, and wary all at once. Though Saeral had been Eldrin's mentor and teacher eight years ago, he was now High Father, while Eldrin held the lowest of Mataian ranks. He had no right even to look directly at this man, much less speak to him.

Uncertain how to conduct himself, Eldrin settled on averting his eyes and stepping back. He would have gone to his knees again, but Saeral stopped him.

"Leave off with that, dear boy. There's no one here but us. And I want to have a look at you."

Eldrin lifted his face as the man seized his arms and realized with surprise that another reason he had not recognized his old friend—besides the premature aging—was because Saeral seemed to have shrunk. Formerly, Eldrin had looked up to him; now he looked down, head and shoulders taller.

Saeral was surprised, too. "Such height you've gained! Though come to think of it, you *were* all legs when last I saw you." His gray eyes shone; his hands squeezed Eldrin's shoulders affectionately. "You have done well, my son. Belmir can't say enough good things about you." He paused, eyeing Eldrin shrewdly. "I trust you have not taken yesterday's events to heart. You were the victim, not the cause, you know."

Eldrin did not know what to say.

Saeral smiled. "I've heard all about it, including Captain Meridon's clumsy attempts at proselytizing. Surely you haven't let that Terstan get to you? Not after all those years of enduring your brother."

"No, sir, of course not."

"Then why are you down here on your knees before you've even broken your fast? Was not your penance to end at dawn?"

Something about this man had always broken through Eldrin's natural reserve, so that now, as on countless occasions before, he found himself blurting out his troubles, telling about the vision and his concern about his worthiness and the fact that he had not yet felt Eidon's touch during meditations. To his dismay, an expression of alarm flickered across Saeral's face at this last, but it vanished so swiftly that a moment later Eldrin was unsure he'd seen it at all. He concluded with his supposition that the vision had been a warning of his need to work harder at purging the pride of his blood.

"And that's why I've come," Eldrin finished. "I mean to fast and pray and meditate until I find him. Or they have to carry me away."

Again Saeral looked surprised; then he smiled. "Your devotion has always been a wonder to me, lad, and Eidon *has* noticed. He will come." He squeezed Eldrin's shoulders again, then released him and stepped back. "You have pleased me more than you can know. I look forward to the day when you join us in union with the Flames."

A thrill of anticipation danced up Eldrin's back. He nodded, and Saeral answered with a nod of his own.

"His Light be with you, Eldrin."

"And with you, Father."

In three strides the man had passed through a curtained doorway set under the second tier—one of four leading into the vesting rooms and private chambers of the high-ranking Guardians who led the rituals of service.

Buoyed by Saeral's confidence and more determined than ever to attain his goal, Eldrin settled to his knees again, bowed his head, and murmured, "Eidon, Almighty One, lay my doubts to rest. You know I long for you. Please. Touch me with your goodness. Let me know you have accepted me."

He looked into the Flames and let them swallow him up as he began the liturgy, the familiar words tumbling out in a soft, mesmerizing rhythm.

A bell tolled in the distance, then stopped. People moved around him, rustling at the edges of his awareness, driving him ever more deeply into the Flame and the passion of his desire. Like the bell, the people went away, too. Occasionally pain shot up from his knees and hunger gnawed at his stomach. His throat ached; his voice grew hoarse. He put the sensations down, sacrificing his discomfort and weakness to his need. His body trembled, swayed. He held it up with force of will, weeping, pleading, beseeching with all the power of his soul.

And then it happened.

The scent of roasting grain tickled his nose as a cold pressure enfolded his body, an eerie sense of otherness crackling with energy. Gooseflesh prickled the back of his neck, and he squirmed, feeling suddenly, horribly like a fly in a spider's web, about to be cocooned in silk. Coldness seeped into his skin. He gritted his teeth as the ethereal embrace tightened. Rising fear and revulsion banged his heart against his chest, rapid-fire beats that powered the blood into throat and temples. His breath quickened; his hands clenched the railing.

Then he flinched, crying out as a cold tongue of inhuman awareness slid into his soul, and terrified aversion erupted like molten rock.

The tendril withdrew as swiftly as it had entered and the cold pressure on his skin vanished with it, leaving him sick and shuddering. Head swimming, he sagged forward, bracing his brow against the rail as he gasped back his breath and fought the rising gorge in his throat.

Gradually his pulse slowed and the nausea in his gut subsided. He sat back on his heels, the Flames leaping before him, and slowly understood: the god in the Flame had touched him. At long last, his years of labor and yearning had borne fruit. He should feel euphoric and triumphant. Instead, it was as if the invading tendril had taken all his emotion, leaving only flat, shocked emptiness.

# CHAPTER

# 4

*Eidon has finally touched you,* Eldrin told himself as he went looking for Belmir. *That's all that matters. He's touched you.* The feelings of revulsion and fear were clearly another manifestation of his deep-seated unworthiness—which explained why he had not been touched sooner. All-knowing Eidon would have realized he couldn't have handled it, might even have been driven from the Brotherhood by the shock of it coming before he was ready.

Now he understood what even a month ago he might not have: it wasn't so much revulsion he'd felt but the keen awareness of the gulf, the incompatibility between himself and a being ineffably *not* human. Naturally his pride would find such power threatening. Next time would be better.

He found Belmir emerging from a meeting with the other Initiate disciplers on the second floor of the library. Seeing Eldrin, the older man guessed immediately what had happened.

"You found him," he said, drawing Eldrin aside as the other Guardians flowed around them and down the hall to the stairway.

Eldrin nodded, smiling.

The older man clapped his shoulder affectionately. "I never doubted you would. Just as I don't doubt you'll make a fine Guardian." He pushed his spectacles up his nose and glanced down the hall. "We've decided to postpone the Initiation. The boys trapped on the barge have only just arrived. We're hoping three days will get everyone settled down. The Procession will have to be redone, but the Festival of Arms will have begun by then, so the crowds shouldn't be as large."

"Will I be able to participate this time?"

Belmir smiled up at him. "A touchy subject. But most are agreed that the best way to deal with this nonsense about your taking the throne is to ignore it."

"I should sign a letter of abdication," Eldrin mused. "Take myself back out of the line of succession."

"A good idea, though I'm not sure even that would satisfy. It will take years of nothing happening before people believe it. And I imagine some won't until you're in your grave." He sighed in exasperation. "Well, I have an audience with the High Father. I will bring him your good news. The other Initiates are at choir practice in the Chapel of St. Elspeth. You can join them there."

"Yes, Master."

But before Eldrin reached the chapel, a stubble-headed, first-year acolyte accosted him, waving the large introduction card of a nobleman.

"B-brother Eldrin? You have a v-visitor." The boy bowed awkwardly, struggling to catch his breath. With trembling hand he gave over the card, and Eldrin felt a pang of empathy. That trembling was not born of nerves alone. Well did he recall his own early months in the novitiate: every movement monitored and scheduled, every moment spent in the company of others, every day filled with more tasks than could be done until fatigue became a constant companion. He had withstood it without undue distress, but many of his novice mates had not. Tics, tremors, ungovernable fidgeting, wandering concentration—they plagued many of the boys. Some had broken under the strain and left.

He smiled at the lad. "How long since you took your vows?"

"Two months, Brother."

"Well, you've survived the worst." Eldrin glanced at the card and did a double take. Carissa? What was his sister doing. . . ? Oh, the Festival of Arms. Her husband, chief of the border lords, must have come down for the contest, bringing her with him. And she, seizing the opportunity, had come to see Eldrin. For the first time in eight years.

Trepidation tempered his rising delight. As fraternal twins he and his sister had been inseparable throughout childhood, and she'd been devastated by his decision to enter the Mataio. They had argued hotly during the weeks before he left. Afterward her letters had been brief and cool. That, of course, could be due to their having been censored, but as far as he knew, she'd never forgiven him.

The boy was eyeing him nervously. "Shall I t-tell her you are unavailable, Brother?"

"Of course not. Where is she?"

"B-by the pool in the g-guest's garden. I c-could lead you there if you w-wish."

"Please."

The garden lay across the main court, west of the Keep itself. Graveled paths wound between hedges of redhart and hockspur and beds of smaller herbs laden with fragrant purple-and-white flowers. Downslung branches of tall, stately weepers provided shady bowers for meditation or counsel, their yellow, fleshy blossoms abuzz with bees and hummingbirds.

The boy led him to a small court with a stone-lined pool and looked around. "I had t-trouble finding you, Brother. She was t-to have been escorted here, but . . . p-perhaps she did not stay."

Eldrin doubted that. He swung round searching, then heard a familiar voice ring briskly over the hedges. "I've been waiting over half an hour, Brother! I will be put off no longer."

With a nod of thanks to the acolyte, Eldrin headed for the voice. Rounding a spherical bush, he spied a tall, amber-gowned figure near the rear portico, half hidden by the weeper that stood at the path's bending between them. She'd cornered a young Initiate Brother.

"But you must know everyone here, sir!" she exclaimed. "How hard can it be to find him?"

The Initiate, shorter than she, had retreated up against a pillar, hands offered placatingly. "I'm sorry, my lady," he said. "There are many newcomers this week." His gaze caught on Eldrin. "Here comes another. Perhaps he will know where to find the one you seek."

"As it happens, I do," Eldrin said, coming up beside them, straight-faced.

Carissa whirled to confront him. "Then, why is he not . . ." She trailed off, blue eyes wide. He couldn't keep from grinning then, while the Initiate retreated hastily.

The last time Eldrin had seen her, his twin had been a chubby, freckled adolescent. Now she was a beautiful young woman, slender and graceful in a full-skirted gown of amber silk. Her thick blond hair was twisted into ropes at the crown and netted into a club at the nape of her neck. Soft tendrils framed a smooth complexion with features gentler than his own, though she shared his straight, narrow nose and deep-set blue eyes.

Those eyes traveled over him now, head to toe and back again. "Plagues, Abramm!" she croaked. "Your hair's nearly as long as mine!"

"I'm told it grows exceptionally fast."

"And you're so tall. And you look so much like—"

"Like Father. I know."

She grimaced. "Well, except for the hair, of course."

"And a few other attributes."

They looked at each other and burst into laughter. She flung her arms around his neck. "Oh, Abramm, it is so good to see you again!"

After a moment Eldrin pushed her gently away. He was sworn to chastity, and even touching a woman, sister or not, was frowned upon. "It's Eldrin now," he murmured.

They stood awkwardly for a moment. Then he said, "Have you come down for the Festival, then?"

"Rennalf has, yes." She stroked the folded paper fan looped to her wrist. "And I'm going to Thilos in a couple of days. To visit Aunt Ana."

"Ah."

Again they fell into silence.

"Of course," she burst out, "I won't go until after the contest. I'm hoping desperately someone will beat Gillard." She flicked him a nervous smile. "He needs to be taken down a notch. Or three. Trap Meridon, the sword master's son—you remember old Larrick Meridon, don't you?—anyway, Meridon—he's captain of the King's Guard, by the way—he almost won last year. Some said he threw the match for fear of the trouble Gillard could make for him, his being a Terstan and all, but—" She broke off with a grimace. "I'm babbling, aren't I? Sorry. I am just *so* nervous . . . seeing you. After the way we parted, I mean."

He regarded her wordlessly, still trying to catch up.

She stole a glance at him. "I said some hateful things."

"We both did."

"Aye." She turned the fan in her fingers.

Eldrin clasped his hands behind his back, wondering what to say next.

"It's just . . ." She let her hands fall to her sides, drew a deep breath, and looked up. "When you left it was like having my arm ripped off. I hardly knew what to do with myself."

"I never meant to hurt you, Riss."

"I know. I'm not trying to make you feel bad. I mean, the way Gillard tormented you, you had to get away."

"That wasn't why I took the vows."

"You did it because you wanted to serve Eidon, yes." But she was only parroting his words from eight years past, still not understanding.

"Anyway," she went on, "I just wanted you to know I'm not angry anymore." She met his gaze and smiled. "But I have missed you."

He felt he should say he'd missed her, too. But truly, there'd been no time or energy to miss anything, and with his thoughts turned more and more to Eidon, no room for the past.

When he held silence, she averted her eyes and stroked the gilded edge of her fan. Then abruptly she snapped it open, stirring the air in front of her face. "My goodness! I'd forgotten how stifling summer gets down here!"

"I know what you mean." Relieved, he gestured up the graveled path. "Shall we find a place to sit? It'll be cooler in the shade."

She fell in beside him as they walked. "The heat seems to get worse for me every year," she went on. "And, of course, last year I didn't even come down on account of the baby so—"

"Baby?!" He whirled to face her. "You have a *child?*" Of course, she must. More than one, no doubt. She'd been married seven years, and it was her duty above all else to produce an heir for her husband. It just hadn't occurred to him that his sister, his childhood companion and co-conspirator, could also be the mother of a pack of toddlers.

She did not rise to his joy, did not look at him at all. The fan worked convulsively. Her voice, when it came, was nearly inaudible. "He was born too early, and we lost him. Just like his brother before him."

Eldrin winced, wanting to kick himself, and mumbled an apology.

She shrugged. "Eidon makes all things right. Isn't that how it goes?"

*For those who love him,* Eldrin thought, dismayed by the bitterness in her voice. He said nothing, not wanting to rub salt in what was clearly an open wound, and stopped beside a shady bower, lifting a blossom-laden branch for her to step under.

"Anyway, that's the real reason I'm going to Thilos," she said, heading for the marble bench at the base of the weeper's gray trunk. "They're supposed to be good at fixing that sort of thing."

"I will petition Eidon on your behalf," he said gravely, settling beside her. She thanked him, but again he sensed her insincerity, and again they lapsed into uncomfortable silence. A bee buzzed nearby; birds chittered in the branches enfolding them. Then a group of stubble-headed acolytes swarmed up the paths, flitting from plant to plant, clipping leaves and stems with tiny scissors, and dropping their treasures into sackcloth bags. An elderly Guardian accompanied them, stopping at various shrubs to lecture his charges on identification and usage, lectures Eldrin had heard numerous times and had even given on occasion.

As the group moved on, Carissa seized on the man's last topic. "Hockspur? Isn't that the one that makes you susceptible to suggestion? The one they're always slipping people at parties?"

"Aye." He chuckled, grateful for something to say. "Hardly anyone makes it through their first year of the novitiate without falling prey to it."

"They gave it to *you*?" She leaned toward him eagerly. "What did they make you do?"

"Well, some people are more susceptible than others."

She grinned. "Don't tell me they had you barking like a dog."

"Fortunately, I'm one of the few with a natural resistance. It only makes me sick to my stomach."

She shook her head wryly. "You never did like being out of control. Must be that infamous Kalladorne will—of which you got a double portion." She paused. "I wonder how Gillard would react."

"Carissa—"

"Oh, I'm not going to do anything. It's just fun to contemplate the possibilities. He has gotten so full of himself these days."

Eldrin offered a noncommittal murmur, preferring to avoid the topic of their obnoxious younger brother.

Before he could come up with a new subject, she giggled and said, "Remember the time you stuck that tail in the back of his belt just as he set out to lead the Parade of Arms? The one with the black-and-white stripes? Remember? It looked ridiculous. And he never knew. Kept wondering why everyone was snickering in his wake. I've never laughed so hard in all my life."

Eldrin smiled briefly. "He broke my nose for that one."

She laid a hand against her cheek, her eyes widening with dismay. "I'd forgotten about that."

Eldrin shrugged. "Of all the things I left behind, I must admit Gillard is the least mourned." Even now it was all too easy to conjure up impure feelings of hatred and anger and resentment. Not least because his brother was apparently unchanged and as unchecked as ever.

He watched a hummingbird whir at a yellow flower on a low-hanging branch behind his sister's shoulder. The bird, a dull gray-green in the shade, suddenly turned and looked right at him, sending an inexplicable chill up his spine.

Oblivious to it, Carissa snapped out her fan and stirred the air again, sending the bird darting away. "So, where were you yesterday?" she asked. "I went to the Procession, got a place right near the dock, but you weren't there."

"They took me off earlier."

"Ah, on account of the rioting," she guessed. "Raynen said they might do that."

She eyed him thoughtfully, then shook her head. "Every time I look at you, I get amazed all over again." She touched the lock of blond hair that had fallen forward over his shoulder. "You look . . ." She flushed. "You look like a real-and-true Guardian."

"I *am* a real-and-true Guardian. Or nearly so."

"Yes." She rested the open fan in her lap and looked at it, caressing an edge. After a moment she drew breath to speak.

He cut her off. "Don't, Riss. You know I won't change my mind."

"Things are different now."

"Not for me."

"Of course for you."

He snorted. "All I've ever wanted was to know Eidon and serve him. That's not changed."

"Maybe not, but it doesn't matter. That's the point." She turned on the bench to face him. "We're Kalladornes, Abramm. That makes us pawns—of the people, of politics, of power. What we want doesn't figure into the mix."

"I am not a Kalladorne anymore, Carissa. I am a servant of Eidon."

"Not a Kalladorne?" She waved the fan dismissively. "Do you have any idea what's going on in this city right now?"

"If you mean the nonsense about Saeral putting me on the throne, yes. I know."

"It's not nonsense."

"It most certainly is."

She pressed her lips together again, then turned away and resumed fanning.

"Carissa, how could I be king? I lack the temperament for it, I have no military background, and I don't know wools about politics. The Table of Lords would laugh me out of the Chamber."

"Not as many as you think. A majority approved your reinstatement to the succession."

He huffed. "In any case, Saeral would never stand for it. It's not at all what being a Guardian is about."

She continued fanning, studying the tips of her amber slippers. "If you were king, could you not enact laws that would further Eidon's interests?"

"Eidon's interests are only furthered by the work we do for his Flames."

"With you on the throne, that work could include driving heretics and practitioners of evil out of the realm, making sure people lived pure and virtuous lives. You could clean up the drunken excesses of the court and bring the lecherous barons into line." She looked up at him. "Would that not strengthen the power of the Flames?"

He stared at her, again bereft of words.

She grimaced and shut the fan. "Oh, come, Abramm. Why can't you see it? Saeral has been using you from the day he met you!"

"*Using* me?"

"Leading you along, convincing you that you were weak and clumsy, that he was the only one who cared or understood."

Eldrin smothered a convulsion of anger and turned from her. "I don't want to hear this, Carissa."

"You wanted him to be the father you never had," she persisted. "So you believed him, refusing to see what he was doing to you, refusing to take the responsibility for changing things yourself."

"You're speaking blasphemies. And I had a father."

"Not one who loved and praised you."

He stood up, forcing himself to breathe deeply. *His name will be my peace. . . .* "You'd better go."

She stood to face him, eyes flashing. "You know, of course, that Saeral was on a pilgrimage not one league from where Father and Aarol were murdered? And Elian didn't die of the consumption—he was poisoned. Just like Stefan didn't *fall* down the King's Court stair. Now there's only Raynen between you and the throne."

Eldrin stared at her, reeling. He felt as though he were in another of his horrible nightmares. How could she be saying these things? His own sister!

She laid a hand on his bare arm. "Saeral will kill him, Abramm. Just like he killed the others. Then he'll put you on the throne and the war will start. Gillard will lay claim, and the Shar lords will support him. The Nunn will favor you. They'll call it a holy war. The realm will be torn apart, thousands will die, and in the end, Beltha'adi will get the spoils." She paused, studying him, her eyes bright with passion. "You always wanted to be a hero. Well, here's your chance. Because you are the only one who can stop this."

He was drowning in the flood of her words, choking upon the whirling mingle of truth and lies, struggling to get his mind around it all, struggling even to breathe. Apparently she took his silence for acquiescence and plunged on, her lowered voice throbbing with excitement.

"Raynen's prepared to offer you a sizable stipend and a vessel of your own. It's the one I'll be taking to Thilos, in fact. No one has to know you're with me; no one should know, in fact. Once we're there, the boat's yours, and you will be free to do whatever you want. Travel, see the world, visit all those scholarly places your heart once yearned for . . ." She smiled. "Have a real life."

He stared at her. Silence stretched between them, broken only by the thundering of his own heart and the rustling of the birds in the tree.

Finally she frowned, pressed her lips together, then stepped back, the emotion bleeding out of her. "He'll send for you this evening. Think about what I've said. Please. For all of us."

She ducked under the blossomed branch and hurried down the path, the rustling of her skirt and the crunch of her footsteps quickly swallowed by the birds' chirping chorus.

It was several minutes before he moved. Releasing a long, ragged breath, he sagged back onto the bench. Belmir had warned him his resolve would be increasingly tested the closer he got to the final decision. But this had taken him completely by surprise.

# CHAPTER 5

Sunset's florid light filtered through the horizontal slits high in the coach's sidewalls, glinting off the hair, nose, and chin of Eldrin's Haverallan companion. Rhiad sat in silence on the bench across from him, Guardian amulet gleaming on his throat like a scarlet eye.

Raynen's summons had arrived an hour ago, and Rhiad himself had brought it to Eldrin, informing him that he would serve as Eldrin's escort. Relieved as he was not to have to face his brothers alone, Eldrin found the Haverallan's presence unnerving. Neither of them had spoken since they had boarded the coach at the Keep gates, Rhiad apparently deep in meditation.

Eldrin knew he should be following the man's lead, but his mind was hopping around like a sparrow in a tree, too distracted by memories and worries to stay focused.

He had run through the encounter with Carissa at least a hundred times since she'd left him, arguing with her in his mind, knowing now the things he should have said when shock had held him silent. And yet, every time he reached the suggestion that his brothers' deaths had not been accidental, his thoughts snagged. He reminded himself that there was no proof, that it was all coincidental and no thinking person could believe otherwise—until the next time he cycled back to the suggestion, and his thoughts snagged again, and he wondered with exasperation what was wrong with him.

The coach rolled to a stop, and he heard the muted voices of their driver and the palace gate guards. Across from him Rhiad started out of his trance and reached up to adjust the interior lamp, dangling between them from the coach's ceiling.

Warm light bloomed across the spartan interior, and as the coach rolled forward again Rhiad fixed his entire attention upon Eldrin. "Are you ready for this?"

Eldrin shrugged. "I've been through it before. Many times."

"Things are different now." The coach leaned slightly as it rounded the circular drive that would take them to the front door.

"I've already made my decision," Eldrin said. "There's nothing they can say that will change it."

A smile quirked Rhiad's lips. "Just keep your wits about you, Brother, and you'll do fine."

The coach slowed, then rocked to a stop in a chorus of creaks. The door opened and a blue-liveried footman stepped back as Eldrin descended into a forgotten world.

The palace soared around him, ablaze with light, its east and west wings enfolding him like the jaws of a trap. Spires and cupolas jabbed the darkening sky, and rows and rows of golden windows gleamed down at him. As with the Great Sanctum, he had forgotten the size of the place, the intimidation of its grandeur.

A marble stairway ascended before him, ranks of blue-tabarded House Guard forming a gauntlet through which he must pass to reach the doors at the top. Standing at attention, not one of them looked at him; nevertheless the old aversion to public appearances uncoiled in his middle. For a moment he wanted to climb back into the coach.

Two men in green detached themselves from the guards' blue ranks. As one hurried away up the stair the other approached, and Eldrin recognized Captain Meridon immediately, decked out in the dress uniform of the King's Guard: a badge of crossed white arrows emblazoned on an emerald tabard belted over white blouse and breeches. With his wide-brimmed, white-plumed hat and short emerald cloak, he looked quite dapper. One golden chain of rank looped across his chest. He still wore the rapier and the ram-headed dirk.

Eldrin met his gaze uneasily, confirming what he had earlier observed—there was no trace of the sarotis in those cold, dark eyes. Meridon must be newly ensnared.

They exchanged an awkward greeting as Rhiad came up beside them. Meridon flicked him a glance, followed by a nod that was barely civil, then escorted them up the stair. Inside, courtiers packed the lamplit atrium, a glittering crowd of curling wigs and satin doublets, lace cravats and jeweled rings, beribboned walking sticks and sweeping bell-shaped gowns. The air was thick with the mingle of unwashed bodies and strong perfume, and the hall echoed with excited chatter—chatter that silenced instantly when Eldrin entered and all eyes turned toward him.

Meridon led him through the parting crowd to the outer salon where yet more courtiers awaited, watching avidly. Beyond this a guarded door opened into the second salon, larger by half than the first, with a gleaming black-and-white tiled floor and a high arching ceiling decorated with gold leaf. Chandeliers hung along its daunting length, and padded benches lined the periphery, interspersed with man-high porcelain lamps. On the expanse of silk-covered walls hung massive framed canvases depicting great moments in Kiriathan history.

This room was not as crowded as the outer salon, but there were still a good number of courtiers, mostly men now, many of them wearing the long curled wigs that were just becoming fashionable when Eldrin had entered the novitiate. These were complemented by a new species of gaudily laced and beribboned doublet, and short, puffy breeches ending at mid-thigh. A number of the men carried wide-brimmed, feathered hats, and a few had even decorated their faces with the painted-on stars and hearts that eight years ago had been the sole province of the ladies.

They stood in clusters about the gigantic room and, like the others before them, had fallen silent upon Eldrin's entrance, heads craning and every eye turned his way.

Meridon's booted footsteps echoed loudly around them as they proceeded across the gleaming floor, the soft slaps of Eldrin's and Rhiad's sandals and even the whisper of their robes audible in the ringing silence. He risked brief glances at the men he passed, knowing they were high lords of the land, some of the richest and most powerful nobles in Kiriath—or at the least, their sons and relatives—but he recognized very few. As a prince he had had few friends, and as fifth-born, had not been required to keep a presence at court. His older brothers were expected to mingle with the men they might one day rule, but the possibility was so remote for a fifth-born, the precaution was never taken.

Now it was no longer remote at all.

For a moment he could hardly breathe, touched as never before by the reality of how close he stood to the throne. His father and brothers were dead. *Dead!* Men in the prime of their lives—healthy, vigorous, active men. All gone in the space of six years—and not even in wartime.

Uneasiness rattled through him, calling up a most disconcerting memory of that cold tendril lashing into his mind. He shut it off, shoving both thoughts aside, aghast at the treachery of his own mind. Of all things to think about—now, neither would help him through the coming interview.

They were almost to the great doors at the far side of the room when one of those ten-foot-high panels flew open and a big man with short white-blond hair burst through, the door barely caught in time by the startled doorman. Seeing Eldrin and his escort, the man stopped short, and Eldrin recognized his younger brother instantly.

Gillard approached slowly, staring. Heavy-lidded ice-blue eyes gleamed beneath white-blond brows. Though at nineteen Gillard was a year and a half the younger, he loomed over Eldrin—as he had from earliest memory. A good half-head taller, he had a massive upper body that was accentuated by a form-fitting, conservatively adorned, forest green doublet. Like Meridon, he wore both rapier and dirk at his belt, sheathed in golden scabbards.

He stopped in front of Eldrin and whistled low, shaking his head. "I'd heard you'd arrived. Everybody's saying it's now clear that Mother really had twin girls. I see what they mean."

It felt as if bands of iron had tightened around Eldrin's head and chest. He swallowed on a dust-dry mouth.

Gillard stepped back, cocking his head, then reached out to flick the lock of hair that dangled over Eldrin's arm. "Plagues, little brother! Look at this hair! Half the ladies here must be dying of envy!" He began to walk a circle around Eldrin, smirking and chuckling. Around them the courtiers watched, no one moving, no one making a sound. The blood rose hotly to Eldrin's face.

Gillard came back to the front, hooked a big thumb into his belt, and shook his head again. "It's a good thing Uncle Simon's not here. He'd die of apoplexy. The rumors will be bad enough."

"Your brother," Rhiad declared loudly at Eldrin's side, "has given his life to the service of Eidon and the deliverance of this land from the evil."

Eldrin's face flamed the more. He wished Rhiad would stay out of this. With Gillard it was always better to keep silent and let the insults roll. Argument only made things worse.

Gillard snorted. "Everyone knows the real reason he joined your little holy club, *Master* Rhiad—to get out of Barracks. He knew he couldn't survive it, so he ran. As for delivering the land—plagues! He can't even deliver himself from insult. Can you, little brother? Couldn't even show your face here without your holy friend to hold you up."

"Have a care, Your Highness," Rhiad murmured, "you tread near blasphemy."

"Blasphemy? Don't make me laugh."

Meridon, who stood a step ahead and to the side of Eldrin, now managed to draw his eye. "My lord?" he said quietly. "The king awaits."

"Ah yes, the king." Gillard drew back, chuckling again. "I'd suggest you listen to him, little brother. Because, Mataio or not, if you make any claim to the throne and—"

"Prince Gillard," Rhiad interjected, "are you threatening us?"

"Merely stating fact." Gillard's pale eyes narrowed, and he shifted his gaze to the Haverallan. "So long as I live you'll never get your filthy Mataian fingers on the Crown. Count on it." With a mocking nod, he shoved past Eldrin and stalked away.

As the smacking of his footsteps faded, Eldrin swayed with a wave of light-headedness. Suddenly his stomach hurt and his knees quivered violently. Deliberately he drew a deep breath, then unclenched his shaking hands, aghast at the sudden desire to heave one of the porcelain lamps against the wall and see it smash into a thousand pieces. It was an old, familiar feeling, the frustration of an injustice that was never righted, no matter how hard he wished it, no matter how hard he fought it. Gillard always won. He had forgotten how impotent it made him feel—and how furious. Probably because he hadn't felt this way in . . . well, eight years.

He closed his eyes, seeking control. *His light is my refuge. His name is my joy. . . .*

"Your highness?" Meridon murmured, drawing his attention again. They continued on.

It was only when they reached the great door to the royal audience chamber that Meridon informed them Eldrin alone would attend the king.

Rhiad protested vigorously. "You wish to get him alone so you can fill his head with lies and confuse him. I will not allow it!"

"Unfortunately, it's not your choice to make, sir," Meridon said.

"Perhaps not, but it is *his* choice." Rhiad looked at Eldrin expectantly. Meridon's gaze followed.

Eldrin became abruptly conscious of the guards and servants and courtiers, a good dozen or more in immediate earshot, Gillard's words still rankling in his mind. *"Couldn't even show your face here without your holy friend to hold you up."*

"Your Highness?" Meridon prompted.

"Stop calling me Your Highness!" Eldrin snapped, immediately regretting his loss of composure. He drew another calming breath and glanced at Rhiad. "It's all right. I told you, I've been through this before. They aren't going to change my mind."

Rhiad's face was closed, blank, and though his words were quiet, they were infused with a persuasive power that bordered on command. "Brother, I do not think this wise. It is not the same as before, and I must question why the king is so intent upon getting you alone. It can only be to neutralize any influence I, as your counselor and mentor, might have upon you. I insist that you allow me to accompany you."

His dark eyes bored into Eldrin's. A faint, odd scent touched Eldrin's nostrils, and for a moment he felt as if his will had been gathered up and hurled along in a current of intent not his own. He opened his mouth to speak the request and closed it in sudden irritation.

Here he was, being the very puppet everyone was accusing him of being. He broke eye contact and said very deliberately, "I'll be fine, Brother. But thank you for your concern."

With that he turned and followed Meridon into the king's audience chamber. It became immediately clear that most of the courtiers in the salon from which Eldrin had just come must have been recently evicted from this one, for it was nearly empty. Half the size of the room Eldrin had just crossed, it was similarly lit—with chandeliers and pedestaled lamps—but devoid of benches on which people might sit. There could be no sitting in the presence of the king, who alone sat on a golden throne atop a curved, three-staired dais. Only his personal servants and bodyguards attended him. All others had been dismissed.

Meridon stepped immediately aside as he entered, leaving Eldrin to cross the floor between door and dais on his own. Kneeling and uttering the traditional "Your Majesty" felt immensely strange in front of Raynen. As he bowed his head, he kept seeing the boy version of the man, charging into a flock of hens out back by the kitchens, swinging his wooden sword and hollering at the top of his lungs.

Then Eldrin's amusement turned to horror as he was beset by the throat-clenching, stomach-churning vision of having to do this to Gillard someday.

"You may rise," Raynen said. "Thank you for not making a scene."

"It won't matter, you know," Eldrin said, the king's words allowing him now to look up.

Raynen smiled slightly. "We'll see."

Eldrin had always thought Raynen the best looking of his kin. Tall and fit, he cut an elegant figure in a closely fitted doublet of black satin, its row of black buttons glittering down the front. Like their father, he wore his blond hair short beneath the golden circlet of his office. His face was rounder than Eldrin's, but they shared the same stern Kalladorne brow line, and the short honey-colored beard that edged Raynen's jaw was the same hue Eldrin's would be if he let it grow.

Now the king dismissed his servants and stood, motioning for Eldrin to stand as well. "Walk with me, Abramm, and we will talk."

An unexpected request, but Eldrin could only acquiesce. Raynen led him through the door at the chamber's rear, waiting in the gleaming corridor beyond for Eldrin to come abreast before starting on again. Meridon followed a few steps behind them, the remaining four bodyguards trailing respectfully out of earshot.

At first, though, there was nothing to hear. Eldrin continued to be discomfited by the unreality of the circumstances. Raynen had been a rowdy, carefree boy, active and impulsive, an excellent horseman with a ready laugh and a soft spot for animals of all kinds. He'd been something of a protector to Eldrin in their youth, if he happened to notice Gillard's abuses.

"I understand there is some question of your suitability as Guardian material," Raynen said abruptly.

Eldrin blinked, disarmed by the unexpected direction of Raynen's discourse. He frowned. "Well, of course I am the first Kalladorne to—"

"I mean more specifically. I mean that after eight years you are the only Initiate who has not yet felt the touch of Eidon in your meditations."

Eldrin stopped in his tracks and stared at him, stunned speechless. Shock turned to indignation. "Where did you hear that?!"

Raynen shrugged. "I am king. I hear a lot of things. If I didn't, I'd be dead." He glanced back at Meridon. "So it's true, then? You have not been touched?"

Meridon, who had stopped a stride behind them, was regarding Eldrin as intently as Raynen.

Eldrin lifted his chin. "Actually, he touched me this morning."

"Ah." Raynen nodded. "As soon as Saeral found out, no doubt. I'll bet that was a shock for him. He must've taken immediate measures."

Eldrin felt the blood drain from his face as he recalled the flash of dismay on Saeral's face, the assurance Eldrin would soon feel the touch he sought, the timely fulfillment of that assurance. . . .

"And how did it go for you, hmm?" Raynen pressed. "Did it make you uncomfortable? Did you fight it?"

Eldrin drew back a pace. "I don't believe that's any of your business!" he cried. "King or not!"

"You did fight it!" Raynen crowed. He glanced smugly at his captain, then continued down the hallway, striding so rapidly that Eldrin had to hurry to catch up. He was writhing with shame and dismay, all the disappointment that first touch had left in him—disappointment he'd largely buried—now rising to the fore. And here were all the doubts come back again, stronger than ever and haunting him at the worst possible time. If there was ever a moment he wished to appear strong and committed, it was now, facing his family. And already he had bungled it.

But how could Ray have known? Had it happened before? To another Kalladorne? He wanted desperately to ask, yet asking would reveal the very mental confusion he was determined not to show.

They climbed a back stairway, then strode down a narrow, paneled hallway into a silent chamber, empty but for its benches. War implements decorated the walls. Ancient and modern both, all had at one time or other been wielded by one of Eldrin's ancestors: Alaric's broadsword, Eberline's longbow, Ravelin's halberd, maces, dirks, crossbows—even his own father's rapier.

The door at its far end led into a paneled, low-ceilinged chamber, its fireplace empty, several pedestaled candle lamps providing illumination. Their reflections glowed in the tall night-darkened windows stretching along one wall. A wooden table gleamed in front of them, chairs lined along it like soldiers at attention. His father's war room.

Stepping into this place was like stepping back in time. Suddenly Eldrin was a boy again, called to face his sire for yet another dressing down. Meren had spoken to him only in this room, as if he were embarrassed to acknowledge paternity anywhere else. So powerful were the recollections that for a moment Eldrin fully expected to see the big man standing behind the high-backed velvet chair at the far end of the table. But there was no one now, his father dead, gone. The realization sparked an unexpected sense of frustration and loss.

"Please," Raynen said, waving at the chairs before the empty hearth. "Sit down."

"I prefer to stand."

"Suit yourself." The king moved to the sideboard and poured himself a drink. As the liquid chuckled into the glass, Eldrin realized that, except for Meridon, who had followed them into the room, they were alone. The other bodyguards had remained in the hall outside.

Glass clinked as Raynen replaced the stopper, then turned to face him, leaning back against the wooden cabinet.

"Carissa told you what I propose to offer you?"

"A stipend and a Thilosian fishing vessel, but I—"

"It's not a fishing boat, it's a merchantman. A fine one. The stipend's five hundred thousand sovereigns. That should be more than enough to see you through years of travel in high style. If you invest along the way, you'll end up a very rich man."

"The idea of living solely for the maintenance of my own pleasure does not appeal to me, brother. Even assuming there will be places to go and things to invest in five years hence."

"You refer to Beltha'adi, I think, and his notions of world domination."

"He has to be stopped."

"Indeed, he does." Raynen sipped his brandy, eyeing Eldrin thoughtfully. "But he will not be if you refuse my offer."

"I will not seek your crown, Ray. I have no desire to be king."

"It's not you I'm worried about."

"Oh, come, you can't honestly believe Saeral will try to kill you."

"Kill me or, failing that, find another way to get me out of the way. I can think of several points he could work."

Abramm lifted his chin, weighing his words. "Like the fact you are a Terstan?"

The barest flicker of an eyelid revealed Raynen's discomfort.

As for Eldrin, it took a moment for the lack of denial to register. Then his eyes flicked to the black fabric over his brother's heart where the mark of heresy lay. A slow revulsion swelled in his chest, pushing against his heart and throat as he took a small step back.

Raynen set the snifter down. "It is unfortunate they told you. I am sure it will prejudice you against anything I might tell you—which naturally was their intent. Even so, it must be said. This may be your last chance to hear the truth.

"You Mataians claim to believe there is a great spiritual battle going on around us. A battle of cosmic proportion waged between the forces of good and evil, which we ourselves cannot see. Eidon versus Moroq, light against the dark. In that we share a common ground."

"But only in that."

"Not quite. We share a reverence for the Words of Revelation. And a mutual regard for Eidon."

Eldrin frowned. "You have been deceived by evil."

"How do you know that, Abramm? You say the mark I wear is the touch of Moroq, but how do you know you are not the one who has been deceived?"

"It goes against all that is—"

"Neither Word says anything about Holy Flames. Nor of a brotherhood, nor of making oneself worthy by the performance of any deed. They speak only of Light—Eidon's own Light, bought by the death of his Son and freely bestowed upon any who desire it. It lives, not in the heart of some stone building, but in the hearts and flesh of the men who accept it."

Eldrin scowled at him, vibrating with outrage, a breath away from bursting into a furious refutation of such evil and heretical claims. A free gift? Eidon was pure righteousness! So unbelievably perfect, so far above mankind, no person could even look upon his face and live. To suggest he would offer his precious Light to anyone who asked for it was preposterous, a violation of all that he was, a disregard for his perfect purity, and the perfect purity of his Light. How could his Light possibly reside in the flesh of those who were still weighed down with the power and the cares of the flesh?

But Eldrin held his tongue, knowing there was no point in arguing theology with this . . . this *Terstan*. And that was whom he was dealing with. Not his brother, not the king, but a man ensnared by evil.

Raynen glanced at Meridon, who frowned and shook his head slightly. The king's eyes came back to Eldrin speculatively, and they held their gaze for a long moment as Eldrin braced for another onslaught. Instead, his brother deflated with a sigh and pushed off the sideboard to pace the table's length. At the far end he turned, and when he spoke he had returned to his original tack. "The point is, you're being used, and it's time you woke up to the fact, time you saw just how badly this all could end."

Eldrin rolled his eyes. "Yes, yes. Carissa's already sung this song. I don't need to hear it again."

"I don't think you heard it the first time." Raynen folded his arms, scowling.

Eldrin scowled back. "Saeral is High Father of all the Mataio, Eidon's Hand and Voice in the land. He could not possibly be the murderous manipulator you're making him out to be."

"Our kin were not the only casualties, you realize. Did you know that of the fourteen Guardians ahead of him in succession, nine fell into disgrace or madness and three died? The last two were so intimidated they readily stepped aside." He paced back up the row of chairs, waving an arm. "Ask around. It's easy enough to prove. Of course, nothing can be traced directly back to him. The deaths were 'accidents.' And one can't blame madness on a man in court."

"Indeed."

Raynen stopped behind the chair across from Eldrin, gripping the tall back with both hands. "But the accumulation of evidence, the sheer coincidence of it—"

"Perhaps it is indicative of Eidon's hand in the matter, promoting the man he would have at the head of his Mataio." Eldrin frowned at him. "You ask how *I* can know I am not being deceived. Well, I could ask you the same. Father hated Saeral from the day he arrived, and you were always Father's son. I think you believe he's evil because you want him to be."

"I believe he's evil because he is. I saw him kill our Father, Abramm. And Aarol. I was there."

That gave Eldrin pause. "I thought they were mauled."

"Yes, but not by creatures of this world." He whirled to pace alongside the table again, stopping halfway back to glare out the window, arms once more folded across his chest, features reflected in the glass. For a long time he stared into the darkness, and just when Eldrin had decided he was not going to continue, he spoke. "Shaped like night herons, but not herons. Not birds of any kind."

In the reflection his face grew vacant with remembered horror. "Black as ravens, with needle-sharp beaks and white-hot eyes. Tens of them, stabbing at him, at his face and arms and chest. When he went down, Aarol tried to drag him to safety, but they turned on Aarol, too . . . both of them screaming and screaming, and I . . ." He braced a trembling hand on the window frame.

Eldrin stood rigidly, chilled to the core. Black as ravens, needle-sharp beaks, white-hot eyes. "Feyna." The word whispered out of him.

Raynen's head snapped around. "They are not myth."

Perhaps not, but Eldrin had never seen one, had never known anyone who had. The First Word warned of them frequently, creatures spawned by Moroq's rhu'ema. Born of the passions and blood of human flesh, they had flesh themselves and thus the power to strike directly, blow for blow in the physical world, something the rhu'ema themselves could no longer do. The Flames supposedly kept Kiriath clean of such things.

Uneasily, Eldrin glanced at Meridon, still standing beside the hearth, watching them closely.

"I was hiding in the bushes," the king said, looking back into the night. "I couldn't move, though I wanted to run for my life. When the screaming stopped, I watched the creatures fight over their bodies. Suddenly they all took wing. I thought they had sensed me, that I would be next, but then a man came out of the wood, cloaked and cowled. Several came and perched on his shoulders. The others just kept flying. He stood over the bodies for a long time before he began to laugh. And there was nothing human in it. As he left he walked past where I crouched, and I saw his face clearly." Raynen's gaze came back to Eldrin's. "It *was* Saeral."

His words plunged into silence. Eldrin stared at him, rooted to the floor, shaken by the conviction in his brother's voice, the certainty in his eyes, but unable to accept this final, damning accusation. At length he forced a laugh. "But, of course, there's no proof, is there? And no one but you saw this awful thing."

"No." Raynen turned from the window. "No one but me."

"Well then . . ." Eldrin gestured vaguely. "It's your word against his."

Not to mention all common sense.

Frustration darkened Raynen's face. "You think I'm lying?"

"No." He believed his brother was telling him the truth so far as he understood it. But it was night, and he'd just witnessed a monstrous evil. He could have seen anything. "I just don't believe it was Saeral you saw." He wondered if his brother had been a Terstan as long ago as when their sire had died.

Something in his face must have given his thoughts away, for Raynen's expression soured. "You think I'm mad. The crazy Terstan king." He shook his head, turned again to Meridon. "You were right. He's beyond hope."

"Maybe not, Sire. May I have leave to speak?"

Raynen gestured for him to proceed. The Terstan turned to Eldrin. "You asked for proof, Your Highness—that Saeral is not who he seems to be, that you are being used. . . . There is a chamber below the vesting rooms that encircle the Well of Flames. A secret chamber, reached only by a hidden passage."

Eldrin cocked an ironic brow. "I'm just a Novice Initiate, Captain. I'm not allowed into the vesting rooms."

"Take the south opening, go down three doors. You'll find the panel in the wardrobe at the back of the room. Make sure you go during the day."

"And how is it that *you* know about this place?"

"I have been there in my service to your brother. More than once, in fact."

Eldrin started. A Terstan in the heart of the Holy Keep? Impossible.

"It's very important that you go during the day," Raynen reiterated soberly.

Eldrin scowled at him. "Don't worry. I'm not about to violate Eidon's rules of sanctity just to prove this madness wrong. I already know it's wrong."

"Not Eidon's rules, my lord," Meridon corrected, drawing his gaze. "The Mataio's." The Terstan paused, his brown eyes deep and strangely piercing. "When you were touched this morning—did it really feel like Eidon? You've studied the Words for eight years, and I am told you've longed to know him all your life. Do you really believe revulsion and terror would be your strongest feelings if you were truly meeting him?"

Eldrin's heart suddenly thundered in his ears. How did he know? How could he possibly know?

"Go to the room, my lord. Then you'll know for sure, one way or the other." He glanced questioningly at Raynen and, when the king nodded, stepped to the door and pulled it open. Clearly the interview was over, but for a long moment Eldrin couldn't move, unnerved, still, by the way the man had hit so precisely on the discomfiting elements of this morning's touch. Elements he had refused to identify until now. But how had this man, this Terstan, known that?

"Highness?"

With a scowl, Eldrin broke free of his thoughts, bowed his good-bye to the king, then strode past the captain into the weapons-lined antechamber and back to Brother Rhiad.

CHAPTER

# 6

The Midnight Hymn crescendoed as the Flames surged upward in the midst of the bowl-shaped Sanctum, a scarlet column reaching for the high, domed window. On the third and highest tier, standing among the other Novices, Eldrin gripped the railing before him and stared in awe, his skin prickling with its power. He had never seen the Flames burn so brightly. From the lower levels they must be breathtaking, a beacon of hope that chased away the darkness.

The Flames subsided as the hymn's last notes faded to a hum, and Guardians from the lower tiers poured into the aisles, descending to the Sanctum's central floor. Encircling the dais, the holy men formed into lines at the four compass points and converged on the Flames, each quartet casting their sin-laden oaken slats down the slope of the white marble moat toward the central Flame.

Eldrin watched from the lofty tier, his eye held by the cross-shaped pattern of light and shadow moving both toward and away from the leaping Flames, the slats fluttering through the air as they were cast into the well. Visually mesmerized, he found his thoughts returning to the inner turmoil that had kept him awake since he had returned from the palace over three hours ago.

Brother Rhiad, still smarting from the way he had been treated and incensed that a dangerous heretic like Meridon should be so close to the king, had questioned Eldrin closely on the ride back. It had taken Eldrin's full powers of wit and self-control to keep the man from guessing just how much the meeting had distressed him—and how much of it Eldrin kept to himself. He said nothing of Raynen's probing with regard to his being touched by Eidon, nor of Meridon's uncannily precise description of that troubling experience.

His conscience pricked him for that. Were not sins of omission as bad as flat-out lying? And yet he would have told the Haverallan everything had the man asked. He just hadn't asked, being more concerned with debunking the king's tale of their father's death. And with whether they had given Eldrin anything. That seemed a particular concern. "You're saying they gave you nothing, then?" he'd asked for the third time in a row. "No trinket? No gift? No family heirloom?"

"No, sir."

"How about a brooch or a signet? Or . . . or a good-luck stone."

*A good-luck stone?* "No, sir, they gave me nothing at all."

"Nothing. You're sure?"

*Of course I'm sure,* Eldrin thought. *How could I not be sure? What's the matter with him?* But he only said, "Yes, sir."

Rhiad had stared into his eyes as if searching for the lie in his words. But truly they'd given him nothing. Only an uncannily accurate description of his troubles with Eidon's touch and an admonition to search for a secret chamber beyond the vesting rooms. An admonition he had kept to himself, as well—which troubled him more than any of the rest. For why would he hold that back, unless some part of him believed the room was real?

As the last four Guardians cast their slats into the moat, the humming silenced, leaving the great chamber filled only with rustlings and an occasional cough as the lines of holy men withdrew up the aisles. The bell of dismissal tolled and Eldrin's companions began to slip away, back to their pallets. Eldrin let them move past him, shoulders bumping him slightly from time to time, until all had gone and he alone remained.

Even then he stood listening and waiting—for what he did not know. Thunder rumbled outside, remnants of another evening storm. The Flames barely flickered above the lip of the brazier now, and shadows hung heavily over the Sanctum. Silently he slipped along the tier to one of the eight aisles that stair-stepped down to the marble moat. At the bottom he stood again before the brass railing, staring into the Flames, recalling how he'd started the day here, full of the anticipation of reaching his goal. . . .

The dancing, throbbing colors pulled at his eye and mind, inviting him to enter. He held back, aversion shivering through him. It was possible another touch would put all his fears to rest, but somehow he could not make himself seek it.

*"You've studied the Words for eight years . . . longed to know him all your life. Do you really believe revulsion and terror would be your strongest feelings if you were truly meeting him?"*

He swallowed hard. His gaze fixed upon the tier above the moat where the curtained doorways led into the vesting rooms. The south one lay directly across the Flames from him.

*This is madness,* he told himself. *You can't go in there. The man must've put a spell on you. Go back to your cell and read the scriptures if you cannot sleep.*

Thunder rumbled again. He drew a long breath and let it out, then turned from the rail to climb back up the stair. And stopped, startled. From the corner of his eye he was sure he had glimpsed someone retreating suddenly behind the curtain covering the alcove just behind him, as if whoever it was hadn't wanted to be seen.

He thought at once of Brother Rhiad, watching him, suspecting he had held back during the interview in the coach. . . .

Nothing moved. Darkness pressed around him, its silence filled only with the soft staccato throb of the Flames and his own beating heart. Slowly he let out his breath, and then annoyance eclipsed the subsiding fear. What was wrong with him? Did he honestly believe Brother Rhiad, right hand to the High Father himself, had nothing better to do than follow an insignificant Novice Initiate around in the middle of the night? It was as ridiculous as all the rest of the suspicions he had entertained this day. He'd become altogether too paranoid. He absolutely must retire to his pallet and cease this useless—dangerous—mental labor.

---

He awoke the next morning to the predawn bells calling the faithful to worship, feeling unexpectedly refreshed. Time and sleep had so dulled the seeming significance of the previous day's events that he could almost discount them. After all, one day's happenings could hardly overturn the accumulated power of eight *years* of days' happenings.

Sunpraise was especially poignant. The dimly lit Sanctum held a peaceful air that presaged the gentle break of dawn. And Saeral himself conducted the ceremony, offering the golden oil of Spirit that sent the crimson Flames leaping skyward. The Morning Song filled the air with sweetness as their united voices anticipated the ultimate return of Eidon's Light in full power, chasing away the darkness and establishing his rule forever.

Eldrin sang with the rest of them, comforted by the familiar stirring of his emotions, the familiar certainty that this was right and true and good. When the first ray of sun caught on the mirrored glass of the high, domed window, igniting it in a blaze of white fire, his heart soared, and he threw up his hands with the others, offering his praise to the Creator. Whatever spell the Terstan had worked upon him, the service and the morning light banished it. He could see clearly again. The Terstan had lied. There was no mysterious room; he *had* been touched by Eidon, and all was well.

The day proceeded quietly, through the morning meal of biscuit and tea, the Initiates' choir practice, and several hours spent studying the Books of Rule and copying out that portion of the Law he had most recently learned. Even to write the holy statutes, St. Haverall had said, was to smite the darkness. And writing was particularly pleasurable to Eldrin—the stroke of the pen, the mindless movements of the arm, the way the ink flowed in dark, wet lines, thick and thin, swooping gracefully across the page. The words sprang from his head, ran down his arm, to return to him through his eyes, a circle that ran upon itself, burning truth into his recalcitrant soul, chasing away the doubts and confusions.

He first heard about the body in the garden just before midmeal, the incredible rumor relayed softly by a fellow Initiate as they stepped through the door of the dining hall. Forbidden to talk once over that threshold, he could not ask for details, and the elders who oversaw the noon repast made no mention of it.

The dark bread and vegetable soup was served out in a customary silence, broken only by the reading of the Praises. But midway through the meal a Haverallan hurried in, spoke quietly into the ear of one of the elders at the head table, and unleashed a relay of whispering that resulted in fully half the elders leaving the room.

Those who remained ensured that the reading of the chapter continued undisturbed, though there were many exchanged glances and lifted brows among those of lower ranks, and concentration upon the Praises was poor.

Finally they were dismissed into the halls, and the rumor mill exploded.

No one seemed to know much, and the tales all contradicted one another. An Initiate/elderly Brother/lesser Haverallan had died in the garden by the back wall—burned to a crisp/frozen stiff/stabbed through the heart. All agreed the man had been the victim of the king's evil henchman, Captain Meridon.

It was said he had flown over the wall on the back of a great feyna and done the deed early this morning. The plants surrounding the scene had been scorched by his power, and the wall as well. Several claimed to know others who had seen him do it, but nobody among the rumormongers in the hall had actually seen anything themselves.

An hour later Eldrin was summoned to a private cubicle on the library's fifth floor, where Belmir told him the full story. Saeral, Belmir explained, was at the palace even then, seeing that justice was done. There had indeed been a murder—a young Initiate, Brother Damon—and Captain Meridon was the primary suspect. His distinctive ram-headed dirk had been found in the victim's chest, and footprints by the garden wall exactly matched Meridon's boots.

The captain was, of course, already in irons, and the High Father meant to petition the king for a speedy trial. Raynen would no doubt try to free his friend from judgment, but both enemies and supporters were already warning him off that tack. The court was in turmoil; a special meeting of the Table of Lords had been called, and the trial would probably be held tomorrow.

The old man shook his head wearily. "It's a grand mess."

Eldrin had listened to his report in thoughtful silence, and now, at Belmir's leave, he spoke. "But why would Meridon murder Brother Damon?"

"You do not know Damon, I take it?"

"No, sir."

"He hails from Fairfield Watch, a slender man, tallish, with hair the same color as yours. Not as long, but he could be taken for you in the darkness, I think." He eyed Eldrin expectantly from behind his round spectacles, waiting for the meaning of his words to sink in.

"You mean they think Meridon was trying to kill me and got Damon instead?"

"That seems the likeliest scenario."

"Not if you know Meridon."

Belmir arched a bushy brow at him. "And do you know him, son?"

"Enough to know he's not the kind of man to leap over the garden wall and kill the first Initiate with blond hair he comes upon. He knows very well what I look like. And I can't imagine him leaving his personal dagger behind as evidence. He may be evil, but he's not stupid."

"He's a Terstan, Eldrin. A fanatic, subject to madness. You have no idea what he's capable of. And his loyalty to the king is well-known."

"You're saying *Raynen* is behind this?"

"Lad, he cannot help but see you as a threat. And they say he's been distraught of late—unbalanced." He shook his head. "I cannot believe all the problems this Initiation has had. I'm beginning to think it will take a miracle to pull it off. In any case, Saeral does not believe your brother will try anything else—it would be political suicide. You can relax." He smiled, sat back, opened the big book lying on the table before him, and suggested Eldrin might want to review the last batch of codices.

Two hours later, Eldrin returned to his cell for afternoon meditation and found that while the surface of his mind had been engaged in the repetition of the codices, the old doubts had been busy underneath it, kindling themselves to new life.

No matter how facilely Belmir might blame it all on Terstan madness, Eldrin could not believe Meridon had murdered that Initiate. Not because of any delusions that the man was above murder, but for the simple fact that Eldrin was certain if Meridon had come after him, Eldrin would now be dead. Besides, he carried no trace of the sarotis that always accompanied Terstan madness and had exhibited, in all Eldrin's dealings with him, not the least hint of insanity.

But if Meridon hadn't done it, who had? And why? And how had Meridon's dagger ended up in the body?

For that matter, why was Damon walking in the garden before dawn? He should have been asleep. Or at least on his way to Sunpraise.

None of it made any sense.

He thought again of Brother Rhiad raving last night in the coach about what a dangerous heretic Meridon was and how he needed to be stopped.

Well, he'd been stopped.

And the king had been deprived of his most loyal supporter, was suspected of having orchestrated an assassination attempt, and was now exquisitely vulnerable to censure, perhaps even to forced abdication should his religious views be made public. It certainly made a convenient route for Eldrin to take the throne.

He sat very still, staring blindly at the open Book of Rule on the desk before him. His chest had grown so tight he could hardly breathe, and his heart thumped a frantic tattoo against his rib cage.

"How can you even think this?" he murmured. "It's heresy." And if it was hard to believe in Meridon's guilt, how much harder was it to believe the theory now presenting itself for his consideration? He dashed the gathering pattern apart, unwilling to consider it further. There had to be another explanation.

Maybe someone who hated the Guardians had jumped over the wall in a drunken fit and murdered Damon.

With Meridon's dagger? Stealing that was a feat not likely pulled off by just anyone. Certainly not a drunken hater of Guardians.

Maybe Gillard did it, trying to derail his chief competitor in the upcoming Festival of Arms.

But the image of Gillard leaping over the wall to murder the unsuspecting Initiate was even less credible than the one of Meridon. Besides, Gillard's feet were too big for the prints.

One of Gillard's retainers, then, or maybe one of Beltha'adi's, a southlander spy seeking to create turmoil in the city!

Each suggestion seemed to grow more fantastic, more improbable. There was no answer. Or rather, the one that fit the most pieces was totally unacceptable.

He clenched his hands atop the open, musty pages, dropped his head onto them, and squeezed his eyes shut. "Oh, Eidon, my Lord. Forgive me, forgive these awful suspicions. I know they are untrue and shamefully disloyal. Please, drive them from my mind."

He repeated his plea several times and finally opened his eyes to focus upon the words beneath his hands, determined to concentrate upon them and nothing else. But he had only read a few lines before another memory assailed him.

*"Do you really believe revulsion and terror would be your strongest feelings if you were truly meeting him?"*

He closed his eyes, moaning slightly as his thoughts tangled all over again. Finally he closed the book, shrugged on his mantle, and left. He did not know where he intended to go until he ended up in the garden, edging up to the place where the body had been found.

The plants were not scorched, nor was the wall, but the gravel had been disturbed, shoved up in little piles like a stormy sea. Probably the result of the king's guardsmen who'd been out here investigating, taking up the body and all. There was blood, too, a small patch of it on the gray crumble. The footprints Belmir had mentioned lay in the soft earth in the bed of hockspur at the base of the wall, the stems and white blossoms crushed and flattened. Only two prints, and then whoever it was had leapt for the wall and climbed over it.

He turned back to the bloodstain. It wasn't very big, but with the heart stopped and the dirk still in the wound, the blood would remain mostly in the body. On the other hand, was it possible Damon hadn't been killed here? Maybe someone stole Meridon's dagger, killed this Initiate, and left his body here to frame the Terstan.

Who? Who would do such a thing?

*"He will kill him, Abramm. Just like he killed the others."*

*"He's using you."*

*"Go to the room, my lord. Then you'll know for sure, one way or the other."*

He stared at the blood, pulse pounding in his ears, sweat trickling down his chest.

If he did this he could be ruined. He could be . . . He didn't even know what the punishment was for a violation of this magnitude. Expulsion? Excommunication? He could even be killed or driven mad by the power of the Flames themselves, angry that he had violated their perfect purity with his wretched unbelief.

But if he backed off, tried to shove this all down into his soul, his faith would always have worms at its core. Doubt would weaken his conviction, sully his purity, compromise his service. And if it could be expunged no other way . . .

*Oh, Eidon, if this is wrong, please, show me, stop me. Don't let me do this!*

As always, his plea received no answer.

Half an hour later he entered the Great Sanctum. Cloaked and cowled as was always a penitent's right, he made his way slowly to the bottom. A handful of others knelt along the railing, deep in prayer or meditation. He walked around to the south, then joined the others—on his knees, pressing his forehead to the rail, his eyes clenched shut. His heart knocked against his chest, and his palms were slick against the brass. His stomach had curled into a tight, hard knot.

He could hardly believe he was doing this. He who rarely violated even the smallest stricture of the codes, who was vaunted for his personal discipline and attention to detail, whom Belmir had pronounced the most obedient Novice he had ever discipled—he stood now on the verge of committing an unthinkable transgression.

But he had to know the truth. Over and over in his Holy Word, Eidon promised his disciples that anyone who sincerely sought the truth would find it. And Eidon must know his heart, must know he meant no harm, that he sought only to prove there was no passage and no secret chamber so he could slay these awful doubts once and for all. Meridon probably did not expect him to seek the place out anyway, had only told him about it to confuse and unsettle him, to birth the very doubts that had been birthed. The sooner Eldrin proved him wrong, the better.

*Lord Eidon, forgive me, preserve me, show me your truth. . . .*

He stood and stepped back, hands clasped beneath the folds of his robe, his head down. Covertly he scanned the Guardians and Initiates in prayer around him, the dancing tumble of the Flames, hissing and moaning in the silence. No one seemed to notice him, but many faces were hidden in the shadows of a cowl, just like his. They could be watching him, and he would never know. He backed another step and let his hands fall beside him. Air stirred around the backs of his ankles, a draft from the corridor behind the curtain. His heart beat so hard he thought it might burst from his chest. Again he scanned his companions. Then he drew a breath, turned purposefully, and stepped through the curtain.

He had gone several strides before he knew it—so focused on the expectation of the outcry his violation would ignite, he had no eyes for his surroundings. But no outcry arose, and no one came after him. Finally he stopped to get his bearings.

A stubby candle in a wall sconce on the curving corridor ahead provided faint illumination. The scents of oil and wood and incense filled his nostrils. Silence pressed upon him, amplifying his breathing into a loud, obtrusive rasp.

Three doors down, Meridon had said. He stepped quietly past the first two, entered the third. The room beyond was pitch black, so he backed out and got a candle from its sconce. The light revealed a small vesting chamber with a lampstand, a bench and basin, and a tall wardrobe carved of dark wood looming against the back wall. And no other door or passageway save the one he had come in through. He searched the room twice, rubbing his fingers over the walls to be sure. There was nothing.

Finally he stood back, relief making him want to laugh aloud. Meridon was wrong! It *was* a trick!

He was about to leave when it occurred to him he had not checked the wardrobe. Hadn't Meridon said something about a secret panel? Renewed uneasiness fluttered in his middle. For a moment he tried to talk himself out of it—he'd been here too long already. Soon the men who would lead the evening worship service would be arriving to prepare. He ought to go before he was discovered.

But he was here now, and it would make all he had done so far a waste if he did not make absolutely sure. Grimly he set the candle on the bench and opened the wardrobe.

The panel behind the ranks of robes had no handle, but it slid aside easily under his touch, revealing a narrow stone stairway curving down into the darkness. Sick with dread, he went back for the candle, then pressed through the robes. The candlelight flickered over walls and steps hewn from solid rock—yet with a veneer as smooth and slick as ice. Dark, tentacled masses clung to the ceiling a little way down, but he did not lift the candle to inspect them. A cold draft, heavy with animal odor, pressed against his face, lifting his hair from his cheeks. His stomach twisted. Hot wax dripped onto his hand.

The last thing he wanted to do was go down that stairway.

Reaching back, he pulled the wardrobe doors shut, then, with a breath of resolve, started forward. Three steps later a wild, unthinking panic gripped him, paralyzing his limbs, pushing back at him with physical force. The candle guttered and the flame shrank to a mere glow at the wick's end.

*Go back. Go back. Go back.*

The stench of evil was undeniable.

He swallowed hard, fought to wrest his trembling legs under control, and by sheer force of will pressed onward.

The terror eased as he descended. The stair spiraled down, the footing slick and treacherous, the walls so close they often brushed his shoulders. Before long he found himself fighting another fear as he grew ever more aware of the tons of rock over his head. Grimly he kept on until the stairway emptied into a small, low-ceilinged landing. Two doorways led off left and right. He chose right and soon came to a short stair ascending to a curtained opening.

Warily he pushed aside the curtain. A blast of icy air roiled out at him, fogging his breath and setting the candle flame flickering.

He ventured over the threshold, the light held out before him. Across from him stood a low couch, carved of black tegwood and cushioned with black velvet. A small silver casket rested on a tegwood table at one end, lid pushed back. Its black satin heart lay empty, but the jewel-inlaid runes on the side of the box raised the hairs on the back of his neck. They were not Mataian devices, nor Kiriathan. They most reminded him of ancient symbols of evil associated with the dark rituals practiced by the barbarians of the north.

Shivering with the intense cold, he turned slowly, playing his light over the niche carved into the glasslike stone to the right. A portrait hung there, hidden in the shadow. He stepped closer, lifting the candle—and nearly dropped it when he recognized the face staring out at him from the gilded frame. It was his own, though very much younger, back before he'd entered the Mataio.

And it was unfinished. He remembered this portrait—how he'd hated sitting for it, and how, adding insult to injury, the picture had disappeared just before completion. He had suspected Gillard, the prank being typical of those his brother used to play on him. Another portrait had been made, of course—another six months of having to sit—and that one had not disappeared. Eventually the incident was forgotten.

He stared at it now, hardly able to believe his eyes, struggling to accept the implications its presence here carried. Surely Saeral had not stolen it. Perhaps he had found it, had . . .

His gaze fell to the silver tray on the ledge beneath it. Three rings rested within a curl of golden hair—one sapphire, one ruby, one a pure gold band. His rings—given up along with his hair when he had entered the Mataio.

What were they doing here?

What was this room?

Or rather, whose?

But he knew the answer to that question, and it was a knowledge he did not want.

*"Saeral has been using you from the day he met you. . . ."*

Eldrin turned abruptly from the niche, letting his feeble light play over the opposite wall. More of the arcane runes had been inscribed into the glassy surface, reflecting the candlelight in a dance of fractured golden lines. He did not know what it was, but he knew that it was evil.

His stomach clenched, and he nearly vomited. Unable to bear the icy, stifling atmosphere another moment, he whirled and pushed through the heavy curtain. His sandals slapped against the cold obsidian floor as he hurried back to the landing and the way out. By then he was in a full-scale panic, gasping out low, tremulous moans, his heart galloping against his ribs. He did not think of the possibility of running into someone, did not think of anything at all save the need of escape, of breaking free from this stifling, frigid world.

He scrambled up the narrow, twisting stairway, slipping on the treacherous treads and dropping the candle in his haste. It rolled back down the stair, but he did not stop to retrieve it, climbing the stair with hands and feet in frantic ascent. His robe kept tripping him, and he hit his head on the low ceiling more than once. The walls brushed his shoulders, closing about him like the gullet of some hideous monster.

By the time he stumbled back into the wardrobe, his breath came in great tearing rasps and his legs would hardly support him. He stumbled out into the shadowed room, which, after the tarry blackness of the stair, seemed light. His leg caught on a robe and jerked it free of its hook and out onto the floor. Pausing, he struggled to fight back from the mindless state of his panicked flight. With trembling hands he closed the back panel, hung up the robe, and secured the wardrobe's front doors. Then he turned—

And froze in his tracks, surprise driving the breath out of him. Rhiad stood in the doorway, watching him calmly.

# CHAPTER 7

Eldrin's first impulse was to turn and scramble back through the wardrobe, but that would only lead him to that horrid room again—or worse. Besides, Rhiad had the advantage of knowing his way around down there, while Eldrin did not.

"The High Father requires your presence in his chambers," Rhiad said softly. "I will take you there." He stepped back into the hall, gesturing for Eldrin to precede him.

Shaking inwardly, his knees so weak he could barely move, Eldrin walked from the room. Rhiad stepped immediately to his side, closing a hand on his arm to steer him down the corridor and into the Sanctum. The great bowl stood empty now, most Mataians at their evening meal. Wordlessly, Rhiad propelled him up the long stair, across the outer foyer, and up a second set of stairs to the High Father's chambers.

Waved through by the secretary, they stepped into a spacious chamber, paneled with oak along one side, lined with narrow, mullioned windows along the other. A wide receiving area preceded a raised dais at the room's far end, where stood a massive desk and chair. Saeral stood with two aides in the receiving area beside the dark, well-swept fireplace, watching as an Initiate Brother lit the last of the several candelabra in the room.

As Eldrin and Rhiad entered, Saeral turned, his gaze falling upon Eldrin. Sorrow lengthened his handsome face, and Eldrin cringed automatically, beset with a sense of guilty remorse in spite of everything. Rhiad stopped him in front of the High Father, but no one spoke until the Initiate Brother and the two aides had left, the door latching quietly behind them.

Even then for a long moment Saeral merely looked at him, the familiar, beloved face as gentle as ever, carrying that indefinable cast of saintliness. As the gray eyes looked into his own, he could feel the compassion, the goodness and light in this man. Suddenly it was impossible to believe he could have anything to do with that awful room below.

Saeral sighed. "Eldrin, Eldrin, Eldrin. What am I to do with you?"

Eldrin had no answer for that.

Saeral turned and walked to the candelabra beside the fireplace, straightening one of the candles that listed in its holder. "You know the vesting rooms are off limits. Now you will not be able to participate in the Initiation ceremony. And I was so looking forward to seeing you finally confirmed."

He turned back, shaking his head. "Still, I cannot lay all the blame at your feet. You are but a boy, and only an Initiate at that. I should have known better than to let you go to the palace." He caught Eldrin's gaze again. "I want you to know that I did *not* kill your father. Or your brothers. You know me, Eldrin. You know I did not do it."

Eldrin believed him completely. It was impossible, unthinkable not to. Yes, he knew this man, trusted him, loved him. He could never—never—have committed such an atrocity.

"Nor," Saeral said, breaking eye contact and settling into the chair at his side, "do I have any intention of putting you on the throne. The idea is ludicrous. You must believe that."

"I do, Master." And suddenly, overcome with shame, he could not look at the man a moment longer. What had he been thinking? How could he have doubted? He stared at the carpet, swallowing at the sudden tightness in his throat.

"You have some idea now, I think," Saeral said, "just how powerful—and dangerous—our enemy can be."

"Yes, Master."

"Knowing is not enough, though. You still lack the power to stand against them. You will lack it until the Flames live in your heart. And now . . ." He sighed again. "Well, we do not know how long it will be before that can happen. You must do a penance. It will have to be severe."

Eldrin said nothing, his chest tight and hot. He had served many a penance, but this would be beyond anything he had yet suffered. He hoped he could survive it.

But Saeral did not pronounce the punishment just yet. Instead he gestured for Eldrin to sit, not in the adjoining chair but on the carpet at his feet.

Eldrin did so eagerly, desperate to show his repentance and remorse.

"Now, my son," the Father said, "tell me about it. What did they send you to find down there?"

Burning with shame, Eldrin studied his clasped fingers. "A . . . a room," he said in small, choked voice. "A room that would prove . . ." He swallowed past the constriction in his throat. "Prove you were what they said you were."

"And did you find this room? This proof?" Saeral's voice was mild, unaccusing.

Eldrin thought of that dark, awful cubicle, with its portrait and the curl of blond hair, and the evil runes on the wall, and in an instant his good feelings vanished, snuffed out like a candle flame. Suddenly his newly gained knowledge rushed back into his awareness, blotting out any notion of Saeral's innocence, assuring him he was in grave danger. He felt the coldness even here, a thick, stifling sense of presence, not unlike the thing that had touched him in the Sanctum, pretending to be Eidon, but not. Fear bloomed in his breast.

"Eldrin! Look at me *now*!"

The command lifted his head and brought his gaze into line with Saeral's before the words had time to register. He was vaguely aware of the amulet on Saeral's throat blazing scarlet, but then the sense of warm comfort and safety returned to him, melting away all fear.

"And what did you see in that room?" Saeral asked him.

"I saw . . ." He frowned remembering it all still, but as through a curtain of gauze. "I saw a dark cell . . . with a portrait of myself . . . my signet rings and evil markings on the wall. And an open casket."

Saeral nodded, tapping his lip with a finger. "Very inventive of him. He's good, I'll give him that." He fell silent, and after giving Eldrin time to mull those words said, "None of it was real, of course. You saw only what Meridon wanted you to see. He must have cast a spell over you while you were at the palace that blossomed when you had found the room."

"Yes, of course." That surely explained it. Though he could not at all remember when Meridon might have done such a thing.

"You're sure he gave you nothing?"

That question again? But Eldrin considered carefully before finally shaking his head. "Nothing, Master."

Saeral *hmphed,* then stood. "Well, you'd better see what it was you really found. Come along, lad."

Together they descended back into the Sanctum, passing through the vesting chambers to a simple door opening onto a perfectly normal stairway lined with walls of mortared stone. At the bottom lay the now familiar intersection, but this time the short stair led to a curtained meditation cell. Like all the rest, its walls were simple stone and mortar with a single niche of holy flame. It stood empty save for an old straw pallet. No dark casket, no portrait, no curl of hair.

Saeral turned to him with a sad smile. "You see? It was an illusion."

Eldrin shook his head. "It seemed so real. And I felt. I felt . . ."

Odd. He felt odd. Right now. As if somehow he were not really standing here in this doorway, but was lying on the floor back in Saeral's chambers with his shoulders pressed to the carpet. He blinked at the vaulted ceiling in front of him. A rustle at his side drew his gaze to the dark bird standing there, watching him. The moment he saw its long-needled beak and searing white eye, he knew what it was.

With a cry of horror, he wrenched against the hands that held him, tried to lift his arm to knock the bird away, but someone else was holding down his wrist. The bird ruffled its feathers, then lifted its beak and plunged it into his forearm.

At the same moment a hand jerked up his chin and the vision vanished. The screaming pain in his arm became distant, unimportant. Once more he stood with Saeral in the underground meditation chamber.

"You can see there is nothing evil here," Saeral said.

"Yes, Master."

"It's just another meditation cubicle, like tens of others."

"Yes, Master."

Saeral sighed. "You'll have to be purged and cleansed of all vestiges of this evil, you know."

Eldrin swallowed uneasily. Absently, he massaged his throbbing arm. The cell seemed to waver around him, the sudden disorientation making him dizzy.

Saeral's eyes narrowed. "I can see it's affecting you even now, trying to reassert itself. We should go." He turned and Eldrin backed out of the doorway to let him pass, then stepped down the stair after him.

His arm throbbed again, fire blazing from his wrist to his shoulder. The room spun and sudden agony wrenched his middle, doubling him over, buckling his knees.

He was on the floor again, pressed to the carpet, the vaulted ceiling whirling overhead, the pain in his wrist like a knife shooting fire into his veins. He was making strange breathy sobs, writhing against the hands that pinned his shoulders, arms, and legs.

*Oh, Eidon! What is happening? What are they doing to me?*

Terror swelled till he thought he would burst with it, feeding off the pain and nausea and this awful cold heat, spreading now across his chest like an invading army.

"Don't fight it, lad." Saeral's voice. "Don't fight it and it'll go easier."

"I've never seen such a strong reaction," someone said.

"He wasn't ready." Saeral again. "But we had no choice."

Eldrin's middle convulsed with terrible pain, and suddenly he was vomiting, vaguely aware of people jumping back, releasing his arms, shoving him onto his side as he retched and retched and retched forever.

A period of grayness followed, then an eternity of bizarre and awful nightmares, of thrashing on a hard stone bed, falling first into cold, briny depths, then into the fiery pit of Torments and back to the cold sea again, shivering and sweating and shivering again.

Time passed. During brief periods of lucidity he found himself lying on a stone pallet in a small room. A tongue of flame danced in the wall-niche just beyond his feet. Sometimes the walls were made of stone, sometimes of shimmering black ice. A man wiped his brow, tended the wound in his wrist, poured liquid between his lips. Sometimes afterward, his stomach knotted into painful cramps that spewed out whatever he'd ingested. Other times he simply fell back into the weird dreamworld of delirium and knew nothing again.

Occasionally he heard voices.

"Is he going to make it?"

"I don't know."

"What are we going to do if he dies? We've told everyone he's in seclusion."

"We'll deal with that when and if it happens."

The light flickered. A door opened and closed. Water trickled between his lips. The voices returned.

"Should we try the feyna again?"

"No. Sensitized as he is, more spore would only kill him. I'll just have to do it the hard way, little by little, step by step, until he gets used to it."

"But that takes so much out of you. And if he keeps throwing you off . . ."

"You think he'll outlast *me*?"

"Of course not. But what if he calls upon—"

"He won't." There was a pause. When next the voice spoke it was closer, softer. "Deep down, you see, he really does want what we're offering. I just have to make him see it."

Eldrin turned the words in his mind, a deep concern pressing him to grasp their significance. But it was too hard. His mind couldn't follow the thought long enough, and finally he let it drift away, returning to the familiar gray void.

Some time later a hand touched him. "Eldrin. Eldrin, attend me."

Groggily Eldrin turned toward the voice.

Saeral faced him, seated on a three-legged stool beside the low pallet. Gently he helped Eldrin sit up, smoothed his long hair back over his shoulders, and finally lifted his chin to bring their eyes together. A soft red light flared from somewhere under Eldrin's own chin, washing over the beloved face, filled now with tender compassion, filling him with warmth and well-being.

"Master," he said, his voice faint and rasping from disuse. "It is . . . good to see you."

Saeral smiled. "Come. Let us go outside for a while." The High Father helped him to his feet, then led him into a warm summer's eve on the shore of Whitehill Lake, where his grogginess fell completely away.

They settled on the sloping grassy bank, wavelets lapping softly at their feet. A nighthawk swooped down, then up. Fish kissed the water's surface, setting off slowly expanding concentric circles. The scent of flowers and grass sweetened the air. Across the lake a couple walked arm in arm, and nearer a flock of white geese glided across the glassy water.

Leaning back on both elbows, Eldrin drew in a deep breath of contentment, feeling as if he stood on the threshold of something great and glorious.

"You have trusted me long, Eldrin," Saeral said from where he lounged at Eldrin's left. "Have I ever given you reason not to?"

"No, Master." He watched three swans glide past, their elegant forms made double on the still water. Reality and reality's reflection. It was hard to tell the difference. The thought seemed to carry great portent.

"I have loved you as your own father did not. You know that."

"Indeed I do, Master." A tinge of the old bitterness ruffled his tranquility.

"If only you knew how I ached at the torment you suffered at your brother's hands, the injustices you were forced to bear. Your father knew, of course, but whenever I addressed the matter, he refused to do anything about it. Said it would make you strong. But it only drove you away."

"Yes," Eldrin agreed. The bitterness deepened, sharpened. Old memories, long repressed, marched through his mind, stirring up old anger and that deep, burning frustration.

"It's no wonder you hated him."

*Hated him. Yes.*

"Hatred is wrong, of course. It feeds the darkness. But you *can* have redress. Eidon is a god of justice. He's promised he will judge the enemies of those who serve him."

An image of Gillard kneeling at Eldrin's feet superceded those of the past, intoxicatingly vivid. Eldrin stretched out his hand, touched the fine white hair on his brother's head, and felt him flinch. What bitterness must churn now in that massive chest. He could almost taste the bile rising to the back of his brother's throat. To have to kneel and murmur words of submission to the one he had so long discounted and disdained must be all but choking him. Perhaps he even felt a measure of fear.

Eldrin smiled. Yes. That was nice. Especially the fear.

"It *will* happen, Eldrin." Saeral's voice came quietly, fervent with conviction. "We can bring it about as surely as we live. Justice *can* be yours."

The desire for that reality surged within him. Oh yes, he wanted it. More than anything in life, he wanted it.

Saeral's face filled his field of view. Beloved face. Trusted face. The gray eyes seemed to suck him into them. "Join us, Eldrin. Come to us and know his power. He wants you just as much as you want him. Wants you never to be spurned and lonely again."

He felt the master's nearness—his warmth, the sweet wash of his breath, the pressure of his arms around his shoulders, embracing him as a father embraced a son, protecting, guiding, comforting. Eldrin relaxed into it, hungry for that approval and acceptance.

And then he smelled the roasting grain, felt the cold pressure close about him, felt that now familiar tendril touch his mind. Again he recoiled in instinctive revulsion. But not so violently as before, for he still held to that vision of the promise it had offered.

The pressure tightened around his flesh, and the tendril began to penetrate, worming slowly, carefully into his soul. Awash with an intensifying sense of safety and comfort, dazzled by a renewal of that vision of justice, for a moment he tolerated it.

But only a moment. As before, his aversion kindled swiftly, fueling a wild burst of claustrophobia, desperate to rid himself of this grasping, clinging *thing*. He jerked away, and his soul convulsed in a frantic cry for help.

*Eidon, I know this isn't you! Help me! Deliver me!*

A flash of white enveloped him, and for the briefest of moments there was pain, an alien rage, a sense of ravening hunger prowling the borders of his soul. The breath crushed out of him; fire and ice rolled through him. Reality writhed and bucked. Then he lay again on the stone pallet in his small cell—limp, gasping, and blessedly alone.

CHAPTER

# 8

Eldrin awakened from what seemed to be his first normal period of sleep in a long, long time. For once his head was clear, his ears weren't ringing, and he could actually string more than two thoughts together at a time. Even so, staring at the black glass-slag walls of the small, windowless room in which he lay, he could not at first imagine where he was.

Some sort of meditation cell, he guessed. In the lower levels of the Keep from the look of the walls. This obsidian slag must be the reality, then, not the stone and mortar Saeral had tried to—

*Saeral.*

It all came back in an instant, tumbling through him in a chaotic wave, devoid of order or logic—the disembodied voices, the struggle in the High Father's chambers, the black cell with its bizarre niche, the pain in his wrist, the cold, grasping presence wrapping around his soul . . . The memory roared through him, pounding away the bulwarks of denial and leaving in its wake the gut-wrenching acceptance of truth: Saeral *had* been using him. From the beginning, he'd been nothing but a pawn, the puppet by which Saeral meant to grab the Crown. All the affectionate pats, the sly, twinkling winks, the words of praise and comfort and approval, the expressions of piety—all false, the snares by which the prey was caught.

He stared at the ceiling's red-lit surface, and something broke inside him. His throat tightened and tears blurred his vision, trickled down the sides of his face.

He had believed Saeral understood him, that he was the only one besides

Carissa who knew how much Gillard's abuse had tormented him, the only one who could see his humiliating inaptitude for soldiering and accept it, encouraging Eldrin to accept it as well and focusing on his strengths instead: academics, religion, the arts. Many a winter day they had passed by the fire, discussing the relative merits of the latest play or the technique of some old master of painting. Sometimes they argued theology or matched wits at the game of uurka or harmonized in duets of lirret and pipe.

He had accorded Saeral the love and respect he had not been able to give his own father, trusting him, emulating him, revering him. It was Saeral who had planted and nurtured the desire to take holy vows, Saeral who had convinced him he was not like the other Kalladornes, was not meant for a life of violence but rather one of righteousness and purity.

And it was all a lie.

A sound in the hallway brought him back to the present, and he remembered that he was a prisoner. He ran through his most recent memories again, hoping desperately they were more nightmare than real. That bird, driving its beak into his forearm—

He sat up, sick with horror as his fingertips danced over the raised ovoid scar just above his left wrist, a scar that had not been there before. A moment later he discovered the amulet at his throat, the woven metal strands of its neckpiece pressing tightly against his skin. He fumbled for a clasp but found nothing, as if the thing had been fused by magic around his neck. It was stout enough it wouldn't be pulled off with bare hands.

Another memory goaded his rising fear. That cold, alien presence that was the real Saeral. It must be one of Moroq's rhu'ema, though how it had penetrated to the highest level of Mataian service, Eldrin could not begin to imagine. Nor did he try. What mattered now was that the thing was here, and it wanted his soul and body for its own.

The notion of being a puppet suddenly acquired new and more sinister meaning.

"Plagues!" He raised a trembling hand to his forehead, feeling sick again. "I have to get out of here."

But the door had no inside latch. With a hand braced against its polished wood, he stood there, fear twisting in his middle, a hairsbreadth from exploding into panic. *Think!* He told himself. *Control yourself and think!*

He turned back, gaze fixing on a pewter flagon and cup standing on the low table beside his pallet. From the talk he'd overheard, they meant to wear him down. They'd want him docile, he suspected, as unresisting as they could get him. He snatched up the flagon, ignoring the sudden awareness of his burning thirst, and sniffed the contents.

Sure enough, the acrid scent of hockspur stung his nostrils. But not hockspur alone. There was something else with it, a faint sour scent . . . ah . . . redhart. To keep him thirsty, so he'd drink more hockspur should he happen to awaken. There was probably even a little badger tail in the mix to dull his wits.

Good. His attendants would not expect him to be awake and alert, and they'd be counting on the hockspur to quiet any notions of escape. Evidently Saeral knew nothing of his resistance to the herb. He just might be able to surprise whoever came to check on him.

Now. How was he going to do it?

He fingered the belt at his waist thoughtfully, then abandoned the idea and took up the flagon instead. The liquid splatted on the slick floor as he poured a bit of it out. Then he lay facedown on the stone slab, one leg braced against the floor, head turned toward the door, hair pushed back out of his way. He draped one arm on the floor, fingers wrapped loosely around the flagon's neck.

Then he waited. His thirst mounted, and the temptation to drink rose with it, but he resisted doggedly, reciting the three codices of Guardian Ordinance to distract himself.

Finally footsteps sounded outside his door, and the bar thumped as it was removed. The door creaked. Light played over his slitted eyelids and a linen rustle approached.

An unfamiliar voice said, "You're right. He's still asleep."

*Plagues!* Eldrin thought. *There're two.*

"Looks like he's come to, though," the first continued. "And had a sip of water. Spilled most of it, too—why do they always have to spill it?"

"He'll be out till midnight, at least," the other voice said, closer now—from within the doorway?

Till midnight. It must be evening, then, or close to it. And midnight was no doubt the time of his next appointment with Saeral.

The cloth rustled again, close by. He smelled stale incense and sweat, heard the sough of the man's breathing. The flagon moved in his hand.

Instantly he drove himself upward, smashing the vessel into the surprised Haverallan's face as he shouldered the man aside and sprang to grab the door. The other Haverallan stared openmouthed as Eldrin charged full into him, bulling him across the hallway into the wall.

Then Eldrin fled, careening down the narrow corridor at full speed, realizing at once the major flaw in his plan—he had no idea where he was going.

Pursued by angry shouts and slapping footfalls, he skidded left at the first intersection he came to, dashed down another empty corridor. Light hung in pools amid the darkness, reflecting along glassy, slag-faced walls. His own footfalls mingled with those of his pursuers, but he did not look back, concentrating on running as fast as he could. He passed several curtained doorways and was about to duck into the next one he came to when a thunderous command reverberated off the rock.

"STOP! NOW!"

The amulet flared at his neck. Pain wrenched his forearm, and his legs stopped moving so suddenly, momentum tumbled him head over heels. He skidded helplessly across the slick floor, fetching up against the slag wall.

Another command echoed down the corridor. "COME HERE." An awful understanding writhed through him as his body picked itself up and turned back toward his pursuers. Seeing he was obeying them, they stopped, waiting while his treacherous legs bore him back to them. Both smiled smugly as he stopped in front of them.

"Now," one said, "back to your—"

He got no further as a robed figure burst from the doorway behind him. A flurry of movement, a pair of thuds, and both men lay on the floor, unconscious. The light under Eldrin's chin blinked out and the pressure against his windpipe released at the same time as the compulsion over his body. He swayed and would have fallen had his rescuer not seized his arm.

"In here," he whispered, shoving Eldrin through the curtained opening from which he had just sprung. Weak-kneed and gasping, Eldrin stumbled into what turned out to be a short hallway lit only by the illumination filtering around a second curtain at its far end. His companion released him and he sagged against the wall, seeking to regain both breath and equilibrium.

The other man, dressed all in black, secured a black fabric tube filled with sand to his belt, then threw back his cowl.

"Meridon?" Eldrin gaped. "What are you doing here?"

The Terstan captain offered a half bow. "His Majesty suspected your decision to seek seclusion might not have been entirely your own."

"But aren't you supposed to be in prison?"

Meridon shrugged. "Technically I still am." He gestured at the necklet on Eldrin's throat. "May I relieve you of that, my lord?"

"I'm afraid it has no clasp, sir, though I—"

But Meridon had already seized it and begun to yank on it, the woven wire biting into the back of Eldrin's neck.

"You're not going to be—"

He felt a tingling sizzle as a blinding light flashed in the darkness, and the necklet sprung loose from his neck.

"How did you *do* that?" Eldrin cried as Meridon flung the thing away and drew a small pouch from his black tunic.

"I'm truly amazed you've resisted them this long," Meridon said, shaking the pouch's contents into one hand. "I thought Saeral would have you safely saddled and bridled."

"I was an idiot," Eldrin said bitterly.

"You never really had a chance, my lord. Here, put this on." He held out a gold chain from which depended a pale gray stone.

Eldrin frowned suspiciously. "What is it?"

"It'll shield you against the power of their command."

"I thought with the necklet gone—"

"They put the feyna on you, didn't they?" Boldly Meridon picked up Eldrin's still throbbing left arm, rubbed a rough thumb over the ovoid scar, and nodded. He dropped it and turned his attention to Eldrin's right arm—which seemed to cause him some surprise. "Only once?" he murmured to himself, rubbing the unblemished skin as if he'd expected more. "But why. . . ?" When he looked up, his face was blank with surprise. "You resisted it."

"Not really. It just made me sick. I think I almost died."

"Indeed." The Terstan arched a brow, and his eyes darted to the chain and its charm, still looped across his palm.

Eldrin eyed it doubtfully. "I'd really rather not."

"At this point, it's the only way you're getting out of here. They'll have felt the removal of their collar, and without this you have no chance. Not with spore in your flesh."

Shouts of alarm and hurried footfalls echoing in the corridor from which they had just come forced a decision. Without letting himself dwell on the possible consequences, Eldrin snatched the chain and looped it over his head.

He followed the Terstan to the curtain at the short hall's end, where they dashed up a short stair, turned right into yet another corridor, then another, and another. Eldrin was fearing they were lost in the seemingly endless warren of passages when they slipped up to yet another curtained doorway and peered into a dimly lit circular chamber. Roughly the diameter of the Sanctum's lowest level, it held concentric rings of knee-high obsidian benches encircling a central brazier of glowing coals. Four aisles cut through the benches in the traditional four-corners cross, a curtained doorway at each end.

A cluster of robed figures stood near the curtained doorway on the right, at the end of the crosswise aisle. Lit only by the brazier of coals, the room lay swathed in deep shadow.

"Here," Meridon hissed, pressing a wad of fabric into Eldrin's hands. "Put it on."

It was the Terstan's robe. As Eldrin complied, Meridon untied the black sandclub from his belt.

"We'll go left," he said, "and hope they don't see us in the dark. If you feel any compulsions to turn around or do anything except run for the opening on the left, fight it for all you're worth." Meridon peered past the curtain again. "You go first. I'll cover you. No matter what happens, just keep moving. Things may get a bit . . . exciting."

"I'm afraid they've already gone well past exciting, Captain."

Eldrin slipped through the drapery, the Terstan on his heels, and they hurried along the curving wall toward the next curtained opening. No shouts rang out, no arcane compulsions took control of his limbs; the men across the room never knew they were there.

Not until he was two strides from their objective and a robed figure stepped through the curtain and into his path, too close not to see him. Eldrin and the newcomer stopped simultaneously, the latter immediately sensing something was wrong. He drew breath to cry out, even as Meridon came around Eldrin's shoulder, swinging the sandclub in a wide arc that connected solidly with the man's head, dropping him like an empty sack.

A questing voice sounded from the men now behind them, someone's attention drawn by the grunt and the sounds of collapse. Meridon's fingers dug into Eldrin's shoulder, shoving him forward as a deep voice boomed off the walls, commanding them to stop. Eldrin staggered, legs twitching, moving as if through cold honey. Beside him, Meridon straightened and let fly the sandclub. The dark tube pinwheeled across the chamber to slam into the head of one of the Haverallans, dropping him as it had dropped the first man.

The compulsion lifted and Eldrin was free to run. He followed Meridon along more mazelike corridors and stairways until finally they burst through a wooden door into the night. Racing around the outside of the Sanctum, they were barely halfway across the main courtyard when the Sanctum doors banged open and what sounded like an army of men thundered out in pursuit of them. Shouts rang across the stone as, alerted by the commotion, the gatekeeper emerged from his booth ahead.

But Meridon was already heading for the garden, Eldrin lagging behind him only a little. They careened along the gravel paths, the Haverallans closing behind them. Suddenly Meridon slowed and stepped off the walkway, pressing through a dark, prickly hedge. As Eldrin came through after him, he stopped beside the wall and cupped his hands for Eldrin's foot. His strength already flagging and his breath tearing at his throat, Eldrin tried to comply.

It was messy, but he managed to haul himself to the top. He was belly down, awkwardly swiveling his legs over the wall, when Meridon scrambled up and over, there to catch him as he fumbled his way down. Then they were free, dashing along the empty street, Meridon in the lead. He skidded into the first alley he came to, Eldrin on his heels, and soon they lost their pursuers in the narrow, twisting passages of Upper Southdock.

By then the air was tearing at Eldrin's throat with every breath, bringing the coppery taste of blood to his tongue. His feet had become lead weights, his legs weak as gelatin, until at last they refused to go another step. He staggered to a stop and collapsed against a rough brick wall. It wasn't long before Meridon came back to sink down beside him. Eldrin sat on the cobbles, heedless of the squalor, back pressed against the wall as he gasped back his breath.

"We can't stay here long," Meridon said presently. In the dark he was only a vague shape peering around the stack of crates beside them. Eldrin heard him sigh. "I'm afraid we can't stay in Kiriath, either, my lord."

It took a moment for his words to register. "What do you mean, Captain?"

"The king sent me to deliver you from Saeral, yes, but also to take you away. You are too great a threat to him. To the entire realm."

"But I am free of Saeral. And I don't intend to—"

"Right now only distance will free you from Saeral. And with the Nunn lords wanting you on the throne, your presence would fuel succession plots and foster rebellion—at a time when Kiriath can least afford it."

"That's ridiculous."

"Perhaps. But it is the king's rule. If you refuse to come willingly, I'm to take you by force."

He could do it, too. Eldrin leaned his head against the wall at his back and closed his eyes, trying to calm the terror, the fury—the hurt—that held him, trying to force his mind to think. He could not surprise this man the way he had surprised the Haverallans in the Keep. Even if he could, he had Meridon's chilling accuracy with the knife to contend with. Still, in the darkness the Terstan's aim would not be as good. And an opportunity might yet arise. . . .

But what good would it do? Where could he go? If Raynen decreed he must leave, and Saeral sought to possess him, he could not hope to elude both for long.

"I'm to be exiled, then?" He opened his eyes and stared at uneven walls tottering over them, separated by a thin line of star-sprinkled sky.

"I'm sorry, Your Highness."

They sat in silence for a time. Then Eldrin burst out with a bitter laugh. "And so I'm to be turned out. Alone and penniless. Or is Raynen still offering the money and the merchantman?"

"The money, yes. But not the ship. However, you will not go alone. I have sworn to defend you with my life."

Eldrin's thoughts stilled, anger overlaid by astonishment. He looked toward the Terstan, a man-form in the dark. Then he laughed again. "You have an odd sense of duty, Captain. You threaten to assault me unless I cooperate with your kidnapping scheme, and in the next breath you swear fealty to me."

"My fealty is to the king. He has charged me with this task, whether I agree with it or not."

"And do you agree?"

Meridon shrugged. "It is the price I pay for my life."

"You have not answered my question."

"It is not my place to agree or disagree. Only to obey. I am but a freeman's son, Your Highness."

"And a strange one, Captain Meridon. For now I'll go with you. It seems I have little choice."

"May I have your word you'll not try to escape?"

Eldrin paused, surprised again and vaguely flattered by the implications. "Yes."

Some time later they reached the river, stealing beneath the forest of pilings that supported the docks overhead until Meridon apparently reached the site he was looking for. There was no one there, nor was there a boat waiting. Only the dark water, lapping quietly at the muddy bank.

The Terstan looked up and down the bank.

"Is something—" Eldrin began.

The other gestured for quiet.

Eldrin's neck prickled a warning the instant before a heavy, stinking net dropped upon him and a hand clapped over his mouth. He was dragged, struggling, back up the shore to the warehouse they had recently skirted and shoved through a door, net and all. Meridon was thrown in atop him, and the door clicked shut. Light filled the room as a foul-smelling man bent over him, pulling away the net as another bound his hands.

Left alone after that, he risked pushing himself to a sitting position as his eyes adjusted to the lantern light. Meridon sat beside him, also tied. Four ragged hoodlums ranged the long, narrow room, one peeking around the canvas that covered the window.

"What is this?" Meridon demanded. "Who are you?"

But their captors only growled at them to be silent.

Shortly the door opened, and a tall, robed figure stepped in. Eldrin's chest constricted. How had Saeral caught up with them? Were even the ruffians in Southdock under his influence?

Then the man in the robe thrust back his cowl, and Eldrin gaped in astonishment at his younger brother.

"Prince Gillard!" Meridon cried, leaping to his feet. "What is this about? What are you doing?"

"What am I doing?" Gillard raised his blond brows and chuckled to himself as he swaggered forward. "I am saving the kingdom, of course."

"Saving the. . . ? But I have the matter in hand, my lord. He has agreed to go into exile willingly."

"I never thought he wouldn't." Gillard's pale eyes fixed on Eldrin. "But if Ray were to die, my little brother here would still inherit the Crown, a position he is woefully unfit to fill."

It was too much. From that deep place in Eldrin's soul a door opened and fury burst out of it. Wordlessly he exploded upward, smashing shoulder first into his brother's belly, his momentum carrying both of them backward to the floor.

A flash of white briefly overlaid the warm lantern light as, with a roar, Gillard flung Eldrin aside. He hit a wall, the air woofing out of him, stars wheeling before him.

Somehow Meridon had gotten free. One of Gillard's henchmen sprawled on the floor, unconscious. A second slumped dazedly against the wall, while a third clutched a bloody slash on his upper right arm. Knife in hand, Meridon crouched before Gillard, the point of Gillard's rapier pressed to his throat, just under the right ear.

Gillard grinned wolfishly, breathing through his mouth. "I could kill you so easily, swine. The bare flick of my fingers would do it." Blood welled at the tip of his blade, trickling down the side of Meridon's neck. "Drop the knife," Gillard barked.

Meridon's blade clattered to the floor. The single uninjured henchman scooped it up.

"Now, hands behind your back."

Again Meridon complied.

"I told you to bind him with chain," Gillard snarled at his men. "Why didn't you?"

"Well, er . . ." said the one with the bloody arm. "It's just that—"

"You didn't think it mattered," Gillard snapped. "Fools! Did you at least bring them?"

"Aye, my lord." The able-bodied man hurried to the back of the room, rustled about, and returned with the chains. They clinked and rattled as he locked the manacles around the Terstan's wrists.

Gillard returned his attention to his brother, leering once again, and a reckless contempt welled up in Eldrin. "You may have the rest of the world charmed, Gillard, but I know what you are: a scheming bully who doesn't know—"

Gillard's free hand smacked open-palmed against Eldrin's cheek, knocking him into the wall, blinded and breathless.

"You seem to have forgotten how to speak to me, brother," Gillard said. "I trust you will not forget again."

Eldrin shook his head, gathered his faculties, and snorted, undaunted. "What does it matter? I don't have much longer to live anyway, do I?"

Gillard feigned hurt. "Kill my own flesh and blood? What do you take me for? One of your Mataian hypocrites?" He slid his rapier into its scabbard, then hooked his thumbs into the belt again. "I may hate to claim kinship with you, but I'll not commit fratricide. No, I act on orders of the king."

"Liar!" Meridon cried.

Gillard looked at him quizzically. "Exile was never the plan, my Terstan friend. It held too many risks. If either of you came back, Raynen would be sorely embarrassed. He has helped a condemned murderer to escape, after all. He'd be forced to abdicate. Personally I don't think you're worth the trouble, but he cares for you." His voice hardened. "It is that alone which spares your life. Be grateful."

They glared at one another, but Meridon said nothing.

"So what do you mean to do with us?" Eldrin demanded.

Gillard glanced at him; his lips quirked. "There are those who can be quite accommodating when one has need of disposing of live embarrassments. I'll even make a little profit off of you."

Meridon hissed, every freckle standing out on his suddenly pale face. "He's your own brother, my lord."

As comprehension dawned, Eldrin all but fainted.

His brother looked from one to the other of them and laughed. "Ah. I knew it would be worth coming down here. You should see the looks on your faces!"

Still chuckling, he turned to one of his men. "Strip 'em. And cut off that miserable hair. I don't want anyone to know he's Mataian."

"No!" Eldrin exploded. "You can't—"

"I can do whatever I wish," Gillard snapped.

His henchman gripped the front of Eldrin's tunic and jerked downward, the ripping sound loud and obscene in the silence. Another man grabbed a fistful of hair.

"You'll pay for this, Gillard," Eldrin gritted, fury rising again. "Eidon will see that you pay."

"Eidon?" Gillard looked mockingly skyward. "I don't see any bolts out of heaven, little brother. Perhaps your god does not care as much as you think. If he exists at all."

He motioned again. Something crashed into the back of Eldrin's head, and the boat room vanished into darkness.

# LAND OF DARKNESS

PART TWO

# CHAPTER 9

The Princess Carissa, Lady of Balmark, waited in the royal gallery outside the king's apartments the next morning, staring at the gold-framed portrait in front of her. Fog-softened light filtered through mullioned glass to her left. A mumble of conversation and laughter from the king's court drifted up the stairs at the hall's end, but here she was alone.

The boy in the portrait stared back at her—strikingly blue eyes in a pale face framed by thick blond hair. Even at twelve Abramm had worn his hair longer than Father liked, the straight locks curling up at the ends where they fell against his lace collar. Mama had encouraged it—part of her ongoing battle against the Kiriathan heritage her husband revered and she detested. Over the years she'd molded Abramm into her own private statement of defiance, a weapon she sadly did not live to see deployed. It was only after her death—and perhaps in part because of it—that Abramm had entered the Mataio.

He looked so young, so naïve . . . so fragile. . . .

Carissa twined her fingers, her middle quivering. *What has happened to him?*

Four evenings ago her twin had met with Raynen and refused his offer of stipend and vessel. The following morning a blond Initiate from Fairfield Watch was found murdered in the Keep garden, Trap Meridon's ram-headed dirk in his heart. Scandal swept the court as Meridon was arrested and charged with murder, and that night fear stalked her dreams as she followed Abramm down a dark corridor. Vague anxieties alternated with sharp premonitions of danger that shook her to trembling wakefulness, and by morning she knew he was in peril. When Raynen declared Meridon's trial postponed a day—pending acquisition of new evidence—she set off for the Keep, determined to speak to her twin.

Only to find he had disappeared.

"It may be," confided the Guardian at the gate—they would not let her onto the grounds themselves—"that he is in one of the meditation cubicles."

He said they could not violate the sanctity of private meditation until her brother had been missing several days at least. And it would have to be approved by the High Father.

Frustrated, she went to the palace. But Raynen would not see her either, cloistered with his law-readers and investigators as they prepared for Meridon's trial. At last, frustrated and exhausted, she returned to her flat in Springerlan—and a second night of dark rooms and nameless heart-pounding fears.

Meridon had been tried and convicted yesterday and was sentenced to die this very morning. Indeed, his head had rolled at dawn, though the event had been overshadowed by the riot of rumors that burst simultaneously from the Keep. Supposedly Abramm had failed the test of the Flames two days ago and trespassed into the innermost parts of the Sanctum to hide himself away. Last night he'd emerged to attack the High Father himself, then fled in a frenzy of violence no one had dared try to stop.

Several of the highest Haverallans wore bandages, including Saeral himself, who wept openly and proclaimed his consternation over this unexpected betrayal. His chief aide and head of the Order of St. Haverall, Brother Rhiad, had personally spoken with Carissa, sincerely distraught at the turn of affairs but suggesting such madness was not unexpected when a man failed the test of the Flames. She'd wanted to hit him, and she believed none of it. Not in her wildest imagination could she conceive of her gentle, scholarly brother doing such a thing, Flames or not. Nor did she believe he could have failed the test of the Flames. No man had been more devoted—or worthy—than Abramm. More convincing than anything, though, was the dream she'd had last night, the third in as many nights and the worst of the lot. It was clearly Abramm who'd been in danger, not Saeral, and she was determined to get to the bottom of things.

Across the gallery behind her a door opened, and she turned as Prince Gillard stepped from the king's chambers. In the moment before he realized she stood there, she glimpsed an expression of pain and helpless grief on his bold features. Then he looked up and it vanished.

"Riss!" One white-blond brow arched as he drew up in front of her. "What are you doing here?"

"I should think it obvious," she replied.

He shrugged his massive shoulders. "Ray's not seeing anyone."

"He saw you."

"Aye, well . . ." His glance lifted to Abramm's portrait behind her. The corners of his lips twitched. "I missed you at Meridon's execution." His ice-blue gaze came back to her.

"Why in the world would I wish to attend that?"

Gillard shrugged. "I thought you had a crush on him once."

"A *crush*? He is a Terstan, for Haverall's sake." She had to admit, though, she did find it dismaying to think of Meridon dead, for he'd always been the perfect gentleman, undeniably likeable, despite his distasteful religious persuasion. But a crush? Absurd. Raynen, on the other hand, loved him like a brother, and she knew the necessity of ordering Meridon executed had to have been devastating.

Gillard pulled at the ruffled cuff of his blouse beneath his gray doublet sleeve. "You've heard about Abramm, I presume?"

"I've heard a lot of nonsense and lies!"

"Oh, I don't know. More than Guardians saw him, after all. I think he has gone mad, and no surprise there." He took her arm to steer her around. "Come."

She shook free of him. "Stop it! I mean to see Ray, and I'll stay here until I do."

Again pain flashed across his face. "Ray is not in any condition for—"

"Perhaps not," she interrupted, "but he knows a good deal about what's going on, and I intend to have some answers."

He cocked his brow again, and the pale eyes hooded. "Do you, now?"

"Don't be snide, Gillard."

He regarded her a moment, then relented, his mien softening. "Carissa, I'm serious. He's . . . on the edge."

"On the edge of . . . oh." With understanding came renewed disgust. "First Abramm's mad, and now Ray. How convenient for you."

"It is not like that." His voice was soft and low. Suddenly he looked like a lost little boy, and she recalled then that he hadn't even reached his twentieth year. For all his size and bluster, he was in many ways still a child. "Spend five minutes with him," he added, "and you'll understand."

She frowned, disconcerted by this uncharacteristic vulnerability—and abruptly afraid. Drawing her dignity about her like a shield, she tossed her head. "I fully intend to, little brother."

As she started by him, he pressed a hand to her arm. "Riss, look at his eyes."

She stared up at him, frozen, searching for the flicker that would belie his words. She found none—no bravado, no smugness, no teasing. Only genuine grief. He released her and strode away, booted feet smacking the gleaming parquet floor.

As he disappeared down the stair, the door to the royal apartments opened again and the chamberlain called her in.

The royal sitting room was high ceilinged and grandly sized, like all the palace rooms, dwarfing furnishings and inhabitants alike. Blue-and-white-striped, satin-upholstered chairs and couches stood on thick, blue, brushed-thread carpeting of paisley design. Dark tables decked with flowers or statuary provided accents. On the hearth a fire burned unnoticed. Her older brother awaited outside on the balcony, facing outward, arms braced on the stone balustrade.

Birdsong greeted her as she stepped through the glass-paneled balcony doors and joined him. He did not acknowledge her presence, so she waited in silence, hands resting lightly on the railing.

A black-and-white terrace stretched below them, deserted in the foggy morning. Normally one could see Kalladorne Bay and the port from this vantage. Today, cedars spired half-hidden through the mist on the terrace's far side. On its near, uphill side an ancient oak lifted gnarled branches bright with spring leaves and alive with a flock of sparrows. In the distance the university clock began to toll, and from the room behind, the mantle clock started up as well, a beat behind its larger, deeper cousin.

As the last strike faded, Raynen spoke. "They watch me all the time, you know. The birds." He stared at the oak, the sparrows chirping and hopping and fluttering from branch to branch. "They watch and laugh."

Carissa flicked a startled glance at him. She could not see his eyes from this vantage, but the rest of him testified to his distress. His blue doublet wrinkled off drooping shoulders, as if he had slept in it. Above the line of his beard, the usually clean-shaven cheek bristled with days-old growth. Deep crevices pulled downward from his nose and eye, and his skin shone as pale and translucent as the fog that swirled around them.

"They tell me to jump," he went on, still staring. "Then they laugh at me."

She laid a hand on his arm. "Come on, Ray. Let's go in."

He glanced down at her and she recoiled. His eyes crouched in deep shadows, red-rimmed and bloodshot, and curving along the edge of his right iris rose a pale crescent of curdled tissue.

The sarotis.

They had been watching for it since Raynen had converted to the Terstan religion six years ago. Meridon's influence, Gillard had said, and she did not doubt it. Raynen held the Terstan in altogether too high an esteem. Now he was paying the price.

"You see it, don't you?" he whispered.

Horror closed her throat. Her vision misted and she looked away, blinking back tears. He turned and stalked back inside.

*Plagues!* Gillard was right. She had heard rumors of Raynen's increasing paranoia, his hallucinations, his fits of temper, and recently, the talk of suicide. . . .

She glanced at the birds in their foliage-bright tree. They had gone still and silent. She swallowed and, drawing a breath of resolve, followed her brother into the palace.

He was slumped before the sideboard, pouring himself a drink with shaking hands. Kiriathan whiskey. At nine o'clock in the morning.

"You haven't asked me how Therese is." He tossed off the red-gold liquor in one gulp, the cuff of his sleeve sliding back to reveal a scab-crusted sore on his wrist. Her eyes fixed upon it, new horror piling upon old.

He slammed the glass onto the sideboard with a loud crack, then turned to brace both hands and backside against the cabinet, rheumy eyes fixed upon her.

"I didn't know there was cause for concern," Carissa replied hastily. Therese was Raynen's wife, now six months pregnant with what everyone hoped would be his firstborn son and heir. "Is she all right?"

"Went into labor last night. Delivered the child this morning. Dead. Like the others." His voice was flat, his words driving like spears into her breast.

Stunned, she sank into a blue-striped chair. "Oh, Ray . . ."

He laughed, the odor of alcohol wafting from him. "It's my punishment, you see. Don't dare cross the Mataio or they see that you pay. Her nurses say there's been a lot of bleeding. She may die." He sighed. "Perhaps I should end it all, just as the birds tell me."

"You're talking nonsense."

"Nonsense?" He waved a hand. "What do you know?"

"Nothing. That's the problem." She gripped the chair's wooden arm and leaned toward him. "What's going on, Ray? Why did Meridon kill that Initiate? And what's happened to Abramm? I cannot believe he is mad."

"Why not? I am." Raynen crossed his arms and met her gaze evenly. "And it's certain Abramm has seen horrors that would unhinge the stoutest mind." His eyes lost focus, and he dropped his chin to his chest.

Carissa stared at the wall above him. No wonder Gillard grieved. He was watching the brother he had looked up to all his life crack apart.

"Trap didn't kill that Initiate, you know," Ray said abruptly. "Rhiad probably did it."

"*Rhiad!* Why?"

Ray lifted his head. "Abramm was close to figuring out who Saeral really is. They needed to distract him and to discredit us. It worked against them, though, for it drove him to trespass into the depths of the Keep and find the truth. He surely looked into the face of evil, and they caught him. I sent Trap to pull him out. . . ." His gaze wandered the room; then he closed his eyes and drew a deep, shuddering breath. "Ah, what have I done? My loyal friend. My own brother!"

His face convulsed with agony, and he stalked halfway across the room, swayed a moment, and collapsed onto a white satin couch, face in his hands, harsh sobs ripping the silence.

Carissa gaped at him. What had he done? She sprang to his side and gripped his arm, giving it a little shake. "What's happened, Ray? What are you talking about?"

He shook his head, mumbled into his hands. "Why did I listen to him?"

"Listen to *who?*" Her fingers pressed the steely muscle beneath his velvet sleeves. "Raynen, for Haverall's sake, tell me what you did!"

He regained himself, sniffed, and raised his head. "Saeral is a pawn of the rhu'ema. He meant to possess Abramm. I had to get him away, so I sent Trap to free him, supposedly to take him into exile."

She released him and sat back, struggling to make sense of his words. "Captain Meridon? But he was executed—"

"Not him. A substitute."

The words took a moment to register. "A substitute! Plagues, Ray! You killed an innocent man on that block this morning?"

The king shrugged. "Hardly an innocent—he was awaiting execution for strangling his wife and children." He lapsed into silence, staring at his lap.

Carissa frowned. "So Meridon was with Abramm when he fled?"

"Yes. He's the one who probably got Saeral—assuming the snake is truly injured, of course. He was to take Abramm to the river, where he was told a vessel would carry them out to one of my ships. Only . . ." He looked up at her. "Understand, Carissa, I did what was best for the realm. If either of them ever came back, the kingdom would be driven into chaos. I had to let Gillard do it."

"Do what?" It was all she could do to keep from shrieking at him.

"He sold them to the night ships."

She gaped at him, stunned. "You sold your own brother into slavery? He'll die, Raynen. He's obviously Kiriathan. Some Esurhite will buy him for their Games, and they'll kill him."

"Not the Games. He's too weak for that."

"So he wastes away laboring in a salt mine. What's the difference? You've as much as murdered him, either way."

The king's face crumpled, and he hunched over again. "Aye."

She looked away, feeling ill. At her side a Thilosian vase sat on the end table, eggshell thin, lime green and orange swirling around blood-splotched flowers. It magnified the nausea swirling in her . . . then triggered a sudden, pulse-quickening notion.

"*Windbird* is nearly ready to go," she whispered. "He's only been out a day. If we sail tomorrow, I can buy him back in Qarkeshan and—"

"No!" Raynen gripped her arm, his bloodshot eyes wide, the lightning shift of his emotions unnerving. "No. Don't you see? Saeral wants him. Saeral would possess him, rule through him."

"Ray—"

He shook her arm, fingers biting into her flesh. "You must tell no one! If Saeral learns the truth, he'll go after him. Abramm cannot come back, Carissa. You must forget him."

She stared at him, filled with the desire to jerk away and wash herself.

"Promise me you'll not go after him. Promise me."

"Never!"

"Carissa—"

A bird chirped loudly on the balcony, and he wrenched around. Sparrows perched along the railing like judges on a bench, all of them staring inward with bright, watchful eyes. Raynen erupted with an inarticulate cry and ran to seize the poker from the rack of hearth tools. "The door!" he exclaimed, fighting to untangle the rod from its holder. "You forgot to shut the door. Now they've heard us."

He wrenched the poker free, the rack falling with a crash as he lurched into the table at Carissa's side. The Thilosian vase shattered on the floor, green, orange, and red shards spraying the carpet. He ignored it, rushing to the balcony, swinging his poker in wide, frantic arcs. "Get out! Get out!"

The sparrows exploded upward in a whir of wingbeats and took shelter in the oak tree. Raynen stared at them, panting. When he returned he closed and locked both doors, then drew the drapes. "They're his servants," he told her, turning. "He sends them to spy on me. He'll send them after you, too. You must be careful."

Footsteps thundered in the adjoining apartments and the chamberlain burst into the room, stopping abruptly, the other servants clustered at his back. His gaze flicked from Raynen to Carissa. "Is anything amiss, Sire?"

"No, Haldon. Thank you."

"The vase fell," Carissa offered.

Haldon noted it and beckoned for a page. As the lad ran for broom and pan, another servant stepped through the side door, holding an auburn-haired, freckle-faced boy by the ear. "Were you aware you were being spied upon, Majesty?"

Raynen went rigid, his gaze fixed upon the youth. "Not you, Philip. Of all people, not you!"

"Your Majesty, please!" the boy cried. He appeared to be in his early teens. "I . . . it wasn't intentional and—"

"Why were you spying on me? Who paid you?"

"No one, Sire."

"I'm sure he meant nothing by it, Majesty," the chamberlain said. "Give him a caning or a night with the dungeon rats, and he'll learn better."

The boy paled, looked from one to the other of them, and then, for a moment, intently at Carissa. He had round gray-blue eyes, an upturned nose, and he looked familiar.

Suddenly he kicked the shin of the man who held him, twisted free, and fled back into the other rooms. The servants gave chase, all manner of thuddings and shoutings erupting from the rear apartments.

Raynen stood death-pale, eyes fixed upon the doorway through which the boy had fled. He drove a hand through his hair and began to pace, shaking his head. "Not Philip. I can't believe it. But you never know. He is so powerful. He can have anyone. Anyone."

He looked up, his red eyes haunted. "Remember that, Riss. He watches us always, even here in my own chambers. Light's grace! What am I to do? Spies on every hand, trusted men turned against me, my own family."

The chamberlain touched Carissa's arm and leaned close. "Milady, I think it would be wise if you left. He will not notice—"

Raynen cried out and hurled the poker at the balcony door. It bounced off the velvet drape and clanged to the floor. "Stop laughing. Stop laughing!" He put both hands to his ears and fell to his knees.

Carissa glanced at the servant and nodded, then withdrew, using the man's body to shield herself from the king's view.

Outside in the gallery she paused and leaned shakily against the doorjamb, her middle churning.

Sarotis. It was true. He was finally going mad, and Abramm was on his way to Qarkeshan because of it.

Her eyes fixed on the portrait of the blond-haired boy on the wall across from her. Memory flashed of Gillard smirking at it earlier. *He* had suggested this horrid plan, she was sure of it. The one to carry it out, the one who stood to benefit. . . .

Anger hardened into resolve. *Do nothing, indeed! Not on your life, Raynen Kalladorne.*

CHAPTER

# 10

Clad only in iron manacles and the collar that chained him to his immediate neighbors, Eldrin stood resolutely on the dirty beach at Qarkeshan, lined up with hundreds of fellow captives for the pre-auction inspection. While the morning sun seared parts of his body never before exposed to its light, well-dressed buyers of all nationalities strolled past him under fabric shades borne by attendants.

There were Thilosians in their eye-clashing layers of brightly colored clothing; sedate, white-robed Qarkeshanians; Andolens in their distinctive beehive hats; long-faced Draesians; leather-clad Chesedhans; Sorites from beyond the headwaters of the great Okaido River; and most numerous of all, the sour-faced, mahogany-skinned Esurhites.

Gold-pierced and ritually scarred, the Esurhite lords wore their dark, long-sleeved, hip-length tunics in defiance of the heat and studied the proffered humanity lined out before them with shrewd dark eyes.

Seeking new warriors for their insatiable games of combat, they hardly spared Eldrin a glance. And rightly so—four weeks of seasickness, intense emotional turmoil, and maggot-infested biscuits had reduced his already slender frame to skeletal proportions, rendering him unsuitable for their purposes. An odd thing to be thankful for, perhaps, but he was thankful, his ravaged spirit clinging to this small indication that Eidon might not have abandoned him after all.

It was a curious thing to stand completely naked before the cool dispassion of these lookers, to be pinched and prodded like a bullock, to have foul-tasting fingers thrust into his mouth, his eyelids pulled back, his face swiveled back and forth, his earlobes yanked. He had no idea what the earlobe yanking was about, but it was not his place to ask, to say anything, in fact. Thankful he was prodded less frequently than the other slaves, he could only stand and let them touch whatever they wished.

He did so with unexpected detachment, as if it were happening to someone else, as if he were not participating but merely watching. And there was much to watch. If not the myriad buyers, then the great Bay of Salama behind them, teeming with the maritime traffic of scores of nations. From the tall, three-masted sailing ships of the north to the narrow, sharp-prowed galleys of the windless south to the tiny coracles of the local oystermen, they careened about the bay, a riot of flags and sails and flashing oars dancing above the turquoise water.

Eldrin exercised his mind trying to identify them and was entertained by the frequent near misses and occasional collisions, the arrival and departure of various vessels, the setting and reefing of sails, and most fascinating of all, the coordinated strokes of the galleys' banks of oars rising and falling in perfect unison to propel their vessels across the water at startling speeds.

Just now he watched one such vessel, a lean dart of silver and black, flash across the water, heedless of the craft it sent scuttling out of the way. Official or not, the galleys had right-of-way by virtue of their superior speed and seaworthiness—only the tall sailing ships had the bulk to inspire them to caution.

The rhythmic pump of the oars slowed, and then, all at once, every sweep lifted in perfect accord, held high in the air as the vessel's momentum carried it onward. Another flash and the oars dropped into the water. The craft slowed dramatically, the off side of oars stood up again, and it eased neatly against a slot along the pier jutting out from the quay to Eldrin's left. It was a competent piece of maneuvering, and he marveled that so many men—slaves at that—could work in such flawless concert.

A group of Esurhite noblemen had been slowly making their way down the line toward him while the galley docked, but he had expected them to pass him by like all the others. Realizing one had stopped before him, he startled from his musings in mild alarm. And when he saw the look of keen-eyed interest in the man's face, the alarm turned to fear.

The man was shorter by a head than Eldrin himself but lean and hard, with a powerful chest and shoulders and an aggressive thrust to his chin. Black hair, liberally threaded with white, was pulled back tightly into a nape knot, accentuating the pockmarked face and parrotlike nose. A crescent-shaped scar gleaming on one cheekbone marked him a member of the aristocratic Brogai caste, and the line of gold honor rings glittering up the side of his left ear bespoke a past steeped in violence.

Undoubtedly he was a Gamer.

Brows narrowed, he looked at Eldrin's face intently, tapping his lips with a broad, scar-webbed hand. One of his two companions joined him, a younger version of himself with a mustache and only two rings in his ear. The newcomer glanced at Eldrin, then turned astonished eyes upon his—father?—muttering in their harsh southlander tongue, his tone clearly questioning.

The Esurhite lord replied, and a chill shot up Eldrin's spine when he heard the word *Kalladorne* sandwiched among syllables of gibberish. Frowning, the younger man offered an argument punctuated with a drag of sharp knuckles across Eldrin's prominent ribs. He then went on to grab Eldrin's hand, gesturing toward the smooth skin on its palm, and pointed finally to the scribe's callus on the middle finger. His father continued to tap his lips, then made another suggestion. It only triggered another round of knuckle dragging and pinching, the son's derisive tone igniting a dull warmth of resentment in Eldrin's breast.

When he'd finished, the older man grabbed Eldrin's chin, forcing his face to one side, studying the profile, explaining further to his companion, and again that *Kalladorne,* oddly accented but clear enough, leapt out among the foreign words. His chin jerked back around, Eldrin found himself staring into the man's hard dark eyes. Memories of Saeral burst into his mind, riding a gale of wild panic that drove him reflexively backward, wrenching free of the man's grip.

The two Esurhites stared at him in surprise. Then the elder's low voice spoke rapidly, and he smiled, his expression bright with interest.

Instantly Eldrin realized how his action had been taken—not as panic, but as aggression and pride—the last impression he wanted to give to men who might be considering his aptitude for fighting.

The man seemed on the verge of decision when the third member of his group arrived—a slight, strong figure, dressed in the same loose tunic and breeches as the younger man of the group, only this one was . . . a woman. Eldrin regarded her in surprise, not only because she wore a man's clothing and went with her face unveiled in a culture that punished such scandalous behavior with death, but because her honey-colored features were startlingly beautiful. High cheekbones, full lips, dark, long-lashed eyes with a hint of almond shape.

The younger man spoke rapidly to her, and those lovely eyes flicked Eldrin's way, then narrowed as she snorted with obvious derision. Astonishingly it pierced him to the core, smiting him with the awareness that he wore not a stitch. For the first time that morning he felt gut-clenching, throat-closing mortification. The sea breeze became suddenly cold, taunting his nakedness, and he was beset with the compulsion to turn away, cover himself, sink into the sand while the hot blood rushed into his face.

Meanwhile the old champion apparently related his suspicions about Eldrin's Kalladorne extraction, pointing to his blond hair, his brow and nose, and maybe his eyes, blue as the sky in a land where most were earth brown.

The woman regarded him more thoughtfully now, a crease between her slim brows. She, too, dragged a knuckle down his ribs, felt his skinny arms, picked up a hand and ran cool fingers over the scribing callus. Her voice was as riveting as her eyes, soft and fluid, the Tahg rolling melodically off her tongue.

She dropped his hand, evidently offering her conclusion as the younger man nodded approval. Her utter disdain galled again, mingling with Eldrin's still-choking embarrassment to trigger an eruption of the scalding self-contempt he had come to know well in recent weeks. Why shouldn't she dismiss him? He was a weak, spineless, jelly of a man.

In the end the master was dissuaded, shrugging in sudden capitulation and continuing down the line. Eldrin stared at his feet bitterly, nursing that old, impotent desire to prove them all wrong—to be something besides the weak nothing he had become.

He blinked and brought himself up. *Are you mad? If they'd done anything but dismiss you, you'd be sleeping in one of those galleys out there tonight.*

He permitted himself a sigh of relief, and gradually his frantic heart slowed. Deliberately ignoring the Esurhites lest he inspire second thoughts, he watched a tall figure in yellow and green stride down the line toward him. Jewels winked from the man's fingers and nose, and gold chains piled his chest. A Thilosian in all his gaudy array, he walked rapidly, as if searching for something specific he did not expect to find, trailed by a set of bored retainers.

He passed Eldrin with hardly a look, passed the Esurhites, now discussing a much brawnier specimen some three men down. Eldrin returned his gaze to the sea, and suddenly the Thilosian was back, stopping in front of him, gesturing at the nearest of his retainers.

Another inspection got under way—hands first, the scribing callus rubbed, the skin examined closely, then teeth, eyes, and the inevitable earlobe check.

*"Haeka t'a dow,"* the trader murmured.

Of all the languages here, Thilosian was the one Eldrin halfway understood. *Turn him around.* Seized by sudden inspiration, he obeyed the command before anyone could touch him, gratified by the murmur of surprise drawn from the men now at his back.

"You speak the tongue of truth?" the Thilosian asked.

*"Tyi,"* Eldrin replied, turning to face him again—a risky move that fortunately went unpunished. He continued in the same tongue. "I can read and write, too."

"Indeed?" Cold black eyes regarded him from a narrow face that betrayed not a hint of emotion. Then the man snorted and stalked away, not even looking at the other slaves now.

Eldrin watched him till the trader was out of sight, a vague hope kindling within him.

Then he noticed the Esurhite Gamer studying him again. As their eyes met, a dagger of fear pierced Eldrin's heart, and he looked away. Thankfully the woman drew the man's attention back to the object of their current consideration, and Eldrin was forgotten.

His thoughts returned to the Thilosian and the vague hope evolved into possibility. Suppose the man purchased Eldrin as a scribe and brought him back to Thilos? Eldrin's aunt was queen there. If she were to learn of Eldrin's plight, she would certainly see him freed. . . . Then he could return to Kiriath and deal with Saeral.

It made a tidy, logical sequence of events. A way of deliverance, perhaps.

Once he would have regarded the possibility with excitement, full of confidence it would be fulfilled because he knew Eidon, knew his word, knew himself to be worthy of his promises. Now he wondered if he knew anything at all.

The last few weeks had seen him plunged into a crisis of faith unlike any he'd ever known. As his body reclined in the darkness of the hold, a far more powerful darkness had fought for the dominion of his soul. He'd been wild with emotion at first, furious with his brothers and tortured by bitter self-contempt for his own weakness. A weakness that seemed all encompassing. He was a fool, an incompetent, and a coward all at once.

The worst of it was that for the first time in his life, he found no comfort in his faith. His faith, like his life, had been shattered by betrayal. Now the long-troubling doubts swept through him like a firestorm, and truths he might once have easily put aside refused to be denied.

The High Father of all the Mataio, the so-called Hand and Voice of Eidon, was indwelt by a minion of Moroq. He said praise and made sacrifices to the very Flames that were supposed to drive his kind out of the land. What could that mean, Eldrin had thought in those early days, but that the Mataio was not of Eidon?

But if *it* was not Eidon's, what was? The power of the Terstans? Power free for the asking that destroyed the very flesh and minds of those who carried it? Impossible.

Or perhaps truth lay with some obscure faith from a faraway land. Or was it that Eidon did not exist at all? That the attempts to know and serve him were but the products of simple minds and cowardly hearts, as his uncle had always claimed.

But Eldrin could not accept that, either, and for days—weeks—his thoughts ran round and round, turning on each other, swallowing each other, contradictions upon contradictions, all without conclusion. Finally, exhausted and frustrated, he stopped thinking at all. And some time after that, he came back to the shreds of his longest-held beliefs. That Eidon must exist—else, where did all creation come from? That he must be good to balance the obvious evil in the world. That he must somehow be knowable—else, why would men seek to know him?

From there it was a simple step back to the Codices of Life, so deeply ingrained after eight years' study they often sprang unbidden to his brain. He considered all the men he had known, all the precepts he'd been given, and finally, almost in spite of himself, he came back to them, at least in part.

Did Saeral's evil condemn the whole Mataio and all the men in it? Eldrin was only a Novice Initiate. There was much he did not know. Perhaps there *was* an explanation that reconciled the presence of a rhu'ema in the heart of the Keep that was supposed to ward it. Eidon's ways were many and mysterious, after all. No man could know them all.

As for Eldrin's present predicament, had he not been taught that suffering was good for the soul? That it served no purpose to question? That men must accept what they've been appointed, knowing that in the end Eidon would make all things right?

Perhaps it was illogical, perhaps it was foolish and even weak, but he had nothing else to hold to. And now he knew himself to be a very weak man. So he allowed himself to consider the scenario he had concocted, allowed himself the tenuous hope that events might yet unfold in his favor and his faith might yet be restored.

The official inspection period lasted until midmorning, when the slaves were gathered together by their various owners and herded toward the auction area at one end of the beach. There, under the looming presence of the city's dingy white walls, they were watered and portioned out into a series of stock pens. Rickety, palm-thatched shelters provided some shade, though not nearly enough for a group of people newly emerged from weeks of lightless existence.

Everywhere he looked, Eldrin saw bright red skin. He would himself be blistered by the end of this day and was already feeling sick from the heat. He could not, however, bring himself to stand in the shade when there were others who would have to endure the sun in his stead, so he sat along the outer fence, head down between his hands, trying to not think about anything at all. It was cause for mild rejoicing when the auctioneer's voice rang across the sand and stone and the business of buying and selling human flesh at last got under way.

He was not selected for auction until midafternoon, by which time the clouds had thickened enough to temper the sun's fire and even spat intermittent rain sprinkles. As he was prodded from the pen with the five other slaves to whom he was chained at the neck, he recognized Meridon, bearded and filthy, as one of another five moving down the aisle past them toward the auction block.

They had not been together in the hold, apparently filling holes vacated by deceased cargo, so he had not seen the man except for a brief, watery glimpse earlier when they were disembarking from the three longboats that had ferried them ashore.

Unlike Eldrin, Meridon still looked strong and fit, his gold shieldmark gleaming in the gray light. As he shuffled past, his eye snagged on Eldrin, recognition flickering through the dead expression on his face. His glance dropped to Eldrin's chest, then away with a bitter twist of the lips. No more than that and he was past, obscured by the men in his wake and the traders who sidled past them in the opposite direction.

Eldrin glanced down at the object of Meridon's attention, feeling a twinge of guilt. He still wore the gray stone Meridon had given him in the Keep to protect him from command. Though his captors had taken all else, they had left that, almost as if they had not noticed it. That he still wore it was as strong a measure as anything of the spiritual uncertainties in his soul.

Saeral had feared Raynen had given him something during their meeting in the palace, and Eldrin suspected this was the object of that fear. He would never forget the feeling of his own body doing the bidding of someone else, and he never wanted to experience it again. Perhaps this stone was a manifestation of evil—perhaps not. Perhaps Eidon found it offensive, but it had saved him where Eidon had not.

The stock pens framed a semicircular yard presided over by a raised wooden platform at the far end. Here stood the auctioneer with the current object of bidding. The auction was proceeding slowly, interest at a low ebb. Indeed, as Eldrin watched from his place in the wings, most of the offerings generated few bids. Several brawny barbarians sparked the crowd's interest—most of whom were Gamers—but it was only momentary, the bidders busy eating and talking among themselves.

Then Meridon mounted the block, and a buzz swept the crowd. The auctioneer had not even finished his introductory utterance before someone shouted out an offer and the bidding erupted. From the first it was intense, almost frantic, men trying to outshout each other, goaded on by the rising bids.

Renowned for their savagery and spectacle, the Esurhite Games pitted men against men and animal. It was said rhu'ema sponsored them and that dark magic was much a part of them. Few competitors survived for long, and

Meridon, fit and athletic as he was, with that gold shield of magic glittering on his chest, was a perfect candidate.

The bidding continued for some time before a sale resolved and Meridon was led away. The furor died at once, and by the time Eldrin stepped onto the block, the crowd had thinned considerably. He spotted his Thilosian prospect off to the right, surrounded by his entourage, looking more bored and resigned than ever.

The auctioneer went through his introductory spiel, grabbing Eldrin's hand and pointing to the scribing callus and then to his hair and eyes before falling into his repetitive request for bids. None came. Eldrin's heart sank. He hadn't considered the possibility no one would buy him. What would the slavers do then? Make a sailor of him? Sell him to the Qarkeshan government? To the mines?

The auctioneer droned on, entering the cycle of intonation Eldrin had come to associate with the end of a bidding session. At the very last moment a harsh voice arose from left of the platform, stopping the flood tide of syllables. Eldrin, who had been watching the Thilosian in expectation, now turned in wary surprise. His knees almost deserted him when he saw who had bid—the hatchet-faced Esurhite Gamer who had earlier shown interest in him for his Kalladorne looks.

The auctioneer started in with the new bid, while heads swiveled all across the gathering toward the bidder. The Esurhite's two companions stared at him as if he were mad. The auctioneer cycled again into his ending, and now the Thilosian whom Eldrin had expected to bid in the first place called out an answer. Again the auctioneer cycled through his request for a higher bid. Again, at the very end, the Esurhite accommodated.

His son spoke to him forcefully, frowning darkly. All around, the few Gamers that remained now looked at Eldrin more closely, some laughing outright, others conferring hastily with their assistants before offering bids of their own. Looking annoyed, the Thilosian topped them all.

By then the Esurhite's companions, both afire with indignation, seemed to have convinced the man to desist, for though he was smiling with amusement, he did not outbid the merchant. The auctioneer rattled on, and the bid finally closed in the Thilosian's favor.

From what Eldrin could figure, he'd sold for less than a tenth of what Meridon had brought. He told himself it was insane to feel disappointment over that observation, but he did all the same. Even as a slave, it seemed, he was worthless.

He was dragged off the block, freed of his collar, and given over to a burly, heavy-featured man he recognized as one of the Thilosian's retainers. The man gripped his upper arm tightly, steering him alongside the crowd to the back where other men in the same uniform stood guard over a group of naked male slaves. All of them were dull-eyed barbarians, considerably haler and brawnier than Eldrin and probably meant for hard labor somewhere.

It dawned on him then that things had worked out exactly as he'd anticipated. The Thilosian had bought him. Would he shortly be on the way to Thilos and his aunt Ana?

No. To his bitter disappointment his new master's retainers hustled him and the others into a cart and headed not toward the waterfront but up a long, switchbacking lane to the front gate of a hilltop villa overlooking the town.

Only Eldrin and the tall Thilosian were let off, the latter immediately consigning him to one of the servants waiting at the gate. As the Thilosian disappeared into the villa, Eldrin was taken around to the back and handed off to a fat, sour-faced man in a linen tunic. Clearly displeased with his assignment, the man brought him to a small yard behind the kitchen and there, in full view of the workers going in and out, scrubbed him down like a pig for slaughter, taking no care whatever for his burned and tender skin. Still damp, he was given a short-sleeved tunic and belt to wear, then compelled under strict supervision to shave the stubbly beard from his jaw. A stout, granite-faced woman came out to trim his raggedly shorn hair into the neat bowl-shaped style the others wore, and finally he was led into the villa itself to meet his new master.

CHAPTER

# 11

The Princess Carissa stood on the quarterdeck of her Thilosian merchantman, *Windbird,* straining for another glimpse of the departing shore party through the glut of vessels teeming in the Bay of Salama. The launch carrying Captain Kinlock and his twenty-five men had just vanished around the bow of a tubby Draesian fishing hulk, leaving her well and truly trapped on *Windbird.* At least until their return.

The bitter frustration of it—to have come all this way and not be able to go ashore—boiled up in her again. Even if the decision to stay behind *had* been her own. Even if she knew full well it was for the best. As Kinlock had so patiently pointed out, she *would* be more hindrance than help—she didn't speak the languages, her presence would discomfit the men he meant to see, and she was bound to draw unwanted attention both to herself and to Abramm, wherever he was. Furthermore, needing to protect her ashore, Kinlock would be unable to disperse his men, significantly reducing their search power.

All were eminently reasonable objections . . . but she hated it anyway. A new burst of exasperation made her pound the railing with a fist and curse being born female.

"Ever been to Qarkeshan before, milady?" First Mate Danarin came clumping up the companionway to join her, blinding in a lime green vest, yellow sash, and violet britches. The captain had left *Windbird* in the handsome Thilosian's hands while he went ashore, another aspect of the situation that rankled. She neither liked nor trusted Danarin—he wore way too much jewelry, for one thing—and she found it especially irksome that her icy manner never fazed him. Even now the brown eyes met hers boldly and white teeth flashed in a confident grin.

She returned her gaze to the harbor, scanning more intently than ever. "Never," she said.

They'd dropped anchor in the bay's less populous northern half, cut off from the main spread of the city by a short finger of land looming off the starboard bow. Rocky quays and wooden piers jutted from its length, cluttered with moored vessels and bustling with activity. Large white buildings with red-tiled roofs reared beyond them—the many warehouses and shipping company offices that lined the waterfront. Where the stubby peninsula joined the mainland stood the tall gray walls that had once bounded Old Qarkeshan, long since outgrown. More white-and-red buildings interspersed with clumps of greenery swirled around them, then swept upward toward the high ridge that paralleled the bay.

"See that dome there?" Danarin said, gesturing past her to the massive gold-and-blue structure rising at the upper edge of the old section. "Used to be the Temple of Aggos. When the Thilosians invaded they converted it to their seat of government."

"The Sorvaissani's palace?"

"So they call it, but he doesn't live there. Mostly it's offices and archives, though that dome houses a huge stateroom. They've got business records that date back to the Cataclysm. That's where we'll find Prince Abramm, I wager."

She pointed her spyglass at the gleaming dome and its subordinate buildings, heart pounding in her throat.

"Unfortunately that'll make it harder to get him back. Qarkeshanian bureaucrats delight in twitting royalty. Makes 'em feel important. Better if some waterfront warehouse merchant bought him. They don't use as many slaves, but if the prince can do figures as well as write and speak Thilosian . . ."

"He *is* good at figures," Carissa said, sweeping the glass up the hills overlooking the bay to the villas perched atop them amidst buffers of greenery. Those white marble enclaves, every bit as grand as the Sorvaissani's palace, would be other likely places to find a newly purchased slave.

From the villas she scanned down to the beach left of the peninsula, site of Qarkeshan's infamous and highly lucrative slave trade. Just now a good hundred or more bearded, naked men stood in ragged lines on the dirty sand, prospective buyers passing slowly among them. But after only a moment's inspection, she lowered the telescope with shaking hands, her stomach suddenly churning. Abramm might have stood on that beach as recently as two days ago, stripped and chained like all the rest. The thought of her proper, sensitive, easily embarrassed little brother exposed and inspected like a common ox made her writhe with empathetic humiliation.

Again that wild impatience surged up in her. She had thought the voyage here was agony, but it was nothing compared to this frustration of being forced to wait in idleness and speculation while others acted somewhere out of sight. Surely Kinlock was ashore by now. Perhaps even making contact with his friends. Perhaps at this very moment he was discovering Abramm in their possession and it would all end soon. Or perhaps not. Perhaps the friends knew nothing. Perhaps . . .

She swallowed the rising emotion and wrenched herself back under control, lifting the scope to begin a deliberate search of the men on the beach, studying each tiny figure as carefully as she could.

"He won't be out there, milady," Danarin said beside her. "It's been two days at least since he arrived—probably more."

Gritting her teeth against the sharp remark that sprang to her tongue, she continued studying the men, searching out the blond heads among them and glad they were far away. "Do they bring them out there every day?"

"Pretty much. Especially this time of year. They'll auction them off this afternoon."

"What about the slaves no one buys?" She did not know if there were any, but it seemed a likely possibility.

He shifted beside her, a whisper of fabric on fabric and a clink of gold chain. "Oh, they go out to the salt flats, I'd imagine. Or the galley ships."

She glanced aside at the five black, long-prowed galleys bobbing at anchor not a stone's throw off the port bow. Narrower than *Windbird* across the beam, each sported a tall, curving stern with a red awning stretched across its quarterdeck. The foredeck stood bare to the sun, cargo lashed to the rails and down the middle of the main deck. Along the sides of the hull, she could see the slaves' faces through the gaps from which the big oars protruded. With the latter now lifted just above the water and those long, pointed prows, the galleys looked like a flock of malevolent, winged sea serpents.

She swallowed the hot lump of anxiety that had risen in her throat. Surely he wouldn't be there. Anyone with eyes could see he'd never survive as a galley slave. But would he do any better in the salt flats?

She swallowed again and returned to her study of the beach. *We'll just have to find him in time, that's all.*

*Oh, please let him be with the merchants. Or even the bureaucrats.*

A crewman approached to report the not unexpected disappearance of their stowaway, a boy they'd discovered some four days out of Springerlan. No doubt more than a few of the men on board had gotten their start at sea the same way. Abramm himself had attempted it once, shortly before he'd entered the Mataio, only to be thwarted by his bodyguard's last-minute intervention.

The odd thing about this stowaway was that for some reason he'd brought along his dog—a huge, grizzled bloodhound. Perhaps it was his only friend. She'd assumed the beast had been thrown overboard, but from what the crewman was saying to Danarin now, she guessed not.

The man left with orders to call off the search, and Danarin sighed beside her. "He was probably in the longboat when it went ashore for supplies. Hiding under the tarp." He shook his head. "I hate it when they get off free like this."

"You don't think he paid for his passage, sir?"

"A caning and a few weeks' hard work is nothing, milady. Certainly not enough to discourage others from seeking to do likewise. And if we don't discourage them, they'll be on us like a plague of rats."

He had braced both elbows on the quarterdeck railing and was looking up at *Windbird*'s three bared masts. He wore no blouse under the green vest, and though his muscular arms had, in their first week at sea, been ravaged by the sun, now they rippled coppery tan in the morning light. Gold armbands gleamed a warm accent, and an emerald stud glinted in his right ear. Tendrils of black hair blown free of his short seaman's pigtail danced against the narrow beard that edged his jaw and mouth to undeniable advantage.

For all she disliked him, there were times looking at him made her shiver with delight. The reaction annoyed her so deeply it usually sent her scurrying to the big stern cabin that served as her quarters, where she might take herself to task for her foolishness.

The man had hired on the very morning *Windbird* had sailed from

Springerlan, replacing his predecessor, who'd broken a leg in a barroom brawl the night before. That alone roused the suspicion he was the king's man, but when she coupled it with the ease with which they'd slipped out of Springerlan and the absence of any subsequent pursuit, her suspicion became near certainty.

Kinlock accused her of making sharks out of dolphins, since men came aboard under such circumstances all the time, but she didn't care. *She* saw the way Danarin worked himself into the captain's good graces. *She* noted his tactful manipulations and keen sensitivity to the reactions of others. . . . He'd be a marvel at court. Probably was, or Raynen wouldn't have sent him. It gave her some small satisfaction to be alone among those he courted to realize it and resist. Even if some idiot part of her did insist on shivering when she looked at him.

As if sensing that very shiver, he glanced at her now, his brown eyes laughing into her own. The smile broke across his tanned face, and she tore her gaze away, hot cheeked, railing at herself all over again. She felt some bit of satisfaction to see, out of the corner of her eye, his smile fade. He was still looking at her, however, and she was on the verge of sweeping off to her cabin when he spoke.

"You are very brave, milady, for all you are a mystery. I do not know many women who would've dared what you've dared. Certainly not many Kirathan women."

She flushed the more under his praise, telling herself he was only trying to manipulate her again and refusing to give any weight to the warm pleasure his words sent rushing through her. Shrugging, she said, "I was going to Thilos anyway."

"Thilos, not Qarkeshan. Northern women don't come to Qarkeshan anymore. Too many have disappeared."

"So I've been told," she said wryly, recalling the lengthy arguments she'd had with Cooper, her retainer, over the matter. Cooper stood behind her now, straddle-legged, armed, and alert. If she glanced at him, she would probably be rewarded with an infuriating look of smugness.

"It's said," Danarin went on, "that many a black Brogai veil hides golden hair and blue eyes these days."

She snorted, as much for Cooper's benefit as Danarin's. "Rumors, sir.

Nothing more." She glanced at him with narrowed eyes. "Are you trying to frighten me, Master Danarin?"

He drew back. "Why would I want to do that, milady?"

"A good question, sir. Perhaps because you wish to discourage me?"

"Discourage you?" He smiled that bone-melting smile. "I doubt very much that I could. Perhaps I seek only to caution you." He glanced over his shoulder at the nearby galleys, his meaning clear.

The smile faded and he drew himself up straighter, frowning. "Well. Looks like our Esurhite neighbors are finally stirring."

Mahogany-skinned men in dark tunics had been lounging under the deck awning of the closest vessel for most of the morning. Now the emergence on deck of a man in a long purple tunic brought them standing to attention as he consulted with one of them. They seemed to be discussing *Windbird*, for they were clearly looking at her, the midday sunlight flashing off the gold in their ears. Now and again one would gesture in her direction, and finally the man in purple drew out a telescope and aimed it at Carissa.

Startled by this blatant intrusion on her privacy, she fancied she could almost see the man's eye through the dark circle of the lens. Then Danarin moved between them, blocking her view with his.

"Perhaps you would care to retire to your cabin now, milady?"

"Surely you don't seriously—"

"We do lack a full crew at present. He apparently does not."

"But he already knows I'm here, so what—"

"We don't know what he knows, milady. Or what he thinks." He paused, dark eyes boring into her own. "Certainly the more opportunity he has to study you, the greater will be his temptation." He paused again. "You *are* a very beautiful woman."

The shiver ran through her again. No one had ever told her she was beautiful before. Not like this, anyway. There had been nothing dry and objective in that declaration. Even now his eyes burned into her own, stirring up that exasperating heat.

She swallowed, then stepped back to glance again at the Esurhite. He still had the glass on them, as if he had known his patience would be rewarded. She backed into the shelter of Danarin's screening form, hoping the movement looked casual. He wouldn't dare to attack *Windbird* here, would he? Not in broad daylight with all these other vessels about.

But . . . it was said that galleys like these owned the southland seas. That they prowled the mist-bound waters, boarding whatever ship they wished, taking whatever they wished, all at the great Beltha'adi's behest. If so, how much power would Qarkeshanian authorities have over them?

A sense of acute vulnerability washed through her.

She lifted her chin, still unwilling that Danarin should see her unease. "Perhaps you are right. It is nearly time for dinner, anyway." It was on her tongue to invite him to join her, a not irregular invitation, given their respective stations. She caught herself just in time, but he saw it all the same, dark eyes laughing into her own. With a *hmph*, she caught up her skirts and fled to her cabin, her man, Cooper, following silently.

To her surprise it was Cooper who served her meal a little while later.

"Where's Doughty?" she demanded as he set the plate of boiled beef and biscuit before her. "Why isn't Doughty serving?"

"He's ashore, milady," Cooper said, standing tableside, army-erect, dark eyes straight ahead. He wore his graying hair and beard cropped short, military style, and though he was well into his forties, he was still strong and vigorous, a man whose life and duty had centered on the task of keeping her safe since her earliest childhood. "Procuring supplies, I believe," he added. "Unless the captain's got him looking for the prince, too."

"Oh." She pushed at the stringy meat with her fork. "I don't suppose there's been any word or sign."

"No, ma'am." They were under orders to bring her word immediately if there was, so this was no surprise.

"And the Esurhites?"

"Their master appears to have gone below."

"Or possibly ashore."

"I think not."

She frowned at the meat and pushed it again.

"His men are keeping a close eye on us, milady. I would recommend you not venture on deck until *Windbird*'s crew returns."

She stifled a most unladylike curse and stabbed at the meat. "I can't believe I've come all the way to Qarkeshan only to be held prisoner in my own cabin!"

"Better that than the inside of one of those galleys."

She snorted bitterly. "As if that could be any worse than what I've already suffered at the hands of my dear husband."

His dark brows drew together. "It could and it would. Bad as Rennalf acted, he *was* restrained by the fact you are a princess of Kiriath." He tilted his head toward the port bulkhead. "Those men would see you as only a slave, to use however they wish. I don't think you even begin to comprehend what that would mean."

"Of course I comprehend it!"

He cocked a dubious brow. "So you *did* notice the women standing on that beach today when you were sweeping it with the scope? Standing among the men, every bit as bare?"

Heat flooded into her cheeks. She had seen them, just not really *noticed* them. Bad enough to think of Abramm out there.

"I know what Rennalf did was inexcusable," he murmured. "By the Flames, I *know* it! But it was nothing compared to what would happen to you in Esurhite hands." He paused. "Are you aware the Brogai customarily share their women with any who guest in their homes?"

Her entire face was flaming now, and she could no longer meet his eyes.

After a moment he said softly, "Is that why you're doing all this? To get away from *him*?"

It was the wrong thing to say. Instant anger burned away her embarrassment, and she rounded on him fiercely.

"Abramm has been sold into *slavery*, Cooper! How is it you keep forgetting that? How is it you keep forgetting that if I don't free him, no one will? It has nothing to do with *Rennalf*!" She leaned away from the table, frowning up at him. "Why do you keep haranguing me about this? If you didn't want to save Abramm, too, why didn't you go straight to the king when I first told you my plans?"

He wasn't looking at her anymore, his swarthy face gone gray, short whiskers bristling over his jaw as he clenched his teeth. For a moment he looked almost stricken; then the blood rushed back into his face and anger knit his brow.

It was a low blow she'd dealt him and she knew it. By rights he should have told the king—honor demanded it, and Cooper was nothing if not honorable. That he hadn't clearly still played havoc with his conscience.

She laid a hand on the man's arm, drawing his eyes back to her. "We *are* going to rescue him, Coop. Kinlock will find him, and as soon as he does, we'll head home and it will all have been worth it."

If anything the scowl deepened and his face went darker. "As you say, milady." He straightened his shoulders and returned his gaze to the stern window. "Will there be anything else?"

She studied him a moment, rankled anew by his prickliness. "Yes. I'd like some more of my books. *Peoples of the Southland*, Gavilan's *History of Ophir*, oh, and *The Song of Gaishar Murin*. I haven't read that one in a while."

A crease formed between his brows. "Those are all packed away in the hold, milady. It'll take hours—"

"If you're going to make me stay in this cabin, I need something to do. And I've read everything I have."

For a moment he hesitated, then sighed. "Very well. I'll have one of the men—"

"No, no, no! I don't want those cretins going through my things! You know which crate it's in, and you know what I'm looking for. I want *you* to do it."

He fixed her with a dark, suspicious gaze, reminding her just how well he knew her. "You'll not be using this as an excuse to roam the decks, lass," he warned.

She returned her attention to the now cold food on her plate. "I'll do whatever I wish, Cooper, and thank you to stop ordering me around. Now, please get the books."

She felt his scowl, but in a moment he was gone, closing the door quietly behind him.

With a sigh she sat back from the table, dropping the fork and pushing the plate away.

Cooper was a dear—far more a father than the king had been—and his strong arms had ever been available to a little girl in need of comfort. To the young woman, as well. She truly did not know what she would do without him.

But his idiotic sulk was growing intolerable.

She got up and went to the stern window, watching the ships bob and careen about the gray waves, wishing she might at least have a view of the shore. Nothing was going as she'd hoped, and she thought this waiting might drive her mad if it didn't end soon. Where *was* Kinlock? He could've at least had the decency to send someone back with word. But, of course, that would mean one less man looking for Abramm.

With a sigh she pushed off the bulkhead and flounced onto the narrow bench, depression seeping into her. It was Cooper's talk of Rennalf, of course. Any reminder of that unhappy time awakened the old feelings of sorrow and shame and despair. Truly she *had* come here to rescue Abramm, but she couldn't deny there were other, more complicated, motives at work.

After all, the trip to Thilos was supposed to have solved all her problems—her womb made fertile and strong, her husband's affections restored, the mistresses with their hateful bastards evicted from her home, the nasty whispers of unclean blood at long last silenced—yet she had abandoned it in a heartbeat when the opportunity arose. Yes, what she was doing was important—vital, even—but underneath it lay something darker, something Cooper had very nearly nailed.

She'd spent seven years in the barren, windswept reaches of Balmark. Seven years rubbing shoulders with a people as cold as the land they inhabited. Perhaps, had she produced the expected heir in that first year, things would have been different. But she had not.

In fact, during the entire seven years, she'd conceived only twice, and neither child survived to term. After each loss her husband took a mistress. The first gave him an unwanted daughter, the second, ten months after Carissa's most recent loss, a son. The precious, long-awaited, first-born son of Rennalf, Earl of Balmark. Never mind he wasn't legitimate. A son was a son, and what a celebration there'd been—bells tolling, horns blasting, people cheering. The dancing and singing and feasting lasted nearly a week. . . .

Meanwhile, Carissa found herself shunned, disdained, answering to the now revered mistress, and caring for the bastard son like a common nanny.

No one back in Springerlan knew the whole of it. It would have started a war. More than that, it was all too . . . humiliating. Besides, Raynen's similar troubles producing an heir made her wonder if the gossips weren't right, if maybe the House of Kalladorne *was* cursed.

She had contemplated suicide in the dark days after that birth—thought of walking out into the wasteland surrounding the castle and letting it suck the life from her. She could have become one of the lost souls searching the barrens for victims to haunt. Certainly she had enough sorrow to qualify, and it would be no struggle to find a candidate worthy of her attention.

Returning to Springerlan had been a last grab at life. And when she'd arrived, when Raynen had approached her with his plans for Abramm, it was like being reborn. She had not known till then how deeply she mourned—and *resented*—losing Abramm to the holy men, how fiercely she'd come to hate the Mataio for what it had done to her family, and especially what it had made of her twin. More than life itself, she'd wanted him to see its hypocrisy and evil.

Yet nothing had gone as she'd hoped. And though the decision to rescue him had been largely impulse at the time, she saw now the deeper, darker reasons. Balmark held nothing for her; she did not believe even a son would change that. And with Raynen on the road to madness, Kiriath offered precious little, either. The only person she really cared about and who—she hoped—still cared about her was headed for a life of slavery in Qarkeshan. A pawn, like her, to be used and cast aside at the whims of others.

Well, she wanted no more of being a pawn. Perhaps the plan *was* mad, but it was her plan. And when they found Abramm, she would *make* him see the truth, make him see that neither the Mataio nor Kiriath held anything for him. Together they would mold new lives for themselves, unshackled from duty and politics and scheming monarchs, free at last to choose their own fates instead of bowing to those chosen by others!

Galvanized by the vision welling within her, she leapt up and began pacing, restless and impatient as never before. When the knock came, she was so certain it was Kinlock back with news of Abramm, so beside herself with eagerness, she flung the door open without a thought.

Danarin stood on the threshold, looming over her, his face fixed with a cold, hard look that sent an icicle of fear jabbing through her excitement.

"Milady," he said, "you have a visitor."

He moved into the room, forcing her to step back. A broad-chested figure in purple followed him. As the stranger entered, Carissa recognized the hatchet-faced Esurhite from the galley anchored beside them and nearly choked.

The Brogai crescent scar gleamed on his pockmarked cheek and gold honor rings ran up the side of his left ear in number too great to count. Though he stood no taller than she, he bristled with aggression and confidence, and she saw in him a man accustomed to having what he wanted.

She turned to Danarin, aghast. Why had he let this man aboard? Why had he brought him to her very cabin?

Danarin wore no expression. "This is Katahn," he said. "He is a dealer in fabrics and jewels."

The newcomer smiled, but the expression did not ease her. "I understand," he said in flawless Kiriathan, "that you are seeking a man who may have been recently auctioned—tall, blond, aristocratic. With very blue eyes."

Sudden interest eclipsed her fear. "You've seen him?"

The Esurhite shrugged. "The description fits many who come through this market, but I think perhaps I have. In fact, I nearly bought him myself for a scribe."

Wariness tempered her hope. She withdrew to the sectioned table, then turned to him, fingers resting lightly on the waxed wood. "How can you be sure, if the description of him was so common?"

Katahn laughed. "Because I have looked upon your face, my lady, and the resemblance is plain. What is he to you? Brother?"

"What he is to me is none of your affair!" she snapped. Then, in a smoother voice, "What do you know of him?"

"I know where he is, for one."

When he did not go on, Carissa cocked a brow. "Well?"

"In Qarkeshan, information is a valuable commodity."

"I see." She considered a moment, then went to her sea chest and drew out a blue purse. "I'll give you twenty Kiriathan sovereigns."

"Thirty."

She studied him, annoyed, but reminding herself it was the way of these southlanders ever to bargain. "Twenty-five."

He grinned and held out his hand. As she clinked the coins into his palm, he said, "Your brother was given to Ekonissima."

"And who is that?"

"The Goddess of the Sea, my lady, patron goddess of Qarkeshan. The slaver was in need of a blessing, so he gave him to her temple." Katahn hesitated, studying her keenly. "It doesn't happen often, but they do make *dalloi* of grown men. Or he could function as a consort."

"Consort? You mean . . ." Carissa shook her head. "No. Abramm would never do that. He's taken vows of celibacy."

"Abramm, is it?" Katahn's dark eyes glittered. He looked like a snake in a quail's nest, and Carissa cursed her wagging tongue. "He's the fifth son, is he not? A long way from the throne. No wonder he entered your religious orders." His eyes bored into her own.

Aghast and alarmed to realize how much she'd just revealed, she turned from him and walked to the table. "We were discussing the Temple of Ekonissima?"

"Ah yes. If he refuses the position of consort, they will undoubtedly make him dalloi."

"Which is?"

"One of the temple eunuchs, my lady."

She choked and swayed against the table.

"If I act quickly, I might free him unharmed, however," Katahn said. "For a fee, of course."

"We can free him ourselves, thank you," said Danarin, with a sternness that untracked Carissa from her thoughts of Abramm and sent them back to her suspicions regarding the Thilosian.

The jewel trader smiled. "I doubt that, sir. I intend no offense, but the goddess does not sell back gifts. You will have to steal him. It would take time for you to learn the layout of the temple, where he is being kept, the arcane safeguards, of which there are many. By that time—"

"How much do you want?" Carissa interrupted.

Danarin gaped at her.

"A thousand of your sovereigns now," Katahn said. "Two thousand when I return with him."

"Three thousand sovereigns!" cried Danarin. "You're a thief and nothing more. I say you haven't seen him at all and only mean to trick us."

Katahn glanced at Carissa. "He has a mole on his . . . uh. Hmph. You probably haven't seen that one. How about the scar that angles across his left shoulder, like so." He moved a hand in demonstration.

Carissa frowned. "Gillard gave him that when he was ten."

Katahn favored her with a courtly nod, his eyes flickering with odd intensity.

Danarin turned to her in protest. "Milady, we needn't give in to this robber's wiles. We can free the prince ourselves."

"He was taken yesterday afternoon," Katahn warned. "They may have already determined he is not suitable consort material. You really haven't much time."

"A classic trick, that," Danarin sneered. "Giving us no time to think or confirm the truth of what you say! Milady, wait for Kinlock. He'll know best. Don't let this scoundrel take your gold."

Carissa looked from one to the other of them, torn. She did not trust Katahn, though his claim was supported by his knowledge of Abramm's scar. And if he spoke the truth, they had no time to spare in dispatching a rescue. But with only Danarin available to command it . . .

No, if she had to choose between these two, she would pick the Esurhite. Already he had passed up the chance to buy Abramm. If she made this rescue worth his while, she saw no reason why he wouldn't deliver.

She exhaled sharply and turned to Katahn, fighting to keep the tremor out of her voice. "Very well. But don't think I am so stupid as to give you one thousand sovereigns unearned. I'll pay you four thousand—but only after you bring me my brother."

"How do I know if I can trust you?" Katahn countered.

She smiled. "I suppose you don't. But you came to me, after all. And you do have twenty-five pieces of my gold already."

His brows narrowed. "It will be dangerous."

"My paying you now would hardly make it less so."

He blinked. She saw acceptance come into his face. "You drive a hard bargain, my lady. I'll need something to convince him I really do come at your behest, however. A ring perhaps?" He gestured at her signet, sparkling on her right hand.

"Certainly not! You may take my earrings." She unfastened the sapphire teardrops. "Abramm gave them to me years ago. He should remember them."

Katahn continued to frown, looking hard at the earrings. Finally he opened his hand and took them from her. "We should be back around dawn. You must be ready to flee the moment you have him. Ekonissima does not look kindly upon thieves."

"We'll be ready, sir."

# CHAPTER 12

On hands and knees, Eldrin scrubbed the tiled floor of the villa's sacred *teppuh*, his back a fire of throbbing welts and bruises that made any movement difficult. They came courtesy of the majordomo's bundled rattan, a double measure of strokes today—one for the error he had supposedly made in his copy work, one for protesting he'd made no error. And he hadn't. He was sure of it.

Nor would Ghoyel show him the mistake—which testified as convincingly as anything of the fact the hard-faced man was merely using it as an excuse to ply his rattan. He was still angry about the bowing incident, no doubt. Or perhaps he thought new slaves needed frequent beatings just to get it into their heads that they were indeed slaves.

At least he hadn't found out about Eldrin's audience with the Vaissana. He'd have killed him if he had, even if it was an accident. Well, almost an accident.

Four days had passed since Eldrin had come to the villa, and he'd had beatings on two of them. He'd not met his new master that first day after all, but he was taken to the majordomo, Ghoyel, who informed him he had become the property of the Vaissana Sisnayama, a high official in the Qarkeshan Sorvaissani's administration. Ghoyel would be the Vaissana's hand upon him, and he was to obey all commands swiftly and precisely or suffer the consequences. He must also observe the rules of the house and of the teppuh, under whose strictures the house resided. The majordomo proceeded to read a list of regulations, far too many to remember on a single hearing and most so esoteric he would be hard-pressed to remember which to do when, even if he drilled the list daily.

Infractions, Ghoyel informed him fiercely, would be punished by the rattan or worse.

He'd given Eldrin a list to copy and, when the work was deemed satisfactory, brought him to the dusty office that became his prison and set him to work on the stacks of lists, inventories, and bills of sale that awaited. As the majordomo turned to go, Eldrin had ventured to ask when he might speak with the Vaissana—and received a sharp smack across his bony shoulders for the impertinence.

"Slaves do not speak to the Vaissana," Ghoyel had informed him. "Slaves have no reason to speak to the Vaissana. They have nothing to say that could possibly be of interest to the Vaissana. And for a slave to speak to him, to even look at him—especially one with blood so tainted it turns the skin white—would be a grievous affront to the Vaissana's purity and would, of course, require the severest of punishments."

He jerked up his long, narrow chin and left Eldrin to his copying.

He'd worked until twilight, then was brought to the kitchen by the fat old man who'd first cleaned him—a sour-tempered, mahogany-skinned Esurhite named Whazel. Among the lower servants he was apparently the only one who spoke any Thilosian at all, but his accent was so thick, and his syntax so bad—to say nothing of his foul mood—Eldrin's attempts at communicating were useless.

The others avoided him with suspicious frowns. He deemed it another reaction to his "tainted" blood and decided he didn't mind. Hopefully he would not be here long. Fat Whazel showed him his bed—a dusty straw pallet in one of the storage rooms.

The next morning he had made his acquaintance with the sacred teppuh and the goddess Ekonissima, whom the household of the Vaissana Sisnayama served and worshiped. Taken at first light to the pond before the domed, circular teppuh, Eldrin was subjected to a ritual cleansing in its holy water, then taken back to the kitchen for breakfast. A second day of scribing followed, during which he began to encounter documents inscribed not in the scrawling Thilosian but in the mysterious jagged characters of the Tahg. He worked all day, until his hand was cramping, his fingers ached, and his calluses were tender to the touch. His back ached, his eyes burned, and his head throbbed. Throughout the day he had thought of nothing more than eating his ration of fish and flatbread and falling onto his pallet.

Instead, Whazel had brought him to the teppuh again, where this time he was ordered to enter the shrine to cleanse the statue with water, replace the oil in the flaming pan, and clean away the day's offerings of flowers and food. Finally he was to prostrate himself in front of the goddess before bowing himself out of her presence.

It was the drop that burst the dam. He had refused to bow.

And received his first beating. He was also denied his dinner, but by then he was too miserable to care.

Another day of inventories followed, and that evening he was again charged with rinsing the statue and replacing the offerings. This time, Whazel and the others watching him sidelong, he joined them on the floor without protest, in too much pain to risk another beating and hating himself for his weakness.

On the fourth day—today—even holding the pen had become torture. And since he had no idea what he was copying, he had to make himself take extra care to be sure he replicated each dot and stroke precisely as he saw it. Fat Whazel, for all his cynical exterior, had taken pity on him. "You carry flag down," he'd growled in his innovative Thilosian.

And when Eldrin gaped uncomprehending, the Esurhite waved an age-gnarled hand in the general direction of the main villa, down the hill from the servants' section. "I no take flag."

Flag, Eldrin knew by now, was the word Whazel used for whatever documents he referred to.

"I pain much today. You take. Go down."

And so Eldrin had his introduction to the main house, trying desperately to remember all the rules Ghoyel had read at him the first day: wash your feet before entering, turn only to the right, never retrace your steps, never meet anyone's eyes, take care not to look at your own reflection in the floor. . . .

He managed to make his delivery to the Vaissana's assistant secretary, but on the way out, unable to retrace his steps and bound to turn only to the right, he had ended up in a part of the villa he did not think he should be in. When he saw the Vaissana himself stride into a room ahead of him, he knew it. He couldn't go backward, however, so he had to pass the doorway, slowing and glancing in as he did.

Seeing the man was alone, he seized the opportunity and stepped into the room. The Vaissana would never let Ghoyel beat him once he understood who Eldrin really was.

For a moment, though, standing inside the door, he had not known what to do. Then the Vaissana looked up, his brows arching in surprise. "Ah, my new scribe. I understand you are working out well. Good. We have been in sore need of a scribe ever since . . . well, no matter. What are you here for?"

"Might I have leave to speak, sir?"

The Vaissana had frowned ever so slightly, then waved a swarthy hand of permission, and so, standing awkwardly before the man's great desk, Eldrin spilled out his tale. His audience had listened with obvious distraction, puttering with the documents littering his desk and not looking up the whole time Eldrin spoke. When Eldrin at last fell silent, it was with sinking heart, for the Vaissana behaved as if he weren't even there.

He was on the verge of tiptoeing out of the room when the man looked up. "A Kalladorne prince, you say?"

"Aye, sir."

"And your sister is Queen of Thilos?"

"My aunt, sir."

"Ah. Your aunt. And I suppose you think this startling revelation will now move me to free you?" The swarthy face regarded him expressionlessly yet with a light of mockery in the dark eyes. "Just like that, you think, after I paid good money for you?"

"My aunt will reimburse you. *I* would reimburse you once I return to Kiriath."

"Naturally." The man returned his attention to the papers in his hand. "My secretary has a remarkable eye, it seems, the way he picks the gold from the dross."

"Sir?"

"Oh, come, boy. All slaves have been kidnapped in one way or another. And many claim to carry royal blood, though I fail to see why you would make such a claim, scrawny as you are. You're obviously no good for the Games, and your antecedents carry little weight here. In point of fact, yours are not as impressive as those of some of your fellows. Old Whazel, for example, is of the line of Dorsaddi chieftains. Now that's a pedigree to be proud of. But he still has to scrub the floor and empty the latrines."

He flicked his fingers. "You may go."

Eldrin was disbelieving at first, then angry. But when he returned to his office, he had found Ghoyel awaiting him, rattan in hand.

He thought at first the majordomo had learned he'd seen the Vaissana and gulped with sudden fear. But it was only a mistake in the copying. And then the protest. And then the double portion of strokes and the sentence of spending the rest of the day scrubbing down the tile, in addition to tending the goddess, with Whazel there to supervise.

Now bitterness cloyed the back of his throat, and he found himself repeatedly blinking away tears that had nothing to do with his throbbing back.

He was not unfamiliar with the scrubbing of floors—he'd done his share at the Watch. This was different. He had chosen to be at the Watch. Submission there had been to Eidon and to Eldrin's own goal of becoming a Guardian. Submission here was . . . merely submission. And there could be no goals of anything, it seemed. Not for him.

Not for a slave. And he was, indeed, a slave.

The cold, stark reality of that fact was hitting him hard now, as it had not in the slaver hold, nor on the beach, nor even while he was being auctioned off like a horse.

His throat tightened. Was this it, then? The finish of his life, lived out here in this foreign land, scrubbing floors, forced to make obeisance to dumb stone figures?

"It pass. Many days enough." He looked over his shoulder at Fat Whazel sitting on the low wall of the Holy Pool, watching him. "Better if not fight. Better if *eschu'acha*."

*Eschu'acha? That must be the Tahg.* He'd finally figured out that the reason Whazel was so hard to understand was because if the man didn't know a word, he just threw in the Tahg equivalent.

Scowling, Eldrin turned back to his work, scrubbing more vigorously.

"No think that, first. But days enough pass. Forget."

Eldrin snorted.

"Is not bad life, *hechami*."

In the trees above them, the crows burst into raucous calls, fighting over something. Eldrin grimaced as the movement of dipping his brush into the bucket pulled at his welts. Water splatted the tile in a gleaming arc.

"You think run, eh?" Fat Whazel said. "I see you think." He laughed. "I try run. Long past. I say you, too. No good think."

The crows silenced. The sound of the brush's bristles rasped into prominence, a rhythmic sawing that allowed them to hear the voice of the cook berating one of her staff in the complex below them.

"Five times, I run. Make try. No do."

Eldrin dipped his brush into the bucket again, glancing over his shoulder. "They caught you?"

Whazel regarded him soberly. The look of amusement with which he generally favored Eldrin was gone, replaced by something dark and grim. "All time. Each. Yes. I *gabuchai* . . . uh . . . I beat. Forty beat sometime. Look scar."

He turned and loosened his belt, pushing the tunic back from his shoulders to reveal mahogany-toned rolls of fat, crisscrossed by ancient white scars. "I strong. Like *ayya*. I Dorsaddi." He shrugged the robe back up.

"*Last of the Dorsaddi chieftains,*" the Vaissana had said.

"I serve Sheleft'Ai. I know escape come, eh? Like you. Last time they be sure no *ul Kanut akkad*."

Eldrin stared at him, feeling he was being told something important, having no idea what it was. *Ul Kanut akkad*?

Whazel frowned, seeing Eldrin's confusion, then slapped a hand to his chest. "I Whazel ul Kanut. No *ul Kanut akkad*. *Akkad*, uh . . . carryname." He held the hand out palm down, hip high beside him. "No carryname. Ever."

He held Eldrin's gaze with his dark eyes, willing him to understand. And suddenly, with a chill that drove deep into his middle, he did. "No heirs, you mean," he whispered. "You can sire no children." They had made a eunuch of him.

"*Tyi,*" Whazel said, nodding. "No children. You make trouble *hechami*, they do you same. No *hechami akkad*."

Feeling as if he were about to vomit, Eldrin looked away, fixing his gaze upon the brush in his hands.

"I serve Sheleft'Ai," Whazel said quietly, "but he no stop them. No care me, no help me. . . . Why care I him? They want me serve Ekonissima—I serve. She help. You see. She give *shemofena*. *Shaarisa*. You see."

He fell silent. After a moment Eldrin glanced over his shoulder at the life-sized statue of the robed, extremely well-endowed goddess standing at the head of the teppuh. Attended by a pair of leaping porpoises, she straddled a flaming, dish-shaped altar, her legs wrapped in seaweed. Sea snakes crept around her arms, her generous mammae, and into her hair to rear proudly from her head. The marble of which she'd been wrought was painted in vibrant hues of green and blue and flesh tones, but it was her glass eyes that most unnerved him, for they looked almost alive and seemed to watch him, no matter where he went in the shrine.

He shuddered and went back to his scrubbing. "All she gives me is the crawls," he muttered in Kiriathan.

"What you say?"

"Nothing."

When he had finished with the floor it was late afternoon and time to prepare the altar for evening. He poured oil into the flat pan between Ekon-issima's ankles, careful not to disturb the pale yellow-green flame that leapt from its surface. Next he swept the crumbs and pieces of bread and fruit—remnants of the morning's food offering—from the tiered shelves at her feet. Putting these into his bag, he began to collect the dead and wilted flowers. A number had fallen to the floor, disturbed by the animals that had come to feed on the foodstuffs.

As he bent to pick them up, his wrist suddenly throbbed, writhing beneath his skin like something alive. Startled, he straightened and examined it. The feyna scar gleamed across his wrist, an ovoid paleness that just might be a little darker than he remembered, though it had been a long time since he had looked at it. It still felt as if something crawled beneath his skin, but the only thing that moved was his pulse, throbbing visibly just below the thumb joint.

He opened and closed the hand, then shrugged and bent to continue collecting the wilted buds. Again his wrist throbbed, but he ignored it, picking up a pale, curled blossom—

It writhed in his fingers as a white energy surged down his arm to blast the thing from his grasp. As it hit the floor he saw it was no wilted flower bud but a pale beetlelike creature, multi-legged and multi-sectioned, already scurrying for cover behind the idol.

With what must have been an oath in the Tahg, Whazel exploded beside him, slamming his sandaled foot upon the escaping insect and grinding it dead. As he bent to examine his handiwork, Eldrin fought to stay standing, his whole arm throbbing with an intensity that made him dizzy and breathless.

Muttering in the Tahg, Whazel hurried out of the shrine, returning with a stick. Snatching the bag from Eldrin's hands, he stabbed the carcass and lifted it into the sack. Then stabbed the other flowers on the floor to bring each into the sack. None appeared to be more than flowers, but as soon as he'd collected them all, he seized Eldrin's elbow and steered him out of the shrine.

Casting the bag aside, he turned to Eldrin, frowning. "You ward *staffid*. How do?"

Eldrin blinked at him. The initial pain was fading, leaving in its wake the familiar throbbing and now a hot nausea in his gut, high up under his heart. He had no idea what the man was talking about.

Whazel shook him slightly, then grabbed his hand, unfolded the fingers, frowning at it. He rubbed a thumb over the ovoid scar, lifted his face to Eldrin's and said again, "How you ward staffid? Tell now."

Eldrin shook his head, baffled. "I . . . I don't know, Whazel. I didn't even know . . ."

Whazel's eyes had dropped to Eldrin's chest, and his frown deepened. He burst into a stream of agitated Tahg, seemed to realize Eldrin couldn't understand him, and backed up, gesturing at his chest. "What this *eluka*, eh? Burn tunic, burn staffid?"

Eldrin glanced down in surprise. A charred hole gaped in his tunic, acorn-sized, positioned just over his heart where the . . .

He pulled the Terstan talisman out from under the tunic. It was unchanged, still looking like a common river pebble. Clearly *it* had not burned his tunic.

"What is this staffid you talk about?" he asked, letting the stone drop with a light thump against his chest.

Whazel stared at it. "Shadowspawn," he said absently. "Staffid take other faces. Bite. Make sick." His tone shifted into a vibrating intensity. "How you get eluka?" he asked, eyes never leaving the stone.

Eldrin glanced down again, puzzled. The talisman remained completely unremarkable. His nausea, however, was mounting. And his arm still ached and crawled. "A friend gave it to me."

"It have many power."

Before he knew it, Whazel had plucked the thing up to peer at it more closely. He murmured in the Tahg, his tone growing puzzled. "Eluka inside. Can't see . . . too bright. You know what is?"

"Too bright? What are you talking about? It's just a—"

"Ayii!" Whazel jumped back, dropping the stone, his brown eyes so wide the whites showed. *"Kai sheleft,"* he murmured, staring at it, shaking his head, muttering on in his strange language. Finally he looked up at Eldrin. "This eluka Dorsaddi."

Taking a guess, Eldrin shook his head. "No. It's a Terstan eluka. I got it in Kiriath."

"Dorsaddi," Whazel insisted, supporting his claim with another run of incomprehensible muttering. It seemed all he could do to make himself stop and find the Thilosian words he needed. "Inside. Sheleft. Ah . . . er . . ." He stirred his hand as if that might call up the word. "Sheleft—shield. Gold shield in eluka. Sheleft. Dorsaddi sheleft. You must give it me."

He reached for the stone again, but this time his fingers hadn't even touched it when a current of energy leapt out of it, making them both flinch.

Whazel looked amazed. He stared at the stone as a starving man might regard a ripe apple. He licked his lips, eyes climbing to meet Eldrin's. "Please. Give it me. I Dorsaddi. Mine."

Eldrin shook his head, which was throbbing now along with his arm, as much from confusion as from his reaction to that staffid. "I . . . it's not Dorsaddi, Whazel. It's Kiriathan."

Whazel was reaching for the stone yet again, as if he couldn't help himself, not aggressively now but in wonder. Eldrin braced for another shock, but this time the stone permitted Whazel's tentative touch. Its power flared gently, the warmth almost pleasurable. Whazel seemed not to notice, but when he pulled his finger back, the stone clung to it, lifting away from Eldrin's chest.

They both stared, breathless, astonished, watching as the marble swelled, its perfect orb malforming into an oblong, then dividing slowly in the middle until there were two stones. One on the end of Eldrin's chain—and falling back now to thump against his breastbone—the other balanced on Whazel's fingertip, swelling steadily. The Dorsaddi stared enrapt, like a man gazing into paradise, his face aglow, his eyes radiant.

He rolled the stone—clearly as solid as the one Eldrin still wore—between his fingertips, murmuring in the Tahg something that sounded like a litany, something that repeated the words "sheleft" and "Sheleft'Ai," the god he claimed he no longer served.

Eldrin swallowed uneasily and massaged his throbbing arm, completely at a loss.

Whazel fell silent, letting the stone roll into his upturned palm. Slowly he closed his hand upon it and stood stock-still, blank eyed, a strange smile on his face.

Then, right in front of Eldrin's eyes, so clearly seen there could be no doubt, a golden shieldmark appeared in the red-brown skin over the man's heart, gleaming softly between the neck edges of his tunic.

CHAPTER

# 13

Horrified realization doused Eldrin like a wave of icy water. Yanking the amulet over his head, he flung it away as if it were a viper. It skidded across the tile to fetch up against the side of the Holy Pool, and immediately a crow swooped from the trees to snatch it up. As it flapped back into the shadows, Eldrin rubbed the skin on his chest, dizzy with relief at finding no golden shield.

Whazel still wore that silly, blank-eyed smile.

*A Terstan. By all that's holy! I've just witnessed the making of a Terstan.*

He backed another step. Then as Whazel finally stirred, as his eyes began to blink, Eldrin turned and fled up the path to the servants' compound. He had worn that stone for over four weeks now; it was a miracle he was not himself corrupted. He'd been a fool—a *fool!*—to have taken anything from a Terstan.

*They are devious, clever, cunning. . . .*

He didn't see the man in the path ahead of him until they nearly collided. As he back-stepped madly, renewed alarm swept through him.

"At your ease, Abramm," a rough voice murmured in Kiriathan. "I mean you no harm."

Eldrin stopped dead. "Who are you?"

"A friend. Come to rescue you." The stranger pressed a wad of dark fabric into Eldrin's hands. "Put this on."

Beneath the robe's dark cowl, light glinted off a swarthy face, long of nose, too hidden in shadow to see clearly. The man read his question before he could ask it. "Your sister sent me. The Lady Carissa. Just sailed into Qarkeshan today." The man directed Eldrin's attention to the bay stretched out below them. "You can see her merchantman there, just north of the point."

Eldrin turned to study the tall ship, one he had watched sail into the bay that very morning, before his encounter with the Vaissana. Carissa *had* owned a merchantman. The one on which he was to sail with her to Thilos. The one that would have been his own had he taken Raynen's offer.

The man held out a pair of sapphire earrings. "She gave me these to prove my claim."

Eldrin stared, reality pinwheeling around him. *Is it true? Is she really here?*

Hope rode the back of his astonishment as he looked again at the merchantman, topsails treble-reefed and glowing golden pink in the sun's lowering rays.

"There you are, you miserable rockworm!" Ghoyel's voice shrilled in the gathering twilight, echoing across the compound. Eldrin whirled to find his mysterious deliverer vanished and in his place the advancing majordomo, rapping his rattan against his thigh in sharp, jerky chops.

"You dare to soil the Vaissana's purity, dare to thrust your filthy presence before his face and speak to him? You have known nothing of my wrath as yet, worm. And if you run—"

A swirling, swooping of shadow descended upon him from behind, collapsing him senseless onto the path. Eldrin gaped in dismay as blood welled from a temple, dark as pitch against the dusky skin. He looked up. The stranger stood before him again—dark cloak swaying around dark boots, his face still no more than glints of light off nose and chin.

"Hurry now," the man said. "He'll have drawn someone's attention."

"Did you kill him?"

The stranger seized the fabric from Eldrin's idle hands and shook out a cowled cloak much like his own. "No. Now are you coming? Or would you prefer to stay here and face the consequences of that?" His head jerked toward Ghoyel's too-still form.

"Tyi, hechami," Whazel said quietly behind him, the voice bringing him around yet again. His eyes went at once to the new-made shield gleaming on the old man's chest.

"I lie them. They say you do, but no matter if gone."

The stranger was already settling the cloak over Eldrin's shoulders.

"Find free life, hechami," Whazel said. "As I find mine, eh? Sheleft'Ai, he not leave afterward, I think."

His dark eyes flashed, and for a moment Eldrin saw in them the man he'd once been—lean and strong and proud.

Voices echoed now from the servants' compound, and the thud of approaching footfalls warned that time was short.

Eldrin nodded at the old servant. "Thank you, Whazel. I'll not forget this."

A heavy hand settled on his shoulder, pulling him around and into the foliage beside the path. They scrambled over the wall as an eruption of outraged voices shattered the evening quiet. Eldrin's rescuer led him briefly along the road that skirted the villa, crossed it in a pool of shadow, then skidded down an embankment planted with succulents. Running now, Eldrin followed his guide across another road, through more wet foliage, down an alley, over a wall. . . .

The loud, clear note of a horn sounded over the city as the last of the sun's rays faded. "They've raised the alarm," Eldrin's rescuer observed quietly. "Now we'll have to step carefully."

Out of breath and still feeling nauseated, Eldrin welcomed the slower pace. They moved in bursts, creeping through the shadows, darting across the light spots, keeping an eye on all who shared the way with them.

They spent a number of hours crouched beneath the branches of a pungent-smelling bush in someone's garden, then hunkering in a broken-down stable farther on, and finally pressed against the damp, fishy-smelling stonework of an alcove in a blind alley while a search party poked through the shadows not three strides away from them. It was deep into the night when they finally reached the waterfront, passing numerous quays before Eldrin's rescuer led him out along one to a moored dinghy. Directly across the water from them, a little over a double stone's throw, Carissa's merchantman floated at anchor, veiled in a light mist and dimly illumined by its night lanterns. The scallops running lengthwise down her hull and the snake-haired goddess at her bowsprit—Ekonissima, he knew now—betrayed her Thilosian heritage.

Hope exploded within him, strong and fierce and redemptive. *Oh, Eidon, forgive me for doubting, and thank you. Thank you!*

Tears blurred the world as his throat tightened with emotion. All the fears and doubts and empty despair—all for nothing. If only he had trusted, he could have saved himself so much misery. If only he had believed . . .

On the waterfront behind them a dog began to bay. Eldrin only laughed to himself. Even if the search dogs were on to him, they'd never catch him now. As his rescuer climbed down into the dinghy, songs of thanksgiving rang through Eldrin's head.

*Wonderful are his ways! Who can know them?*

*Oh, Eidon, I will never doubt you again! I will serve you with all my might and make myself pure and never turn from your ways.*

His rescuer moved into the stern sheets as one of the four oarsmen aboard joined Eldrin on the quay to help him down. The oarsman looked familiar, but Eldrin was too ecstatic to do more than grin back.

Ashore, the baying hound drew nearer.

The oarsman seized Eldrin's arm, suddenly impatient, and Eldrin looked up, annoyed. Light from the boat's lantern gleamed off a young mustachioed, parrot-nosed face, a crescent cheek scar, and two gold ear hoops. Eldrin gasped with recognition.

The man grinned at him, nothing friendly in his expression.

Eldrin looked to *Windbird* again and saw now the curve-sterned silhouettes of a gaggle of galleys anchored just this side of her, shrouded in the misty darkness.

"No," he breathed.

Down in the boat, his rescuer threw back the cowl of his cloak, revealing that bold hatchet face with its pulled-back hair and multitude of gold earrings.

The Esurhite Gamers.

In a heartbeat he twisted free of his captor and fled up the quay, dashing toward shore as the baying hound drew nearer, its voice frantic, ear-piercing. Eldrin angled left as it burst upon him. It was a big brown hound, towing a boy on a leash, its nose to the ground, its tail slashing the air.

He expected others, officers of the city, men from the villa, civilians. But there was only the boy and the dog.

The Esurhites, who had hesitated as the dog approached, now thundered after Eldrin. He yelled at the boy to go back, and the lad stopped, but the hound raced on, tearing the leash from his hands.

No time. Eldrin angled off the quay, feet landing painfully on sharp, wet stones. He slipped, touched water—

Purple light flared in the darkness.

"STOP." The voice was not loud, but it carried an authority impossible to resist. Eldrin's body wrenched itself to a stop, teetering at water's edge, arms windmilling.

Behind him, the baying silenced with a yelp.

Now the Gamer loomed on the quay above him, thumbs hooked into his belt below an amulet that glowed like a malevolent eye. He grinned. "I knew there was fire in you, my Kiriathan prince." He spoke in the Tahg to the men beside him, and they descended to Eldrin's side. Rough hands hauled him back up the quay, then bound and gagged him.

The boy hung limply in the grip of a henchman, his pale face streaked with tears. Beyond them lay the still, dark form of the dog. Did they mean to take the boy to their galley, too, then? Surely he was too young. . . .

As Eldrin was shoved into the shore boat, the Gamer stuffed a folded parchment into the boy's belt and gestured to *Windbird*, now a dim and indistinct shape behind the rapidly thickening mist. He spoke softly, then jumped down into the stern sheets of the dinghy and they shoved off.

The boat slid silently across a sea of black glass, oars dipping and rising in near silent unison, heading for the nearest of the galleys. All too soon they were swinging up alongside it, a rope boarding ladder tumbling down from the gunwale as the oarsmen secured their paddles.

The Gamer stood and pulled Eldrin to his feet, chuckling softly. "You are far too trusting, hechami," he murmured. "Let that be your first lesson for the Games: never trust anyone but yourself."

Eldrin stared at him.

The Esurhite's grin widened. "You are going to make me a very rich man, Abramm Kalladorne. A very rich man."

# CHAPTER 14

Carissa lurched up in her bunk, breathing hard, staring into the darkness. Something awful had happened. She had dreamed. . . .

A round gray stone hanging in the air, a dog's frantic baying, a dark figure looming up to drag her into a dark hold where scarred, malevolent faces leered around her in a purple light. A symbol of glowing lines floated up from the shadow, a rampant dragon filling her vision, exploding her brain into terrible, burning pain—

It was only a dream. Yet her head and chest and arm still burned, and nausea spun in her middle.

She sat holding her head in her hands, catching her breath and feeling the pain ebb. Something had happened to Abramm, again. This was like the dream she'd had before they'd left Springerlan. The dream she'd had years ago when Gillard had lured Abramm to a secluded corner of the palace and beaten the spit out of him. Humiliated, hurting, miserable, Abramm had crawled away to a hiding place and collapsed. They never would have found him if not for Carissa's dream.

She didn't understand this linkage she had with her twin, didn't know if he had reciprocal dreams about her—she only knew it was real and should be acted upon. Except . . . she had no idea what action to take.

She got up and poured water with trembling hands, sloshing some on the thin carpet beneath her feet. The tallow dip burned dimly on its brass pan, casting ogrelike shadows on the cabin walls as she gulped the water. Images whirled before her mind's eye: the shadowed hold, the dark faces, the glowing dragon. . . .

A horrible suspicion made her drop the ceramic cup to the table with a clatter, then tear her cloak from its peg and wrench open the door.

Cooper slept outside, as was his wont, sitting with his back to the bulkhead, legs bent up, head drooped forward. Careful not to wake him, she hurried past onto the deck.

A mist had come up in the night, swathing harbor and sky in thick black wool. Two lanterns hung athwart the ship's waist, their light constricted into muzzy yellow pools, limning the crewmen's huddled forms, asleep on the planking but ready to rouse and make sail at a moment's notice. Though in this breathless mist, sail would do *Windbird* little good.

She paced to the port gunwale. The lanterns of one of the neighboring galleys showed as blurry lights in the darkness, but she could just make out the dark hulls, five of them, still there. Somewhere a hatch shrieked, followed by muffled thumping, then silence. The faint aroma of roasting meat waxed then waned on the air.

She grimaced, caught in a flurry of agitation. Part of her wanted to awaken the captain and send him over there to assure her that Katahn wasn't intending betrayal after all. As soon as the Esurhite had left yesterday she'd been beset with doubts—that he was really a Gamer and hadn't bought Abramm earlier because he didn't know who he was. Maybe because of her, Abramm would be plucked from the kettle and thrown to the flames.

True, the captain, upon his return, had affirmed the difficulty of freeing Abramm from the temple and said he'd heard a rumor that a slaver had recently delivered a number of young men over to the temple priestesses. Moreover, the activity they'd observed ashore this evening was indeed due to the search for an escaped slave, though Kinlock believed the man had belonged to one of the villa owners, not the temple.

Still, with all the commotion tonight, if Katahn *had* freed Abramm, he might well and sensibly have gone to ground, might even now be making a run from shore.

She stared into the darkness, every sense straining for something that might foretell his approach.

*Windbird* creaked around her. A cricket sang somewhere below. The scent of burning tobacco wafted on the still air from the lone sailor at watch well forward of her. Around him lay his slumbering mates, their snores muffled by the mist.

If Katahn had come out and bypassed *Windbird* to go straight to his own vessel, the watchman would have notified Danarin. . . .

Suspicion wrenched at her again. What if he had? What if Danarin had deemed it unimportant and done nothing? That way, Katahn would take Abramm, and Danarin's orders from the king would be fulfilled.

She hurried forward to ask the man herself, but he assured her there'd been nothing. Clearly the Esurhite had not returned.

*Go back to bed,* she told herself. *There's nothing you can do here.*

Sleep, though elusive, did claim her finally, and the next thing she knew gray daylight filtered through the wide stern window. Her first thought was that no one had come to her with news of Abramm's rescue. Her second was that the ship still stood at anchor.

Quelling incipient panic, she washed her face, combed her hair, and pulled on a blue woolen shift. Cooper stood awake outside the door now, giving no sign he had ever been other than standing there at attention. She passed him without comment, avoiding his gaze.

Captain Kinlock stood near the starboard companion in counsel with Danarin and the second mate. As she stepped into the cold, misty morning, they turned to her of one accord, their faces grim, and her heart fluttered.

Immediately she turned to the port railing and the five black-hulled galleys. They were gone.

She stared at the empty place on the gray water and her knees turned to jelly. "Please, no," she murmured. *Not that. . . . He'd never survive that. . . .*

"I'm afraid so, lass," the captain said, proffering a wide white envelope. It was grubby and crinkled, but she recognized the fine paper, the watermark of Haden's Mill. Her name was flawlessly and flourishingly lettered in black ink on the front:

*Her Royal Highness*

*The Princess Carissa Louise Mariellen Kalladorne Balmark*

The wax wafer was broken—Kinlock had read it first. She frowned at that but said nothing as she withdrew the note. In the same beautiful calligraphy she read:

*Your brother was actually sold at auction five days ago to a wealthy official of the Qarkeshanian government who employed him as a scribe—a dreadful waste of his potential, in my opinion. I could not have told you that, of course, or you would have never sent me to rescue him, though I must confess, your gullibility surprised me. It is a prime example of the stupidity of your people and a demonstration of why it will not take us long to conquer you.*

*I will make far more than four thousand sovereigns on your royal brother in a single match. Warriors will bid with each other for the amusement of defeating him in the arena. I will, of course, do all that I can to prepare him for his contest. Obviously the longer he lasts, the more money I make. Perhaps you will find comfort in that.*

*In Destiny,*

*Katahn ul Manus*

"Our stowaway and his dog there"—Kinlock gestured to the ship's waist, where an auburn-haired youth stood watching them beside a grizzled bloodhound—"caught up with them just as they were leaving. The kid's lucky he's not with them now. Katahn gave him the letter."

She advanced to face the boy, who was all arms and legs, with the big floppy feet of adolescence. The top of his head just reached her shoulder, and his curly hair flew wildly save for that which someone had gathered at his nape and tarred into a tiny pigtail. Like the caning and forced labor, it was one more rite of initiation imposed upon all those who dared stow away.

It hadn't cowed him, though. In fact, the erectness of his carriage along with a certain fineness of feature and the direct way he met her eyes made her think he might have been a nobleman's son. In fact, he looked familiar, now that she thought of it. And as she knew too well, noblemen's sons could have as good reasons to run away as any other.

She wondered why he had come back with the letter, though. And how he had managed to be in the right place and time to get it in the first place. The sense of familiarity washed over her again, more urgently now. She had seen him somewhere. Recently.

At one of the parties she and Rennalf had attended in Springerlan?

"You saw the man this Gamer took?" she asked.

He nodded. "He was dressed funny, and his hair was short, the way they wear it around here, but I'm sure it was Prince Abramm."

It wasn't at a party. The palace maybe? But he was too young to attend court, so . . .

"Have we met before, boy?"

The boy's face went dead white, every freckle standing out in sharp relief. All his confidence evaporated. He swallowed. "I . . . don't think so, my lady."

He could've been a page. Many young men of noble blood served in that capacity at the royal residence. Except she wasn't likely to notice any particular page. They were like furniture—useful, always there, but you didn't really look at them. So why would she—

The page from Raynen's apartments. That's who he was. The one caught spying while she'd been there, who'd twisted free of the chamberlain and fled.

Suspicion rose crazily within her, her passion reflected in the rising alarm on his face. She seized his arm, waving the letter before his nose. "Did you write this? Where is he? Where have you hidden him?"

He flinched backward. "My lady, no! The Gamer took the prince. I swear it. And he gave—"

"Who are you? Why are you on this ship? Why were you spying on the king that day? Tell me!"

He grew even whiter, gray-blue eyes flicking to Captain Kinlock and Danarin, who had come up behind her. "I—"

She shook his arm. "Did Saeral send you? Where have you hidden my brother?" She realized this accusation was absurd, realized she was out of control, but could not seem to stop herself.

"Saeral?" the boy choked. "Never!"

"Wait!" Kinlock interjected. "You were spying on the king?"

The boy wilted. He looked at the deck, then said quietly, "I had to know what was going on. What he'd done with my brother."

"*Your* brother?" Carissa demanded.

"Captain Meridon, my lady," the boy said.

Carissa gaped, seeing the resemblance now, plain as day.

"I knew the man they executed wasn't Trap," he added hurriedly, "that whatever was going on, the king was behind it. When you came in that day, my lady, I was dusting in the next room. It was hard not to hear you. Then he starting talking about Trap and I—"

"And you thought you'd conduct your own private rescue?" Empathy overrode Carissa's anger.

But the boy's face hardened. "He's a Terstan, and you were interested only in the prince. I thought, if I slipped along, I would cause no trouble and buy him free in Qarkeshan."

The words stung, and for a moment Carissa said nothing, embarrassed. Then, "So why the dog?"

The boy shrugged. "He's my brother's, and he knows his master. More than that, he's got a nose some say is magical. That's how I came upon the Gamers last night. Newbold followed Trap's scent to the pier, and I found them. And it *was* Prince Abramm, my lady. I saw him before we left Springerlan—the night he came to the palace—so I know what he looks like."

He fell silent, remembering. Then his brow furrowed. "There was nothing I could do. After they left, I tried yelling out to you, but some men came around, so I had to hide and wait for dawn before I got someone to bring me out here."

"Have you read this?" She waved the letter.

He shook his head. Then he drew a big breath and looked right at her, hands tightening at his sides. "Will you be going after them?"

Going after them? She'd hardly accepted the reality of Katahn's letter. Even now her mind was busily scurrying after alternative explanations, possibilities, scenarios—anything but admit and accept the awful truth that Abramm was on a Gamer's galley, destined to die in a Gamer's Tale—and all at her own hands.

A torment of guilt broke over her, hatching inquisitors of self-recrimination. If she'd never contracted with Katahn—no, if she'd never come to Qarkeshan in the first place. If she'd stayed on course for Thilos, done what her husband and her royal brother had wanted her to, then . . .

Then what? Abramm would live out his life scribing for some wealthy Qarkeshanian? Better than dying in the Games, perhaps, but . . .

Oh, what did it matter? The fact was, Abramm was in worse trouble than ever, and it was all her fault. More than that, she was the only one who could get him out of it.

" . . . don't see how, I'm afraid," the captain was saying.

"Of course we're going after them," she broke in.

Kinlock frowned at her. "But, milady—"

"I've seen the maps. This southern sea is a maze of islands. You can't go a day without running near one of them. We could restock and rewater at will. We might even be able to do some extra business on the side. And even if it takes a day or two to load, with her sail power, *Windbird* can easily—"

"There is no wind, milady."

"—overhaul that galley. . . ." She stopped. "No wind?"

"Three leagues south of here, they say, it dies altogether. Sailing vessels are becalmed, and the crews die for lack of water. If they are not plundered by pirates first. Or the Esurhite navy."

She stared at him, frozen, fingers braced lightly on the slick surface of the gunwale beside her.

He frowned. "I'm sorry, lass, but I won't sail *Windbird* south of Qarkeshan. Dismiss me, if you will, but I'll not take us all to our deaths."

Carissa felt as if her body had turned to hard, brittle clay, as if it would break and crumble into a thousand pieces if she so much as breathed. The frustration, the bitter disappointment, the terrible grief and guilt rose up to overwhelm her.

Katahn had tricked her, had taken her money and her brother and fled, knowing there would be no wind. Knowing she could not follow.

*Eidon, he is* your *servant! How can you do this to him?*

Rage swelled up through the other emotions. Fists clenched, she whirled from the men and leaned against the gunwale, not breaking, but still brittle. She felt very much like hitting something. Like screaming and ranting and raging.

But she said nothing, staring blindly at the mist-bound harbor, clutching her arms about her chest, gripping them as she gripped her self-control.

Kinlock stepped up beside her, close but not touching.

*Plagues! How can there be no wind?* "It's not natural," she protested.

"No," Kinlock agreed. "It's a peculiarity of the region—the calm and the fog. It has been so for centuries. Some say 'tis the Shadow of Moroq."

A launch bobbed out to the side of the nearest vessel. Beyond, another rowed toward shore. Seabirds circled in the mist above, their mournful cries providing counterpoint to the thumpings and clanking of the three men scraping the deck behind them. Smoke from the cook fire tainted the salt air, tickling the nausea in her stomach.

*I will make far more than four thousand sovereigns on your brother in a single match. . . .*

Her throat swelled, aching sharply. Tears scalded her eyes. She drew a deep, ragged breath. *I will not cry. I will* not.

Kinlock touched her shoulder. "I'm sorry, milady."

"I know." She swallowed, but it was as if a bone were caught in her throat.

"It is up to Eidon now," Kinlock murmured. "And to Abramm himself. He is a Kalladorne, after all. And he has more steel in him than people think. I was not easy on him the summer he sailed with me. Pressure only makes him dig in harder, and Kalladornes are renowned for their skill at weapons. It may be that some hidden talent will surface."

"He won't fight." She dashed at the tears, blurring her vision. "He's taken that stupid vow, and he'll stand by it. As you said, pressure only makes him dig in harder."

She wished Kinlock would argue with her, but all he said was, "Perhaps he will escape." A platitude, offered without conviction.

Suddenly the horror of it closed on her. She turned from the railing and fled to her cabin, letting the tears come.

As the first storm of grief abated, the door, left unlatched in her haste, bumped open. A whiff of doggy odor preceded a cold, wet nose pressed against her arm, snuffling. She looked up to find Newbold the hound regarding her with his droopy eyes. His long tail waved tentatively. She wiped her face, then scratched behind his ear. He stepped closer, upper lids closing so that the red lining of the lower lids was all that remained. He leaned against her hand and sighed.

When she stopped he sighed again and settled by her bunk as if to sleep. She drew a kerchief from her belt and blew her nose, then noticed Cooper standing in the doorway, blocking the boy from entering and muttering angrily about the dog and audacity.

"It's okay, Coop," she said. "Let him in."

The older man glared over his shoulder at her but gave way, and the boy approached, offering an uncertain bow. He couldn't be more than twelve or thirteen.

"Sit down." She gestured at the locker behind him. "What's your name?"

"Philip, my lady."

"And are you marked with a golden shield like your brother?"

His chin went up proudly. "I am, my lady." To prove it, he pulled open the neck of his tunic and showed her.

Struggling to hide her dismay and disgust, she wondered why she had asked. Because she'd hoped it wasn't true? Because it made her angry that anyone would do such a thing to a child? Marking them with evil like that, sentencing them to the life of madness and deformity and ostracism?

She blew her nose again and, deciding to ignore the shield, said, "Well, Philip, I'm afraid our quest has been in vain."

He leaned toward her, forearms braced on his knees, eyes bright. "There are other ways south, my lady. You could hire transport, mercenaries. . . ."

"You must think I'm richer than I am."

"I know you brought funds. I have some as well."

She sighed. "You have hope your brother will survive. Mine will be dead in a week."

"I don't believe that, my lady. I don't believe it is chance they are together. Eidon has a purpose in all of this."

"Eidon!" She barked a bitter laugh. "Only fools rely on Eidon, boy. Or babes too ignorant to know better!"

His face fell, hurt showing plainly on the open features. She felt disgust at herself for allowing her own bitterness to dig at him. In an effort to make up, she changed the subject. "How do you know they are together?"

"Because the man who wrote you that letter is the same man who bought Trap at auction five days ago. The story's all over the docks—biggest price a slave's ever brought, and since he's described as a red-haired Kiriathan Terstan in obviously fine condition . . . well, it has to be Trap. And as long as he's with the prince, he'll look after him, my lady. You can count on it."

She smiled sadly. "Your brother is as much a slave as mine. He won't have opportunity."

Philip lifted his chin, and an obstinate look came into his eyes. She thought he wanted to say more about Eidon and was glad when he did not.

"What if your brother does live, my lady? Like the captain said, he is a Kalladorne. My father said he could've been good if he'd wanted to. That he was just a late bloomer on account of his illnesses."

"Your father." Larrick Meridon. The royal sword master, one of the most respected trainers and swordsmen in the realm. Was he a Terstan, too? She shook her head. "He won't fight."

"What if he does?"

"He won't. He's made a vow."

"Vows can be broken."

"Not by him."

Again she had the feeling he wanted to say something and kept it to himself for fear of her reaction. He regarded her a moment more, then stood. "Well, *I'm* not giving up."

"You can't do it alone."

"I'm not alone. I have Newbold. And Eidon. He's seen us this far; I believe he'll provide a way." He lifted his chin as if defying her to gainsay him.

She grimaced. "This is not Kiriath, Philip. The ways here are treacherous. Within days you'd be captured as a slave and Newbold would be put into a stewpot. If you're lucky. Besides, you don't even know where they've been taken."

"They'll go to Katahn's estate on the island Ne'gal. He'll train them there. After that, they'll be taken to one of the great arenas for their first contest, and there'll be no trouble learning where that is."

"What good is knowing where he is if we can't get to him?"

"I believe a way will open, my lady."

He did, too. Without a shadow of doubting. Well, he had a lot to learn about life, and it was certain this adventure he proposed would teach him many ugly truths.

Still, something in his confidence drew her—like the promise of the sun glowing above the barren flats at Castle Balmark, gathering with infinitesimal slowness before it suddenly cast the ice-cloaked world in gold.

If she went back to Kiriath . . . could she live with knowing she had left Abramm to die at the hands of that Esurhite snake because *she* lacked the courage to go on? Wouldn't the guilt eat at her soul until it consumed her if she never made a try of putting things to right?

And perhaps Abramm *would* abandon his vows and agree to fight. Why should he give his life for a god who obviously cared nothing about him?

Buy passage? They could do that. Selling *Windbird* and all her stores would net them a hefty sum. They could easily continue their guise as Thilosian traders—might even make a profit at it. Cooper could certainly pass for Thilosian.

But she couldn't. And yet, what had Danarin said? *"Many a black Brogai veil hides blond hair and blue eyes. . . ."*

*No! What am I thinking? I can't go wandering around Esurh. It would be ten times as foolhardy as what I've already done.*

And Cooper would have a fit.

CHAPTER

# 15

As Abramm was taken aboard Katahn's galley that first night, as he was chained to one of the thwarts below and a hot iron pressed into his left biceps, as the stench of his own burning flesh filled his nostrils and he almost passed out from the pain, he said nothing. Did not protest, did not curse, did not cry out.

For even before that, when he had looked into Katahn's face and listened to him crow, realizing that the worst of the worst was happening and no deliverance was coming, something had torn loose in him.

Eidon was not in the Flames. Perhaps he was not anywhere at all, but certainly he had no hold on Eldrin's life. The Flames were a fraud—his years of service to them a waste. Now he could no longer delude himself. Now he must face the unfaceable: that he was a slave, that he was to be put into the Games, and that his only way out would be of his own devising.

*"Religion is the crutch by which the weak hobble through life,"* his uncle had liked to say. *"It is for men who cannot stand on their own two legs and face what they are dealt. Instead they hide and whine and hope for magical deliverance from life, from disasters usually brought on themselves by their own poor decisions."*

Finally he saw the truth of his uncle's accusation, for thus it had been with him—a crutch, a shield, a wall behind which he hid from life. An excuse for his failures and inadequacies.

In one piercing, overwhelming flash of insight his whole perception of his life shifted, and he saw himself for a naïve, cowardly boy, manipulated by his own fears and a pathetic need for the approval of a family that offered only scorn.

The wall was gone now. Shredded. Blown away. No more hiding. No more excuses. No more dependence on some divine hand to direct his every move and keep him safe from the trials and heartaches of life. It was all gone. He felt oddly purified.

And achingly, sickeningly empty.

He was chained in the hold to the first starboard thwart, facing astern. His captors laughed among themselves and spoke mockingly to him, but he could not understand their words. It wouldn't have mattered, anyway. Their abuse was a small thing, swallowed up by the cold chasm within him.

After they departed, he sat motionless in the whisper-filled darkness, his poisoned, branded left arm cradled to his stomach, shrieking its pain. His heart pounded slowly against his breastbone. His legs ached and trembled. Around him came soft sighs and creaks and rustlings. He sensed a man sitting beside him in the dark, heard the sough of his breathing, felt the warmth of his body.

A galley ship.

He turned the thought over in his mind, still half disbelieving it, while a bleak terror swelled beneath his consciousness. He had done his share of labor around the Watch but nothing like what faced him now. With his slender frame scrawnier than ever, how would he survive?

*I won't,* he thought dully. *Gillard has won at last.*

And after that, *Why?*

The word echoed aimlessly in his head, finding no answer, only the great, fathomless emptiness, swirling like a wind across a barren, rocky field.

Somehow he fell asleep, rousing to foggy daylight, a clatter of chain, and a deep bellowing. He lay curled on the hard bench, his ear aching where it pressed against the wood. Iron anklets pulled painfully against his feet.

He sat upright.

To the right, crates and barrels were stacked to the ceiling, a central island that blocked his view of the offside oarsmen. Ahead, more cargo jammed the stern, framing the ladderlike companionway that led to the upper deck. Light checkered through a grate at the top. More filtered through the long oar slot on his left, washing over the hunched form of his bench mate, collapsed now over the oar. Its handle end was anchored beneath a ledge directly in front of

Abramm's feet, the massive blade now up, out of the water.

Glancing back, he found himself sitting the second bench in a rank of fifteen—thirty men in all. Like his own bench mate, a few of them were slumped over oar handles, but most lounged easily, regarding him with unveiled curiosity.

Abramm's gaze returned to the man at his side, then out the slot beyond. Silver water, lined with gentle ripples, swept away from the ship to meet a dark runner of foliage-cloaked land. The boat was not moving, the air breathlessly still.

Somewhere a fire crackled—its smoke scent tickled his nostrils alongside the aroma of roasting meat. Laughter sounded above, mingled with thumping footfalls. Behind him someone rustled and a liquid trickle was chased by the reek of urine.

Finally he forced himself to look at his left arm. It still throbbed, the flesh swollen and angry around a palm-sized, dark red scab shaped vaguely like a rampant dragon.

Branded like a common ox.

His stomach turned. His hair would grow out and his dignity could be restored, but this he would have with him always.

And then he laughed aloud, the sound high-pitched with incipient hysteria. He was chained to the deck of a galley, a Kiriathan in the hands of an Esurhite Gamer. The brand was the least of his troubles.

The bench creaked as his companion shifted, and a hoarse voice spoke. "So you *are* alive."

The man still hunched over the oar, but now his head was turned to face Abramm, curly hair backlit by the fading light.

Abramm gaped. "Meridon?"

The other smiled wryly, closing his eyes. Weariness carved his freckled face, his eyes sunken and shadowed, his features gaunt beneath the mat of his beard. His arm muscles twitched and quivered as they rested on the oar handle, and his left hand, dangling loosely against the oar's smooth grip, showed a bloodied palm. Scarlet and brown smears on the wooden handle spoke eloquently of how the injury had been acquired.

He had been rowing recently. Which meant they were no longer in Qarkeshan.

So long did Meridon sit without moving that Abramm wondered if he'd fallen unconscious. Finally, though, he spoke again, his voice rough and harsh. "After they chained you here last night, you sat like one enspelled. Then you fell over and nobody could rouse you, not even when we were called to oars. I thought I shared the bench with a dead man."

"Not yet."

Meridon's dark eyes opened, and he stared at Abramm blankly. Then his eyes glazed and the lids dropped over them. "Guess they figured out who you are. Can't find a much bigger name than yours." Meridon sighed deeply. "I'm sorry, my lord. You deserved none of this."

"I am not your lord," Abramm said bitterly. "Not anymore."

The dark eyes opened again, regarding him dully. "No," the man slurred, "I suppose you aren't."

Again his eyelids drooped, and in moments his breathing deepened into sleep.

A little later the hatch shrieked open, and four dark-clad guards thundered down the companion bearing two steaming pots and some wooden bowls. Two disappeared on the far side of the central cargo wall as the rich scent of roasted goat and onions set Abramm's stomach into instant ravenous reaction.

He shook Meridon awake and shoved the bowl into his bloody hands barely in time to catch his own as the guards moved on to the next row.

The stew's heat warmed both bowl and hands, and his mouth watered ferociously. He did not think he had ever known such hunger. Eagerly he thrust his fingers into the thick brown gravy, plucked out a hunk of steaming meat . . . and halted.

*I will abstain from corrupt food . . . shunning the meat of animals. . . .*

As Meridon revived to gobble down his own food, Abramm stared at the meat in his hand. A small enough morsel, but if he ate it, he would, for the first time, deliberately violate a sacred vow.

*And does that matter?* asked a dry voice in his head. *If the Mataio is a lie, your vows are meaningless.*

A moment more he hesitated, then slowly, deliberately, he put the meat into his mouth, chewed, and swallowed. He fished out a second chunk and instinct took over. As he scraped the last of the gravy and lentils from the bowl, the guards returned, offering more stew—which he accepted—along with loaves of dark, coarse bread and pots of brackish water.

Toward the end an audience had gathered near the companion, the guards watching him with broad amusement, though he could not imagine what was funny.

Finally, with mocking bows and raucous laughter, they departed. The hatch squealed down and banged into place, then stillness settled over the hold. He felt a little queasy now—payment for overeating. At least they were to be fed well. When the time came to escape, he wouldn't be too weak.

He looked down at his leg irons, the chain held by a stout iron pin driven deep into the dark wood. *Who are you kidding? You're not going to escape—you're going to die.*

He glanced at Meridon, asleep on the bench again. *He's had all he can take, and you're not half what he is. You probably won't last the week.*

Gillard's laughter echoed in his mind, and Abramm ground his teeth.

*No*. Deep within him resistance stirred. No, Gillard had not won yet. Each day that Abramm survived was a day he took from his brother and made his own.

*I will not give up that easily. I will* not!

The next day his determination was tested to the limit. By afternoon his back was a raging, bloody fire, the remains of his tunic hanging in ribbons around his waist, courtesy of the innumerable blows of the oar master's rope quirt. His limbs felt like sodden wool, trembling perpetually now, and his hands had cramped into claws around the oar handles. Though Meridon was sharing the punishment for his weakness—and doing all the work—Abramm could not force another ounce of effort from his aching, failing flesh.

When at last the beat ended, he could not even help Meridon anchor the oar, could only sag back onto the bench. Every muscle in his body throbbed an aching rhythm: arms, shoulders, chest, back, legs, buttocks—even his jaw hurt. The cotton strips he had torn from his tunic to shield his hands from the friction were soaked in blood. The decking beneath his feet was likewise bloodied from blisters on the soles of his feet, formed and torn apart by the constant need to brace himself as he pulled the heavy oar toward him.

He gave no thought to escape now. If they had broken his chains and told him to walk free, he could not have done it.

The oar secure, Meridon collapsed as usual across the long grip, and shortly Abramm fell forward likewise. His muscles continued to twitch, and time and again he felt like he was still rowing. It was all he could do to choke down a few mouthfuls of stew—which had definitely not set well with him last night—before he fell back across the oar. An image of his old feather bed taunted him—a cloud of soft, clean-smelling sweetness.

He was half-conscious of someone gripping his hands, smearing something onto the ravaged palms, but he could not rouse himself enough to know if it was dream or reality.

The days that followed were an unending nightmare of straining, agonized muscles and blistered, bleeding flesh pitted against wood and water, driven on by the throbbing drumbeat and the merciless quirt.

After a time that quirt hovered over him of its own power, its wielder unperceived, only the knotted rope and the stinging pain. Later the hand that swung it returned, and at times that hand was Saeral's, or Brother Cyrus's, or his father's. Most often, though, it was Gillard who drove him, laughing and mocking. As the days passed and the pain and exhaustion mounted, it became for Abramm a battle of wills—Gillard striving to push him beyond what he could endure, Abramm refusing to give up.

Day melded with night. Pain and Gillard and the motion of rowing became his only realities. Even in his sleep he rowed and felt the quirt and heard his brother's laughter, the mocking high-pitched sound setting his teeth to grinding.

He wondered occasionally if he were going mad, muttering a litany of determination under his breath in time to the beat. *I won't give up. I won't give up*. It became his personal rhythm, driving him on and on and on. *Survive for just another day. Endure for just another hour. . . .*

Then one morning he noticed the pain had lessened. That Gillard no longer held the whip, nor did he command the drummer. His hands and feet were healing, calluses thickening where blisters had been. His breath no longer ravaged his throat with each exertion.

Best of all, he received only four blows of the quirt that day. There came a time soon after when he received none at all. Each new day brought a significant reduction of the pain, and in its absence his thoughts returned to rationality. Eventually he realized he would survive, and the knowing filled him with wonder.

One evening he sat with his back against the deck walk, chewing the last of a piece of bread with an almost giddy sense of success. Meridon faced forward, eating as well. Since the first day they had spoken not a word and hardly even glanced at one another, each occupied with his own private torments. Even so, Abramm felt a powerful bond with the man, forged of shared misery and the need of working together in constant synchronous rhythm. More than that, Meridon represented the only link with his past. Abramm could speak to him in his own language, and the Terstan would understand him.

Suddenly that was important. Suddenly he wanted very much to hear Kiriathan. To be understood and answered, as if in doing so he could lay hold of that which he had lost.

"What were you doing there that night?" he asked abruptly. "In the Keep, I mean—how'd you know where to find me?"

Meridon's beard bristled slightly, as if he were clenching his teeth, and Abramm realized he had asked the wrong thing.

The Terstan sipped deliberately from his water cup, then said, still facing forward, "I knew where they were likely to be holding you, though not the exact cell, so I was searching, hoping to find you before it was too late."

He fell silent, a hardness settling around his eyes.

Abramm studied him, surprised by the depth of his own compassion. "Ray was your friend."

Meridon looked down at the wooden cup in his callused hands. "Or so I thought."

"You know he probably wasn't involved in this. Gillard lies as easily as he speaks."

"He was involved," Meridon said flatly. "It was likely his idea."

Abramm frowned, watching an orange cat slink down the companionway and disappear around the bottom rail post into the darkness. He glanced at Meridon again. "Granted, I didn't know my brothers well, but Raynen was always an upright sort. It was important to him to do the right thing. I can't believe that—"

"He was afraid," Meridon said bitterly. "And I was a threat. To him it would have seemed the only thing he could do."

"Afraid?" Abram's voice rose with incredulity.

For the first time Meridon looked at him, pain, and now anger, in his eyes. "Do not judge him too harshly. He was under pressures you know nothing about."

Abramm held the man's gaze evenly, but somehow he felt reproved.

The Terstan looked away. After a moment he sighed, drained his cup, and passed both it and his bowl to Abramm, who set them with his own on the central walkway.

Above, the men laughed and jeered at one another.

Presently Meridon spoke again. "He had the potential to be one of Kiriath's finest kings. But he never got over watching your father die."

"You speak of him as if he's the one dead."

Meridon snorted and bent to pull the canvas flap across the oar slot, blocking the flow of chill night air. "He may be. In any case, the man I knew most certainly is. You're right. He did have a fine sense of duty. Now he has only the fear."

"Of Saeral?"

"And Prince Gillard."

"Gillard?"

Meridon met his gaze again, the hard light back in his eyes. "Gillard wants the throne and always has. Raynen wears a Terstan shield and suffers from the sarotis. By now that fact has certainly become apparent—to Gillard, at least, if not to the realm at large. With you out of the way, he is the undisputed heir. It is only a matter of time before he convinces Raynen to abdicate—or the Table of Lords to remove him." He sighed. "The worst of it is, Gillard's more vulnerable to Saeral than Raynen."

Abramm remembered the spell Saeral had cast over him—the trusted face, the quiet lake, the sense of utter security. And into that, the promise of the fulfillment of his most cherished dream. . . .

Yes, Gillard would be vulnerable.

But Kiriath was a long way away now. A lifetime away. And odds were heavy he'd never see it again.

Weeks passed. Abramm's beard grew long and thick, even as his stomach grew tight and hard; cablelike muscles bulged through the skin on his legs and arms. In time he found a curious pleasure in hauling on the oar and feeling the power of his own strength go down its length to press against the water and move the ship forward.

Meridon changed, too—muscles and tendons and veins rippled beneath skin that held not an ounce of fat. A thick beard camouflaged the boyish look of his features, and his curly red hair now flopped over his forehead and ears and down the nape of his neck.

The gauntness left his face, and though at first his brown eyes were haunted with a pain not physical, after a time he came to terms with it. Eventually he spoke freely, even animatedly, of his past and his family.

Born of common stock, the first of six children, Trap Meridon had four sisters and one brother. His youth was spent divided between summers afield, looking after his mother's herd of prize goats, and winters in town, working at and then attending the School of Fence his famous father ran in Sterlen.

His first mention of the school had jolted Abramm, for he had forgotten the old swordsman was the man's father.

Taught by a master from birth, and being an apt pupil, Meridon was accepted at the school a good two years before most boys even tested. By the time he was fourteen he was already winning competitions.

He met Raynen at a Fairday in Sterlen that same year. They were finalists, not in sword but in archery. Both lost out to age and experience, but they struck up a friendship, being of an age.

"In those days," Meridon explained, "Ray never thought he'd be king, with four brothers ahead of him and Aarol's wife already expecting. And he was never particularly concerned with titles and status. We took an instant liking to each other and spent the rest of the fair together.

"Then some older boys thought it would be fun to pick on a Terstan—me. There was a fight, and Ray stood back to back with me, two against five. We were winning, too, and then one of them pulled a blade." He paused, and when next he spoke, his voice was low. "He was the first man I ever killed. Turned out he was a duke's son. There was trouble, and even though Ray supported me, I was a commoner and a Terstan. It was decided I should leave Sterlen. Ray was going on progress to the borderlands and asked for me to be his squire. I've been in his service ever since."

Of Abramm's past they spoke little, though not for lack of interest on Meridon's part. He attempted to draw Abramm out more than once, curious as to how he'd come to join the Mataio. Abramm always changed the subject. The past held shame and failure and betrayal, and thinking of it only made him more aware of the emptiness that now dwelt within him. Thankfully, Trap never pushed, and it was for that, more than anything, that Abramm appreciated him.

One day, after the oars master had halted them unexpectedly at midmorning, a group of guards trooped into the hold, brandishing crowbars. In astonished disbelief Abramm watched as the pin that chained him to the deck was levered free. Then he was reeling on the deck walk, disoriented at standing upright for the first time in he didn't know when.

The five galleys had anchored in a quiet, mist-hung cove surrounded by steep, rocky hills sparingly dotted with strange, fleshy gray-green plants. Shaped like leafless stumps, crowned by myriad groping arms, they looked like something spawned of Moroq's Veil, malformed and hostile.

Wavelets kissed a tan, pebbly beach and lapped the base of the cliff on the left. At its midpoint, apparently built into the rock as much as on the shelves that notched its face, hung a massive complex of white-walled buildings with multitudes of balconies and tall, arched windows and latticed breezeways. A waterfall trickled between them, running down the cliff face to the sea, its margins crowded with lush vegetation.

Ten of them were ferried ashore in the galley's dinghy under the direction of the Gamer's son. While they waited for the other boats to discharge a similar cargo, Abramm studied the villa above, intrigued by the dark birdlike statues standing guard in the crags above it. Or at least he thought they were statues—until one unfolded great, dark wings and flapped away.

"Veren," Trap said softly at his side, seeing the direction of his gaze.

"Rhu'ema spawn?"

The Terstan nodded grimly, his golden mark gleaming in the gray light. "All the guards a man could need. I expect we'll get a demonstration."

As soon as all the men had gathered ashore, one of them—a tall, stringy, pale-skinned Chesedhan—made the break for freedom. The Esurhites had seemed unconscionably lax in this regard, laughing and talking with hardly a glance at the prisoners they were allegedly guarding. So inattentive were they, even Abramm gave thought to attempting flight, but Trap's grim prediction—and his own conviction that it was intentional—stayed the impulse.

Sure enough, the Chesedhan had barely reached the edge of the beach before the Gamer's son stepped toward him, held out a hand, and shouted one word in the Tagh, the wide medallion on his chest flaring with purple light. The fugitive wrenched to a halt as if he'd hit the end of a lead.

The hatchet-faced Brogai spoke again, his gold earrings glittering, and the Chesedhan turned stiffly, his eyes so wide Abramm could see the whites of them even at a distance. He expected to watch the man walk woodenly back, but instead the Gamer addressed them all, babbling in a language Abramm doubted any of his audience understood. He seemed to be asking a question.

Now he smiled, waved a hand, and the tension on the Chesedhan's body relaxed. The man gave a start, glanced around in confusion, and stood there.

The Gamer spoke again, waving his hand, clearly encouraging the fugitive to run. The other guards watched, grinning.

*It's a trap,* Abramm thought at the man. *Don't fall for it!*

But the Chesedhan was panicked and finally bolted. He'd not taken three steps when a great black shape swooped upon him, its wingtips brushing the ground as it surged skyward again, clutching something in its talons. On the beach, amidst a dark, spreading stain, sprawled the pale, headless body of its victim.

Abramm swallowed bile and looked away. Around him, others gagged and retched.

The Gamer spoke condescendingly, no doubt assuring them of the futility in attempting escape. His gaze never wavered from Meridon, standing at Abramm's side, as if somehow he more than the others needed this warning. Finally the Gamer barked a command, and his men leaped to the task of jerking their charges into line and escorting them through an elaborately carved iron door at the base of the cliff.

A maze of passageways so low-ceilinged Abramm had to stoop to avoid hitting his head led to a dark, musty room. There they were divided among the squadrons of waiting overseers who sheared off the matted, lice-infested hair on their heads and faces, scrubbed them down in tubs of foul-smelling solution, dressed them in leather loincloths, and finally prodded them into a sandy-floored arena, where a group of dark-tunicked men awaited them.

Bracketed torches burned around the room's circumference, and above them shadowed balconies reached back into the rock. Only one was lit, and in that one stood Katahn himself, accompanied by the woman from the beach at Qarkeshan. An irrational warmth swept Abramm at the sight of her. She'd no doubt expected him to die in the galley, and it felt good to have proven her wrong. And this time he at least had a loincloth.

The Gamer began to speak, using again that flawless Kiriathan with which he had tricked Abramm into trusting him. "I make my money in accordance with how well my warriors perform. Some of the greatest champions of the Games have come from my stable."

Abramm realized suddenly that this speech was primarily for his benefit.

Not only was Katahn looking right at him—but also, except for Meridon, none of the other men here were likely to understand Kiriathan.

"My handlers are well experienced in training," the Gamer continued. "They'll tolerate no laziness, incompetence, or cowardice." He gestured toward the group of scarred, hard-eyed men gathered under the balcony.

"You will fight here first," Katahn said. "If you do not perform to standard, you will be punished. If you continue to perform unacceptably, you will be culled. If you are to fight for me, you will win or die."

He fell silent, lips quirked in a half smile. Then he turned away.

One of the handlers growled something in the Tahg, and the others divided the trainees into pairs, spacing them out about the yard. The handler assigned to Abramm—a weaselish man with a bad complexion and a tag of black hair sprouting under his chin—held out a sheathed rapier, hilt first.

Abramm stared at it. *I will touch no weapon of warfare. . . .*

Another vow to be broken. And there was the First Word, too, forbidding the killing of others. But why was he thinking of that now? Had he not put all that behind him? He cared no more for Eidon than Eidon cared for him.

And if he refused this blade, he would be killed. Royal blood or not. He could learn to fight and try to save his life in the arena. Or he could be culled right at the start.

Setting his jaw, he reached forward, wrapped his palm about the rapier's leathered grip, and pulled it from the sheath. The blade was old and dulled, only a practice piece. But as he tightened his grip on the shank and hefted the weapon for balance, old memories roused.

The tag-bearded handler smiled, displaying a gap where his front teeth should be. Then he turned to the barbarian who had been paired with Abramm. As he, too, was offered a blade, Abramm's gaze caught on Meridon, standing across the yard, regarding him soberly. Of all present, the Terstan alone understood the full significance of what he had just done.

Brother Eldrin was well and truly dead.

CHAPTER

# 16

Months later, in one of the many sandy-floored practice chambers of Katahn's training enclave, Abramm circled a brawny, loincloth-clad opponent, his rapier at the ready before him. In the weeks since his arrival, this blade and the practice floor had become his life. From first awakening in the morning to the moment he collapsed on the pallet in his tiny cell at night, he thought of nothing but the blade and how to use it: angles, positions, parries, feints, counterparries, counterfeints, strategy, tactics, conditioning. He even did it in his sleep.

The work paid off. In his first match he had been disarmed in moments, had lost twenty-two consecutive matches thereafter. Then suddenly he did not lose any more—except to the handlers, and even those matches were getting closer.

Today he had faced a fellow trainee named Brugal, and from the moment he had crossed swords with the powerful northlander, Abramm had known he would win this match, too.

Brugal was a monster of a man, heavy boned, thick muscled, with long arms and legs. His reflexes were good—he was not slow like many large men—but he was stubbornly convinced that it was bulk and strength that won battles rather than quickness and finesse. So far that assumption had served him well—he had not lost a match since he'd arrived.

Sweat gleamed now on his magnificent musculature and beaded his face above his blond beard, soaked his curly hair. His eyes, chips of blue ice caught in bone caverns, burned with aggression and impatience. He did not yet realize he was outclassed, that Abramm was smarter than he and more skilled. A little faster, too. He saw only the size differential and what he perceived as a fear of engagement on Abramm's part.

He was right in that—Abramm knew himself to be no match for him, brawn against brawn. So he stayed away, parrying the other's strikes easily and dancing out of reach, around and around, as the bigger man grew ever more frustrated and impatient.

It occurred to Abramm that he was, himself, enjoying this. His muscles were warm and fluid, a thin film of perspiration slicked his nearly naked flesh, and his bare feet fell light and sure upon the sand. He felt strong and quick and alive.

The two handlers watched slit eyed, with that unnerving fascination that always came over them at times like this, as if they hoped one or the other of the combatants might overstrike, with the result that blood be spilled or death attend the match. Abramm had learned early of their fascination with death.

Brugal struck again now, lunging low. But instead of backing away, Abramm parried the blade right and stepped in to the left, striking simultaneously with the dagger in his left hand, a killing blow that would have slid up between the barbarian's ribs to his heart had Abramm not pulled his stroke.

He felt a swift surge of satisfaction as Brugal gasped and swore and drew back in defeat. Abdeel, the handler with the tag of chin hair and missing front teeth, called a halt. Since the end of the first week of training, a killing blow always brought the same result—the end of the match and punishment. Already the diminutive Esurhite was turning for the griiswurm in its box, tucked into a niche in the black slag wall.

It would be the first time for Brugal.

The barbarian's pale eyes sank even farther into his skull. He backed a step, then with a furious roar, threw himself at Abramm, striking with sword and dagger both, again and again and again. Abramm parried frantically as he backpedaled out of reach and sought to reestablish an offense.

Rage dulled the man's already limited intellect. It did not take much to disarm him: a feint left, right, and then committing left again, a flick of the wrist and Abramm's blade laid a cut across the meaty base of the barbarian's thumb. The tip caught behind the handguard, and with a grunt Abramm jerked up and away, flinging the weapon free of a grip loosened by cut tendon.

Abdeel strode up behind the barbarian, clucking disapproval, and kicked his legs from under him. As the big man tumbled to the sand, the Esurhite smacked him alongside the head with his training rod and snatched the dagger from his hand. Meanwhile, the other handler, an oafish fellow named Dumah, disarmed Abramm. Together the two Esurhites dragged the reeling barbarian to the wall where a pair of shackles dangled against glassy stone.

As they locked the metal bracelets around Brugal's wrists, he snapped into full awareness, the whites of his eyes encircling pale irises. Faint mewlings forced their way up from his throat as Dumah smeared streaks of thick white *hamar* on the barbarian's face. Abdeel approached with the box. "Well, first time for you, eh, Brugal?" He held the vessel atilt near Brugal's cheekbone, and a gray tentacle ringed with purple groped past the box's lip, reaching for the white streak of hamar. The big man panted, straining his head backward against the wall to escape that probing arm. It touched the white streak gently, and Brugal screamed, his face gray, his whole frame shuddering. The tentacle grabbed hold and the rest of the griiswurm's body rolled out of the box, sucker arms slapping down one after the other across the man's face, securing a hold, muting the sound of his screams as it covered his mouth. Blood limned the edges of its arms.

Abramm watched unmoving, keeping his eyes fixed upon the suffering man, keeping his thoughts away from the fact that he had caused the man this pain.

*It could as easily be you*, he told himself.

Indeed, it had been in days past. He remembered suffocating fire that squeezed the screams from his throat until it was raw, then the debilitating sickness afterward, the nausea, the fever, the bone-shaking weakness. It was not as bad as what he'd known after the feyna, not so bad as to interfere with his training, but it was certainly enough to give him a miserable night.

He had no desire to experience it again, and now, even though he had won—and had done so twice—if he showed anything save cold, compassionless attention, he would wear those shackles himself, and it would be his body that banged and shuddered against the wall, his voice that echoed off the stone.

Brugal went limp, blood dripping from his beard to his chest. Abdeel came to collect the griiswurm, holding the box in which new hamar had been placed up against the creature. The gray limbs groped for the edge and pulled itself in, leaving Brugal's face a web of bloodied welts.

Abdeel glanced at Abramm, then at Dumah, who grinned. Both men turned to Abramm, and a sickness settled in his middle. They stood before him, leering, box held near his face. Abdeel jabbered something he couldn't make out. It didn't matter. He knew what they wanted—for him to try to flee, to struggle, to show his fear. . . .

Dumah fingered hamar onto Abramm's cheekbone, and Abdeel presented the box. The gray tentacle crept over the edge, waving inches from Abramm's nose, tiny, white, chitinous grippers lining its ventral surface.

He tore his gaze away and stared forward, keeping his face expressionless.

The box drifted closer as they teased him. But just before the gray finger could touch him, Abdeel pulled the box away, and the two men laughed heartily.

Abramm stood firm and unexpressive, though sweat popped out anew on his brow.

Dumah painted another strip along the sensitive inner crease of his left arm, and again Abdeel presented the box. This time, they let the tentacle touch, his skin seeming to rip apart at the point of contact, the cry that left his throat unstoppable.

At once the feyna scar began to throb.

The cell door opened and a third handler stepped in. Red light reflected off his freshly shaven head, and Abramm recognized his taut, spiderlike form with dismay—Zamath.

Of all the handlers, he feared Zamath most. Though Katahn's servants were to a man cruel and capricious, Zamath was the worst. A member of the infamous Broho, the elite personal guard of the Brogai caste, he was given to unpredictable acts of viciousness toward associates and trainees alike. Abramm had seen him slice off one trainee's finger, watched him crush another's kneecap. The ear he wore on his chest was that of a Dorsaddi chieftain, he boasted, a trophy won in the Games years ago.

Now he stood just inside the door, taking in what was happening with a slow leer that revealed his pointed teeth. When Abdeel and Dumah turned to him, he waved them to continue.

Abramm controlled his rising alarm with iron will. As Abdeel stroked a line of hamar across his belly, just above the edge of the loincloth, Zamath watched with a faint, expectant smile—watched Abramm's face and eyes. Especially his eyes. The Broho was more sensitive to expressions of fear and pain than any of the others and took almost spiritual delight in manifestations of either.

Four more times the griiswurm kissed him before the unique sibilance of Zamath's voice cut them off. Abramm understood enough of the Tahg by now to get the gist—Katahn had sent for him. Or so Zamath said. Abramm had been trained to never relax his guard. One never knew when a handler might spring from some shadow or around a corner, pummeling the unsuspecting with his stout wooden rod. At mealtimes, on the morning group run, in the middle of the night in his cell, even in the latrine, Abramm had been attacked. Thus he did not wholly believe Zamath was bringing him to Katahn until, bathed and robed in clean black silk, he was delivered to the house guard waiting at the gate of the training complex. Even then he didn't relax, for the novelty of the situation still made it perfect for an ambush.

After the dark, cramped warrens of the training center, this upper enclave seemed unnervingly bright and open, despite the foggy conditions. The various buildings were linked by breezeways, stairways, and soaring bridges, all overlooking the broad, leaden sea stretching away beneath a leaden sky.

The house guard brought him to one of the uppermost buildings, a wide, circular chamber with arched doorways opening along its outer half onto a railed balcony. A split-level polished wooden floor sported Thilosian rugs in bright blue and green. Low tables, tall potted ferns, and strategically placed fabric screens comprised the room's furnishings, and the tang of incense sweetened the air.

Guards and servants stood discreetly about the lower level, where a bevy of veiled women sat on pillows near one of the archways, busy with handwork involving lots of gold thread. The moment Abramm entered, they all looked up, then fell to whispering and giggling behind their veils.

Katahn waited alone on the upper level, an elegant figure in midnight blue, reclining before a low table set with a silver tea service. He had been staring out to sea as Abramm entered but now turned briskly from his contemplation. "Ah, you're here," he said in Kiriathan. "Come and sit."

He gestured at the pillows across the table from him.

More ill at ease than ever, Abramm crossed the room, girls giggling energetically, though he was careful not to look at them. He settled onto the pillows, still half expecting someone to jump from behind the nearest screen and try to behead him. Or for Katahn himself to throw the table and tea service in his face and whip a longsword from his nest of pillows.

But the Esurhite only snapped his fingers, and a servant woman stepped from behind the screen to pour the tea. Abramm recognized her at once as Katahn's companion in Qarkeshan, though she seemed even more beautiful than he remembered. She wore no man's clothes now, but rather a sleeveless white gown of layered silk, overlapping in front and tied at the waist with a thin gold cord. Waist-length coffee-colored hair flowed loose around her shoulders, framing those regal cheekbones. Her dark eyes, hid beneath long lashes, focused down now upon her work, her long, slim fingers pouring green tea into the silver cups.

Abramm found himself unable to breathe, mesmerized by all that silken hair and honey-colored skin, the delicate jawline, the graceful neck, the plunging expanse—

She was handing him his own cup now, jolting him back to himself, startling him with the realization of where his eyes and thoughts had gone. He looked up into her cool gaze and saw a glint of amusement.

"She is beautiful, is she not?" Katahn said.

Abramm glanced at him, embarrassed that his expression had been so easily read.

"Her name is Shettai," the Esurhite went on. "She is Dorsaddi. You've heard of them?"

"Of course." Legendary merchant-warriors who traced their ancestry to pre-Ophiran times, the Dorsaddi had for centuries maintained a thriving civilization within a maze of gold-rich canyons called the SaHal. For five hundred years after the fall of Ophir, the SaHal had stood closed to outsiders, except for the well-guarded trade route through its middle. No one passed along it without Dorsaddi permission, an edict enforced, it was said, by the power of the Dorsaddi's god, Sheleft'Ai.

"Their defenses were believed to be unbreachable," Katahn said. "Hundreds of armies destroyed themselves trying, so when Beltha'adi proposed his expedition, many said he was mad. He was not the first to have gone against them for the sake of *or'dai*—blood vengeance. But he was the only one with the power of Khrell to help him."

Khrell was one of the Esurhite gods—son of Aggos, brother of Ret, husband of Laevion—and sponsor of war, death, and order.

"I heard Beltha'adi had human help," Abramm said. "Working on the inside." Immediately he wondered why he'd spoken. Was he deliberately trying to provoke the man?

Katahn only raised an ironic brow. "Dorsaddi greed and a woman scorned? True. But it was Khrell who showed him how to stir that up. And Sheleft'Ai who let it happen—either because he abandoned them or was too weak to help them." He sipped his tea, regarding Abramm over the cup's silver lip. "Much the same as it was for you, I think."

It was as if a current leapt from his eyes to Abramm's, rushing through his body, prickling all his skin. His heart suddenly pounded, his stomach twisting with forgotten pain.

"Eidon. Is that not the god you Kiriathans serve?" Katahn continued.

"Some do, yes," Abramm said.

"The Dying God, he's called?"

"We call him Almighty. Lord of Light. Creator of the world."

"Ah. Like Sheleft'Ai. Perhaps he was exhausted, then, from all of his work."

Abramm scowled at him. He had not thought of Eidon for months, and the reawakening of the memory was painful in the extreme.

"Strange, though. There can't be two creators. So one of you must be wrong. Unless both of you are."

"I wouldn't know," Abramm said tonelessly, finally managing to drag his gaze from his captor's and apply it to the cup in his hands.

"He marched all the way to Hur," Katahn said after a moment. "Sent more than five hundred thousand of the blasphemers to the Dark Abode and took many more for slaves."

Belatedly Abramm realized he was talking of Beltha'adi again, recounting now the infamous March of Death—retribution for the centuries of abuse the Esurhites and their ancestors had suffered at Dorsaddi hands and also for their long years of prosperity and supremacy. Having breeched SaHallan defenses, Beltha'adi had shown no mercy. The Dorsaddi paid with their lifeblood, their families, and their lands. Those not killed were taken as slaves, and Hur was fouled beyond redemption.

"They were not weaklings, the Dorsaddi," Katahn went on, "for all their blasphemous ways. Many have refused to bend to servitude, choosing suicide over slavery. There are few left." He glanced at the woman. "Shettai, you see, is quite rare. A true princess of the line of Hur. Sister, in fact, to their current king. If you can call a man king who rules so little and so provisionally."

"But the March of Death was over two hundred years ago!" Abramm protested. "Surely she is—"

"The SaHal is too vast and convoluted for even Beltha'adi to have gotten all of them the first time around. Even today survivors remain among the rocks—little bands nursing delusions of rebellion. Our Supreme Commander conducts periodic forays to round them up. I was on one such foray when I found her, as tough and courageous a warrior as any of them and only fourteen. That was ten years ago, and she hasn't changed a whit."

He traced the edge of her chin, drawing Abramm's attention back to her incredible beauty. She looked at her master askance, not as one subservient but as one only pretending to serve. On the beach, Abramm remembered, she had not even pretended much.

"Perhaps it was her youth that persuaded her not to take her own life," Katahn mused. "Or my charm." He chuckled, letting his finger drop along the slender neck and drift to the edge of her robe. With a grimace she knocked the hand aside, delivering what sounded like a rebuke. Katahn answered her sharply, and for some moments they engaged in a verbal duel, their meanings hidden in the Tahg but an inexplicable respect for one another evident in their manner.

Katahn burst into laughter, and Shettai cocked her head at him saucily so that Abramm gulped again, shaken anew by the power of his attraction to her. He was close enough to smell her spicy scent, to reach out, if he dared, and touch her. The thought made his flesh grow warm and his heart pound. For the first time in his life he found himself longing to bury his hands in a woman's hair, to stroke her skin, caress her curves. . . .

He realized suddenly that Katahn had spoken to him and struggled to put these unfamiliar—and dangerous—desires back into the place from which they'd sprung. "Your pardon, sir?"

The man's dark eyes laughed at him. But he only said, "I was merely remarking on the fact that many believe it was the fall of Hur that unleashed the power of Khrell. That soon all the world will be under his dominion."

Abramm shrugged, feigning indifference, though he was glad for the change in subject. "I know too little about your Khrell to comment." Shettai, he noted to himself, was more interested in the potted fern at his side than she would ever be in him.

"Come, come, my prince," Katahn persisted. "Surely you have an opinion. Your sister said you've taken religious vows."

"Vows to a god who, as you have just pointed out, abandoned me." Perhaps he was not so happy with this subject change as he had thought. "They are nothing to me now, sir. Thus I have nothing to say."

"You have abandoned him as he has abandoned you, eh? But still you must believe something. When you die in that arena a few months from now, where will you go? To the Dark Abode? To the Eternal Plain? To that dreadfully boring Garden of Light you northerners anticipate? I've never understood the draw of that one. . . . But then, your Tormenting Fires hold even less appeal, so perhaps it's all relative. But how will it be decided where you go? I know you have opinions, my prince. Tell me what they are. Tell me what you think."

He leaned forward eagerly, like a glutton might approach a favorite dessert. Abramm frowned in distaste, sensing in the man the sort of person who merely enjoyed the intellectual exercise of debate but believed nothing himself. A man who had never known the ecstasy in devotion and surrender nor the agony of betrayal and disillusion.

"I think I am a slave," Abramm said finally. "And that my life resides wholly and completely in that sword you've given me. If I learn to use it well, if I learn to win with it, I *won't* die in that arena." He was suddenly angry—with himself for the weaknesses that had brought him here, with Katahn for his intrusive, cold-blooded interest in it all, with the entire hopeless, wretched situation that, despite his determination to survive, would likely see him dead, and then . . . But no, he did not want to think about that, which made him angrier than ever. So now he glared at the man, defying him to probe further.

Katahn's expression had gone curiously blank. Finally he smiled, a slow, knowing smirk. "There *is* fire in you, my prince. And steel, I think, even though you've descended from a race of pigeons. I begin to see how you survived the galley ship. And why your handlers have been so surprised. . . ."

His handlers were surprised? That was news. As far as Abramm could tell, he was little more than a dog to them, worthy only of beating, taunting, and torturing. His thoughts drawn back to his arm, he realized its throbbing had worsened and would likely worsen more before it improved. He hoped he could complete the rest of his training routine today without mishap.

With a sigh Katahn shook off his reverie. "I confess you have disappointed me, my prince, for I was looking forward to a lively debate. . . . But perhaps you can indulge me my other passion." He drained his cup and set it on the table, then drew his legs beneath him and sat upright. "You do play uurka, don't you?"

Abramm blinked and lifted his gaze. "Not since I was twelve. It was forbidden in the Mataio."

"Ah yes, the religious vows. But why forbidden?"

Shettai began to remove the tea service.

"It's a game of warfare, sir," Abramm said, keeping his eyes away from her. "Capturing territory, sacrificing men . . . strategy, tactics. Not at all suitable for those who would pursue peace."

"Peace." Katahn made a face. "Were you any good?"

"I held my own. I was only a child, though."

"Mmm. It seems I will face yet another disappointment. I was so hoping, as royalty, you might give me a fair challenge. Few of your subjects seem to know how to play properly."

The table cleared, Shettai brought out the uurka game board, the carved white and black pieces stored in its deep central pit. As she attached the supports to each of the four corners, Abramm remarked that it was a fine set.

"I gave up two fine fighters for it. It better be."

Thankfully Shettai withdrew to a respectful distance as Katahn arranged the game pieces. "I spent some years in your land," he explained, "so I know your people and customs well. Most of it I disdain, of course, but the game caught me. It is obviously a corruption of our jackal and crow, but I like the elegance and trickery you have introduced into it."

"It is an old, old game."

"Esurhite to be sure." He set the last game piece into place and looked up. "Are you ready?"

"Whenever you wish."

"You may go first, then."

They fell silent, concentrating on the board between them. It soon became apparent to Abramm that his opponent played like no one he had faced before—not ineptly nor stupidly, but with the flavor of a very different mind. His plays were unexpected, at times foolishly daring, yet effective. In the end, however, several moves before it became obvious, Abramm realized he had won.

Which forced him into an all-too-familiar dilemma. Should he go ahead and play it out honestly or make a faulty move? The price for defeating Gillard when they had played as boys had been a pummeling. But if his brother caught him deliberately throwing the game, the abuse only worsened. To be pacified, Gillard had to think he had won fairly. And Katahn, in many ways, reminded him of Gillard.

If Abramm won now, would the man fly into a rage? He could not help but think of Zamath's ear medallion, the brace of fingers collected by some of the other guards. He tugged at the whiskers beneath his lower lip, considering. What was to be gained in his winning? Only the solace of his own pride, perhaps. But—blast it all!—he didn't *want* to lose to this cunning weasel. And since Katahn would surely demand a rematch, Abramm could always lose to him then.

Thus he played the match out to win, struggling to conceal his satisfaction—until it struck him that he had forgotten the range of attack Katahn's archer commanded from its current position. True, Katahn had done everything to disguise it, had executed a laudable campaign of deception, in fact, but his skill was no excuse. Abramm should have seen it.

He watched Katahn take the field and end the game, feeling annoyed now that the initial shock had worn off. The Esurhite sat back, grinning. "Excellent!" he exclaimed. "You have the makings of a formidable opponent. In fact, had you not fallen victim to overconfidence, you would have won today. Let that be a lesson for you in the—"

He was cut off by an outcry at one of the doorways below, and they turned to see a shaven-headed man in scarlet robes stalking across the lower level toward them. His ancient, weathered face was a storm cloud of concern, and a young man in Brogai black—Katahn's son—followed in his wake, mirroring his agitation.

The bald man—Abramm guessed he was a priest from the filigreed medallion he wore on his chest—stopped beside the low table, eyes widening at the sight of Abramm. Then he whirled to face Katahn, fell to his knees, and burst into a torrent of agitated Tahg.

That Abramm was the subject of this outburst was evident from the way the stranger repeatedly gestured at him. Unfortunately, he understood only a few of the man's words. Words like "kill him," and "Khrell," and "lose all."

When he had finished, Katahn continued to regard him with a mask of imperturbability, but Shettai released a soft, scornful laugh.

The priest made an emphatic gesture, glaring first at her, then at Abramm. He launched into another diatribe, but Katahn lifted a hand, silencing him. Summoning one of the guards, he arched his brows at Abramm and said, "We will play again, my prince."

There was nothing for Abramm to do but follow his guard from the room, the priest's renewed efforts at persuasion pursuing them onto the balcony—*"Meraka nae do!"*

*Kill him now!*

# CHAPTER 17

Abramm returned to his routine, fearing every moment might be his last. So far as he knew, he'd never seen that priest before, could not imagine what he'd done to provoke him. Had the man received some sort of vision? Was he even a priest, or something else entirely? And how much influence did he have over Katahn? Clearly some, or he could not have marched into the Brogai's private chambers unannounced and unimpeded. But Katahn had not seemed intimidated, and Shettai had laughed outright.

At length he forced himself to put it all aside, resigned to yet another infuriating aspect of being a slave—that of having to live in ignorance while others decided one's fate.

In any case, he had more immediate concerns facing him. His arm, as expected, grew worse through the remainder of the afternoon, and by his last match he could hardly grip the dagger with which he parried his opponent's blows. He prevailed, but his win was not clean, the deciding stroke powered by desperation not skill.

By the time he was returned to his cell, all he wanted was to collapse and be left in his misery. Unfortunately, during the day someone had brought in an additional straw-filled sleeping pallet, the sight of which made him groan with dismay.

He'd been through three cellmates already, not knowing what became of them, and not caring. They were always surly, always bigger than him, always perversely determined to make his life miserable until he finally stood up to them and put an end to it. He'd realized after the last one that he'd save himself a lot of grief if he put them in their place at the start, but that was the last thing he wanted to do now.

The new man had not arrived yet, so perhaps someone had miscounted and the sack would not be used after all. But when the dinner detail shoved two portions of pork-lentil stew and bread under the railed door he knew there was no mistake.

The sight and oniony smell of food made his gorge rise, so he merely drank the water and settled back against the wall, eyes closed, willing himself to sleep. A key grating in the lock jerked him from a half doze, and he sat forward to meet the new man—someone shorter than Abramm for once, though well muscled, with curly red hair and beard, and a golden shield glinting on his bare chest. Abramm's jaw dropped. *"Meridon?"*

As the door clanged shut, the Terstan looked even more astonished than Abramm. Then he grinned sheepishly and dropped onto his pallet. "Well, this is a pleasant surprise," he said. "I was all set to fight for my dinner."

Abramm shoved the tray toward him with a foot. "You can have all of it as far as I'm concerned."

Meridon glanced at the two full bowls and hunks of bread, then regarded Abramm more closely. "Are you ill?"

"They put the griiswurm on me today. It always makes me sick. Go ahead." He gestured at the food.

Clearly uncomfortable, Meridon pulled the tray toward him. "I thought you won all day," he said. "Word is you gave old Brugal his first taste of the wurm."

"I did. But you know how the heathen like to play." He frowned as he caught another whiff of the familiar but out-of-place scent Meridon had brought in with him. Incense, maybe? But what. . . ? And then he understood. "You've been with Katahn."

"I have indeed." Meridon spooned stew into his mouth. "All afternoon, in fact, no thanks to you. He fancies himself quite the religious scholar."

Abramm dropped his head back against the wall and smiled at the ceiling. "So he got his debate after all. And did you make a Terstan of him?"

Trap snorted. "All he wanted was the debate. He was quite disappointed with your failure to cooperate, I might add."

"So he said." Abramm shifted into the corner, his throbbing arm cradled in the bend between hip and thigh. He closed his eyes, trying to ignore his discomfort. And then a startling thought made him stiffen and look around. "Was the priest still there when you arrived?"

He wasn't, nor, after Abramm related the incident, could Meridon make any more sense of it than Abramm had.

"You needn't worry, though," he added. "Katahn has no plans to eliminate you. In fact, he told *me* he's thinking of working us together—as the Kiriathan Prince and his Faithful Retainer. Supposed to contribute a 'highly desirable dramatic element' to our performance."

"Really." Abramm stared at the ceiling again, watching a tuft of cobweb wave slowly back and forth with the vagaries of the air currents. He sighed. "Well, I must say I'd welcome you covering my back, Captain."

"As I would you, my lord."

It took a moment for those words to sink in. Another to acknowledge their quiet sincerity.

Meridon met his surprised glance with a sober smile. "You have progressed beyond all . . ." He gestured helplessly. "Well, I can hardly believe it. In fact, I *didn't* believe it until I saw you fight yesterday." He shook his head, and . . . was that . . . *approval* in his eyes? "No question you've got the Kalladorne moves, my lord. My father was right about you."

Abramm found himself abruptly flummoxed. In the first place he could hardly believe the man was serious. And in the second, he had no idea how to respond to it, no idea what to do with this sudden warm pleasure flooding through him, save that he ought to conceal it. Just in case he really was reading the man wrongly.

Meridon, busy emptying the second bowl now, had pursued a different line of thought. "Saeral came into your life when you were what?" he asked. "Eleven? Twelve?"

"Ten."

"About three years before you'd have entered Barracks, then. Years in which you might have been expected to bloom."

"Gillard started defeating me in the sword rooms long before Saeral came along."

"Still, Saeral clearly exploited the situation."

Abramm went back to watching his cobweb, not much liking the direction in which the conversation was going.

"I wonder if he worked both sides," Meridon went on. "Encouraging you to pacifism and helplessness while one of his minions urged Gillard toward increasing belligerence. You must've been dreading the prospect of entering Barracks with him."

"And rightly so. He would've killed me."

"Was that your idea, or Saeral's?"

Abramm looked at him, startled. "Mine." But was it? There had been hints, allusion . . . He shrugged. "He would have, in any case."

Meridon regarded him thoughtfully. "I'm not so sure."

"You don't know how it was between us."

"I know enough. And I've seen what you've done here."

"Barracks isn't like here. It's less controlled. Gillard would've risen to the top, gathered his little group of admirers, and come after me when no one was looking."

"And you, with your back against the wall, would've folded?" One of Meridon's red brows arched. "I think not, my lord. The matter would've come to a head. And once you stood up to him things would have changed."

The same way, Abramm realized, things changed when he'd stood up to his bullying cellmates.

"You might have become friends."

"No," Abramm said. "He hates me too much for that. He has from the day he was born, though why, I've never understood. He was always stronger, bigger, better. What was I to him, but an embarrassment? You'd think he'd just ignore me."

Trap set the now empty second bowl atop the first on the tray, then leaned back against the wall and clasped his hands upon his bare abdomen. "You were much more than an embarrassment, my lord. You were in some ways the bane of his life."

It was Abramm's turn to lift a brow of disbelief.

"Look at it from his viewpoint. You're smart, handsome, artistically accomplished, genteel, and religious—the only son your mother considered worth anything. An opinion she expressed regularly and loudly, as I understand it. Even Raynen was jealous. As for Gillard—from the day he came into this world you were ahead of him, the bright and shining star in his mother's eye."

"Aye, and *he* was the bright star in our father's. And our uncle's and our brothers' . . . and most of their peers', as well. Rightly so, given their standards." The old bitterness rang in his tone.

Meridon regarded him oddly. "And that bothered you?"

"Of course it bothered me! I was a Kalladorne and a miserable failure at the most valued characteristic of the line. I spent hours on the practice floor trying to improve—and never did. The day my *baby* brother defeated me . . ." He trailed off, feeling the humiliation as if it were yesterday, hearing the laughter and the vicious jibes. Old pain twisted in his belly, and he clenched his fists, his thoughts skittering forward over all the subsequent humiliations, both on the practice floor and off—the cruel jokes, the lies, the beatings threaded through his past like thorns on a string.

Across from him Meridon sighed. "Yet it didn't win him your mother's regard, did it?"

Abramm's pain transmuted all at once into hot, wounded indignation. "What is this? You expect me to sympathize with him? After what he's done?!"

Trap gestured dismissively. "I doubt it's given him much pleasure. And anyway, it wasn't he who put us here, nor even Raynen. It was Eidon."

"Eidon?!" Abramm gaped at him.

"We're here for a reason, my lord."

"A *reason*? Khrell's fire, man! How can you still believe such a thing? Eidon, indeed! Isn't it obvious he doesn't exist?"

"Not at all."

"I gave him eight years of my life!" Abramm said bitterly. "All I ever wanted in exchange was to know him. You have no idea how many times I begged him—*begged* him—to show me how to do that. But I never got an answer. All I got was betrayal and suffering and abandonment."

Aggravated by his passion, the pain in his arm flared with such intensity he gasped, then had to swallow down the bile rising in his gullet. Eyes shut, he dropped his head back again and gripped the hard muscles of his left forearm as if that might stop the flood of fire pulsing out of his wrist.

For a few moments he poised on the brink of lurching for the relief bucket. Then the pain faded and he began to relax. Presently he heard Meridon's straw bag crackle, heard the extended rasp as the tray of empty bowls was shoved toward the door, then another crackling as Meridon stretched out on the pallet. A long, low sigh gave way to silence, broken only by the distant thumps, clanks, and muffled voices of their keepers out in the service rooms.

After a time Abramm lay down, too, reclining on his good side, with his back to his cellmate and his face to the wall. He'd lain there a few moments when Meridon spoke again, his voice quiet but firm with conviction.

"You're wrong, my lord. Eidon does exist. And he hasn't abandoned you or your request. It's just that his answers don't always come the way we expect."

Abramm gritted his teeth and said nothing. Years ago his mother and uncle had argued religion in front of him. His mother had condemned the arrogance of unbelief, while Simon railed against religious delusion and supplicants participating in their own deception. Faith, he'd said, was the absence of thought. It was believing the impossible, despite all sense and solid evidence to the contrary.

Abramm had expected an outraged rejoinder from his mother. She'd surprised him with her quiet, almost condescending confidence. Simon, she'd said, would do better to confine his arguments to subjects about which he had some knowledge.

He'd had no answer to that, and Abramm had been terribly impressed. That calm conviction had inspired him for years afterward. Now he knew it to be misplaced. She'd been deceived, as he himself had been, and in the end Simon was right.

The corridor echoed with the clatter and rasp of the dinner trays being removed by the cleanup detail. The sounds grew louder as they approached, faded as they moved away, and once more near-silence reigned.

By then the shoulder on which Abramm lay had begun to ache, so he rolled over. That was worse, so he sat up and wedged himself into the corner again. His head felt like a melon ready to burst, and the stone was cold against his bare back and shoulder. He suspected it wouldn't be long before he needed that bucket after all.

"May I see your arm?" Trap's voice jarred through his agony, surprisingly close.

He opened his eyes but did not lift his head. Meridon crouched on one knee beside him, regarding him gravely.

Abramm let his eyes rest on the ceiling with its shivering cobwebs. He swallowed on a dry mouth, then turned his wrist, lifting it so Meridon could look. He heard a faint hum, felt a sudden warmth, and a clear, fist-sized globe of light flared to life in front of him, floating above his knees. He gasped and flinched against the wall, but it only bobbed benignly, delicate as a soap bubble.

Terstan evil. It had to be. And yet—it was beautiful. Bright and clean and pure. It had been too long since he had seen light like that. He could almost feel the warm sun beating down upon him, see the blue sky arcing overhead, smell the summer grass. For the first time since he'd come to this dark, mist-bound land, he realized how deeply he craved the light of a clear day.

"I could ease this if you'd let me."

Abramm tore his gaze from the orb. Meridon gestured at the scar on his wrist, the purple, ovoid mark, moist now and raised, throbbing visibly like some misplaced heart under red, tender skin.

He met Meridon's sober gaze. "How do you mean?"

"It's the feyna spore that's making you sick. The griiswurm's activated it. I can put it back to dormancy—can even burn some of it off in the process. You'll feel better right away."

Abramm glanced at the bubble of light, drifting slowly toward the wall at his side. His eyes flicked to the shield on Meridon's chest. He remembered the protective talisman this man had given him in Kiriath—how the round gray stone had replicated itself under his own chin in the teppuh. He stifled a shudder as he remembered Whazel carrying away the replication on his finger and then the shield burning into his fat chest.

"It'd just be your arm," the Terstan said, guessing his thoughts. "It won't change you."

Abramm shook his head, swallowing down new nausea. "I'll be all right."

It was a moment before Meridon shrugged. "Suit yourself." He flicked the orb with a finger, and it vanished, shadow enfolding them once again.

"No!" The word sprang from Abramm's mouth all unexpected, so full of dismay it shocked him.

Immediately another orb blossomed in its place. Meridon stared at him questioningly.

Abramm blushed. "I . . . uh . . . does it cost you to leave it?"

"Not at all." He settled back on his own pallet.

Abramm feigned indifference. "It's been so long since I've seen—"

He was interrupted by a snarl and a sharp babble of Tahg as a dark figure loomed outside the cell and violet fire burst the lock. The man jerked open the door and leaped in.

As Abramm dove instinctively aside, he recognized the gleam of Zamath's head, the filed teeth, the long-nailed fingers coming at him, dark against the flare of violet light at his chest. But the Broho wasn't after him. Though the sphere had winked out the moment Abramm first moved, Zamath swatted at the place it had hovered as if in a frenzy, then turned upon the Terstan.

"*Anahdi!*" he growled, jerking the man up by the throat and slamming him against the wall. Meridon kicked him and wriggled free as Abramm rammed a shoulder into the southlander's back, driving him against the wall—only to be flung across the cell a moment later. He crashed into the wall and sagged onto his pallet, violet splashing across his vision. Through a haze of purple he saw Zamath fall upon Trap like a madman, striking him again and again, faster than humanly possible, all the while cursing softly. *"Anahdi! Beshad!"*

Suddenly the other handlers crowded into the cell, jabbering excitedly. Abramm saw nothing but legs and feet, could pick out only a few words in the babble. Then they were gone, Meridon with them. One paused to fasten a chain around bar and frame so the door held, and then Abramm was alone, stunned by the viciousness of the attack.

The room whirled again, and he spent the next few moments bent over the relief bucket. When at last he was released from his agony, Meridon was screaming somewhere down the hall.

*But they can't kill him,* he assured himself. *He has to be able to fight.*

After a seeming eternity, the screams grew hoarse, then fell silent. Abramm sat clutching his arm and was very near to praying, though to whom he would have prayed he did not know. He only knew he did not want Meridon to die.

Finally the slap of footfalls heralded the handlers' return. The chain rattled, the door swung open, and Meridon was thrust into the cell.

Abramm caught him as he fell, his hands slipping over hot, wet skin. The handlers laughed, said something about angering the gods, and departed. Gently Abramm lowered the man onto his pallet.

Even in the poor light he could see the angry, bleeding griiswurm welts crisscrossing the Terstan's face, arms, and chest, each lined with pale, bubbling blisters. There were so many it was hard to find a clear patch of skin, and already Meridon was burning with fever and shaking violently.

He coiled inward on the straw bag with a moan, doubling around his stomach and struggling to his knees. Abramm shoved the relief bucket in front of him just as he began to vomit. Once started, the tide did not turn for some time. Meridon's convulsions wracked him with a power and savagery that was frightening.

Abramm could do no more than hold him up until the spasms passed and he sagged against Abramm's side, as cold now as he had been hot before. He dragged a quivering hand across his polluted beard and swallowed. "Are they gone?"

"Yes."

Meridon pushed weakly against his ribs. "Let me go, then. And get back."

"But . . ." Abramm swallowed his protest and complied. The other man crawled onto his pallet and collapsed face down in the crackling straw. A faint buzzing filled the chamber, building to a mellow hum. At the same time Abramm's skin prickled as of lightning about to strike, and Trap's body began to glow.

Abramm leapt to his feet.

The glow intensified, hurting his eyes, though he could not look away, held by fascination as much as by fear. It thickened around the Terstan's form, a bright, white cloud, flashing with silver-and-gold coruscation.

Footfalls down the corridor broke the spell, and he snatched the blanket from his own pallet, draping it over the other's body, fearing the blaze might burn through it as the stone had burned his tunic back in Qarkeshan. But though the light was so strong it shone through the weave and blared up under the folds, it did not harm the fabric itself.

As the footfalls drew nearer, he dragged his own pallet around to the foot of Trap's and sat with his back against the barred door to block the view of anyone standing behind him.

He had just settled when the guard reached him, pausing briefly at his back, then moving on. Dropping his head back against the bars with relief, Abramm became immediately aware again of the throbbing in his arm. He was sure Trap's Terstan magic was aggravating it, but to move would make Meridon visible from the door. He could only sit and try to ignore his discomfort.

The night passed in a miasma of wakefulness and unpleasant half-dreams until finally he lay awake for good, listening to the rising clatter of pans and wooden bowls echoing from the kitchen. His arm had somehow come to rest against Meridon's foot, which had strayed, along with half of the rest of him, from under the blanket. He immediately noticed that his pain had subsided, along with the nausea and fever, and that, despite his poor night's sleep, he felt rejuvenated. The second thing he noticed was that Meridon was breathing evenly, that his flesh was cool and—

Abramm peered at the man's back, face, and arms. The griiswurm welts were no more than a network of threadlike scars, when they should've taken days to heal.

A wave of gooseflesh spread up Abramm's arms. He looked at his own wounds. Not yet scars, they were well on their way toward healing, nonetheless. And the feyna scar was once more white and flat, when it, too, should have taken days to subside. . . .

Meridon stirred, then sat up groggily. "What is that awful smell?"

His gaze fixed on the relief bucket beside him, then flicked to Abramm as memory returned. "You're all right! I thought—since it was right over you—they would think . . ." He rubbed his eyes. "I thought I heard someone screaming, but I guess it was just me."

Hurried footfalls echoed in the silence, and three men stopped outside the cell, clanking chain and lock as they freed the door and swung it back. Abramm drew his feet under him warily as they entered, startled to recognize Katahn himself, clearly furious. When he saw the Terstan up and well, however, he stopped dead. Then he called for a torch, and when his underling brought it, he stood staring at Meridon's face and chest. Beside him Abdeel gaped in even greater astonishment.

Katahn spoke to him sharply. Abdeel protested in a rapid stream of the Tahg, and they left without another look at the northerners, Katahn's voice echoing angrily in their wake.

Nothing more came of the incident, though they did not see Zamath for over a week, and when he returned he was sullen and reserved and never worked with Meridon again. Nor, thankfully, with Abramm, either. Trap was right about their new alliance. After that night, they were worked as a team, back to back, shoulder to shoulder, facing at first three, then four, and sometimes even six assailants. With Trap's added instruction, demonstration, and encouragement, Abramm improved more rapidly than ever.

Katahn continued to summon him for games of uurka, which Abramm won as often as his master. Every game was followed by an analysis of strategy and tactics, and he soon realized this was as much a part of his training as what happened on the practice floor.

Shettai sat with them occasionally, and Abramm wondered if Katahn noticed that Abramm always lost when she did. Despite her cool, condescending manner, his infatuation with her burned on. He'd learned to control the outward evidences, at least, according her the same cool indifference she accorded him. But always after he saw her, she haunted his dreams. Often they woke him, and always they shocked and perplexed him. He wondered if he was in love with her, only to remind himself that in her eyes he was but a weak-willed, pigeon-hearted Kiriathan slave whose scrawny ribs she'd knuckled and rejected back in Qarkeshan. He did himself no favors hoping her opinion might change. Best to put all the raging desires back into their box and concentrate on staying alive.

Thus the weeks passed until finally, inevitably, the morning came when he and Meridon were taken not to the practice floors but to the beach. There they and a handful of their fellows boarded a trio of galley ships that immediately set sail for the site of their first official competition.

The training period was over.

# CHAPTER 18

The razor flicked along the side of Abramm's jaw, Zamath's hand quick and sure as it cut the beard from his face. Abramm stared up at the red canvas awning suspended directly in front of his line of vision and clenched his teeth, trying not to think of who held the blade, trying not to consider just how helpless he was before it.

They'd arrived here in Vorta yesterday, just in time to take part in the opening procession of warriors last night. Dressed only in their loincloths, they had, with the other slaves who would participate in the coming contests, been marched in a long line around the sand-packed oblong floor of the Ul Manus Arena for the crowd to inspect. It had been a long, humiliating evening, after which they'd returned to the galleys for the night. Katahn had slept in, but his fighters had been wakened early and already put through their practice routines. A few had even been taken off to the arena for their matches.

It wasn't until after the midday meal that Katahn gave orders for Abramm and Trap to be prepared. The guards had fallen upon them with glee. Abramm did not know what had become of Trap but surmised it was a fate similar to his own, for a second group of guards clustered on the far side of the foredeck's covered area.

Abramm sat in a straight-backed chair, his hands tied to its arms, his feet to its legs. The whole had been tipped against a barrel, forcing his head back and exposing his throat to Zamath's blade.

The Broho was entertaining his audience, handling the razor with elaborate flourishes, always just in control. Abramm knew full well the man was trying to scare him, knew also that he had succeeded. But he was not about to show it.

"That's a long nose he's got there," one of the onlookers called. "Maybe you should give it a trim."

By now Abramm's command of the Tahg was good enough he could catch nearly all the meaning—and wished he couldn't.

A muttered comment at the back of the group sparked them all to laughter. Zamath laid his fingers to opposite undersides of Abramm's jaw and flashed the blade before him, close to his nose. "It *is* long," he agreed. "But without it he wouldn't be as pretty. And Katahn wants him pretty."

He lifted Abramm's chin and slid the razor up his throat. Abramm gripped the chair's arms and fought the compulsion to swallow.

"Am I making you nervous, your *highness*?" Zamath mocked. He pulled the blade back, then drew it along Abramm's brow, scraping away the beads of perspiration and shaking the moisture free. The guards laughed again.

*"Yelaki!"* they called. *"Yelaki hashta."*

Yelaki—coward. He'd heard a lot of that last night.

Zamath leaned over him and laid the razor along his other cheek. A few swift strokes and it was clean, the blade coming to rest disarmingly against the lobe of his left ear.

"Aye, Zamath!" one of the men called. "He could fight as well without the ear, and it'll be hidden anyway. Cut it off!"

"Aye, Zamath. Add the Kiriathan prince to your Dorsaddi chieftain!"

"Cut him, Zamath. Let us see him squirm."

The razor pressed upward. Abramm kept his eyes fixed upon the planes of pink-and-red canvas overhead, his arms aching from the death grip he had on the chair. With effort he forced himself to breathe regularly.

Pressure mounted against the point of his earlobe's attachment, and then a tracery of pain laced outward along neck and scalp and cheek. Something hot dripped down the side of his neck.

Zamath leaned close, putting his face eye to eye with Abramm, his filed teeth gleaming against the darkness of his mouth. His eyes flashed with madness.

"Your life is in my hands, *yelaki Kiriatha*," he whispered. "You are weak, and I am strong." His voice had grown harsher, oddly resonanced. "With a twitch I could take your ear. Or cut the vessel beneath it and watch your life's blood spurt across the deck."

His breath was fetid, his lips close enough to kiss. "Have you ever seen it?" he rasped. "I can make it shoot like wine from a barrel, rich and red with *elak'a*."

The drip down Abramm's neck now trickled over his shoulder and chest. Sweat beaded his brow again, and the pain was making him sick. He wanted to look anywhere save into Zamath's face, but that was what the Broho wanted—cringing submission. So he stared unblinking into those mad eyes and refused to be cowed.

"Zamath!" Katahn's voice cut into the spell. "Aren't you finished with him yet?"

The slow upward cut of the knife halted, and then with a sudden final jerk, Zamath pulled away, cursing under his breath. Abramm swallowed hard, feeling faint, the side of his head shrieking its agony. *The maniac must have cut off half my ear,* he thought. But he could not move his hands to find out, could only sit and endure as the blood ran down his neck and over his chest.

Katahn pressed through the dark-clad men, took one look at Abramm, and turned on Zamath in a furious tirade. The Broho stiffened, lips skinning back from his teeth as the light flashed off the razor in his hands. Katahn halted. In that moment they reminded Abramm of two vicious dogs, faced off, not quite sure who was the stronger.

Katahn stood stiff and straight, silent now, staring hard. The air crackled with challenge, and Abramm recalled that Katahn had been a famous arena warrior himself. There was more than the weight of past glories in that stare, however, for suddenly the Broho deflated. Wheeling wordlessly, he flung aside the razor, pushed between two guards, and stepped out of sight.

Katahn turned to Abramm, grabbed his jaw and swung his face sideways to examine the ear. He fingered it gently, sending white starbursts tumbling past Abramm's vision.

"It'll heal," the Brogai lord pronounced finally. "Sew it up and get him dressed." He glanced in the direction Zamath had taken and muttered, "I should cage that madman."

Abramm breathed a sigh of relief.

Abdeel sewed up his ear and shortly released him from the chair. But the humiliation was not over. With much laughter and jeering, the guards dressed him in white doublet and stiff, puffy breeches that ended at midthigh. An only slightly exaggerated rendition of the latest trends in Kiriathan fashion, it was so copiously trimmed with ribbons and lace he felt like a cloth merchant's notions rack. High-heeled white ankle boots and a faded purple cloak completed the ensemble.

Next he was tied down again and a short, slender man—one of Katahn's personal servants?—came to paint his face. White lard-textured pigment provided a mask over which the man drew thin red lips in a wide jester's smile and long black lines radiating from his eyes. A curly white wig secured with a golden headband—his crown?—completed the costume.

All the while, the guards roared with laughter, mocking him with mincing gestures and high-pitched voices and falling upon each other in their mirth-made infirmity.

Beneath the paint, Abramm's face burned. Rage and frustration knotted in his chest, twisting his stomach painfully. It had been like this in the arena last night, marching before that jeering crowd, pelted with rotten fruit and old sausages, the anger and bitterness simmering higher and higher until he was actually looking forward to the chance to silence their laughter.

He joined Meridon by the railing outside the canopy, and if it were not for knowing it had to be Meridon, Abramm would not have recognized him. He also wore a dandified doublet and ballooning breeches, both emerald hued. The doublet and under blouse were unbuttoned at the chest to reveal his shieldmark. Like Abramm he wore a long curly wig—his was black—and face paint, all white, with a red sad-mouth brushed in over his lips, drooping black brows, and a small black tear inked in on one cheek.

As they eyed each other Abramm muttered, "I suppose I look as ridiculous as you do?"

"We'll have our vindication, my lord."

Katahn strode from the stern cabin, wrapped in furs against the day's dank chill, his Brogai amulet gleaming on his chest. Shettai followed, swathed in black today with a sheer half-veil covering her lovely face. At the sight of his Kiriathans, the Brogai lord grinned widely and nodded. "Perfect. Get them cloaked, and take them over as soon as my boat returns." He pulled a large gold watch from the pocket in his tunic, glanced at it, and nodded again. "The timing should be perfect. Remember—be discreet. If you draw a crowd, you'll be late."

His son Regar and the red-robed priest, Master Peig, came on deck then. The priest scowled at Abramm but said nothing as he followed the others over the side. Shortly the shore boat heaved away, oars flashing as it glided through Vorta's bustling harbor toward the dock and the gray-walled city looming above it.

Cloaked, cowled, and escorted closely by Zamath, Abdeel, Dumah, and the others, the Kiriathans drew little more than casual interest on their walk from the dock to the Ul Manus Arena. Built on a low hill at the city's midst and crowned with the colorful banners of the twenty-two Houses of the Brogai, the arena's entrance ramps thronged with arriving spectators. Zamath bypassed these for a busy service tunnel that descended into the arena's stinking, bustling underbelly, where a network of low-vaulted chambers housed rows of iron-barred cages along a curving central aisle. Men, women, and children occupied those cages, as well as beasts of all kinds, both predators and prey. The Games, Abramm had learned from his talks with Katahn, were not so much about fighting as about killing and death. Death, Esurhites believed, was a part of life and not to be feared. Great power was released at the moment a soul was liberated from its flesh, power that might be conferred upon those who witnessed it. For some it was a spiritual experience, a linkage, however brief, with the power of Khrell himself.

And so, there was not only combat between equals, not only the great dramas played out in all their gory finality, there were sometimes simple contests of hunter and hunted, the lion against the lamb, albeit controlled and directed by a Game Master for maximum suspense and impact.

Hearing about it in Katahn's spacious gallery over a game of uurka and a cup of tea was quite different from suddenly finding himself a part of it all. Those people in that cell over there, scrawny and dead-eyed men, women, and children—they were no warriors. And if not warriors, they must be victims, herded into the ring to act out some past event or prognosticated future.

Which was exactly the role he and Trap were expected to play. Yes, they would be given weapons, but no one, not even Katahn, expected them to live.

As a Game official hurried up to them, Abdeel pulled back their cowls for inspection. The official had seen them unpainted last night, and now he started, then chuckled openly. His assistants laughed as well, exchanging dry remarks with the handlers as the official got down to business. He peered closely at the Kiriathans, making them turn around before him, then checked the number on his list against that on the bronze bands sealed—with magic, it seemed—round their wrists yesterday. Finally he examined the bands themselves and, finding nothing amiss, approved them for admittance.

"And you're here none too soon," he informed their handlers. "They're up after the Dorsaddi Deliverer, and he's in the wings right now."

They were brought to a holding area before a pair of wooden doors, filled with men and women dressed in Kiriathan high-court finery—frills of lace and ribbon and satin—and long wigs of every color. Like Abramm and Trap, their faces had been painted white and onto that, in red and black, various comical expressions—prissy heart mouths or wide silly grins, round red cheek spots or mournful, downslanting brows complete with painted tear.

They sat or stood silently, staring at the floor, at the wall, or into space, their eyes dull and empty.

A young woman in a yellow gown sat dully on a bench, tears streaking the painted happy face she wore. She looked up as Abramm and Trap entered, examining them with dead, disinterested eyes. Old eyes, though Abramm guessed she was younger than he was. Two other women sat beside her, staring into space.

"Why are you here?" Trap asked one of the men in the Tahg. When the stranger only looked at him blankly, he repeated himself in Kiriathan.

That sparked a stirring of interest. The man's eyes flicked from him to Abramm and back. "We're your courtiers." He hesitated, looking at Abramm again. "You're supposed to defend us. It's the Fall of Kiriath—Beltha'adi meets the Kalladorne king." He flashed Abramm a look of bitter reproach, then turned away. "But they always give us imposters," he muttered.

Abramm understood his feeling easily enough. Everyone here must know, despite their behavior to the contrary, who Abramm was. He'd been paraded around last night for all to see, spectators and fellow participants alike, his name blared out clearly, even accented by the Tahg.

They knew.

How many times had they taken part in this "Fall of Kiriath"? How many defenders pretending to be king had failed them already? Here, at last, their masters gave them the real thing, a man of royal blood, and instead of vindication, they could only believe he'd bring them the worst humiliation of all.

For if they knew of him, they could only know what he had been—the weakest of the Kalladorne brothers. Little Abramm, the pious servant of Eidon. The smallest, the least talented, the poorest trained. A boy who'd spent the last eight years of his life studying how not to fight. In their eyes, having Abramm Kalladorne as their defender would be worse than no defender at all.

Looking at them now, with their eyes downcast or deliberately averted, none of them wanting to have to acknowledge his presence, he felt something harden within him. For the last six days he had dreaded this hour, knowing full well that fighting at practice was not in the least like fighting for real. Old doubts had resurfaced, strengthened by an all too vivid capacity to imagine the possibilities for failure. Would he panic? Freeze? Forget everything?

These warriors he would face had killed hundreds of times before. He had never killed a man in his life and wasn't sure he'd be able to do it if he had to.

But now, seeing these people—his own countrymen, sharing his fate—a long-dead sense of duty resurrected within him. He was a prince of Kalladorne blood, the object of his people's respect and tribute, for which he owed them nothing less than the sacrifice of his own life to their service. Even his entry into the Mataio had reflected this, for he'd given up as much as any soldier—more, even—to do it, and all for the sake of the realm and the people within it.

If he was no longer Brother Eldrin, he was yet Prince Abramm. If he no longer served the Flames, he still served his countrymen. And now more than ever he understood the power and the reality of the threat that menaced them. When he entered that ring out there, he would be fighting not only for himself but also for the reputation of his family and his homeland and for these individuals who shared this cell with him. Individuals with faces and names, with eyes ashamed to look at him but whose ancestors had revered and trusted his own. He wanted fiercely to be worthy of that trust, to restore their faith, and most of all, to wipe the despair from their eyes.

The crowd's roar drew him to peer through the crack where the double doors met. He'd seen the arena last night, a walled oblong of sand surrounded by steeply rising tiers of seats. Now, though, the stands were packed with screaming spectators, making the smallish ring seem even smaller and more intimate.

At the moment black-tunicked warriors swaggered across the sand amidst bloodied figures in Dorsaddi ochre. As the few survivors were herded together by the victors' subordinates, the champions strutted and postured before the audience.

"And so the Dorsaddi fell," the Taleteller intoned, "and the SaHal remains dead to this day. Let all who defy the gods take heed. None can stand against the power of the Black Moon. None can—"

"NO!" One of the surviving Dorsaddi broke free of his captors. Dodging the bodies and preening victors, he challenged the gilded box on the far side wherein sat the elite of Vorta, among them the infamous Beltha'adi himself.

"You are wrong," the man cried out in the Tahg. "Sheleft'Ai has not forgotten, nor will he suffer your arrogance much longer. Even now the Deliverer is coming to slay you. Within two years the sand will drink your blood and the Dorsaddi will rise again!"

He stood straight-backed and proud, his bloodstained robes swaying around him. No one moved or breathed, every eye fixed upon him.

From his distant vantage, Abramm could see no more than a slight shifting amidst the figures in the shadowed box—heads turning, a hand lifted—then, from the adjoining box, where sat the warlords' Broho, streaked a violet plume of death. In an eyeblink it crashed into the Dorsaddi's chest and exploded out his back. He stood for a moment, head high, chin up, as if it did not matter that he no longer had a heart. Then he pitched forward, falling in an attitude of supplication, his arms reaching out ironically to the great Beltha'adi before him.

Profound silence followed. Then a group of workers hurried out from the far gate to carry him away. The Taleteller began again, his deep voice making the doors shiver.

"None can stand against the power of Khrell. None can stand against the power of Aggos. Let all who defy them take heed and know: As Sheleft'Ai has fallen, so will they. All will bend the neck to Khrell. In his name, we will rule as we are destined and even the white-skinned infidels to the north, who strut in their debauchery, will one day eat the dirt before him.

"Hail Khrell! Hail Beltha'adi! Hail Destiny!"

"Hail Khrell!" the crowd roared. "Hail Beltha'adi! Hail Destiny!"

# CHAPTER 19

The inner cell door squealed as Abdeel and Dumah hurried in with their charges' swords, withheld as always until combat was about to begin. They strapped on the harnesses for both longsword and dagger, gave them grins that were anything but friendly, and hurried out again.

A moment later the arena doors swung open, and Abramm gasped to see what they revealed. The sand had vanished, replaced by a gleaming gold-and-lapis court from which a long, marbled stair rose to a railed platform. White partitions, some appearing solid, others clearly illusion, rose up here and there around the set. High overhead a massive chandelier depended from a vaulted ceiling that looked for all the world like it must block the view of the spectators at the higher levels, and yet, he knew it did not. It was an illusion, like all the rest. Double-sided, appearing solid from one vantage and as the sheerest veil of gauze from the other.

But he was ready for that, having seen glimpses of the phenomenon in the parade last night. What astonished him was that this set was a near-perfect replica of the king's court at Whitehill.

The courtiers had hurried out when the doors opened, busy taking up their positions, while Abramm stood entranced. Now he heard his own name blare across the arena, fractured miserably by the Tahg, and the crowd fell silent. With a glance at Trap beside him, he drew a deep breath, straightened his shoulders, and stepped into the light.

It was only a moment before the laughter began, and once begun, it escalated quickly. People pointed and slapped each other's backs; they screamed and squealed and howled, doubling over and falling on top of each other in their mirth. Abramm walked with his head high, his back straight, his eyes ahead, as he'd been taught as a child, ignoring them. Taunts flew out of the general melee. *"Yelaki Kiriatha! Hashta kermaad!"*

He slid into that place of calm detachment, as on the beach at Qarkeshan, thinking what a curious thing it was to be mocked and disdained by people who knew nothing about him. Even more curious that they should do it with such vehemence.

The strains of a popular waltz started up around them. At once the courtiers began to drink and prance and primp, apparently having been coached, or maybe just making it up, for no one Abramm had ever seen at court acted like this.

The girl in yellow met them at the court's "entrance." Her tears had dried, and she avoided their eyes as she guided them up the stairs to the platform where Abramm was to sit on the throne. Another ran up the stair with empty silver goblets, wagged her finger at them, as if they were naughty boys, and hurried away.

The stentorian Taleteller—Abramm could not imagine how he made his voice so loud—launched into his introduction. The Fall of the King of Kiriath, this act was called. With somebody or other as Beltha'adi and somebody else as Beltha'adi's second—not that *he* would find anything to do today. The joke was received with a surge of laughter and applause.

Abramm was then introduced as playing the role of the King of Kiriath, courtesy of Katahn ul Manus himself. "And in the role of His Majesty's retainer we have the Heathen Shield Trap Meridon, formerly of the Kiriathan Royal Guard. Or so Lord ul Manus claims."

Wrathful, contemptuous screaming greeted this announcement. Pieces of rotten fruit splattered the outer edges of tile and sailed through the ghost wall that stood between Abramm and the audience on the court's far side.

The courtiers postured and bowed and fluttered, the men directed here and there by the women, tripping and reeling exaggeratedly as they slopped wine down the fronts of their doublets. The crowd laughed contemptuously.

"Drunken and dissipated . . ." said the Taleteller as the men grabbed at the women and tore at their gowns. "Indecent and immoral . . ." The women welcomed the advances with embarrassing writhings. "They are unable to control their lusts, unable to make themselves worthy of any real god's attention. Only the Dying God will have them. Serving such a god, they know not how to fight or die like men, nor will Eidon be able to defend them. They are fit only to be conquered and ruled by their betters!"

The Taleteller's voice rang stridently, igniting the crowd. The roaring, screaming voices filled the arena like a living thing that pulsed and quivered, tearing at ear and heart and belly.

Light bloomed on the far side, illuminating a door in the arena's wall, now trundling open to admit a troop of black-and-gray-garbed soldiers. Amidst them strode one clad and cloaked in gold, a black crescent moon standing atop the crown of his helmet. Impossibly, the crowd's passion rose another notch, screaming Beltha'adi's name.

With a wail the courtiers scurried to a corner of the set, crowding together like frightened hens. As the newcomers reached the main court most of the soldiers stopped near the courtiers and only the substitute Beltha'adi and one other drew their swords. Advancing casually toward the foot of the stair atop which Abramm sat on his throne, they waved to the audience, exchanged jokes with their followers, and barely glanced at their opponents.

Abramm stood up, feeling a strangely familiar rage.

The crowd began to chant. *"Yelaki! Yelaki! Dormod anahdi!"*

From Abramm's side came the hissing rasp of Meridon's blade as he drew it free of its scabbard. Abramm's hand closed upon the hilt of his own sword, hesitated.

*I will touch no weapon of warfare.*

*Violence feeds the Shadow.*

He swallowed. Could he really kill another man? And if he did, was he any better than his opponent?

He watched the men laughing up at him, listened to the crowd calling for his blood, remembered the Dorsaddi just before him, heart blasted out of his chest. And knew the answers to both questions.

Yes. And Yes.

As he pulled his blades free, something changed within him—his pent-up frustration finally found release. Suddenly he was no longer helpless. Alloying with all he had endured and seen this day, his anger forged a fierce determination to deflate their self-righteous assumptions of superiority.

He glanced at Trap, received a barely perceptible nod, and together they leaped down to meet the two who would challenge them, closing with them in a burst of aggressive parries. The two fell back, made awkward and desperate by surprise.

Abramm's opponent overparried one time too many. Before Abramm even realized what he had done, his own blade had slid under the southlander's weapon and up through the man's ribs. Blood blossomed on the golden tunic as Abramm pulled the blade free. He glimpsed a dark, surprised face as the Esurhite fell to his knees.

Meridon's man sagged to the marble floor an instant afterward, the battle over almost before it had begun.

But even as Abramm drew a shaky breath, hardly daring to believe it *was* over, a flash of metal caught his eye and he turned, lifting his weapon instinctively, deflecting the blow of one of the soldiers who had spontaneously assumed the role of backups for the first two.

Another was closing from the side, and he felt Meridon step around behind him back to back as they battled the four who had taken up arms at the fall of their comrades.

Blood pounded in Abramm's ears as he parried, lunged, and ran his opponent through the forearm, drawing a howl of pain as the man's weapon clanged to the marble floor. The disarmed Esurhite flung himself at Abramm with bare hands, and Abramm's dagger slipped between the side slits in his armor, just as he had practiced a thousand times. The soldier fell forward, and Abramm jumped back, jerking his weapon free and slamming into Meridon. He twisted left, blocked an incoming thrust with the dagger, and whipped his longblade around, slashing his opponent's arm.

A reddish haze had sprung up around him, blotting out all but the new antagonist in front of him, whom he saw with exquisite clarity—the hate-filled eyes, the clenched teeth, the rivulets of sweat streaming down the dark face. He could hear the Esurhite's breathless muttered curses and could see that the man was caught in the grip of a self-righteous fury that did not allow him to acknowledge that he faced a superior opponent.

Abramm was surprised at the man's sluggishness, at the way he seemed to telegraph his every move and struggled to keep his blade in time with Abramm's. It was a simple matter to parry his slow thrusts, to ignore his awkward feints and pay him for the failure with a stab to the leg, the arm, the waist. The man grew angrier by the moment, and before long he fell for a double feint that left him open to Abramm's killing stroke, in and out in an instant. The wild eyes widened, then rolled back as he toppled to the floor.

It was over. Six southlanders lay dead or wounded on the tile, surrounded by a rapidly dissipating haze. The distant roaring had stopped, replaced by the pitiful cries of the injured. Blood streaked and spattered the tile, and there was far more of it than he'd expected. He felt suddenly cold and weak, a great shudder staggering him.

Then Trap was at his side, gripping his arm, pulling him up and around. When he tried to resist, tried to look back over his shoulder, his friend shook his arm. "You did what you had to do, my lord."

Abramm swallowed and stared at him, heartsick and bitter. "Is that how you deal with it? Just ignore it?"

"Be thankful it's not you lying on that floor. Because it easily could have been."

His brown eyes bored into Abramm's, bearing the truth deep into his soul. Yes. It *was* supposed to have been his blood that stained the tiles.

The haze was gone now, and finally he noticed the crowd. Its shocked silence filled the arena with palpable force. He realized then that the man in the golden tunic, the one with the black crescent moon helmet, lay among the dead. The portents in that event—coming on the heels of the Dorsaddi's prophesying—struck even him, raising the hairs up the back of his neck.

He stepped back, his gaze falling at last upon his courtiers. To a person, they gaped at him with wonder and outright worship in their eyes.

He looked back at them, wiping the sweat from his upper lip on his sleeve, smearing red paint on the fabric. He was surprised to find himself panting.

Suddenly, to his utter astonishment, each of the courtiers went down on one knee. "Hail Eidon!" they cried. "Hail Abramm, King of Kiriath!"

A rumble arose from the spectators as, in the Broho's box across the ring, a man stood and stretched wide his arms. As the Kiriathan courtiers screamed and cowered, the king's court disappeared, and Abramm found himself standing on packed sand.

The man's chest swelled as he drew breath, then opened his mouth in a bellow that flung forth a gout of violet fire. Abramm toppled backward as it slammed into his sword, sending it sailing through the air to land with Trap's in a twisted, smoking heap on the sand some ten yards away.

At Beltha'adi's side, Katahn had leaped up, jabbering and gesticulating furiously. Already Zamath and the others were rushing in, interposing their bodies between their charges and the box and hurrying them out of the ring.

Katahn met them in the corridor not long afterward, bursting with excitement. "Wonderful!" he crowed. "And that bit with the courtiers at the end? They'll be falling all over themselves to get at you next time."

Shettai, who had trailed in his wake, looked at Abramm as if she'd never seen him before, while Abdeel and Dumah swirled out cloaks with which to enfold them. The chamber throbbed with excited babble as news of the Kiriathans' victory spread. . . .

Until a familiar high-pitched voice cut through it all, producing an instant shocked silence.

Katahn's priest, Master Peig, stood in the aisle, shaven dome gleaming, dark eyes glaring, Regar at his elbow in silent support.

"You must kill them both, Lord Katahn!" the man said again, his voice hard and condemning. It echoed away to silence, every eye in the packed chamber suddenly fixed upon the two men.

Katahn laughed. "Do you have any idea how much money these men will make me in a single season?"

"Greed brought down the Dorsaddi, Katahn." Peig paused, narrowed his eyes. "I told you not to make a warrior of him. I told you this would happen. But you paid no heed, and so your task is harder. I tell you these two carry the mark of destruction. If you do not destroy them, Katahn ul Manus, you will lose everything. *Everything.*"

The silence could not have been more absolute. Even Katahn seemed momentarily taken aback by the intensity of the holy man's warning. For a long, horrible moment Abramm feared all his grasping after survival, all he had sacrificed and endured, would come to nothing after all.

Then Katahn smiled. "How many of your prophecies have come true in the last year, Master Peig? Half of them? That's probably too generous. A quarter, then? And if we consider the last handful of years, how many times, then?"

The priest jerked up his chin. "They have all come true, sir; it is only the interpretation—"

"A prophecy is useless if not properly interpreted before its execution, sir. And considering your record, why should I believe that this time you've done it correctly?"

Master Peig ignited in a flaming rage, loosing a volley of words Abramm had no hope of following. When Katahn clearly still resisted, his son Regar jumped in, but he, too, argued in vain. Finally Peig surrendered with a bitter epithet and strode away. A moment longer the son regarded the father, tight-lipped, clearly distraught. Then he too took his leave.

Katahn watched them go, smirking openly. He made some irreverent comments to his men, then gave orders concerning his slaves' treatment and rewards and departed.

Shettai lingered, her gaze once more on Abramm. Their eyes met for a long, fierce moment, as if she searched for something of vital importance, and he thought again of the slain Dorsaddi's earlier prophecy to Beltha'adi. *"Even now the Deliverer is coming to slay you."*

She turned away finally, and it seemed to him there was something very like a secret smile upon her lips.

# THE WHITE PRETENDER

PART THREE

CHAPTER

# 20

Scratching the staffid bites on the back of her hand, Carissa stepped from the tunnel onto the iron bridge spanning the inlet between New Xorofin and Old. It shivered under the weight and movement of the people thronging about her, the spaces between its iron gridwork allowing a dizzying view of the depth over which she trod. From this height, the dilapidated houseboats lining the inlet's steep shores were reduced to small ragged boxes, and the fisherfolk who lived on them, mere dots in the distance.

With an uneasy gulp, she lifted her gaze skyward, having to tug and push at her face-veil to align the eyeholes enough to see. Through the bridge's ranks of iron girders, Old Xorofin's dark, lichen-encrusted guardwalls loomed forbiddingly atop the opposing cliff, its ramparts bristling with guards barely glimpsed past the crenellations. Nervous guards. Suspicious guards. Guards ready to quash the slightest twitch of rebellion, should it come.

More of them stood at the bridge's end ahead of her, checking travel documents and baggage, their gray tunics stark against the dark maw of Old Xorofin's entrance tunnel. The anxiety that had smoldered in her belly all afternoon twisted restlessly, and she drew a deep breath to settle it. There was no going back now.

Bodies pressed her from all sides—Cooper in his Thilosian finery to her left, her Esurhite serving girl, Peri, smashed up against her right, Philip's dog pressed against the back of one of her legs, and the youth himself constantly stepping on the heel of the other. Their Esurhite retainer, Eber, followed at

Cooper's flank, and all around them, close and hot and stinking of old sweat and stale onions, were strangers.

Robed and hooded, hatted and turbaned, laden with the bags and bundles and slingsacks that marked them visitors, they laughed and jabbered, pontificated and proclaimed, excitement billowing around them. Apprehension fueled the milieu as much as anticipation, for the great spectacle slated to unfold in Old Xorofin's famous amphitheater tomorrow afternoon would surely change all their lives. If the rumored uprising did occur, some might be dead or maimed or imprisoned. And Carissa . . .

Carissa would be changed as well, though perhaps sooner than tomorrow. The anxiety twisted again, harder, almost taking her breath away. After two years of mishap, delay, and frustration she was about to get her first glimpse of the most famous champion in present day Esurh, the man they called the White Pretender. The man she hoped was her brother Abramm.

She still hardly dared believe it would happen in light of all the mind-numbingly bad luck she'd endured. But surely nothing could go wrong now. They'd arrived in plenty of time. There would be no more sinking boats, no pirate attacks, no unexpected, superstitious detours. With only two small bags, they offered little reason to be stopped, and Old Xorofin's great *Val'Orda* opened its public seating on a first-come, first-served basis, so tickets could not be sold out in advance. Finally, the route from the warriors' compound to the amphitheater was well-known and access to it was unrestricted. If all else failed, she could see him there.

Truly, she had no reason to fear another frustrating failure now.

Unless . . .

She glanced aside at Cooper, who was scowling at something up ahead. The brilliant oranges and greens of his Thilosian merchant disguise set off his swarthy skin, and the gray, spiked goatee and mustache of current Thilosian fashion gave him a sophisticated aura, enhanced by the gold gleaming at his neck and ear. It was undeniably true, as Philip had pointed out to her on the foredeck last night, that Cooper had taken to his part well. True, also, that he was in complete control of this expedition, despite his apparent deference to Carissa. For the first nine months he'd been the only one who'd known the language, and with women forbidden to speak to any man not their husband or blood relative, he alone made the contacts, cut the deals, and saw to the travel arrangements. It wouldn't have taken much to—

*No!* She faced forward again. That was a horrid accusation, and she would not indulge it. Cooper was an honorable man; he'd die for his honor. He'd die for her. She was a wretch to think for even a moment that he might betray her.

Philip was just tired and frustrated—as were they all—and searching for a way to explain their failures that did not discredit his god. Moreover, he'd clashed with Cooper from day one, so it wasn't surprising he blamed the older man.

Beside her that older man now grunted with displeasure. "They're changing shifts, as I feared. The new fellows'll likely be itching for a search."

"Well, we have nothing for them to search."

"So long as you keep your head down and your mouth closed, *masim*." Masim—beloved. Their travel papers called her wife, a designation neither of them welcomed but which was clearly safest for her. A daughter was more likely to be seized for an officer's pleasure than a wife. But a wife had less freedom.

His dark eyes flicked to Peri, who was clutching Carissa's arm, and his mouth tightened. The girl had been with her a year, hired to bolster the credibility of their disguise. Cooper had not wanted her to bring Peri today. *"If they seize her,"* he'd warned, *"I'll not resist them."* She'd accepted that because she knew if she'd relented and commanded Peri to stay, he'd have been at her to remain on the boat, too, while he went alone to seek out the truth. She'd agreed to a similar arrangement in Vorta months ago. She wasn't doing it again.

The line moved erratically, and sure enough, the four new guards soon found someone to harass, while everyone else had to watch and wait. Like their counterparts in other areas of Esurhite bureaucracy, they delighted in these small flauntings of power, twitting all the world while they carried out their petty little procedures.

Carissa dropped back onto her aching heels, scratching the staffid bites again and thinking how much she hated this place, how tired she was of being ordered around, of being at everyone's mercy, of being afraid all the time. Afraid of being discovered, afraid her friends would suffer for her decisions, and most of all, afraid it would be for nothing.

She hugged her arms and refused to go down that road again. She was here. She would see it through.

Ahead, the guards had gone through all the bags and sacks and, having pulled off some hapless woman's veil, now conferred among themselves. After a moment, one of them led her into the tunnel, and not even the men she was with protested.

The line started moving again, and before long Carissa and her companions were shuffling up to face the soldiers. The guards' uniforms were fancier than she was used to seeing—trimmed with gold braid and piping—and huge purple flags emblazoned with black moons flanked the tunnel opening, proclaiming Old Xorofin's status as the administrative heart of Beltha'adi's empire, but beyond that, there was nothing to distinguish it from any other Esurhite city she'd encountered in this wretched land. Dark, dirty, and stinking, right down to the familiar stench of rotting flesh now wafting out of the tunnel. Esurhite jurisprudence demanded public display of its sentences; thus at every city's main gates there stood a grisly promenade of impaled miscreants, some still alive and moaning, others long dead, but all reminding visitor and native alike of the severity of Esurhite judgment.

A wave of aversion flooded her. For a moment she thought she absolutely could not walk through another one of those gauntlets of death. She was certain if she tried she'd go insane with the horror of it. She drew a deep, shaky breath and horror transmuted into anger. What was the matter with these people that they couldn't bury their dead? That they had to decorate their cities with rotting corpses? They were all mad. Mad!

Cooper handed their travel papers to the sour-faced officer and submitted to the pat down initiated by the officer's subordinate. Philip and Eber were also searched for hidden weapons, but the women were left alone. Their two small bags were pawed through and cast aside, and just when Carissa was sure they'd passed muster, the officer in charge asked about Newbold. Something about trailing hounds and Beltha'adi.

Cooper replied calmly, in flawless Tahg, having absorbed the language as thoroughly as he'd absorbed his trader's role. The animal was an old friend, past breeding age, he said. If the Great One wished to have him, he would gladly give him up, although he had much finer, more vigorous animals at home in his kennel that the Supreme Commander might find more to his liking.

The guard scowled at the dog, and the dog ignored him, his droopy brown eyes as dull looking as ever. With his aged white face, Newbold certainly did not appear a creature befitting a Supreme Commander. But with these men, one never knew. Most of them were so desperate for advancement they'd seize upon anything with the least bit of promise.

Beside her, Philip stood stiffly, as tall as Carissa herself now, though he hadn't yet lost the leggy look of adolescence. He'd proved himself a promising swordsman of late, hardly unexpected for the son of Master Larrick, and if he'd had a sword, Carissa did not doubt he'd be on the verge of unsheathing it. Cooper had warned him this might happen, made him agree not to protest if they took the dog. But now, in the face of it, she was not sure he would comply.

Fortunately it did not come to that. With a grunt, the officer thrust the yellowed papers into Cooper's hands and motioned them into the stinking tunnel as he turned to his next victims.

By the time they reached the inn Cooper had been instructed to seek, Carissa's mood had darkened from anxious, impatient discontent to a full-blown foulness that had her snapping and spitting at everyone. When Peri tried to help her remove the veil and headcloth, she slapped the girl away and yanked them off herself, angrily tossing them in a heap on the ancient, filthy carpet, despite the likelihood a staffid—or a rat—would find its way into their folds. And when the girl brought her the food they had sent up—fish stew heavily laced with onions—she shoved the bowl away with such force it hit Peri's arm and tipped over, spewing its noxious contents across the table. That set off an eruption of vitriol that ended with the girl cringing and weeping in the corner.

Which only triggered another flare of annoyance and a stern order to be silent. Peri complied as best she could, and in the ensuing quiet Carissa's anger turned to a self-loathing so bitter she nearly wept herself.

"Forgive me," she said finally. "You deserved none of that. I don't know what's wrong with me."

*It's this city,* she thought. *Dark and cramped and stinking. Swags of onions everywhere you look, sewage in the streets, the guards and the mist and the people always afraid and suspicious. And those horrid statues of Khrell!* Squat, ugly-faced little men with fires burning in their bellies, they sat on every corner. She hated them with a passion that was truly irrational. As if they symbolized all she detested about this land.

Peri ventured from the corner and timidly cleaned up the mess, then took the bowl away, returning with a fresh portion of stew, a piece of dark bread, and a cup of the vile Esurhite *kassik*. With most of the water unfit to drink, the bitter, mildly alcoholic poor-man's brew was their only alternative. Carissa loathed it. But she drank it.

Cooper strode in a few minutes later, his face tight and angry.

"What now?" she asked as he dropped onto the grimy, musty pillows across from her.

"The boy. He's gone off to find his brother. Probably be picked up before the night's half over." He pulled the *corba* of stiff green felt from his head and threw it on the table before him. "But if that's what he wants, so be it. It's no concern of ours now."

Peri set his food before him, and he picked up the bread, pulled off a hunk, and dipped it into the stew. Only when the bowl was half empty did he speak again. "Seers say the rains'll come early this year. Maybe as soon as three weeks."

Kinlock had been wrong about there never being any wind here. For two or three weeks in late spring, land and sea alike were lashed by a furious, near-continuous succession of storms. Violent winds and pounding rain blew off roofs, knocked over trees, and turned dry wadis into angry, churning rivers that flooded the lowlands and stopped all travel for the duration.

She tore off a piece of bread but couldn't bring herself to dip it in the oily stew. "We'll be gone by then."

"Will we?" He regarded her from beneath gray-sprinkled brows, his face eerily underlit by the oil lamp on the table.

She ate her bread and said nothing.

"They say some kind of sickness broke out in the Sorite sector a couple days ago."

"Probably onion poisoning."

He cocked a brow.

She gestured at the swags on the walls. "They live with them, breathe them, eat them. It can't be good."

"They're saying it's plague."

"Hmm." She ate another piece of bread, grimaced as she chased it down with kassik. "So what have you learned about *him*? Will he be on display tonight?"

"The innkeeper's sent someone to find out." He fell silent, concentrating on his eating, and she felt his disapproval, radiating from him alongside the heat from the lamp between them.

Finally his bowl and plate were empty. When Peri came to take them away, Carissa sent her mostly full bowl, as well. As the door closed behind her, Cooper spoke. "We shouldn't be here, milady. Whether he wins or loses tomorrow, there's sure to be an uprising. They'll close the gates if that happens. Start in with the searches."

"Then we'll just have to see him tonight, before it all starts."

He blew out a breath of frustration. "Lass, the White Pretender is not your brother. He—"

"We don't know that. If—"

"We do!" he roared, coming up off the pillows to glare over the table at her. She stared at him, shocked.

After a moment he sagged back. "You do," he added softly.

Suddenly she was shaking, her stomach pulled into a hard knot. Suddenly she saw the fear that had fueled her tantrum earlier—the cold, keening terror that Cooper was right.

Game authorities claimed the White Pretender was a real Kiriathan prince, but Game authorities were renowned for bending the truth if it served a monetary—or political—purpose. Many believed they were doing so now. Why else was the Pretender always costumed, wigged, and painted whenever he was in public? Why else was he always whisked away so swiftly to a private cell after the contests? Rumor said the man was blond and blue-eyed, but no one Cooper had spoken with had ever seen him uncostumed.

"The Pretender's a born warrior, lass," Cooper said gently. "How can he be Abramm? You of all people know what your brother was, why he took those vows. He was a gentle boy—sensitive and smart—but he was not strong."

"Yes he was. He was! Remember the time we tried to run away to sea? And everything went wrong and I broke my arm and he rowed me all the way back from Bertran's Isle in that storm? He saved my life that night."

"And nearly lost his own."

She looked down at her bite-marred hands, twisting one of her gold rings round and round. It was true. Abramm had been sick for weeks after that adventure.

Her retainer sighed again. "Just for the sake of argument, let's suppose you are right. Let's suppose it *is* him. Did you think to walk up to Lord Katahn and simply buy him free? It won't happen. Whoever this Pretender is, he's beyond the status of a simple gladiator. The way he challenges the Supreme Commander, mocking his claims of divine destiny? And with the Dorsaddi calling him Deliverer?" He snorted. "I'm not big on politics, but even I can see the man has to die. And there's not a blessed thing we can do to stop it."

A mist had sprung up around him, and her throat ached fiercely. "I won't believe that," she whispered. "There's got to be something."

"Now you're sounding like Philip, with his talk of Eidon making us a way," Cooper said. There was, for once, no mockery in his voice. Only profound sadness. He shook his head. "Think, lass. Do you really believe little Abramm could have become this man who is renowned for his skill at killing people?"

She could not speak, could hardly breathe. The mist grew thicker.

He reached across the table to touch her hand. "It isn't him, Carissa. You have to face it—Abramm died on the galley ship. And this White Pretender is exactly what his name implies—a pretender."

The ache in her throat sharpened to knifelike pain, and tears streamed down her cheeks. She swallowed but could not find her voice. Finally she looked back to her hands now in her lap, rings glinting softly in the shadow.

A knock at the door saved her from having to speak. It was a man from the inn. Cooper went out to talk to him and returned shortly, settling onto the pillows without speaking.

"It was about the Pretender, wasn't it?" she prodded.

He picked up his cup of kassik, sipped from it, and finally nodded. "He'll be fighting tonight, as we guessed. A last-chance, all-comers challenge."

He sipped again. The lamp flickered between them, and from the great room below came the sound of muffled laughter and off-key singing.

"I want to go," Carissa whispered.

Cooper shook his head. "The innsman said there'll be no seating—not even standing room—by now."

"We can catch him along the way, then. When he goes back to the warriors' compound."

"He won't be going back. They're keeping him and the Infidel in the Val'Orda itself. To forestall possible rescue attempts."

He fell silent, watching her. She studied her hands a moment more, then lifted her head. "I want to see him, Coop."

"Lass—"

"I have to."

He set the cup down, pain furrowing his brow. "But what difference will it make when after tomorrow he'll be dead, regardless?"

She swallowed down the lump in her throat, but her voice trembled nonetheless. "Because if it is him, I want to see him—at least see him once more before—" Her throat closed, and she looked into her lap again, blinking back tears.

After a moment Cooper sighed. "Very well."

The great Val'Orda stood at the midst of Old Xorofin, linked by a long plaza to an Ophiran temple now devoted to the worship of Khrell. Unlike the city, which was disappointingly small and dirty, the amphitheater lived up to its reputation of greatness. Five concentric rings of torchlight marked its quintuple stories, illuminating the series of bas-relief arches that encircled each level. Some framed niched statues; others looked more like openings to interior chambers. Flags hung limply among the torches at the top, interspersed with huge, dark bird-forms perched on slender pillars. At first sight it stole the breath and numbed the mind, so big it was, looming over them like a glowing, gargantuan crown.

Largest and finest of all the southland amphitheaters, the Val'Orda was one of the few remaining wonders of Ophir's architectural prowess. It was here that the Games' final championships were always played out, here that the strongest warriors triumphed, here that all the greatest contests in the history of the Games had been fought. Tomorrow, it would be here that the insolent White Pretender and his Infidel received their long-due comeuppance at the hands of Beltha'adi's personal guard, the vaunted Broho.

The people were out in force, swirling around it, jostling among the myriad merchants' booths that encircled it and clogged the great plaza before it. The aroma of barbecued goat, fried spima, and sweet, sweet foaming fig filled the air. Musicians, dancers, and jugglers vied with the peddlers banging their pots for the crowd's attention. From time to time a lion's roar echoed over the merrymaking.

It soon became apparent that the innsman had been right about their not being able to see any of the matches. People stood in thick, pressing masses before all the main gates. Only the gate leading down into the warrens beneath the arena floor offered egress, and though Cooper fought her all the way, in the end that's where they went.

If Carissa thought the streets of Xorofin stank, it was nothing compared to the compound of manure, blood, oil, sweat, and death that awaited in the warrens' low stone corridors. Various rooms bathed in the warm light of orange fish-bladder lanterns held ranks of iron cells for men and beasts alike. Here and there, long ramps led up to gates opening into the arena itself, each incline clogged with hopeful spectators. No one seemed to know for sure which one the Pretender would exit from, however, until they found Philip and Newbold.

The pair stood near the north ramp's base, and spying them, Philip waved them over.

"I think they'll come out here, milady," he said, gesturing at the heavy wooden gates atop the ramp. Those nearest were peering between the cracks where the doors met and offering commentary to those behind.

"There are at least six gates, Phil," Carissa said. "How can you be sure?"

"Because this is the way they went in."

"And how do you know that?"

He smiled at Newbold. The dog looked more alert and interested than she'd ever seen him, though that was hardly surprising given the situation. The lions alone had to be of interest to him.

"You're saying he tracked your brother through all this?"

"I told you his nose is good. And the track was fresher when we first got here."

"Perhaps we should go to the last gate," Cooper said from behind her. "That way we'll have two of them covered. Just in case."

She glanced back at him, wondering at the annoyance his suggestion roused in her. It was eminently practical, but she didn't like it all the same. Newbold had already proved himself once, and even if this tracking task was admittedly difficult to the point of straining believability, still it was something more than random chance.

"We'll stay here," she said.

Behind her, Cooper sighed his disapproval.

It was a good decision from one standpoint—if they'd gone, they wouldn't have reached the other gate in time anyway. For they had no sooner settled in to wait than a great shout arose from the arena. It went on and on, so she knew the match must have ended.

Excitement dried her mouth and dampened her hands.

At the door, people hissed and cheered and groaned. She ached to see what was happening, suddenly consumed with fear that if it was Abramm, he would be killed right at the last moment. . . .

She could hear the Taleteller intoning something beyond the warrens' din but could not discern the words. Her anxiety was at fever pitch when the doors ahead trundled open, pulleys and rollers squeaking. The crowd's roar beat at her ears and throbbed in her chest. The group of dark-tunicked handlers who had stood foremost among the gathering atop the ramp hurried into the arena, returning shortly with two men, one in white, the other in green.

Carissa's heart froze. The one in white was about Abramm's height—but he was backlit from the lights of the arena, his face in shadow, and all she could make out was the white paint and the thin, laughing lips of a court fool. He was big, too—broad across the chest and shoulders, his build more akin to Gillard's than Abramm's. Blood stained his white ruffled doublet.

Beside her, Philip clasped her arm, excitement raising the pitch of his voice. "That's him!" he cried. "It's Trap for sure!"

But she had eyes only for the Pretender, straining to see past the paint and the shadow and the long curly wig, straining for a glimpse of the eyes. Someone swirled a dark cloak around his shoulders, pulled up the cowl, and the face was lost altogether. Others had done the same to the Infidel, but she hardly spared him a glance.

The handlers pushed forward now, surrounding their prize warriors with weapons bared. The crowd parted, screaming the Pretender's name. Carissa held her breath. He approached. Only a single line of onlookers stood between them as he came even with her, startling her with his sheer physical size. She wanted to shove forward and rip away the cowl. Instead her eyes fastened on the only part of him she could see—his right hand. The strong, long-fingered hand was light-skinned, as a Kiriathan's would be, but callused and scarred and stained now with fresh blood.

Then he was by her, and she saw only wide, dark-cloaked shoulders and the crowd closing behind him and his guards. Moments later, as he reached the bottom of the ramp and turned into the corridor, he disappeared from her sight.

She stood there, buffeted by those who surged around her, choking on disappointment. He had been close enough to touch, yet she still did not know if he was Abramm.

*But wouldn't I be sure if it was him? Even at only a glance, wouldn't I know him? The way he moves, the set of his shoulders . . .*

Disappointment turned to gall. She swallowed painfully and forced herself to breathe again. That man did not move like Abramm, was too big to be Abramm, and the hand . . . It was no scribe's hand, certainly.

Her gaze caught upon a figure in garish Thilosian costume—yellow and blue and red—standing at the foot of the ramp. He was facing her but staring intently in the direction taken by the Pretender, and the dark aristocratic features were startling familiar. It was Danarin, Captain Kinlock's former first mate.

She had only a glimpse of him, hardly long enough to register the face, before he disappeared into the crowd, and though she hurried down to the main corridor after him, she didn't see him again.

Questions tumbled through her head. They had left Danarin back in Vorta almost eighteen months ago. What was he doing here? Did he, too, suspect the Pretender of being Abramm?

Hope stirred.

Reason tempered it. If it really was Danarin—she was no longer certain—he must be Ray's man, assigned to kill Abramm *and* Trap Meridon.

She thought again of the man who had passed by her, tried to dissect the image of that painted face, tried to find in it something familiar. But all she saw were a jester's laughing lips. And the hand.

Abramm had long fingers. And if he had been trained to fight—

The reality finally dawned on her. Not just fight. Kill.

She turned back to the gate where the arena crew now brought in the vanquished—Esurhite soldiers and professional gladiators who gasped and moaned and cried, or made no noise at all, victims of the Pretender's blade.

*"He is a killer. A born warrior,"* Cooper had said. *"Do you really believe little Abramm could have become this man?"*

The mist was back, blotting out the crowd, encircling the bloodied, moaning soldiers. Pressure closed her throat.

*"Abramm died on the galley ship."*

She had not dreamed in almost two years. Not since Qarkeshan. And that last dream . . . that fiery dragon, that flare of awful pain, the screaming, and then . . . death?

A hand clasped her shoulder. She turned, looked up into Cooper's sad, dark eyes, and let the tears come.

CHAPTER

# 21

Abramm slid his ivory archer three spaces on the diagonal and forced Katahn's shield bearer into the game board's central pit, exposing the Esurhite's king to attack. Then he looked up. "I believe you are besieged, sir." He spoke in fluent Tahg now, thanks to eighteen months of Shettai's private tutelage.

Katahn scowled at the board. "Khrell's Fire! How did you do that?" Abramm had captured or cut off every one of his pieces, leaving Katahn's king with nowhere to go. It was a gambit he'd only recently thought up—daring and risky but, if one's opponent wasn't anticipating it, devastatingly effective. He'd won in six moves.

Katahn continued to study the board in disbelief as Abramm leaned back on his pillows, glancing around for the first time since the game had begun. The spacious top-story, four-chamber suite was one of only six in the entire amphitheater. Darkened, bead-curtained doorways stood to right and left, beside clusters of intricately beaded skulls. At his back, the cool night air wafted in from an open window overlooking the city. Directly across from him, ceiling-high potted palms framed a colorful mosaic of the goddess Laevion breathing life back into the stitched-together pieces of Khrell's dismembered body.

When Abramm had returned to his quarters following his impromptu evening matches, his Sorite slave had stripped off his ruined costume, washed away the blood, sweat, and paint, and dressed him in fine black woolen trousers with a silk undershirt and stiff, knee-length tunic of violet brocade. He was then brought up to Katahn's quarters, where food and wine and nubile, half-clad young women awaited his pleasure.

Left alone with them, he had nibbled the spiced meat and oranges they offered, chewed soft bread, and sipped fine wine. He had listened to them sing and watched them dance to the music of pipe, drum, and kit'el, their curves sliding provocatively in and out of their veils, their dark eyes watching him with seductive intensity.

Though the intent of it all seemed clear enough, it still left him baffled. Brogai custom forbade the indulgence of one's lusts on the eve of battle, and tomorrow he faced the biggest battle of his life. He could not afford to be sick or muzzy headed.

Few men untouched by the fire of Khrell had ever stood against a Broho and lived. But there were those few—men who had resisted Broho magics, who could not be Commanded, who had shaken off the Veil of Fear. He intended to be one of them. Intended, if he had to die, at least to go out with honor, fighting to his last breath. . . . Tonight, of all nights, then, he must abstain.

And Katahn offers him his daughters?

The Brogai Gamer had arrived an hour ago with the uurka board and, seeing the mostly untouched food, had reproved him mildly for his abstinence. Then they'd plunged into the game and the matter was forgotten.

The girls had removed the spiced meat and bread. Now all that remained was a basket of fruit, a plate of golden, crescent pastries, and a bowl of green, honeyed cumlaats. They had put away pipe and drum, and only the kit'el player remained, plucking a mournful melody on the taut strings of her gourd-shaped instrument. Her sisters lounged on bright blue and green pillows below the dais on which the men sat, their young faces scandalously bared, their bodies clearly visible through the diaphanous material of their gowns. They watched Abramm with a vulturine intensity.

As he looked at them now, they giggled and whispered and elbowed one another, their dark eyes flashing with excitement. He felt his face flush again, which only set them off the more.

Shettai, who'd come in with Katahn, sat a little way off from them, her high-boned features sharp and dramatic in contrast to the others' soft, girlish faces. Her glorious hair fell unbound in a river of shimmering dark mahogany down her back. Pearl teardrops gleamed in her ears and on her forehead, and her gown of blue, silver-flecked silk set off the deep honey-gold of her skin to stunning advantage. Had he been in any other frame of mind, he'd be torturing himself with pangs of desire, and even now he wondered idly what Katahn would do if he chose her over the Gamer's own daughters. He was fairly certain that *she* would not be pleased.

She alone did not giggle or smile in invitation, though she watched him closely. It was impossible to tell what she was thinking, which, he had learned in their close association over the last year and a half, meant she was probably annoyed. He knew for a fact that she had little love for Katahn's gaggle of silly girls and even less for being put on display alongside them, for being put on display at all.

"That was very well done," Katahn said, breaking into his thoughts. The Gamer leaned back from the board, turning a grin of open admiration on Abramm. "I am beginning to think I have created a player I am no longer able to beat."

"After tomorrow it shouldn't be a problem," Abramm said dryly.

Katahn's dark brows arched in surprise. "That sounds undeniably defeatist, my golden prince. Most unlike you."

"Unlike you as well, my master." Abramm flicked his gaze significantly around the room, indicating the girls, the pastries, the wine. "I can only conclude this offer of celebration before the fact of victory means that for me you believe there will be no victory."

Katahn held his gaze, the ironic smile still in place, though the dark eyes had gone flat and hard. They seemed slightly less alert than normal, and Abramm remembered the wine he'd smelled on the man's breath when he'd first arrived with the uurka board, remembered that he'd continued to drink throughout the game—which was probably why he'd fallen so thoroughly for that new gambit. But it was also starkly out of character.

The Brogai looked away, the smile twisting at his lips, flaring just slightly and vanishing. He picked up his goblet and, leaning back on his pillows, beckoned for one of the girls to refill it. As she rose to obey, another glided to Abramm's side, plucking a cluster of grapes from the basket as she passed it. She pulled one free and held it to his mouth, pressing herself intimately against his arm.

His pulse quickened, but he kept his eyes off her and accepted the fruit stoically.

She seemed to interpret that as acceptance of her as well and leaned more actively against him, toying now with the gold rings in his left ear. The ear was still tender from the insertion of his third ring last week, an unprecedented honor he suspected sprang more from political and monetary considerations than any deservedness on his part. Though he and Trap had beaten fairly the greatest non-Broho champions in the land, three rings were not normally attained in less than five years. Katahn's son Regar, having but two rings of his own, had reacted to the promotion so hotly he'd joined the priesthood in protest the very next day—an irony only Abramm fully appreciated.

Katahn took a long swallow of wine, then wiped his mouth on the shimmering, gold-embroidered sleeve of his tunic. He gestured with the goblet. "Drink, my prince. You must be thirsty after your exertions of the evening."

"Wine steals the spirit and muddies the mind," Abramm said flatly, quoting the Brogai proverb to the Brogai himself. "I have a battle tomorrow."

The girl was kissing the corner of his jaw just under his ear, her breath a light, fluttery tickle on his neck that inexplicably stimulated even as it annoyed.

Katahn snorted. "A battle which you've already admitted you're going to lose." He took his own advice and drank again, then sat staring distractedly into the vessel, his face seeming more wrinkled and weary than usual. It finally occurred to Abramm that Katahn was no happier over the prospect of tomorrow's match than Abramm. And well he shouldn't be. When it ended he would have lost the two biggest money-makers he'd ever owned—with little chance of replacing them.

Katahn's daughter was becoming decidedly distracting. She had undone the buttons and loops on his tunic's high collar and was now kissing his throat, the flowery scent of her hair oil making his head spin. Katahn said something, but at the moment he could hardly breathe, much less think and speak.

Shettai was staring at him, as were the other girls, as was Katahn himself. Abramm's face burned, and he knew it must be bright red. He shifted away from her, but the girl only pressed at him more insistently. Some of her sisters smirked, while Shettai's lips tightened with disapproval. He knew what she was thinking. *"Men are goats,"* she liked to say. *"Only interested in one thing."*

He'd always taken pride in proving her wrong in that, but at the moment, his treacherous body was hotly ignoring the dictates of pride.

Katahn alone seemed oblivious. He spoke again, irony heavy in his voice.

Grimly Abramm tried to wrench his mind to order. "I . . . I . . ."

Katahn frowned at the girl as if he had just noticed her. He waved a beringed hand. "Sabine, that will do."

She drew herself off Abramm and turned to pout at her father.

"Later you may have him if he chooses. For now, return to your place. Your behavior is unseemly."

She heaved a dramatic sigh and flounced back to her sisters.

Katahn smiled at Abramm. "She likes you. They all do. It's that blond hair and blue eyes. More than that, it would bring a woman great status to lie with the White Pretender. Even greater should she conceive his child."

Abramm's flush spread down his neck and over his chest. He knew only enough of Esurhite sexual mores to be appalled by them. Though great indignation would arise should a woman venture into public uncovered—and any female caught in adultery would be summarily executed—within his own home a man could loan his wives, mistresses, slaves, or daughters to whomever he wished. Still, Abramm thought loaning them to a slave must be highly irregular.

"Did you know Beltha'adi is my cousin?" Katahn said, apparently returning to what he'd been saying when Sabine had been at her most distracting. "He is my father's father's father's father's . . . brother."

He set down the goblet and took up one of the crescent-shaped pastries. "That makes us cousins. And, since he's never in all his two-hundred-sixty-some-odd years managed to produce a son who lived, it also makes me his heir." He chuckled again, then bit off half the pastry.

Abramm regarded him sharply. Katahn might be just this side of drunk, but Abramm did not believe it prevented the man from choosing his words with care.

Katahn waved the remaining pastry half. "But then, he doesn't need one, I guess, with Khrell keeping him forever young. The priests say even if he's slain, he'll live again. That Laevion will breathe life into him just as she did Khrell after Ret hacked him up."

Ret, consumed with jealousy, had laid a trap for his brother Khrell, and afterward called the winds to blow the pieces of ruined body to the far corners of the world, never to return. The birds told Laevion of it, and she sent them after the remains, which she then sewed back together with her own hands. It was a gruesome story, typically Esurhite.

"I understand you northerners have your own resurrection mythology," Katahn said. "Wasn't your Eidon killed and then resurrected?"

" 'Twas not Eidon," Abramm said. "Eidon cannot die. It was his son Tersius. And he wasn't resurrected—he gave his blood and body to form the Holy Flames that stand against the Veil and burn at the heart of Mataian temples."

"Mmm. Your Terstan friend tells a different version."

"The Terstan serves a different god."

"He claims it is the same. That he uses the same books."

"Some of the same books," Abramm pointed out.

"I have copies of all your sacred texts, if you'd like to show me where you differ."

"I wouldn't."

"Mmm." Katahn fell silent, watching his hand finger the goblet, his face once more closed and unreadable. The girls murmured and shifted upon their pillows, their bright, birdlike gazes peppering Abramm with almost physical force. He refused to look at them, blushing all over again and wishing Katahn would get this over with.

"I've heard some believe Beltha'adi is Khrell himself in human form," Abramm said finally. "That he cannot be slain at all." He smiled slightly. "I think it's a claim that certainly ought to be tested."

Katahn looked up sharply, his gaze reproving. "You are a fool, Pretender. You cannot beat him. This Dorsaddi madness of your slaying him—it will not happen."

"I've beaten Zamath."

"Zamath is an excommunicate, a has-been, destroyed by his own madness. You may just as well say you've beaten a gnat. He is nothing of what Beltha'adi is. And you certainly didn't *kill* Zamath, which is what we're talking about. In any case you won't be facing Beltha'adi tomorrow, so the question is moot."

"I may win tomorrow and so have another chance."

"You won't."

Abramm glanced around. "Some few have resisted Broho magics."

"A few perhaps, but it doesn't matter, because either way, you *will* die tomorrow. The people may hope you'll prevail, and the Underground may talk of rescue, but it won't happen. In fact, it won't even be a contest—it'll be an execution. This Dorsaddi Deliverer nonsense must be stopped."

"If Beltha'adi thinks my death will stop that—"

"He's got a full complement of city guardsmen ready to shut down the city and squash any rioting that erupts tomorrow. And two full Hundreds are returning from the Andolen front as we speak. They'll drive into the SaHal and clear out all the rebel nests that have sprung up in the last decade. My cousin is a ruthless man, Pretender. He'll do what he must to hold his power. And it all begins with your death.

"A death that will be neither swift nor clean. You must not merely be defeated in battle, you understand. . . . You must be humiliated, crushed . . . thoroughly broken." He paused to let his words sink in. "The last thing they'll hear from you will be your screams for mercy."

He paused again, selecting another pastry and examining it closely before dipping it into the bowl. "There is, however, another way. One much preferable for all, I think." He bit the crescent in half. His dark eyes flicked up to meet Abramm's. "You could change sides."

"Change sides?"

"I have persuaded my cousin that it would be more gainful to offer you beneficence than execution." He stuffed the rest of the pastry into his mouth, then licked the sticky green syrup from his fingers. "If you swear allegiance to him and to Khrell, that would solve everything. And if you participated in the raid on the SaHal, why, clearly you could not be the Deliverer. Indeed, I believe just giving your allegiance would be enough to take the wind out of the whole bloody movement."

He smiled. "Which would be in all ways the best solution. My cousin has already decreed that you may seek Brogai status at the temple and that he will afterward grant you the privilege of joining the Army of the Black Moon. You would be the first of your northerner race to wear the Shadow's colors. An unprecedented honor."

Abramm sat very still, stunned to speechlessness.

Katahn leaned forward eagerly. "I do not offer you your life alone, my prince. I offer you everything you might desire. I suspect he'd even give you Kiriath once he's taken it from your brother."

"And the price is merely my own treachery, is that it?"

"Treachery?" Katahn frowned. "To Kiriath? Ast! You belong with them no more than a hawk among finches. Why give your life for a realm of cowards? *They* betrayed you. You owe them nothing." He leaned back, fingers steepled beneath his beaklike nose, eyes never leaving Abramm's. "It is our destiny to rule the world, Pretender. I offer you the chance to ride with us, to share in our glory."

The girls had gone silent, listening intently for his response. He could feel Shettai's eyes burning upon him. And he could not deny the offer tempted him.

"I know you for a stubborn man, Abramm Kalladorne. It has saved your life more than once. But there comes a time when stubbornness ceases to serve one's best interest."

Still Abramm said nothing.

Katahn dropped his hands and leaned forward. "You have until tomorrow to decide." He gestured at the waiting girls. "Perhaps the joys they can provide will convince you where words and other pleasures cannot. Choose one to be your companion this night. Or more than one, if you wish."

They eyed him coquettishly, fluttering their lashes, letting some of their curves slip out from the veils. Abramm frowned and averted his eyes. "I prefer solitude."

"If you do not choose, I will do so for you. Sabine seems especially eager to share your bed. . . . But perhaps she is too aggressive for one who once took religious vows. Lege is a quiet girl. Submissive. Gentle. She—"

"I'll take Shettai." The words were out of his mouth before he realized he was going to say them, and they shocked him as much as they clearly shocked her. He saw a flash of unadulterated astonishment on her face, followed closely by something very like pain before the mask dropped back into place.

Katahn also drew back in surprise. "I offer you my virgin daughters and you ask for a slave?"

"You said to choose the one I want. I want her."

The Brogai's eyes narrowed. Then a shrewd look came into his face, riding a half smile that made Abramm think he wasn't nearly so surprised as he'd pretended. Katahn glanced at the slave woman. "Yes," he said. "I do believe she *could* persuade in ways the others would not." He waved at Shettai to obey. "See that he is satisfied, woman, or pay the price."

Shettai unfolded herself expressionlessly and glided toward the beaded curtain on the left. After a moment, Abramm followed her.

CHAPTER

# 22

An alcove with two wooden doors—one of which Shettai had opened—lay beyond the beads. Abramm stepped through it, and she closed it behind him.

An elaborately carved wooden screen shielded the body of the room from the doorway. To his left, a potted palm stood in the corner beside three glass lanterns.

Shettai disappeared around the screen, and he followed reluctantly, not surprised by what awaited in the chamber beyond. To the left, a low table flanked by pillows held a bowl of fruit and a wine carafe and cups, gleaming in the light of a small oil lamp. In the corner beyond it, a charcoal brazier had been lit for warmth. To the right, a large feather-stuffed mattress lay on the floor, tented with translucent draperies hanging from a ceiling hook. Dressed in silken sheets and mounds of pillows, its purpose was obvious. He gulped down a sense of rising panic.

Shettai had gone to the arched balcony opening in the far wall and loosed the flanking swags of beaded curtain to block out the night. She turned and, watching him intently, reached up to the back of her neck. A moment later, her gown's silken overlayer fluttered to the floor, and he gulped again, for the clinging, translucent undergown hid almost nothing of her magnificent body.

Then she was standing right in front of him, unfastening the long line of loops and buttons that kept the front of his tunic together. He watched her breathlessly, mesmerized by her touch and the rising heat of his own desire.

This close he could smell her exotic, spicy scent and feel the warmth of her flesh. Those long, graceful fingers, working steadily downward, roused all manner of wild thoughts. Perhaps she might cherish more than mild affection for him after all. And even if she was simply obeying orders, she wasn't acting as if she detested him. . . . Maybe he would just let her continue.

For two years he had stuffed away this desire, believing it would never be satisfied. Now satisfaction lay within his grasp. And it would be his last night of pleasure—his only night of this particular pleasure, thanks to that stupid vow he'd taken, thanks to the wasted years he'd given to a useless, uncaring god.

The last of the loops pulled free, and she pushed the stiff tunic off his shoulders. As it fell to the floor she turned to the ties of his undershirt. Would it be so wrong to take what she offered, to know what he would never know if he didn't?

But then he remembered the look of pain that had chased the astonishment across her face when he'd chosen her. As the ties came loose, he caught her hands in his own—they were hot and trembling. Her eyes darted up to his.

"You don't have to do this," he murmured. "I'll tell Katahn what he needs to hear. I only chose you because . . ." He smiled. "Because you were the only one who wasn't leering at me."

The startled look faded. Her face became stone, her eyes deep, unreadable pools.

"I won't do anything. I promise."

There was no response. Not the slightest twitch or wrinkle. Except for her eyes, gleaming with moisture, she could have been made of marble.

Clearly she didn't believe him.

Releasing her, he stepped back. "And I *do* have a battle to fight tomorrow."

He turned away, already regretting what he'd done, and strode for the balcony, the beads rattling with his passage.

It was a relief to step into the misty night—somehow the room had grown unbearably hot. He rested his hands on the cold iron railing and gazed at Xorofin, its dark tumble of closely packed buildings huddled beneath the ceiling of ever-present mist. Fish-bladder lanterns hung on posts throughout the darkness, glowing green and lilac, amber and red, like so many evil eyes peering out from their hidey-holes.

He took some deep breaths, and as the internal fire dissipated, his head cleared.

A crowd milled in the plaza below, jostling between the amphitheater's stone perimeter fence and the merchants' booths and tables. Their voices carried up to him on the still air, a staccato mutter punctuated by sharp bursts of laughter and the wheedle of a piper's song. He smelled the hot grease they used to fry the spima worms, the fragrances of incense and baking bread, all overlaying the faint, ubiquitous stench of burning fish oil.

Until that crowd went home—or settled for the night—he had no hope of climbing down the amphitheater's face. There looked to be little hope of it, anyway. The smooth-dressed stone to either side of his balcony sported none of the architectural details that might provide hand or footholds. Nor would knotting the bed curtains together help—all of them together with his tunic would not begin to reach the pavement below.

He stood there a long time, the night chill seeping through his silk shirt. Katahn's offer tumbled tantalizingly through his mind, powered by the forces of fear and desire. He did not wish to die, least of all in the manner Katahn described. He wanted the respect and admiration of others, wanted power and justice. Wanted Shettai.

The image of her in that veil of watery silk made his pulse accelerate and his mouth go dry all over again.

Oh yes. He wanted her.

And he thought it very likely Katahn would give her to him permanently. If he asked.

And swore allegiance to Khrell.

A swell of agitation seized him, and he pushed himself back from the railing, paced back into the room. Shettai sat cross-legged at the low table, swallowed in the violet and gold of his tunic, which she'd draped over her shoulders and which was much too large for her.

He ignored her and strode for the door. But as his hand closed on the latch, he realized Katahn wouldn't let him leave, and asking would only replace Shettai with Lege or that overeager Sabine. Muttering an oath, he strode back through the beads to the balcony, studying the wall below it again. Nothing had changed. Smooth face, brightly lit, guards below . . . There would be no escape tonight.

*"You must be humiliated, crushed . . . thoroughly broken. . . ."*

He had seen men thoroughly broken. Had swallowed down bile as he had listened to their screams, watched them burned, dismembered, skinned alive. For a wild moment, the prospect of facing such torture filled him with terror, and he knew he couldn't do it.

Whip and carrot. Fear and desire.

*"Swear allegiance . . . first of your northern race to wear the Shadow's colors . . . everything you might desire. . . ."*

He was gripping the rail so hard it hurt, horrified to discover he wanted to do it. *Sweet Fires aloft! What manner of despicable thing have I become? How can I even think this way?*

And yet it was there, pressing at him, throwing up reasons and rationales. Katahn was right. His family despised him, the Mataio had betrayed him, and his god had abandoned him. What did he owe any of them? Why should he give up his life for them? Why should he give up Shettai for them?

He hissed another oath, then shoved away from the railing once again and paced back into the room.

Shettai still sat at the table, unmoving, her hands clasped before her, her head bowed. Desire flared in him, tainted with a darkness that matched the awful thoughts in his soul. He tore his eyes from her and, consumed with restless fire, paced to the door and back.

Then onto the balcony again and back into the room. He dropped onto the pillows across from Shettai, poured wine into the cup, and gulped it down, thinking Katahn was right in that, as well—perhaps the best thing *was* to lose himself in drunken stupor.

He poured another cup, but a new thought intruded before he could drink—a real man faced death and danger with his head up and his eyes clear and did not seek to hide from it by pickling his brain with spirits. Uncle Simon had said that. But Simon was a hero, the one real hero Abramm had actually known. Simon would not for a moment consider what Abramm was considering now.

He set the cup down, sick with self-loathing, and drove himself up to stride back to the balcony—

"How many times are you going to do that?" Shettai's voice startled him, drew him around to look at her.

Her dark eyes watched him dispassionately. "You can't escape. You have only to look up to see that."

Outside again, he did so and saw the veren on their stanchions, dark vulturine forms underlit by the glow of red lanterns. He remembered a rocky beach, a man running for his life one moment, his headless corpse sprawled at water's edge the next.

Abramm went back in and dropped onto the pillows.

Shettai watched him drink, then sighed. "You're all tense. Lie down and I'll rub out the knots."

Glancing at the bed, it dawned on him that one of them—he himself—would have to spend the night in a chair or else sleep on the floor. And wouldn't that make great preparation for the battle of his life?

He realized then what she'd said, what she'd suggested, and the very thought set all that raging lust for her loose again. He took another swallow of wine and shook his head. "I'd rather not."

She sat silently for a moment, then said, "I had no idea you found me so distasteful."

Was that *hurt* in her voice? He looked up in surprise. She seemed very small huddled beneath the big, heavy tunic, and for a moment, unexpectedly vulnerable. He hardly knew what to say, particularly in light of how he felt at the moment. It was safer to watch his cup, and so he did. "I don't find you distasteful at all," he said carefully. "I just . . . don't want you to think of me as a goat."

From the corner of his eye, he saw the faint twitching of her lips.

"I've never thought of you as a goat, Pretender."

"Well, I'd like to keep it that way."

"So why did you choose me, then?"

"I told you. I didn't relish the thought of being mauled by one of Katahn's daughters."

"Mauled." Amusement definitely colored her voice.

He studied the cup, rotating it in his hands. "I begin to understand what you mean about goats, I think."

The tension between them was dissipating now, all his wild thoughts settling, fading away, as if he had been insane and was finally returning to his right mind.

The tunic rasped as she reached for her wine cup. "Katahn has made you a remarkable offer."

He grunted acknowledgment.

"One you want to accept, maybe?"

He met her eyes then, those deep pools he sometimes thought he might drown in.

"Want to," she repeated sadly, "but won't."

"Won't I?"

"You are the White Pretender." She traced the cup's rim with a finger. "And you are a man. A stubborn, prideful, glory-craving fool of a man. And men can never do the sensible thing."

"I have no wish to die."

"Then don't." She set the cup upright and looked at him directly. "Tell him you'll join the Black Moon. Swear service to Khrell and allegiance to Beltha'adi."

Her words hung in the air. The dark gaze impaled him, and he felt the conflict begin to rise again.

She looked away, her gaze cool, her finger once more circling the cup rim. "But you won't, will you? You're the White Pretender, after all. The Dorsaddi's great Deliverer." Sarcasm sharpened her voice, and he understood she meant to goad him, belittle him—the prideful, glory-craving fool of a man. Except it wasn't that at all.

"I don't know what I am," he said uneasily. "Only that it's not so easy to walk away from one's past."

"Oh, it is very easy. You just do it."

"But then you have to live with what you've done. With what you've become."

"You would become a great man in Esurh. A respected champion in the Army of the Black Moon. Perhaps even confidant to Beltha'adi himself, given your connections. You'd be riding the wave of destiny."

"A destiny I've spent the last two years of my life fighting to deny."

She studied the cup in her hand, her expression pensive. "I do not think it can be denied. Not in the end. I've seen too many try and fail."

"But if the Deliverer—"

She cut him off with a sharp, bitter laugh. "The Deliverer! He is but the wishful thinking of desperate men who cannot bring themselves to accept the inevitable. Do you know how many times my people have claimed the Deliverer has come? One hundred twenty years ago they rallied round Jonajhur. Fifty past it was Nabal. He, too, was supposed to slay Beltha'adi, but of course he did not. Now it's you, and you're not even Dorsaddi." She snorted. "Which just shows how desperate they've become. Besides, if you don't go over to him, you'll die, and how can you deliver anyone if you're dead?"

He regarded her soberly. "A man doesn't have to be alive to start the fires of revolution."

She went from pensiveness to fury in the blink of an eye, lunging forward to slap the table and snapping out, "You are not the Deliverer, Abramm Kalladorne! You are *not*! There is . . . no . . . Deliverer."

He blinked, shocked by the intensity of her outburst. She seemed shocked herself, quenching the fire at once and slumping back on the pillows.

The hand that lifted the cup to her lips trembled. He saw her swallow. She set the vessel down and studied it a moment before she went on. "Stirring thoughts of freedom and inspiring the courage to resist is all very well, but what's the use of it if it only brings death? All those people talking rebellion—it'll only get them killed. He'll put them down. He always does. Nothing can stand against him, Pretender." Her eyes bored into his own. "If you fight tomorrow, you'll die. And it won't make any—" Her voice ran up the scale and broke apart before she could finish.

Then, right there in front of him, the mask crumpled. She drove to her feet, and he glimpsed a contorted grimace as she fled past him through the beaded curtain to the balcony.

He sat in stunned incomprehension, his heart pounding against his breastbone. Something very like a muffled sob sounded from outside, but only one. When she did not return he went to peer through the beads.

She stood at the railing, his tentlike tunic clutched around her, gold threads glittering in the darkness. From this vantage he could not see her face, but now and then she seemed to shudder. Part of him wanted to withdraw, to leave her to her pain, for he had no idea how he might comfort her, and the implications of what she'd just said had stirred up dangerous imaginings.

The beads rattled as he passed through them. Hesitantly he drew up beside her, wary of an unwelcome reception. She stood unmoving, staring over the city, her cheeks shining with lines of moisture.

He could think of nothing to say and soon felt awkward and stupid. But just as he was about to leave, she spoke.

"I'm sorry." She scrubbed at the tears, clutching the tunic one-handed. "I didn't mean to . . ." She exhaled sharply, then rubbed her upper arms beneath the tunic. She drew a deep breath, and this time the words came out steady.

"One thing I've learned in all this, and that's to keep myself apart. If you keep your feelings inside and never let yourself care too much about anything, you can't be hurt. Men use you—it doesn't matter. People die—that doesn't matter, either. It was a good plan, and I—"

She choked and fell into silence, still rubbing her arms. Then she drew another breath and veered off on a new subject. "That day on the beach when we first found you, you were so pathetic. So weak and scrawny. We couldn't believe Katahn was even looking at you, much less that he'd bid." She chuckled at the memory. "And all the other Gamers were beside themselves, wondering what he was up to. It was too funny when some of *them* bid on you, too!"

The laughter faded, and she stopped rubbing her arms. Her expression grew distant, almost wondering, and she tilted her head, like one working out a puzzle. "I was sure you'd be dead in a week. . . . Never in a thousand lifetimes would I have guessed I'd fall in love with you."

His thoughts, rambling uneasily through the shared memory, stopped abruptly.

She turned to him, her eyes confirming the words, wide and shining with tears. She laid a hand on his arm. "I don't want you to die, Pretender," she murmured.

There was none of her mask now. Love, fear, grief—she laid her heart bare to him in a way he could never have anticipated in a thousand lifetimes of his own. Yet all he could do was stare at her.

It was like being in a dream, where you tried to run but the air was thick as honey, tried to speak and nothing came out. Perhaps, indeed, he was dreaming. Or injured and hallucinating.

Her expression began to harden, the tenderness giving way to bitter hurt. Tears spilled again down her cheeks. "When you chose me I thought . . ." She stopped, lifted her chin defiantly, and dashed the moisture from her face. "But I see I was a fool. Even on your last night of life, what would you, a great northern prince and a *hero* of the people, want with a Dorsaddi whore, eh?"

She lurched toward the doorway. He caught her arm, his head spinning with the scent of her and the force of the emotion finally erupting in him.

Her face came around, etched with hurt and anger, and he stopped her protests with his mouth.

It was an awkward kiss, quick and clumsy—he had never kissed a woman before. Had he stopped to think, he wouldn't have done it now. But there had been no thought. As in combat, there was only time for action, and he had acted.

As he drew away, the cold conviction of error gripped him. What had he done? That was surely the last thing she wanted, never mind what she'd said about loving him.

She stared at him as if she'd been struck by Command, unmoving, her mouth agape, her eyes so wide the whites ringed them. He had, at least, stunned her as much as she had stunned him.

Still she said nothing, just stood there, staring up at him. When at last he realized she hadn't yet wrenched herself free of him and wasn't going to, he bent toward her again. She held her ground and lifted her lips to meet him. Then her hand was pressing against the back of his neck, and suddenly, incredibly, she was in his arms, her intoxicating softness pressed against the length of his body.

The doors on that secret place in his soul blew off, and all his desire and need and love came roaring out, igniting his flesh with fire and filling him with a rising pressure that made his ears ring and his chest feel as if it might explode.

He could not hold her close enough, could not get enough of her softness, her spicy scent, her sweet, warm lips. Yesterday, today, tomorrow—vows and heroes and the looming prospect of a horrible death—it was all blasted away by the wild winds of his passion. There was no thought of restraint, no thought of propriety or consequence. She loved him, wanted him as much as he wanted her.

For a few hours that was all that mattered.

# CHAPTER 23

The morning mist hung chill and damp, heavy with the scent of the sea. Pale tendrils curled around Abramm's head and drifted between him and the balconies to either side of him. It had swallowed most of the city and, from this vantage, rendered even the plaza directly below veiled and indistinct.

He'd arisen a little while ago, pulled on shirt, britches, and tunic in the darkness, and left Shettai asleep in the draperied bed. He should be sleeping himself—he understood now why Brogai tradition demanded celibacy on the eve of battle—but sleep had become impossible.

Last night had been . . . glorious. Never had he known such delight, such intense physical pleasure, such deep contentment and satisfaction. It had faded with the dawn, of course, but it had left behind the sense that somehow his soul had been expanded. It had changed everything. And nothing.

Awakening to find Shettai in his arms, her dark hair spread like a wing across his chest, he'd been totally unprepared for the emotion that surged through him, totally unprepared to find his righteous thoughts of heroism and duty withering before the brightness of a desire magnified for having been expressed and reciprocated. His desire for her, his fear of dying, his agonized reluctance to cause her pain, all the reasons Katahn had advanced for his defection—as well as those Shettai herself had put forth—had all boiled up in a hot surge of decision, and for a moment he was convinced he was going to go over. And then, in the next moment, the heat had transmuted to horror and revulsion and scalding self-contempt . . . only to revert back to longing and rationalization. The cycle repeated over and over. It was the same excruciating duality he'd endured last night, intensified a hundredfold.

Consumed at length with the restless fervor of his indecision, he'd arisen, dressed, and come out here—as if the brightening light and chill morning air might somehow settle him one way or the other.

In the plaza below, lantern keepers were at work snuffing the flames of the fish-bladder lanterns, one after the other of them winking out in the gloom. Last night's celebrants had gone home, replaced by eager fans waiting for seats that would be assigned first come, first served. Many had arrived long ago, still curled beneath their cloaks and blankets in a line that started at the main gate somewhere to his right.

Already the merchants were returning to reopen their wagons and set out their wares, sea gulls swooping around them, seeking booty that had been dropped last night. Soon the sleepy fans were staggering to their feet as the smell of fry bread warmed the air.

The scent triggered memories of distant summer morns, playing tag with Carissa and Gillard and the cousins around striped festival tents. Squealing with excitement, they'd darted between the horses and flags, the ropes and gear and barrels, savoring the sweet scent of the baking sugar-crusted twist-breads they'd soon be eating. . . .

He sighed and pushed the memory away. That was a long time—and place—ago.

More and more people filtered into the plaza, taking their place in line. A good number carried slender sticks topped with misshapen whitewashed diamond motifs that they occasionally waved above the crowd. Supposedly representing himself in costume, the diamonds proclaimed support for the Pretender. Similar sticks bearing silvered crescent moons designated Beltha'adi's supporters, markedly in the minority this morning.

The rising level of babble below drew his attention leftward as a division of gray-tunicked soldiers marched up behind the purple banner of the Black Moon. Forcing the civilians to dive aside, the soldiers bored straight through the waiting line and stopped at the main gate. As their commanding officer began barking orders, men ran to take up posts alongside the gate, then at points along the plaza's outer and inner perimeters.

Another unit passed by them and entered the amphitheater itself.

*Riot control,* Abramm reflected grimly.

No one dared say anything to the soldiers, but as the ticket line reformed, he saw a few resentful shakings of the diamond-topped sticks at the soldiers' backs.

*After today they'll be shaking those sticks at me,* he thought. Or more likely, will have broken them and thrown them in the fire. After today, if he chose in favor of his desire, the White Pretender would be transformed from a symbol of hope and courage to one of betrayal and cowardice.

He frowned, dismayed by the renewal of aggrieved self-loathing, and pushed the thought away. Would he rather be dead? Lose Shettai? Break her heart?

Of course not. Of *course* not . . .

"You're up early, my love." As if his thoughts had drawn her, Shettai slipped up beside him and slid an arm underneath his unfastened tunic. She lifted her lips for him to kiss and he did so, slowly, tenderly, savoring the taste and touch and smell of her.

*Dust and ashes! How can I even think of giving this up?*

When they drew apart she stayed in his arms, looking up into his eyes, searching for the answer he still hadn't given her and clearly hesitant to ask. He wanted to reassure her, to tell her he had indeed decided—that he would never leave her, never hurt her like that . . . but the other side of him kept his tongue frozen and his mouth closed.

After a while he saw the despair move across her face. "You're going to refuse," she said quietly.

It was as if she'd stabbed him through the heart. "No!" His voice came out a ragged croak. "I'm not! I'm going to take it! I am! It would be insane to do anything—"

She laid her fingers on his lips, stopping the flow of words. Then she smiled, that old, ironic smile. "I can see it, even if you can't. And I can't say I'm even surprised, though I had hoped . . ." She trailed off. Her eyes moved across his face, as if she sought to burn his features into her mind. She touched his lips, the rings in his ear, the thick, shoulder-length hair come loose of its knot hours ago. Finally she sighed. "I wish for once you could fight without the costume," she said. "There are those who do not believe you are Kiriathan."

"It won't matter, because I'm not going to fight," he declared firmly, resolve hardening once more within him. "I'm going to take his offer."

He saw the hope flare in her eyes, then fade as she smiled sadly. "I think," she said, "if you were the kind of man who could take such an offer, I would never have fallen in love with you in the first place."

His resolve crumbled, shattered by the impact of her words and the sudden, devastating certainty that they were true. It was the most agonizing, gut-wrenching realization he'd ever made, and for a moment he thought he might become physically ill.

He saw the tears welling in her eyes and kissed her again, fiercely this time, wishing he didn't have to die, wishing he could take Beltha'adi's offer without losing his soul, wishing she hadn't loved him after all, and a hundred other things that weren't going to happen.

Abdeel and Dumah arrived a little while later, banging open the door and clumping into the room, jeering and laughing until they saw her in his arms. They stopped, surprise widening their eyes, followed by a flicker of jealousy and, yes, a light of new respect.

That only made it worse, however. As they escorted him back to the underbelly of the Val'Orda, they jabbered incessantly, tossing out ribald questions and vulgar suggestions that, had he done anything but ignore them, would have roused him to a fury.

Trap sat in the front room of the suite of chambers he and Abramm shared in the lowest level, eating black bread, figs, and cheese. He looked up as Abramm entered, cocked a brow at the sight of him, but said nothing. He looked haggard, as if he had gotten no more sleep than Abramm last night.

As the handlers left them, Abramm dropped onto the bench across from him and stared at the portion of dark, crusty loaf on the plate. The last thing he wanted was food.

He felt Trap's eyes upon him and knew if he sat here much longer the man would speak to him. Wanting conversation even less than he wanted food, he stood and took one of the wooden practice swords down from the wall. Wordlessly he started through the basic cycle of forms, the need to concentrate on technique and sequence effectively keeping more troubling thoughts at bay. When it came to an end, he started the next form, then the next, and the next. Finally, though, he was forced to stop for breath. Leaning the sword against the wall, he stripped off the heavy tunic.

"So it's true, then," Trap said behind him. "He *did* make you an offer."

Abramm froze, crushing the tunic in his fists.

"Brogai status, they say," Trap went on. "Wealth, honor, everything you could want."

"What good is it if you have to sell your soul to get it?" Abramm asked, dropping the tunic onto the bench. He picked up the sword again. Fifth, sixth, seventh, eighth—he ran through the intermediate forms, holding his mind to each nuance of stance and stroke. But inevitably he was once more reduced to weak-armed panting and thoughts he wanted to forget. Shettai in a hundred different images of beauty and softness and sweet, wonderful scent, realities of memory that far surpassed anything he might have imagined. The price of pleasure, it seemed, was the amplification of pain.

And there was nothing he could do to change it.

"We'll probably die out there, my lord."

Abramm stood where he was, staring at the wall, his breath rushing between his teeth, his back to the other man. Sweat trickled down his chest and sides. He didn't know what to say.

After a moment, Trap spoke again. "You're not ready."

At that Abramm finally turned, barking a bitter laugh. "Seeing as I've defiled myself in every possible way by now"—he'd broken the last of his holy vows just last night, in fact—"I'd say you're right. Unfortunately, there isn't time enough to do anything about it." He feigned a start of surprise, then widened his eyes as if in sudden understanding. "But wait! I could take hold of your gray talisman! Let it burn that golden shield into my flesh and then . . . why, *then* I'd be ready, wouldn't I? Isn't that what you were going to say?" He snorted. "Sorry, but it's just too convenient for me to believe."

Meridon regarded him steadily. " 'Those who receive the truth and spurn it shall be without excuse.' "

That was from the Second Word of Revelation. Abramm grimaced. "Very nice, Captain. But frankly, I don't care anymore. Even if Eidon is in your mysterious light, why should I want it? He hasn't done any more for you than he has for me. We're both slaves, marked and unmarked."

Trap smiled slightly. "But very well treated slaves, you must admit."

"Oh yes, *very* well treated. Right up to the point where we're defeated and tortured to death. 'The last thing they'll hear from you will be your screams for mercy,' " he quoted from Katahn's warning last night. He snorted again. "What good is a god who can't protect his followers from harm?"

"He can."

"Then why hasn't he? Or does he take pleasure in making you suffer?"

"Of course not."

"You can't have it both ways, Trap."

"Suggesting he takes pleasure in our pain is blasphemous. But he *has* given us the freedom to choose. Some choose to do sinful, evil things, which have inevitable and ugly consequences."

"Consequences that spill over to others who did not so choose," Abramm added bitterly.

"But that's the beauty of it—Eidon can use those evil deeds and consequences for the ultimate benefit of his servants."

"Benefit?" Abramm's voice cracked with incredulity. He waved the sword at the chamber around them. "You're saying this is for our *benefit*?"

"Yes!" Trap's gaze bored into his own, arresting his outrage. When next he spoke, the Terstan's voice was quietly compelling. "Do you have any idea how much you've changed, my lord? You are not at all the man you were when you left Kiriath. You have become a hero here, the champion about whom innumerable stories and songs are even now being written and spread."

Of course Abramm knew he was a hero. How could he not with his supporters waving their diamond-topped sticks and screaming their approval at every match? He wouldn't be facing the match he faced today if not for their growing adulation and the dangerous attitudes he had spawned in them through his continued success at defying Beltha'adi's claims of destiny and right to rule.

But suddenly, somehow, perhaps because of the way Trap had said it, he saw his newfound status through different eyes—the eyes of a frail and scorned little boy who spent entirely too much time reading adventure stories and tales of the great champions of Kiriathan history. The greatest goal of his childhood, besides knowing Eidon, was to emulate those champions, to become someone honored, admired, sung about. Someone who was emulated by other little boys. It was a dream that had died on the practice floors of the royal school of fencing a good fourteen years ago. A dream, he now saw, that had been realized, in spite of its death and through no conscious choice of his own.

The sword point sank slowly to the stone.

"Can you think of any other way you could have become what you are today?" Trap pressed. "Could it have happened in Kiriath? Would you have made the kinds of decisions that have led you to this point? Would you have even had the opportunity?"

Abramm stared at the nicked and polished length of wood before him, and a chill swept up his spine. No. He would not have.

"How can you say he has not been with you, Abramm?" Trap demanded softly. "Using you for his glory even though you continue to reject him."

Denial welled up. "You're wrong! I'm no hero in his eyes. I have killed—"

"Defending yourself against those who would kill you. The Words forbid murder, not self-defense."

"But I have hated—I have struck in anger. I have defiled myself in every possible way. Last night I—" He broke off, not yet willing to verbalize that confession, even knowing Trap must have guessed what he'd done. "I have . . . I have hated him. *Cursed* him . . ."

"And even so, he has not abandoned you."

Abramm looked down at him, into his eyes, and felt all at once as if he were sliding down a bright hole, slipping away, losing control, his mind captured and enspelled by Terstan power. . . .

His forearm tingled, jerking him free of the spell. "I don't believe that!" he cried, an irrational anger flooding into him. "It was *Gillard's* treachery that brought me here." He swept the sword up sharply, blade hissing through the air. "And it's the power of Beltha'adi's evil that keeps me here."

He started into the next form, stepping and slashing with rapid, angry strokes that only gradually settled back into the smooth precision that normally characterized his practices.

The next time he stopped, Trap was no longer looking at him, was instead watching his own fingers crumble the dark bread on his plate. His lips were pressed tightly together, his face closed and hard with frustration. Abramm noticed again the dark circles around his eyes, the way his freckles stood out against pale skin, and was struck by a new and alarming thought.

"Are you sick? You look awful."

For a moment he thought the Terstan meant to ignore him. Finally, though, the man seemed to shake off his sulk and shrugged. "Nothing a little sleep wouldn't cure."

Abramm lifted a brow. He had never known Meridon to lose a night's sleep for worrying. Hadn't he claimed just yesterday to be completely at ease with whatever Eidon chose for him today, death or life, either one? Apparently, alone on his pallet last night, he had not been so at ease after all.

The walls shuddered as one of the lions roared, and they both looked toward the wall nearest the arena proper. The lion fight was scheduled for some three hours before the final and most anticipated match, but Abramm had thought they still had double that amount of time. The creature roared again, and as the subsequent silence stretched itself out longer and longer, Abramm relaxed. The beast was just sounding off. Or else it was feeding time.

Across from him, Trap stood and disappeared into the adjacent sleeping chamber. Abramm went back to his forms. He needed the entire sequence to work himself into a fatigue strong enough to allow him to sleep.

When he awoke it was midafternoon and the Sorite slave who shaved and dressed and painted them had arrived to prepare them for their match. They went through the routine wordlessly, exactly as they'd done scores of times before. Indeed, it was hard now to believe this would be the last. . . .

The slave was just leaving when Katahn's personal secretary burst into the room and thrust a carved jewel case into Abramm's hands. "The master wants you to wear this for the match."

Before Abramm could even slip free the gold catch, the man was gone, door thumping shut in his wake.

Puzzled, Abramm lifted the lid, then felt his face slacken as he saw what lay on the satin inside: a pale, gray, opalescent orb, no bigger than the end joint of his little finger, set into a gold ring hung from a gold chain. It wasn't quite the same as the one he'd had before, the color of this one a little lighter, the sheen more opalescent, but he knew what it was all the same.

He looked at Trap accusingly. "You think I wouldn't recognize this?"

Trap frowned at him, the expression exaggerated by his painted-on sad-face. "What is it?"

"Don't play dumb. I know you put him up to this." He pulled the talisman from the box, dangling it between them. "It's just like the one you gave me when we were escaping the Keep."

"Perhaps, but *I* didn't make it."

"There *are* no other candidates, Captain." Abramm realized then that for some inexplicable reason Trap had reverted to speaking Kiriathan, a language they had not used in months.

"Actually, there is," the Terstan said, still in Kiriathan. A smile might have been tugging at his lips, but the sad-face made it hard to tell.

"What are you talking about?"

"Our esteemed Master," Meridon said. "Why do you think I didn't get any sleep last night?" It *was* a smile, breaking across his face and wrinkling the painted tear on his cheek. "He took the star just before dawn."

Abramm gaped. "*Katahn* wears a Terstan shield?"

"I'm sure he'd be happy to show you, but I don't think now is a good time. If anyone found out . . ." He spread his hands.

If anyone found out, the Gamer would lose everything—wealth, position, family, even his Brogai status. He would be expelled from the caste, condemned to spend eternity in the Dark Abode and ostracized by all who did not wish to join him there. No wonder Trap spoke in Kiriathan.

Abramm's gaze dropped to the stone dangling in his fingers. "So now you expect *me* to take it, too?"

"I'm sure his only hope is that you'll wear it for the match."

Abramm scowled at him.

"You know they'll put you under Command if you don't. I'd have made you one myself if I could have figured a way for you to wear it."

Abramm tightened a fist about the chain. The spore in his arm writhed protest at being so close to the stone, goading his rising anger. It annoyed him that Trap would think him so weak, so malleable. . . . Yet the memory of his own body operating outside his control remained as vivid—and compelling—as ever. He clenched his teeth, hating where this was leading.

"They promised to use only steel with us," he said.

"You know they won't. Not today." The Terstan tugged at the fall of lace under his chin, pulling out an errant fold tucked improperly under the collar band.

Abramm's arm tingled distractingly. He hadn't refused Beltha'adi's offer of clemency yet. Maybe he would surprise everyone—himself included—and accept it. Then there would be no fight, no need for Command, no need for protection.

He stared at the opalescent stone and shifted uncomfortably, feeling Trap's eyes upon him.

"It isn't going to . . . I mean, it won't make me . . . you know."

The brown eyes didn't blink. "Only if you wish it."

"And I will be able to take it off?"

"Of course."

As if that mattered. Still, if he were to accept Beltha'adi's offer—*Oh, plagues! You aren't going to do that, and you know it! Besides, the first thing they'll ask you to do is turn on Trap, so what would you gain?*

It seemed he had no good choices here, no matter which way he turned.

With a sudden jerk he shook the chain open and looped it over his head, the stone thumping benignly against the ruffles on his chest. He scowled at his friend. "Satisfied?"

"I suggest you put it under the doublet. If the Broho see it, they'll snatch it away."

Exhaling annoyance, Abramm pulled the heavy satin away from his chest, picked up the chain, and threaded the stone down behind the froth of ruffles and the slick silk of his under blouse.

Feeling its warmth and hardness even through the silk, he shivered uneasily. "You're sure I'll be able to take it off?"

"You took it off before."

"I know, but . . . it's different now."

Trap's head jerked up, his gaze suddenly intent. "How so?"

"The color's changed. And . . . well, I don't know exactly. Why are you looking at me like that?"

The Terstan's intensity gave way to something that once again could be a smile. "Because for the first time," he said, "I think we might actually survive this."

CHAPTER

# 24

A thunderous roar erupted from the amphitheater crowd around Carissa, and she shuddered beneath her veils. *Someone else must have died,* she thought grimly. *What in all of Torments am I doing here? Cooper's right. Even if the Infidel is Phil's brother, we can do nothing to help him.*

When they'd ascended from the arena warrens last night, the boy had been exuberant. It took real effort for him to curb his enthusiasm in the face of Carissa's disappointment at learning the Pretender was not Abramm, but that hadn't stopped him from persuading her to help him free *his* brother. She wondered now what she had been thinking, for clearly there was nothing they could do. Even Philip had no real plan. *Eidon will make us a way,* he'd insisted. But, as usual, Eidon had yet to come through.

Perhaps if Cooper had not thrown such a fit she would have been more reasonable. But when he outright forbade her to go, she grew incensed. And when he said she was too weak to stomach what went on in these Games, that she'd not last five minutes of them, she grew all the more determined. If he could bear it, so could she.

She'd abandoned that contest early on, appreciating for the first time the vision-obstructing mask propriety demanded she wear. Not only did it shield her from the carnage, it kept Cooper from seeing just how deeply that carnage affected her. Twice already she'd nearly lost her breakfast, and now she spent a good deal of time staring into the darkness beneath the eye holes, scratching her staffid bites and hoping fervently that the horror would end soon. *I should have stayed at the inn with Peri.*

Forced by the crowds to find their place in line outside the gates last evening, she, Cooper, Philip, and their hired retainer, Eber, had spent the night dozing on the plaza's dirty brickwork, and even so they just managed to find seats. The necessity of entering the arena early meant they were there for everything—from the first event, which entailed lions stalking a frightened herd of broken-down horses, to an eternity of demonstrations by the infamous Broho, brethren of the vaunted warriors who would ultimately face the Pretender and his Infidel.

Members of the elite fighting caste of the Brogai aristocracy, the Broho were said to carry the power of Khrell himself in their bodies. That power enabled them to mutilate their own flesh with the tattoos, piercings, and ritual self-infliction of wounds that proved their indifference to pain. It also made them inhumanly strong and quick.

Lions, tigers, huge horned and armored beasts from across the deserts, Andolen prisoners of war, barbarian slaves, sarotis-crippled Terstans, Dorsaddi warriors—the Broho vanquished them all. They killed and maimed with sword and ax, hand and foot, nail and tooth. Tiring of that, they vomited gouts of purple fire that blasted away their adversaries' chests or heads or limbs.

Worst of all was the writhing veil of fear they sometimes set upon their victims, coils of mist that wrapped them in a paralyzing terror neither man nor beast could resist. Wailing, screaming, roaring, their eyes rolling wildly in their heads, the victims stood helpless and pliant as the Broho tortured and slew them, sometimes swiftly, sometimes not swiftly at all.

And this was merely practice for the final match of the day and the famous victims whose deaths would last the longest yet.

The crowd let out another thunderous roar, and for a moment she thought she would suffocate behind her veil.

*This is senseless. Admit he's right, you idiot woman. Do you wish to live with the memories of those brave men being castrated, blinded, and skinned alive?*

She glanced at Philip sitting to her right, Eber's silent bulk looming just beyond him. He looked like a wax boy, his features frozen, pinched.

She touched his arm. "Philip, maybe Cooper's right. Maybe—"

"Go if you wish," he said, staring at the ring. "I'm staying."

"But there's nothing we can do—"

"I can witness his death. And I can remember it." He looked at her, eyes grim and hard. "He will not die like the others." His gaze shifted back to the arena. "The Broho are not the only ones with powers, my lady."

She frowned at him. Meridon was a Terstan, yes, with a Terstan's alleged powers, whatever they might be. But nearly a score of his kind had died here already this morning, and their powers had done nothing to deliver them. Why believe Meridon would be different?

She could not fault the boy for his hope, though. If it were Abramm down there—and she was desperately thankful it was not—she would not have been moved from this bench, no matter how dreadful it got.

The crowd's roar had dwindled to a loud murmur. From the concourse above, she could hear the annoying, minor-keyed melody of a trio of pipers, accompanied by their drummer, wheedling amidst shouts of vendors peddling hot, spicy sausages, fried caterpillars called spima, and wine.

She risked a glance at the arena, found it empty but for the wide oblong of stone sentinels encircling its perimeter. Gray daylight filtered through a central hole in the great canvas ceiling stretched overhead, washing over the churned and bloodstained sand. A faint mist shredded off the stones, drifting upward toward the hole, a mist that had not been there previously.

She glanced left toward the arena's end, where a huge stone image of Khrell had been set into the second tier of seating, grimacing over the playing field. Scarlet flames danced in its fat belly, their light shining eerily through the back of obsidian eyes. Just below it, in the Ringside Tier, a large seating box draped in red was filling now with red-robed, shaven-headed priests. These were the Game Masters who would fashion the arcane illusions that always accompanied the greatest tales.

A quarter of the way around the stadium from the statue of Khrell and his priests, dead center of the oval's length, was a similar box, this one draped and garlanded in gold. For most of the day it, too, had stood empty. Now various robed, furred, and bejeweled Brogai nobles were filtering into it, talking and laughing among themselves.

The box was nearly full when a sudden blast of the long-necked horns from the musicians' gallery cut through the crowd's low rumble. In the wall beneath the Game Masters' box, a pair of tall doors trundled open. As the fanfare continued, two black horses burst out of them and into the light, a gilded chariot flashing in their wake. It carried a man armored and cloaked in gold, holding his crescent-mooned helmet under one arm as he waved at the screaming crowd with the other. The chariot wheeled a circuit about the ring so that all could see their Supreme Commander.

Beltha'adi was a short, beardless, broad-chested man with a hawk nose and a gleaming shaven dome. Ranks of gold honor rings lined both ears, and even from a distance one could feel the power of his personality.

Completing its circuit, the chariot stopped in front of the idol, and as Beltha'adi dismounted, the crowd quieted. Then, before them all and with great solemnity and flourish, he dropped to his knees and pressed his forehead to the sand. The stadium lights dimmed and Khrell's belly fires flared, eyes flickering as if the statue were alive. A cold sense of evil crawled over Carissa's scalp and she shuddered.

Beltha'adi rocked back onto his heels and stood, then rode his chariot around to the royal box. Once he had taken his seat, the doors beneath the idol opened once again to disgorge a line of gray-tunicked soldiers, marching under the standard of the black moon on purple field. A moment later, doors in the wall opposite them disgorged another line of men, these in Kalladorne blue.

The sentinel rocks glowed with a pale light amidst ever thickening mists, and the Taleteller began, his voice deep and resonating. He spoke of the great struggles of the past and of the Brogai tradition of champions facing one another to determine the outcome of a battle. "Our Supreme Commander has continued this practice, requesting always from those who would stand against him a champion, a man to fight him one on one.

"Today we give you a forthtelling of one such conflict, still to come. The day our Great Lord Beltha'adi—Chosen of Khrell, Favored of Aggos, Champion of Laevion—faces the king of the Kiriathan pigeons on the northlander's home soil. A conflict sure to unfold not many months hence. Representing the Great One himself is his champion Oriak ul Ranour, First Lar of the Broho, defender of the Heart of Aggos, the undefeated master of the Val'Orda."

From the still-open doors under the statue of Khrell, a man seemed to float into the arena, his long, black-skirted trousers hiding the movement of his feet. He wore a deep purple tunic, belted at the waist, the sleeves rolled back and tied. His bald head gleamed in the combined light of the idol's fire and the stones' glow, scalp and face mottled with a network of tattooing.

Lines of gold honor rings ran up both ears. A long Broho *elbana* rode in its black, lacquered scabbard at his hip.

Gliding away from the doors, he turned, fell to his knees before Khrell, and pressed his forehead to the sand. Three times he did this, and when he arose to face the screaming crowd again, the amulet at his throat flared purple with the power of his god.

The mists had obliterated the canvas ceiling by then, blotting out all light from above, so that the glowing sentinels stood out starkly in the darkness. Those farthest from the idol shone the brightest, casting their blue-gray illumination on the doors they framed. As those doors opened, the crowd quieted and the Taleteller spoke again.

"Representing the king of Kiriath we have our very own Kiriathan champion, alleged descendent of the royal line of Kalladorne and also undefeated, the White Pretender, and his Infidel, who will serve as his second."

The words sent yet another chill crawling up Carissa's spine, for though she knew they were claiming the Pretender to be Kiriathan and even of Kalladorne heritage, hearing it proclaimed was unnerving.

The doors rumbled to a stop, and the two men she had seen so briefly last night stepped into the ring.

As before, the taller one wore all white—doublet, hose, and those horrid, too-short, ballooning breeches that were the height of recent Kiriathan foppery. From this vantage he looked like a white pear, decked with lace and ribbon and topped with a long white wig and gaudily jeweled crown—the outfit hardly even an exaggeration of the more outrageous versions of current Kiriathan fashion. Again his face was painted stark white with the laughing jester lips and black lines exploding from his eyes in an expression of perpetual surprise.

His companion looked equally foolish—afroth with emerald frippery and a black wig, face painted with a sad-mouth and a black tear falling from one eye.

And yet, despite the absurd costumes, they carried themselves regally—particularly the Pretender. He stood straight-backed, chin up, radiating defiance, and he had a presence about him every bit as mesmerizing as Beltha'adi's. Whoever he was, it was plain to see how he had gained his following.

The crowd erupted all at once, with no apparent cue. One moment they were silent and the next they were screaming their lungs out in a thunderous wave of sound. Not cheering, but not jeering, either—more an expression of savage excitement. White diamonds appeared out of nowhere, reflecting the sentinel stones' light so that they danced and fluttered like butterflies throughout the dark bowl of audience.

The two men moved with long, easy strides, their heads high, their hands resting lightly upon the blades that banged in scabbards at their sides, the weapons a sobering counterpart to their apparel. After all she had endured, their courage caught her heart. *Perhaps we will not see these two quaver and quail before the beasts. It's said there were men who could do it. It's said these two have, in fact, done it. . . .*

The pair strode to ring-center and stood to face the royal box. The swell of voices waned, and a light appeared over Beltha'adi. The Supreme Commander stood and spoke, his voice eerily amplified. "Pretender, you have shown great courage and ability in combat. You have shown us you have the heart of a son of Khrell. As a reward, I will be merciful. Renounce your past, do homage to Khrell, and I will spare your life."

The crowd burst into a low mumble of surprise, mutterings passing back and forth as people asked if he'd said what they thought he'd said, then fading as they waited for the Pretender's answer. The silence intensified until she could hear the softest rustles of the people around her.

Finally the Pretender spoke, his voice ringing through the arena's lofty spaces, deepened and distorted in amplification. "I am a Kiriathan, sir, and I will betray neither my heritage nor my homeland!"

The audience gasped, and Carissa felt a thrill of pride.

"I would ask," the Pretender went on, "why you send a proxy to face me. Why not test me yourself? Surely the Immortal One does not fear the blade of one yelaki northerner."

Beltha'adi snorted and waved a hand. "You are not the king of Kiriath, Pretender."

"No, but it is said I *am* the Dorsaddi Deliverer. Why didn't you choose that contest to be the subject of this tale?"

She actually heard a wave of snickering.

Beltha'adi threw up his chin. "If you survive my champion, Pretender, perhaps I will." He made a slashing gesture, and the stadium went dark.

The crowd erupted again, screaming, stamping, waving its white diamonds as the arena slowly disappeared. . . .

Carissa had heard about the incredible illusory powers of the best Game Masters, had even experienced the work of the lesser practitioners, but it was nothing compared to this.

Where the audience should have been now stretched a gray expanse of sea, overhung with dark thunderclouds, a fleet of galley ships at anchor just offshore. The arena's sandy floor became a grass-hummocked bluff in Kiriath: part of the famous Field of Hollyhocks where the war with Chesedh had ended, where Arnon stopped the Thilosian warlord Danau from taking Springerlan, where Alaric I had led the Gundians against Polark and his hordes to become the first Kalladorne to wear the Kiriathan crown. It lay just east of Springerlan, and she had walked its grassy hummocks in reality. This was a rendition so perfect, she wondered if they had somehow been transported there. A wind blew across the bluff, ruffling the grasses, stirring her mask, touching her nostrils with the taint of the sea. She could even hear the flags as they flapped.

How was this possible?

Below, the two armies stood in their camps, the two champions between them, Broho and Pretender facing one another. The Broho's long, two-handed elbana slid from its scabbard, and the Pretender bared both longsword and dagger. They began to circle, stepping carefully among the hummocks, watching each other, the Pretender with his blades held forward, point first, the Broho with his long sharp steel cocked back at shoulder height.

They circled and circled, watching each other, weighing, evaluating, waiting.

The Broho struck first, taking a little hop forward and swinging out, the elbana's reach twice that of the Pretender's blade. It flashed in the gray light, flashed again as it looped and came back, and again, and again, an easy, rhythmic motion that looked more like a practice form than anything serious. The Pretender hopped back, out of reach, refusing to take one-handed what his opponent delivered with two.

She grew aware of the spectators around her again as they shifted restlessly, and she heard murmurs of *"Yelaki! Beshaad!"* A reluctance to engage was never tolerated. It smacked of cowardice and fear—traits the Pretender had never yet revealed. Or so she'd heard. Then again, this *was* a Broho. And his sword was awfully long, flashing malevolently in the darkness as it looped and swung, looped and swung.

Suddenly the Pretender lunged in after one of those swings, laying his dagger against the Broho's bared forearm and thrusting with his sword. The Broho twisted away and, heedless of the blade at his arm, drove the elbana's pommel down hard toward his opponent's face. The Pretender stumbled backward over the hummocks—and still caught the next swing with his dagger, trapping it with his sword to come in close again.

They struggled briefly, blood dripping down the Broho's forearm. Then the Pretender staggered backward, his sword sailing from his grip. With the Broho slashing after him, he backstepped over the hummocks and tripped, falling flat on his back. The elbana flashed down, a powerful, killing stroke that caught but a slice of doublet as the Pretender rolled away and came up, sword in hand again.

Blood staining one white sleeve, he returned to his ready position, both blades held forward, and the two went back to their quiet circling.

The audience responded with a murmur of approval. The Pretender had not only held his own, but it was the first time a Broho had been blooded all day.

Overhead a sea gull soared on the same wind that ruffled the tunics and hair of the watching armies in the field and again stirred the veil at Carissa's face. Lightning speared the distant clouds, dark over the restless sea and bobbing galleys. A growl of thunder followed moments later.

The Broho laughed. Immediately the wind kicked up a sand skirl between them, and as the Pretender turned his head to shield his eyes, his opponent struck. The blow was blocked, trapped, and the Pretender came in close, sliced his opponent's forearm again, and was flung away.

Again the crowd murmured, and the sound seemed to ignite the Broho champion's ire. He hurled himself forward, swinging his blade with blinding speed, forcing the Pretender to abandon the dagger and put both hands on the sword to block the blows.

The blades pounded against each other in rapid repeating clanks, ending finally in an off-tone clunk that left the Pretender backstepping furiously, his sword a jagged shard barely longer than the dagger. Then he slammed into what looked like solid air and rebounded dazedly as the elbana swooped for his head.

He dropped just in time, sweeping a leg to kick the Broho's feet from under him. As the man fell, the Pretender thrust with the broken sword, missed, thrust again, and scrambled out of range. When he rolled to his feet, he held the dagger again, along with the broken sword.

The crowd roared.

The Broho rose to a taut crouch, the amulet at his throat blazing violet. He shouted a Command, and the Pretender froze. The cheering choked off on the instant, Carissa's voice among them. She had hoped this contest would be different. But clearly it was not to—

The Broho moved into striking range, and the Pretender charged in close, grabbing the elbana's hilt with one hand, plunging the dagger through the man's ribs with the other. The crowd went wild as the Broho flung him off and opened his mouth to deliver another Command even as the Pretender's broken sword spun through the air to bury itself dead center in his chest.

It was a killing blow that did not kill.

The Broho's eyes flared red, his mouth opened, and the dark veil of the Fearspell billowed out, writhing through the air to wrap itself around the Pretender. Again he went rigid, and Carissa screamed at him—along with a thousand other voices—to fight it. He had mastered the Command. Surely he could master this.

Reeling a bit himself now, the Broho plucked the broken sword from his chest and cast it away, eyes still blazing, the glow of his amulet spreading down to the wound. He stood for a moment, staring at his hands as he caught his breath and marshaled his strength.

The crowd roared again, and Carissa's gaze flew back to the Pretender, now shrugging himself free of the Fearspell. Grimly he strode toward the Broho, dagger in hand. The man looked up, saw him, and screamed out a ball of purple fire that plunged straight into the Pretender's chest—

And was deflected in a blaze of white that sent it exploding into the arena wall on Carissa's left.

The force of contact flung the Pretender thirty feet backward, slamming him into another of the invisible barriers and collapsing him senseless on the sand. The Broho advanced to finish him off, but before he'd gone half the distance, the man in white was struggling to his feet, blood bright on his white-painted chin. The front of his doublet was charred and he stared around at the windswept bluff as if dazed.

The Broho spoke another purple bolt at him, and it was deflected as before, this time crashing into the wall directly in front of Carissa with a plume of purple sparks that made all the illusion shudder. Again the Pretender was flung through the air, but this time he missed the invisible sentinel, hit the ground rolling, and came to his feet, not looking so dazed anymore. His wig had been knocked askew, and now he tore it off, revealing blond hair caught into a warrior's knot at his nape.

The Infidel, conspicuous in his emerald costume, stepped away from the men of the watching armies, as did the Broho's second, watching each other as they watched the primary combatants.

The combatants stood eyeing each other, as well, both panting heavily. It looked like the Pretender *smiled*—and then he threw himself forward once more, once more meeting a purple lance that sent him flying. Again the illusion flickered, faltered, then went dark, leaving only the sandy arena, the glowing sentinels, and the great dark bowl of the amphitheater alight with dancing white diamonds and screaming spectators. The sound beat at Carissa's ears and chest and belly, rolling over her like a fierce wind, even as her own voice joined it.

Yet again the white figure dragged himself upright, the front of his doublet now completely gone, revealing the glowing talisman he wore suspended on a chain about his neck. The skin beneath it was red, seared by the heat released in the clash of powers. Red smeared his shoulder and soaked his white britches and hose.

A thrill raced up Carissa's back and scalp at the man's persistence. And yet she wondered what he hoped to accomplish. To drain the Broho of his energy? Tire him out enough to even the odds?

The Infidel had eased closer, but so had the other Broho.

*Let him win. Surely after all this he deserves to win.*

The Pretender's legs wobbled, strengthened. Again he smiled, but this time he did not fling himself at his enemy. Instead he took a sideways course, as if to come round wide in a flank attack.

Purple fire slid inexorably through the air. The Pretender twisted as it hit, and suddenly she understood what he was doing—a heartbeat before the deflected bolt hit one of the arena's six pairs of wooden doors and blasted it to splinters. Not chance. He had been aiming.

He rolled as he hit the ground, came up yelling, and all devolved into chaos as the Kiriathan soldiers rushed into the gap between him and the Broho, leaving him a clear shot at the gate. The other army leaped to the challenge and suddenly a full-scale melee writhed across the sand. She saw the Infidel close in on the Broho champion, running the shaven-headed warrior through the throat with his long Kiriathan blade. As the Broho fell, the Infidel raced to catch up with the Pretender, interposing his body between the Pretender's and those behind them.

In the Supreme Commander's box, Beltha'adi leapt up with a screech that became a violet fireball, flying across the ring after the fleeing slaves. They were still some twenty feet from the warren opening when it hit, exploding in a blinding blossom of white and purple and red.

Slowly the smoke cleared, revealing two blackened bodies sprawled on the sand amidst shards of smoldering wood. In the deafening quiet a whimper left Carissa's raw throat as she stood there stunned and disbelieving. Beside her Philip muttered something, clenching his fists and staring hard at the bodies. She watched him dully, waiting for the realization to hit. Instead he clutched her arm. "They got away!" he hissed. "They got away!"

She stared at him.

He shook her arm and pointed at the bodies. "They're illusions."

For a moment it seemed he was right. Suddenly the two sprawled forms lost substance, becoming ghostly shapes laid over the rubble beyond them, as if they were no more than mist.

"Eidon *did* make them a way!" he cried.

Cooper jerked her free of the boy, and the bodies grew solid again. She blinked, confused, then looked up at Cooper, whose face was tight and pale with worry.

"We've got to get out of here!" he yelled, gesturing at the chaos roiling around them. In the arena below, the armies continued to fight, joined by additional soldiers and even spectators. Four men hacked at the corpse of the fallen Broho, while others—not soldiers—dragged away the bodies of the Pretender and the Infidel. In the stands people screamed and threw rotten fruit, cups, shoes, anything that came to hand. They tussled with each other and with the gray-tunicked soldiers stationed to keep order.

"We've got to get out of here now!" Cooper yelled again and pushed her past Philip into the crowded aisle after Eber.

CHAPTER

# 25

Abramm sensed the approach of Beltha'adi's fireball moments before it hit—a prickly, pressure-at-the-chest feeling that only made him run harder. Trap, just behind him, took the brunt of the blow in a deafening explosion that sent curtains of light billowing around them and hurled them ten feet forward.

Abramm landed on shards of wood, his weapons lost in the force of impact. Gasping back the breath that had been driven out of him, he shook the stars from his eyes and scrambled up again. With Trap at his heels, he dodged an upthrust piece of wooden timber, then leaped a shard the size of his own body. The gate loomed through the smoke ahead, rent with a jagged hole and twisted back off its hinges. In the darkness beyond, people lay pinned and bleeding beneath heavy timbers, some of them limp and still. Still others were picking themselves up dazedly as Abramm and Trap stopped at the top of the ramp leading down into the warrens.

A living sea filled the chamber below them, blocking their way—robed, dark-eyed, dark-skinned Esurhites, who a moment ago had likely been cheering the Broho's victory and eagerly awaiting the northerners' death shrieks.

Abramm stared at them, panting. His left arm was weak and throbbing, the feyna scar alive again. His chest burned beneath the Terstan stone, and his broken ribs knifed him with every breath.

Crouching, he slid a dead man's sword free of its scabbard.

*"Kiriatha."* The word rose in a hushed murmur from the onlookers. "Kiriatha . . . Sheleft'Ai . . ."

The people stared slack faced now toward the arena behind them. Glancing back, Abramm saw the smoke clearing over two bodies, one in white, the other in green, sprawled on the sand where he and Trap had just fallen.

"It's an illusion," Trap murmured beside him. "To make them all think we're dead."

From somewhere in the warrens beyond the crowd, urgent shouts arose—soldiers coming to ensure the illusion became reality. Immediately a one-eyed man in a tan robe stepped forward, gesturing for them to follow him into the path now opening in the crowd. They did not hesitate. As a flurry of hands hurried them along, the soldiers' voices sharpened with anger, and not far away steel clashed against steel.

The robed man led them through a small door into dank darkness. From somewhere he produced a lantern to light their way and they descended an ancient, musty-smelling stairway so narrow they had to turn sideways in places to pass.

They emerged into a large, dark, mildew-smelling drainage pipe, where rats scurried from the light and water gleamed on the floor. A little way down the pipe, a series of footholds led up to a crawlspace that opened into an earthy-smelling grotto tucked under a massive oiled gear. Hanging the lantern on a peg driven into what appeared to be a wall of bedrock, their one-eyed rescuer turned to face them. In the flickering light Abramm could see a slit in the rock at his back.

"We're directly under the arena," said the man. "You'll be safe here for a time. I am Hanoch." He looked at them oddly. "You really are Kiriathan."

A grit of leather on stone and a rustle of cloth heralded a second lantern bearer, its glow preceding him through the slit. He drew up beside Hanoch and pulled down his face-veil, staring at them with the same expression as his companion.

"They are northerners," he said finally.

"The prophecy doesn't say the Deliverer is specifically Dorsaddi," Hanoch said. "And you can't argue Sheleft'Ai didn't rescue them."

"How're your ribs?" Trap asked, close at Abramm's side.

"Could be better." In truth, though he could hardly breathe, he was more concerned about the fire on his chest, terrified of what he might find there after that eruption of Terstan power.

"And the spore?"

"I can fight if I have to."

"You shouldn't if things go as planned," Hanoch said.

The other man was still staring at them, slack faced. "They slew Beltha'adi's champion and lived," he whispered. "It really is coming to pass."

A slow chill slid up Abramm's back, as the stone hanging from his neck burned anew against his stinging chest.

"Yes, and they did not do it without injury," said Hanoch pushing a barrel forward from the shadows. "Here. Sit and let us tend your wounds."

"What do you mean 'planned'?" Trap asked. "How could you know we would escape?"

Hanoch glanced reprovingly at his companion. "Some of us had more faith than others. You won't be the first slaves to disappear from the warrens of the Val'Orda, merely the most famous. Sit."

"We don't have much time," Trap said, sitting. "They'll be able to sense our power."

"This won't take long."

A woman and another man slid through the opening, carrying a water bag, bowl, and bundle of clothing. As they set about tending the wounds and washing the paint from the northerners' faces, Hanoch outlined the plan. In the riot's confusion they would slip out of the Val'Orda and across the city to where an old bolthole tunneled beneath the outer wall.

"We haven't used it in years," Hanoch told them, "and the old cart path in the cliff where it comes out is in bad shape. Part of it's been blasted away completely, but we drove iron pins into the rock so you can skirt it with ropes. The greatest danger is the magic. There's what looks like a tunnel bypass right before you get to the blast. Enter that and you won't get out."

To Abramm the thought of negotiating the sheer cliffs outside Xorofin with nothing more than iron pins and ropes was only slightly more appealing than fighting his way free of the city by open confrontation. Despite what he'd said to Trap, his right shoulder was already stiffening and his chest still hurt like wildfire, even with the pain-dulling salve the woman had slathered onto it.

They exchanged their fighting costumes for homespun tunics, britches, and boots, then the rings were cut from their ears, their hair dusted with powdered charcoal, and darkened lard smeared on their faces. Dark head-cloths and overrobes completed the disguise, and soon they were wriggling back into the drainpipe where more Undergrounders awaited.

"We'll take them out the east door," one said. "Crowd's moving fastest there, and it's fairly quiet."

"What about the lioness?"

"Still free—roaming somewhere in the north sector."

"Where's Tola?"

"Here, sir." A tall blond man raised his hand. With his pale skin, aquiline features, and the three gold rings in his ear, he bore a fair resemblance to Abramm.

Hanoch glanced round at the rest of them. "You all know what to do?"

Murmured assent echoed off the stone.

"A moment, Hanoch," came a familiar female voice from the rear of the group.

Pressing through the gathering, she stopped before Abramm and threw back her hood.

"Shettai?" Abramm cried.

"What are you doing here?" Hanoch demanded.

Shettai ignored him, her eyes on Abramm, looking up at him wonderingly. There was something uncomfortably close to worship in her expression. She touched his cheek. "You *are* alive," she whispered. "There were rumors, but I saw your bodies in the arena. . . ."

And then she was in his arms, embracing him fiercely. He reeled with the feel of her, everything else momentarily lost in the wonder of rediscovering what he thought he'd never have again.

"We have no time for this," Hanoch said sharply. "Why are you here, Shettai?"

She drew back, tears shining on her face, and stepped out of Abramm's embrace to face the Underground leader. "I will go with them."

Stillness overtook the gathering.

Hanoch's dark brows beetled. "Are you sure?"

"They will need a guide."

"Yes, but you—"

"I have not forgotten the way." She smiled wistfully. "And I have been with Katahn too long. It is time for me to face my past."

Hanoch looked at her long and hard, then nodded. "They could have no better guide than you, my lady. Let us go."

The corridor outside the east gate was clogged with people waiting to get out, forced by the guards to bare their heads and faces as they exited by twos. The guards looked tired and bored, eager to get the crowd on its way and not looking very closely.

Nevertheless, when Abramm stepped up and pulled off his headcloth, his heart pounded a frantic rhythm. The guard glanced at him, passed him on—

Then called him back, looking intently into his eyes.

Balanced on the edge of the puzzlement in the man's expression, Abramm debated whether he should make a run for it or hope the guard would pass it off. But before either man's uncertainty crystallized into decision, someone shoved him hard from behind, knocking him into the guard and running past them both.

"The Kiriathan!" the other guard yelled, pointing at the runner. "He's getting away!"

Abramm was shoved frantically aside as the two chased the fugitive down, wrestled him to the pavement, and ripped off his robe. Abramm glimpsed blond hair and the flash of honor rings as the crowd, left unrestrained, surged forward on its own, blocking his view. Not knowing how to redon the veil and headcloth, he didn't. Struggling to stay with Shettai and Trap, he let the crowd carry him out into the plaza. A series of covert connections followed—a narrow alley, a trapdoor in a cobbler's shop, and a cramped, bone-crunching ride across town in the false bottom of a cart—ending an hour later in a cellar near the city's north wall, where they would wait until dusk to use the bolthole.

During that time, the city had grown increasingly quiescent under tightening martial law. A curfew was imposed, the city gates were barred, and a systematic search of houses begun, ostensibly for rebel agitators, though their hosts assured them they would be gone long before any soldiers showed up at their cellar.

Now Abramm sat with his back braced against an earthen wall, knees drawn up, eyes closed, trying to ignore his many aches and pains, of which the feyna scar had become paramount—a hot, writhing presence in his arm. He caught himself fingering the Terstan stone again and made himself stop, dropping his hand to his lap. In the hours since his escape from the arena he had developed a fascination for touching it, obsessed with its oily-slick surface and faint vibration. Memory of the power that had come out of it, that had saved his life and delivered him from the Broho, still unnerved him. He'd been weak-kneed—even nauseated—with relief to find no Terstan shield burned into his flesh when it was over. Even now he wanted to fling the thing away, lest he end up marked yet. But the potential of being Commanded remained too great. He must wait until they escaped Xorofin. Then it was coming off. No question.

The door at the top of the stair creaked open, and Shettai descended with a round loaf and a wedge of white cheese. Settling beside him, she divvied up the bread.

"The woman said we can drink from the barrel there," she said.

"When do we leave?" Trap pulled out his dagger to carve slices from the cheese.

"Soon." Shettai handed Abramm a piece of dense, dark bread. "We'll need time to make it across the blast area before it's full dark. They say there was a rockfall last spring that may cause trouble, too, but once we're past that, the rest is easy."

"Except for the veren." Trap balanced a slice of cheese on his blade tip and handed it to her.

"And a countryside crawling with soldiers," Abramm added. "To say nothing of Beltha'adi's infamous intelligence system, assuming the rumors about that are true."

It was said the Supreme Commander commanded the forces of nature, that he used the birds for ears and eyes and had conjured corridors through the etherworld to transfer agents, even whole squadrons, across great distances of land or sea in moments.

"They're true," Shettai said grimly. "But we have learned to compensate. And once we reach the SaHal—"

"The SaHal?" Abramm broke in, alarmed. "We're not going to Ybal?" As the northern and easternmost of Esurh's archipelagic port cities, Ybal stood closest to the Thilosian-held island of Tortusa, offering by far the likeliest prospect of finding a vessel to take them north.

"Ybal?" She looked at him as if he had suggested they go for a stroll in the plaza. "You are the Deliverer. You must go to Hur and reawaken the Heart."

"Reawaken the . . . What are you talking about? What heart?"

"The Heart of the ancient Wall of Fire, set in place centuries ago by

Sheleft'Ai to protect us. Beltha'adi extinguished it when he invaded. The prophecy says you will raise it again and the Dorsaddi will regain their stronghold, from which they'll drive the Evil One out of Esurh."

Abramm glanced at Trap, uneasy but intrigued. Though he had no idea how this heart might be awakened, the notion carried undeniable strategic appeal. An impenetrable Dorsaddi stronghold in the heart of Beltha'adi's empire would surely disrupt his plans of conquest and thus ultimately benefit Kiriath. Still, as far as he knew, the Wall of Fire was legend, and he was absolutely certain he was not the one to awaken it.

Then, recalling what Katahn had told him last night, he shook his head. "It's already too late. Beltha'adi's pulled two full Hundreds off the Andolen front. They're probably invading the SaHal as we speak."

Shettai smiled. "Shemm will learn what has happened here soon enough. He'll hold them off until we get there."

"Shemm?" Abramm asked.

"My brother."

Trap's brows flew up. "Your brother is a Dorsaddi commander?"

She smiled slightly. "My brother is the Dorsaddi king. And has been almost as long as I've been a slave." Her eyes dropped to the talisman on Abramm's chest. "Knowing that Sheleft'Ai has not abandoned us will give new strength to my people. They will fight as they have not fought in decades." Her smile grew positively wicked. "And the SaHal is not so easy a place to invade."

He shifted uncomfortably. This Deliverer thing was growing less appealing by the moment. The thought of people giving their lives in a delaying action just so he could arrive and fail to do what they were all relying on him to do was not a happy prospect.

Trap spoke up. "If that is the prophecy, then surely Beltha'adi will expect us to go there. How can we—"

"There are many ways into the SaHal," Shettai said. "He does not know all of them."

"And that's where you come in," Abramm said.

She nodded. "That and the fact that my kinsmen tend to kill outsiders first and ask questions after. Particularly when they are being invaded."

"Even knowing the Deliverer is coming?" Trap asked.

"They would trust Sheleft'Ai to see him through safely."

"Great," Abramm muttered.

Shettai shrugged. "But I will be with you, and I will know the signs to make." She smiled at him. "You see, Sheleft'Ai *has* provided a way for you."

He exchanged a dubious glance with Trap. For a moment no one spoke. Then the Terstan stood and took their cups to the wine barrel. As the trickle of falling liquid filled the chamber, Abramm asked how she'd escaped Katahn.

She brushed breadcrumbs from her lap, then folded her legs tailor style. "When you blew the arena doors open, everything went crazy. Katahn turned away, caught up by what was happening. Chaos swirled around us, and suddenly I saw myself free to walk away."

"Surely you've had such opportunities before," Trap said, returning with the cups and passing them round.

"Opportunity, yes, but little desire." She drank, then held the cup with both hands in her lap. "I've been defiled in my people's eyes. By our code, I should have killed myself long ago. I lacked sufficient courage, I suppose."

"Or maybe you have too much," Trap said.

She looked at him dead on, unwavering for a long moment, then shook her head. "You are a northerner. What is honor to you?"

"A little more sensible than Dorsaddi honor, it would seem. If we'd followed your code, your Deliverer would be dead now."

"He is not a woman," she said bluntly.

Trap blushed as red as Abramm had ever seen him.

"My people will have branded me unclean," she went on. "Forgotten. There is every chance they will kill me themselves once they realize who I am."

*"Kill you?"* Abramm cried. "Well, then, you're not going."

She smiled at him, clearly unimpressed by his edict. "I hope that by bringing them the Deliverer I might atone sufficiently to remain alive."

Abramm was already shaking his head. "Absolutely not. It's too great a risk. What if they don't agree?" *And what will they do when I fail to light their stupid Heart?* "You're not going."

"I won't lose you again, Pretender," she said softly. "Where you go, I go." For a moment all the fire of her love blazed in those wonderful eyes, and his protests died as emotion filled his throat and chest. *What did I ever do to deserve her?* he wondered, and then he had to back away, lest such thoughts lead him into an abyss of sentiment that would undo him.

Her gaze dropped to the orb on his chest. "You *are* the Deliverer, you know," she said staring at it. "You must not doubt that any longer."

Her words were an exceedingly effective check to his galloping emotion. He frowned, wishing again that she wouldn't keep going back to that subject and that she wouldn't look so . . . *fanatical* when she did. Most of all he wished she'd stop staring at the talisman that way, for it reminded him entirely too much of Whazel.

He got up to refill his cup from the wine barrel, breaking the spell. Thankfully after that she spoke no more of prophecy and was content to sit beside him, close under his arm, head on his chest. As Trap stretched out for another of his naps, Abramm lost himself in the wonder of being alive and having her to hold in his arms. Though he tried to keep it back, his mind insisted on traveling into all manner of delightful futures, every one of which involved her at his side, slave no longer, but wedded wife, the mother of his children, the light and power of his life. With her beside him, he felt there was nothing he could not do.

Their contact arrived some time later, handing out bags of food and water, a coil of roughly twisted rope, a sling and pouch of stones for Shettai, and the two pairs of swords and small fishnets Abramm and Trap had requested for themselves.

"There's been a patrol nosing around the bolthole opening," the man told them as they divvied up his offerings. "So I'm afraid you're leaving a little later than we'd hoped."

"Where is the opening, anyway?" Trap asked, settling the rope so it looped over his shoulder and across his chest.

"Not far." The man handed Abramm a shuttered lantern as the latter finished tying one of the nets around his waist, then crossed the cellar to a stout wooden door, heavily barred. "You'll turn left outside and go to the end of the alley. There's an old, stone guard shack, long abandoned. The passage is inside. Not too far in you'll find what appears to be a cave-in, but if you keep to the right you'll see a passage through it. From there it's straight to the old cart path." He unbarred the door and pulled it open. "Sheleft'Ai be with you, my friends."

CHAPTER

# 26

They found the bolthole and the passage through the cave-in without incident, crawled on hands and knees through the cramped opening, and emerged easily on the other side. From there the ancient tunnel sloped down to a narrow crack framing the dim, gray light of the outside world. Shettai slipped through first, Trap squeezing after her. Putting out the lantern and setting it aside, Abramm sidled through the gap to join them on a ledge cut into the side of the gorge that separated North Xorofin from Old Xorofin. Sheer rock walls plunged inches from his feet to the narrow cove below, where houseboats floated on black glass, their multicolored fish-bladder lanterns spangling the gathering gloom. On the far side, the northern city's crenellated walls disappeared into mist, and to the left loomed the dark bulk of the iron bridge spanning the gap between the cliffs. Disgruntled travelers packed its length, frustrated by the unexpected closing of the old city.

"This way," Shettai said, scampering goatlike down the slender spur that led to the wider cart path below.

At Trap's gesture, Abramm went next, reflecting grimly that calling this thing a cart path was a grave misnomer. As he walked, his right shoulder brushed rough rock even as the left hem of his robe swung over the edge of the abyss, filled with cool, salt-scented updraft. He fixed his eyes on Shettai and the time-eroded track ahead of her and tried not to think of all those eyes on the bridge behind him, nor the fact that somewhere in the mists above veren glided on the updrafts, searching for their scent. It was said veren could detect their quarry more than a league away.

The trail snaked around uneven walls, and they rounded a bend to find the false tunnel Hanoch had warned about, gaping in a fold of stone across from them. Other openings peppered the wall above it, and Abramm realized they must be tombs. Just beyond the tunnel a huge yellow slash in the rock eradicated all sign of the trail. That would be where the pegs were.

Before they faced that, though, they had to negotiate the newer rockfall, where a slab had peeled away from the cliff face below the trail, reducing the path to a scant two feet in width for a distance of about ten strides. At the far end it narrowed to less than a forearm, but that was only for a few strides before the path widened again.

Abramm eyed the narrow part reluctantly. If the veren came while one of them was stuck on that, it would be disastrous.

Shettai faced the cliff and shuffled sideways along the ledge, careful but moving quickly, her grace and balance never more in evidence. As she reached the narrowest part and slowed, Abramm faced the wall himself and edged out along the constricted section, feeling for handholds. His nose brushed the stone, the smell of iron strong and biting. At his back, air filled his robes, the fabric tugging gently at his shoulders as it lifted.

Shettai reached the far end and turned back to watch.

Abramm was fifteen feet from her when the ledge dropped away beneath him, leaving him to cling with fingers and the balls of his feet. Briefly he imagined plummeting into the depth behind him, floating like a bird for a few glorious moments, then crashing upon the rocks like a rag doll. His stomach knotted, and sweat dribbled down his side. Banishing such thoughts, he forced himself to concentrate on feeling for grooves and handholds in the gritty stone, on moving no matter what. Behind him, Trap's scabbarded blade scraped against the stone, marking his progress.

Shettai had just reached the point where the ledge finally widened again when a hair-raising screech reverberated up the canyon.

"Torments!" Trap hissed behind him. "That didn't take long!"

Shettai looked up past Abramm, and her face went white. He clenched his teeth and breathed deeply, slowly, blotting out everything save the need to move and feel for holds.

Air whooshed around him, and he sensed the creature's bulk, heard a hissing throb of wingbeats. Then it was gone.

"It's circling back," Shettai hissed. "Hurry!"

Abramm planted his left foot on the wide ledge and lurched up beside her. A heartbeat to gain his balance, and he swung round, the sword hissing from its sheath as his free hand untied the net from his waist.

Here it came, bursting out of the mist, bigger than he was by twice and heading straight for them. He shook out the net, feeling as if he were armed with a broomstraw and cheesecloth. Maybe the Terstan talisman would help him again.

The dark wings flared wide to brake, ebony talons reaching for his face. Then, just as he moved to snap up the net, Shettai flung herself unexpectedly in front of him, straight into the creature's grasp. With a bellow of horror, he shoved her aside, stabbing blindly into a thick, scaly leg. His sword point punched through tough skin into tougher cartilage as an odd cold sizzle rushed down his arm. White light blazed at his chest and the veren launched itself off the wall with a scream, ripping the sword from Abramm's hand.

A dark wing slammed into him, hurling him against the cliff wall in a flash of re-ignited agony. He bounced off the stone and went down gasping, trying to throw himself forward as he scrambled for a hold—and found it. He came to a painful stop with one hand jammed into a vertical crack along the ledge's outer edge, the other closed around a sharp, rocky upthrust. One leg was hitched up over the ledge, while the other dangled over awesome space.

Dizzy with the pain and loss of breath, he held very still, gasping, shaking, his heart chattering in his chest. On the ledge before him Shettai huddled against the wall a good five strides up the trail, her dark hair in disarray. Her back was to him, and she appeared to be doing something to her chest. Blood was everywhere.

"Abramm!" Trap called. "Can you move?" Abramm heard a grit of stone behind him, a rattle of scabbarded steel, and realized Trap still clung to the cliff wall and that he himself lay in his way.

Something dark passed behind him, just at the edge of vision. Clawing with legs and feet, he dragged himself onto the ledge and scrambled forward. Trap jumped the last few feet and Abramm caught him, the two of them twisting aside as a blast of air and the sense of the veren's presence warned of attack.

Abramm's net had gone over the edge when he'd fallen, but now Trap was pulling his own free and handing it over as he drew both sword and dagger. Abramm whirled to snare the outstretched talons as Trap plunged his blade into the dark breast, showering them with black blood. A jerk of the net pulled the veren off course and the thing bowled into them, screaming, flapping wildly, then falling away, taking the net with it.

"I hit it too low," Trap said as Abramm peered over the edge after it. "It'll be back."

Sure enough it twisted round as it plummeted toward the dark water, the wings righting themselves, gaining purchase on the air, pulling out of the dive. Abramm stepped back and tore off his overrobe, the garment spattered and streaked with red and black. A glance over his shoulder showed him Shettai had not moved but was no longer beating at her chest.

"We've got to get to the tunnel," Trap said.

Abramm looked at him in alarm. "Hanoch said it was false. That we'd never get out if we entered."

"Better that than this. We need broadswords. Better yet, battle axes."

A great shriek erupted from the bridge, where many of the travelers had climbed up onto the girders for a better view of the contest, their pale forms cluttering its dark lines like an infestation of brinybug. More forms and faces crowded the top of the cliff wall across the way. Many were pointing as they shrieked warning, and Abramm turned to find the veren coming in for its third pass. This time, instead of diving and grabbing at them, it landed on the ledge in front of Shettai and ran toward them, beating at them with its free wing and jabbing its bare, knobby head, trying to spear them with its beak or drive them back off the edge.

They had fought long enough together that they needed no words to communicate. Abramm snapped out with the robe to distract and confuse as Trap charged in, catching the flailing wing with his dagger and lunging in with the sword. But though the blade drove deep into the creature's massive breast and loosed a stream of black blood, it seemed to have no effect beyond enraging the thing.

Flinging the robe at the furiously jabbing head, Abramm leapt in and grabbed it, hands closing upon the hard, pointed beak. As the veren reared back, lifting him off his feet, white light flashed at the corner of his eye and he saw the steel of Trap's blade—now buried nearly to its basketed hilt in the veren's breast—ablaze with Terstan power. Screaming its rage, the veren shook Abramm off, freed itself of the blinding robe, and loomed up over them, wings half open, eyes burning with red fire, beak gaping, A steady stream of black blood poured onto the white blade, some sizzling into acrid smoke where it touched the fiery metal, most flowing on over the basket and down Trap's arm.

The veren's eyes flared again, then suddenly dimmed as the vigor drained out of it all at once. Its wings sagged, its beak lurched drunkenly, and it reeled back off the blade to stand swaying and dazed, its narrow tongue fluttering in the gaping beak. The knobby head turned to fix them with a strangely human hazel eye, recalling to mind the legends that claimed veren were manufactured from men gone too far in Shadow to redeem. Then the whole beast shuddered, threw back its head, and fell face forward on the trail. It gave one last twitching convulsion, then lay still. Trap leapt to its side, plunging his blade into it one more time, just to be sure.

It was well and truly dead.

They heaved a simultaneous sigh of relief, looked at one another with the same sober satisfaction, then shoved the carcass off the trail, watching it plummet to the cove below. As the dark water swallowed it in a ring of white froth a triumphant roar arose from the bridge where the people waved their arms and cavorted in celebration.

*The White Pretender and his Infidel live on,* Abramm thought grimly.

Then he remembered Shettai.

She huddled in a fold of rock beside the cliff face. Blood soaked her robes and stained the wall behind her. A great puddle of it shimmered on the ledge around her, and she was very still, very pale.

Abramm knelt in her blood and touched her gently. She turned her head to him, her dark eyes glazed. For a moment she struggled to focus, and when she succeeded, smiled slightly.

"Deliverer," she whispered. "Go . . . awaken the Heart. . . ." Her gaze fixed on the Terstan orb he still wore. A crease formed between her brows. Staring intently, she lifted a blood-smeared hand to the talisman, the chain tugging against his neck as she grabbed it. He felt a flare of warmth, and her face went slack, her eyes widening. The surprise gave way to a joy and light so vibrant he thought the stone's power was healing her.

"So beautiful . . ." she whispered. "He's so . . ."

Then her hand fell away and she sagged against the cliff, her head listing sideways, eyes open but vacant, the little smile still on her lips. And on her chest, gleaming between the ravaged edges of her tunic, lay a bright golden shield, burnished into the skin over her heart.

Abramm slumped back onto his heels. The mist had closed in all of a sudden, blotting out everything but the beautiful hair, the pale, regal face, the full lips. . . . The eyes looked wrong, though. Staring like that. He closed them gently. Now she was just sleeping. He felt like sleeping, too, but he was so cold. So bone-achingly cold.

The mist crept closer, narrowing around her face and layering a thin veil across it.

He drew a sudden gasping breath that was almost a sob and realized he was shivering and that his bruised shoulder throbbed with a hot agony matched only by the fire in his forearm. His chest ached so fiercely he could hardly breathe, and all over his arms and face little points of searing pain sang in counterpoint.

The changing tenor of the cries from the bridge roused him—no longer celebration but warning again—and he turned in time to see a dark form slide out of sight into the misty ceiling.

A second veren, of course. Beltha'adi had probably sent every one of his pets on the chase. He absolutely could not afford to let the northerners slip through his fingers. Bad enough they'd escaped the Val'Orda.

He heard Trap speaking, but it was as if he were a long way off. "We've got to . . . the tunnel, my lord."

*Yes. The tunnel.*

Why didn't he care? He turned back to Shettai, suddenly immensely weary, almost hoping—

"Abramm!" Trap's hand closed on his arm, jerked him around. Abramm blinked at the other man, and it dawned on him how bad the Terstan looked.

His face was gray, his eyes glazed. His right arm, covered with blood and black ichor almost to the shoulder, was already hideously swollen. Now, as if the effort of rousing Abramm had cost him his last bit of strength, he swayed back against the wall, shaking his head as if he were dizzy.

"What's the matter with you?"

"The veren's blood is poison. Like griiswurm, only worse." Trap shuddered violently. "I can't heal it here. The tunnel is our only chance."

Abramm glanced toward the bridge behind—its occupants still screamed with excitement and fear—then ahead to where the cart path ran into the false tunnel.

In their present condition, they could not go back the way they had come. And negotiating the iron-pegged slash was unthinkable. Trap was right—the false tunnel was their only hope, and not much of one. "Can you walk?"

For answer the Terstan pushed himself upright, refusing Abramm's help and cautioning him against touching the black slime. As he started off, Abramm paused beside Shettai, then snatched up his discarded cloak and bent to gather her up in it.

Though Trap had looked barely able to move, the Terstan surprised him once again, seeming to have tapped into one last reserve of speed and agility. Abramm, burdened with Shettai, fell quickly behind. Her weight pulled savagely at his shoulder, his every breath sent knife cuts of agony through his chest, and his legs wobbled maddeningly. By the time Trap disappeared into the tunnel mouth, Abramm had only covered half the distance. But he wouldn't leave her body to be picked at by the birds or, worse, collected by the soldiers and impaled beside the city gates. Somehow he, too, called on his last reserves and crossed the distance.

The opening loomed just ahead when another screech bounced off the stone, so close and loud it made his ears ring. He didn't look back, just drove himself on, only four more steps, only three, only two. . . .

He heard the hiss of the veren's wingbeats, felt its bulk close upon him as he dove through the opening, startled by a sharp, sluicing coldness, as if he had passed through a waterfall. Barely maintaining his balance, he stopped in his tracks as he found himself in complete darkness. Gasping and wheeze-moaning, he turned back. The opening was gone.

Unnerved, he squatted to lay Shettai on the ground, then put out a hand, feeling for the emptiness that must be there—and knocked his knuckles against cold, unyielding stone.

Careful to keep contact with Shettai, he launched a wider exploration. Trap lay unmoving not far ahead, his skin hot and slick with sweat and blood and the veren's awful ichor, which in here smelled strongly of burning flesh. The tunnel was indeed a trap, a small prisonlike chamber, bounded on all six sides by solid rock, its floor cluttered with rocks and many, many bones.

He groped around the entire chamber twice more before he finally sat down, knees crowded to his chest, Shettai on his left, Trap on his right, the Terstan's shoulder, already hot with fever, digging into his calf. Fingers pressed to his friend's throat found a rapid, fluttering pulse. Trap was not doing very well.

Nor was Abramm, for that matter. *"The veren's blood is poison."* In addition to his other injuries, he realized he was now growing sick himself. Soon he would be little better off than Trap.

He leaned his head back against the stone and exhaled a bitter sigh. To have come this far, fighting free of the Broho, escaping Xorofin, killing the veren—all that only to die like trapped rats? It was not fair. There was no sense in it.

No sense.

And Shettai was dead.

He grew aware of her cooling flesh against his elbow and hip, and suddenly the cold ache of horrible loss lashed him with an intensity that made all his other ills seem as nothing.

Memory flailed at him: Her dark eyes fierce as she flung herself between him and the veren's talons; her soft kiss this morning; the tearful joy with which she'd met him in the drainage pipe after his escape from the Val'Orda; the afternoon, months ago now, when she had so seriously and carefully explained the difference in usage between two very similar forms of greeting, as if understanding that was the most important thing in all the world. He heard again the soft, startling melody of her laugh, saw the regal, bemused smile with which she'd so consistently regarded him—until last night, when she'd told him she loved him.

Like an avalanche it swept upon him, carrying him over the edge of that inner precipice of grief and sorrow. Suddenly he was weeping, his voice ripping from his throat in harsh, wracking sobs that lanced fire through his chest.

*Ah, sweet Fires, Eidon! If you live, why have you done this to me? After everything else! Why this? I don't understand. I don't understand at all.*

He dropped his head into his hands, digging his fingers into his scalp as if they might drive away the anguish.

*"She is with me. And you, Abramm, son of Meren, remain alive to choose."*

He stiffened, the soft hiss of his indrawn breath sharp in the silence around him.

Slowly he looked up. Trap still lay unconscious, but already his flesh glowed faintly with the power of his healing. Barely visible in the darkness beyond him stood a man of average height, dressed in linen tunic and a heavy robe scrolled with interwoven vines. His face, which Abramm saw clearly, when the lack of light should have prevented it, was scarred and misshapen, but his brown eyes—*How can I tell they're brown?*—gazed at him with an expression of heart-melting tenderness.

He blinked, and the man vanished, leaving a track of tingles up the back of his spine. He blinked again but saw nothing more, aware now that he had become very warm, that sweat slicked his brow and chest, and his arm throbbed a tooth-jarring rhythm that overlaid all his other pains.

*Plagues!* he thought. *I'm hallucinating already.*

And then his stomach tore at his middle as if it had claws, and he doubled over, groaning, lurching across the chamber to find a place to be sick without befouling Trap.

CHAPTER

# 27

The line of people seeking exit from Xorofin the next morning shuffled forward toward the gatehouse, bringing Carissa alongside the two bodies which had been impaled there. Morbidly she looked up at them, pulling at her face mask to align the eye holes.

One wore green, the other white, the silk charred, the bodies themselves hacked and burned. Meridon's face was swollen, his eyes burned out. All that remained to identify him clearly were the freckles and curly red hair.

The Pretender's face they had left intact, aside from burning out his eyes. Smudged still with paint, its handsome aquiline features looked strangely peaceful in death, despite the flies that crawled across it. It was most definitely not Abramm.

But then, she'd known it wouldn't be.

They'd been unable to leave last night as Cooper had hoped. The city gates were sealed long before they ever managed to fight their way through the chaos to the nearest of them. There'd been nothing to do but return to their room at the inn to wait for morning and pray somehow the place would be spared a thorough search.

Philip had wanted to go out alone with the dog, until Cooper had pointed out that if he were caught, the Esurhites could use Newbold themselves to find his brother. Or worse, Philip might inadvertently lead them to their quarry himself.

The boy had seen reason, but he hadn't liked it, certain as he was that Meridon had escaped. Nor was that the only certainty he embraced. "I believe the Pretender is your brother," he'd said firmly, almost the moment they had resolved the matter of his going back out.

She'd stared at him blankly, the words hardly registering at first. After the torture and excitement of what had been a very long night and day, she was reeling with exhaustion. When she finally did understand what he meant, her brain didn't know what to make of it, so she just continued staring at him.

"I think he was down there today," the youth went on. "That the man they say is a prince of Kiriath really is."

"Abramm was a scholar, not a warrior, boy," Cooper said gruffly.

"He is a Kalladorne," Philip retorted. "And the way Trap went to him, protected him when he was down—I don't think he would have done that if it wasn't the prince under all that paint."

"He's been partnered with the Pretender for eighteen months," Cooper countered. "They're probably friends. Why wouldn't he go to his aid?"

Philip frowned at him. "Why are you so eager to deny it could be him?"

"Because I knew him. And he was weak and sickly."

"He could have changed—"

"He would have died long before."

"But—"

Cooper slammed a palm on the low table. "Enough, boy! The Pretender is *not* Prince Abramm, and we will have no more talk of it."

Philip's smoldering resentment had flared to flame. "Why are you so determined to keep us from finding him, Master Cooper? Did you swear an oath to the king that you'd not let us succeed?"

Cooper went dead white, an expression Carissa recognized as one of deep fury.

"Philip, you're overstepping here," she interjected.

"Am I? All the while he's been in charge, we haven't gotten close enough to even glimpse the most famous men in Esurh until now. You expect me to believe it was nothing more than bad luck?"

"Oh, Philip, what possible reason could he have for doing any such thing?"

"I already told you—he's the king's man."

"Nonsense."

"And what about that business back in Vorta with Danarin? You never did explain that, Master." His gaze shifted back to Cooper. "What did you pay him for on the eve of the contest?"

"I paid him for his services as our guide and interpreter. You don't think he came with us for free, do you?"

"And the next day he tells us the wrong time, tells us it wasn't Abramm or Trap at all when obviously it *was*."

"If anyone was the king's man," Carissa broke in wearily, "it was Danarin. I didn't trust him from the moment I met him. That's why we fired him."

"Yet still things went wrong, my lady. And it's not Danarin trying to convince you that the man we saw escape tonight is not your brother. Yet Master Cooper has fought us all the way. Always presenting some reason why we shouldn't go, why we can't do something, why—"

"Have you no thoughts for anyone but yourself, boy?" Cooper burst out, as angry now as Carissa had ever seen him. "Can you think of nothing but finding your own brother? Who has, according to you, escaped his slavery without your help. You should be rejoicing, and instead you torment this poor woman by raising false hopes that even you must see have no substance. And for what? Because you know that once she's convinced her brother is dead she'll go home, and you'll have no one to subsidize your own interests?"

Philip had stared at him, stricken, and Carissa saw the truth of Cooper's words written in his face.

"Your brother may be alive, boy," Cooper went on, more gently, "but hers is dead. Let her accept the truth in peace and get on with her grieving."

To his credit, Philip had backed off, looking chagrined and ashamed. There had been no more talk after that.

But long after the others had settled and the silence of deep night fell over them, Carissa had lain awake on her pallet, facing the wall and weeping in bitter acknowledgment of the truth. In time sleep did claim her, if only briefly, and she awoke feeling groggy and apathetic.

Breakfast had brought news that the bodies of the Pretender and Infidel now hung impaled inside the east gate, proof they had not escaped. Even so the rumors still flew—crazy stories about bodies made of mist and two men slaying a veren last evening on the cliffs of the Icthan Inlet. Many swore the two had used the same white fire as had defeated the Broho yesterday and that Beltha'adi was secretly combing the countryside in search of them and that that was why Xorofin's gates had been opened this morning.

Philip had lapped the stories up with such avidity it seemed to take all his willpower not to hop up and down and shout, "See! I told you!"

After the meal Cooper had gone to see about getting passage on a ship, only to find the harbor quarantined on account of an outbreak of plague. With the threat of plague adding to his concerns for Carissa's safety, he decided they would go overland to the port city of Ybal, some sixty leagues north by well-traveled, well-policed road. They'd walk as far as nearby Vedel and buy better transport there. The important thing now was to get out of Xorofin.

Carissa had listened to his plans and explanations without comment, content to let him make the decisions. All she wanted was to escape this horrid land. How that was accomplished mattered little.

Thus they had come to stand this morning in the line of travelers seeking exit at the east gate, filing along beneath the bodies of Beltha'adi's latest vanquished nemeses.

She now found herself staring at the golden shield on the imposter Infidel's chest. Not Meridon, perhaps, but some poor sap. Eidon certainly hadn't delivered him.

The pain in her throat sharpened, and she dashed away sudden tears as the line shuffled forward again. Beside her Philip sighed resignedly and turned from the display.

She felt a fluttering of pity for him, knowing he loved his brother as much as she loved her own. It had to be hard for him to give up. "It really is better this way, Phil," she said softly. "Think how he would feel, knowing you were here looking for him."

A wry smile twisted his lips. "He'd be furious."

"And it would be awful if you got yourself captured when he's just found his freedom."

"Aye." He made a disgusted face. "I've been a fool, I think. This is Eidon's fight, not mine. Wherever he is, Eidon will hold him."

Eidon. The name stirred new threads of bitterness. How many lives had Eidon ruined now? "I've been a fool, too," she murmured. "This whole trip has been such a waste."

"A waste?" His head came round, his blue eyes wide. "My lady, we've just witnessed the birth of a legend! The escape of the White Pretender and his Infidel from the great Val'Orda. It will spread across the land. It will be passed down through the ages. And we saw it. With our own eyes." He grinned up at the corpses. "I'll remember that fight for the rest of my life! It will be something to tell our children! Our grandchildren!"

The words only stabbed new pain into her heart, and suddenly she wanted to cry all over again.

At long last they reached the guardhouse and Cooper was handing over their traveling papers yet again. The guard looked them over cursorily, then gestured at Carissa and Peri.

"And these?"

"My wife and her servant."

The guard flicked a hand. "Lift their veils."

Cooper stared at him, his expression of outrage probably not much feigned. "Is this really necessary, sir?"

"No one passes that we have not personally laid eyes upon."

"I am Liakan Ingsolis," Cooper fumed. "Merchant of fine textiles and rare treasures. I am not a rebel, and I resent being treated like one. You may rest assured your commanding officer will hear of this. From *his* commanding officer."

"Nevertheless, I have my orders."

Cooper looked around as if hoping deliverance might somehow swoop out of the crowd. Yet the crowd itself held them in, cutting off escape. Resignedly he gestured to Peri, who quickly unveiled herself. With a grunt the man turned to Carissa. This time Cooper did the unveiling, lifting the cloth just enough to reveal her face, then quickly dropping it back into place.

It did not work. Frowning, the guard pushed him aside and lifted the veil himself, flipping it over her head to reveal her pale face and blond hair to all. A murmur of surprise arose around them.

"She's Kiriathan!" he declared delightedly. He leered at her, then at Cooper. "Kiriathans are quite in demand at the moment."

Cooper stood rigidly, white faced. "She is my wife, sir."

"Yes, and how much did you pay for her?" The guard laughed, then stroked her cheek with a rough finger. "A spilling handful, I'd say. She's a beauty."

Sudden fear cut through the veil of indifference that had held her since last night. Cooper stood poised at the edge of violence, Eber looming behind him as Philip pressed against her shoulder protectively, Newbold panting at his side.

"Come, pretty one," the guard said, gripping her arm. "The commander, I think, will like you."

A voice rose sharply from the crowd behind them. "Master Ingsolis! Liakan Ingsolis!"

They all turned as a tall, dark-bearded young man hurried up the line toward them. Though he wore the drab shadow-gray of the Army of the Black Moon, he was no soldier. He was, in fact, their former Thilosian first mate, Danarin.

"I was afraid I'd miss you," he said, bowing to Cooper. "Captain Hoag released me so I could escort you. Here are the papers." He handed them to the guard, then looked at Carissa. "Why is she unveiled? This is disgraceful!" Quickly he pulled the fabric back over her head and turned to the guard. "What is the meaning of this?"

"We were told to search everyone, sir."

"Rabble and commoners, yes. This is Liakan Ingsolis. Do you imagine he would be involved with rebel scum?"

The man paled. "I . . . I did not know, sir. He has no baggage, and I have never heard of Liakan Ingsolis. No offense, sir," he added to Cooper. "I am only a poor soldier."

"Very poor," Danarin snapped. "His baggage went through yesterday. His coachman was supposed to return for him last night, but of course no one could enter the city."

"Of course," the soldier said, his dark skin growing darker with embarrassment. He would not look at Danarin. "Uh . . . and where is your mount, sir?"

"In the stable. I will be riding in the coach with Master Ingsolis, you dolt."

"Of course, sir." The soldier folded both sets of papers together and passed them to Danarin. "Have a safe journey."

They hurried through the tunnel gate and down the dusty road outside. "What a story!" Cooper muttered as they strode past the other travelers, most of whom were busy repacking their things. "I'm astonished he believed it."

"Oh, they'll believe quite a bit if you wear the right uniform," Danarin said, smiling. "I can't believe you still have that old dog with you."

"Where did you get that uniform?" Carissa asked.

"Borrowed it, of course."

"Of course."

"The part about the coach was true, though," Danarin said. "Well, it's not a coach, it's a cart, but you're welcome to travel with us. Which way are you headed?"

"Ybal," Cooper supplied.

"On foot?!"

"We'll buy transport in Vedel."

Danarin was shaking his head. "Vedel's been hit with the plague, too, didn't you hear? I suspect that's where the outbreak in Xorofin came from."

"I heard it started in the Sorite sector."

"In any case, Vedel is closed. The only way north is to go around through Jarnek."

"But Jarnek's inland!"

"Yes. The old gateway to the SaHal. And unless you want to go overland without a road, it's the only remaining option. Assuming the plague hasn't spread there, too."

"I don't relish the thought of walking all the way to Jarnek," Cooper said.

"Well, you're welcome to come with me," Danarin said.

"Absolutely not!" Carissa cried, pushing around Cooper to confront the Thilosian. "You have dealt us enough blows. I'll not fall for your trickery again."

"Blows? Trickery? My lady! Why do you charge me with this injustice? Have I not just saved your life?"

"For that I am grateful, but do not think it will cause me to forget how you deceived us at Vorta."

Danarin looked completely flummoxed. "Deceived you? How, my lady?"

"Telling us the Pretender would perform at six when he was really performing at four."

He glanced at Cooper. "My lady, if I did, I do not recall it. It is possible I misspoke, I suppose. Things were confusing that morning. As I recall there was that dispute with the merchant of silks and brocades."

"He was trying to rob us," Cooper added. "Remember?"

She did not remember, because it had been Cooper who'd done the talking and in a language she had not understood. "I remember you arguing with a man. That's all."

"Perhaps I misheard Master Danarin in the confusion," Cooper added. "I was still not proficient in the Tahg."

"It was simply a misunderstanding, my lady," Danarin said. "And even had I done it apurpose, what good would it have done? Surely you could see them at the next contest."

She frowned, feeling confused. He was right, of course. A deliberate attempt at deception would have been pointless. And he had just saved her life. Moreover, if he had at least a cart and a traveling party, he was in better shape than she was, so why bother with her at all? Especially since the whole question of his being after Abramm had become moot.

His attractiveness made it difficult to hang tightly to her distrust. She was so relieved to have been delivered from the Esurhites, and he looked so . . . distressed.

She drew a breath. "Well, perhaps it *was* just a misunderstanding. I was very disappointed that day."

"And you have never trusted me." His dark eyes twinkled, and a corner of his mouth twitched upward. "Have you?"

"I trust very few," she said, lifting her chin.

"Will you come with us, then? It will be safer—the roads will be full of soldiers. This Dorsaddi thing is just beginning, I fear . . . and away from their chain of command, well, some of these men are not always as controlled as one would like."

She frowned at him, wanting to trust him, to like him unreservedly. "Very well. We will go. And thank you for your generosity."

CHAPTER

# 28

*It's my fault,* Abramm thought miserably. *It's all my fault.*

He sat with his back against the wall, clutching a talon-pierced, half-drained water bag. His companions—one dead, one alive—lay on the rock- and bone-strewn floor in front of him. The pale shimmer of the healing power now enwrapping the live one—Trap—enabled him to see them both. And to see clearly the solid rock walls that imprisoned them.

He had crawled reluctantly from the unconsciousness that had followed the vomiting to find his contact with the Terstan's healing session had again reaped unexpected benefits. His nausea was gone and the scar on his arm quiescent. And if his head still ached, it was from being slammed against the cliff. His other pains—shoulder, hands, and ribs—could also be attributed to plain physical abuse, though even they seemed lessened.

He had spent some time clearing away the rocks and bones to make a space where he could lay out Shettai's body properly. Carefully, stoically, he had positioned it on her cloak, straightening her limbs and arranging her glorious hair so that it covered most of the signs of the wound that had killed her, though he left her new Terstan shield in view. Then he sat looking at her, unable to tuck the robe over her as he'd intended.

If only the Terstan's power had washed away his guilt and grief along with the other wounds.

She was dead. Dead at his own hands as surely as if he had held the implement that killed her. If only he'd been quicker on that ledge. Quicker to see what she'd intended, quicker to bring the net to bear so she wouldn't have felt compelled to protect him. *Fire and Torment! What was she thinking? She had no sword, no chance at all!*

If only he hadn't allowed her to come, hadn't given in to his desires to have her with him, hadn't deluded himself with the notion that all would work out well because all had worked out well so far. He'd known what kind of odds they faced. Whatever was *he* thinking not to assume they'd be attacked by veren precisely where they were attacked?

If only he hadn't given in when she'd confessed her love for him. If he'd kept his wits about him then, realizing to let it go any further would only hurt them both, she'd still be alive. Never knowing he'd shared her love, she'd surely have stayed with Katahn, safe in Xorofin . . .

The accusations burned in his breast, adding layer upon layer of condemnation. He had sinned—against Eidon, against the Holy Words, against even the tenets of honor held by the true heroes of Kiriath. It was part of the hero's duty to protect the weaker sex, to honor their chastity and virtue, to acknowledge the rights of the men who were or would one day be their husbands. Yet he had spurned that, had lain with a woman not his wife, the beloved slave of his master, in fact. He had compromised her virtue and destroyed his own, all for the sake of satisfying his own lusts. And he dared to think himself a hero?

A sharp, new nausea rolled up in him, and he groaned, clutching the water bag to his chest as the misery intensified. *I should have died on that ledge, not her!* He deserved it, after all. Sin upon sin upon sin . . . Yes, he deserved it.

And from the look of things, he would be making due payment before much longer. They would most likely die of dehydration, since he had only found the one water bag between them, the others lost along with their food in the battle with the veren. They'd die, trapped like rats in a ship's wall, no deliverance accomplished, no awakening of the Dorsaddi's Heart. Just a quiet, ignominious end, attended and marked by no one. She died for nothing.

He groaned again, and at his feet, Trap stirred.

Abramm swallowed the sharp, hard lump lodged in his throat and wiped the tears streaking his face. Grimly he wrestled his emotions back under control.

Meridon sat up with a groan. A kelistar flared to life, and as always,

Abramm was unprepared for the way it captivated him. The light so clear and clean and beautiful, the sense of a thousand voices raised in joyful song, the warmth that reached down into his soul, spawning memories of sun-drenched afternoons in fields of golden, shimmering grass. For a moment it even overruled the grim specters of grief and guilt and despair that haunted his mind.

But only for a moment. Aware of the Terstan blinking blearily at him, Abramm tore his gaze from it, and the comfort vanished like a candle flame in a gale.

Trap frowned at the chamber around them. "Where are we?" His voice was hoarse, but as before, there was no sign of ichor, no sign of injury beyond the cuts and scrapes engendered by their encounter with the cliff face—and the contest in the arena before that.

Abramm handed him the water bag and, as Trap drank deeply, recounted the fight on the ledge. But when he came to Shettai's death he could not go on, overcome by a fresh wave of grief. It did not seem possible she was gone. Yet there she lay, unnaturally still and stiff, cradled in the cloak and rocks that would be her burial cairn.

His tale forgotten, he leaned forward to adjust the fall of her hair away from her face and, after a long moment of stroking the dark locks, leaned back again.

Trap was staring at the golden shield on her chest.

"She touched the talisman right before she died," Abramm explained.

Meridon's eyes climbed to meet his own. "She is truly free, then."

Abramm swallowed hard and turned aside, blinking back more tears, fighting to control himself, and hideously embarrassed by his failure. He could not speak at all, and long moments went by until finally he dropped his head into his hands and gave up.

"I am sorry, my lord," Trap said quietly.

Still with his head in his hands, Abramm let the grief roll through him. "I was the one who was supposed to die," he croaked. "Not her."

"Only Eidon can decide such things. And she is with him now," Trap went on. "Beyond the veil of tears and shadow, happier than we can imagine."

*"She is with me—"* the ghost-man had said.

But that was a hallucination. Had to be. No man could see Eidon and live. The Words said so. It was all just wishful thinking brought on by shock and the gathering storm of his reaction to the veren poison. It must be.

Mustn't it?

He grew abruptly aware of the Terstan talisman's warmth upon his breastbone. Simultaneously the spore in his arm writhed and a sudden inexplicable fear broke over him. He backed away from the disturbing notions that were presenting themselves.

Hallucination. Nothing more.

"If you could see her now," Trap said softly, "you would rejoice."

There was no doubt in his voice, only a rock-solid conviction that Abramm found himself envying. Even at his most devoted as a Novice Initiate, he did not think he'd ever believed as strongly as Trap seemed to. Now, though he believed almost nothing, the other's words brought comfort. Maybe they were true. If they were . . . it was a wonderful thought.

"Do you feel ready to move on yet, my lord?" Trap asked presently.

Abramm lifted his head. "Move on?"

"I doubt they'll send anyone after us. It'd be easier to box us in and let us die of thirst. We're supposed to be dead already, so this way they won't have to bother with any awkward rumors getting spread around."

Abramm eyed the walls surrounding them. "Where exactly did you have in mind to move on to?"

"We're trapped by illusions, my lord."

"I know that, but . . ." He touched the wall, hard and cold as ever. "What do you propose?"

"We'll just walk through it. But we'll go inward, rather than out. I've had enough verens for one day."

"Walk through it."

"Sure. Watch." Trap stood, still holding the water bag, and walked into the wall at the back of the chamber, the orblight left bobbing on the air currents disturbed by his passing. A moment later he reappeared, plunging back through the wall. "See?" he said. "Simple."

"What's on the other side?"

"More tunnel. Certainly a way out they won't expect us to take."

Tentatively, Abramm stroked the rock's surface. It was still hard and cold and rough.

"Here," Trap said, holding out a hand. "Take hold and I'll pull you through it."

Abramm glanced between hand and wall, then gave a skeptical nod. "Very well. Let me finish with Shettai first."

With great care and deliberation he wrapped the cloak about her, hesitating a long moment before he could bring himself to cover her face. Then, dry-eyed and numb, he covered her with a layer of rocks. Seeming to sense his need to do it alone, Trap made no move to help, watching him in patient silence.

At last it was done. Standing, he drew a deep breath and turned away. Trap held out his hand, Abramm took it, and they walked forward into the wall. The stone hit him hard enough to make his eyes water but gave way like soft butter as Meridon drew him on.

Then he stood at the Terstan's side looking down a dark tunnel. Trap had conjured a second orblight to replace the one that had not followed them through the illusion. Unlike the spell on the outer opening, this one worked both ways, for even though he'd just walked through it, the stone felt as hard and solid as any normal rock.

He frowned at his companion. "How did you know it was there?"

" 'His Light pierces the Shadow and destroys the constructions of evil,' " he quoted. " 'Where Light comes, Darkness must flee.' "

"That's from the Second Word."

"Aye."

Meridon conjured a third orblight, set it carefully against his shoulder—where it clung—and started off, leaving the other one drifting slowly to the ground behind them. After one last, long glance backward, Abramm followed him.

The tunnel was unremarkable, narrow and barely high enough for Abramm to walk upright. Periodic openings led into narrow, empty chambers whose use was at first a mystery. Then they found one that was not empty and realized they were tombs—possibly dating from pre-Cataclysm times when the Ophiran Empire still reigned. The thick layer of dust on the floor looked to have been undisturbed for centuries.

As the corridor wound on and on, tunneling ever deeper into the rock, Abramm began to worry that the only exit might be the way they had come in. When he expressed his concern to Trap, the latter admitted he, too, had considered that.

"But I don't think it's so. The tombs at the beginning were unused, remember, and the chambers few. We're passing lots more now, all used, which makes me think the front door's still ahead. I suspect the opening we came through was carved long after the bulk of the tombs were filled—making an easier way to get into the chambers at the rear."

What he said made sense, but Abramm's concern continued to nag him. With every turn of the tunnel and still no sign of the end, he grew more and more convinced they should turn back and take their chances on the cart path.

Assuming they could find their way back out.

Again he spoke to Trap, and again his friend insisted they were on the right track, that it wouldn't be long before they found the front entrance. But still his uneasiness mounted, spinning out a rising reluctance to go on. Fear nipped at him, cold and stomach-turning, as he grew steadily more convinced that disaster lay ahead. A dead end, a trap, an ambush by shadowspawn—perhaps even the veren awaited them at the end of this trek.

It disturbed him, too, that he walked among corpses, and he began to think perhaps he was already dead and just didn't realize it. A cold sweat broke out upon him, the spore throbbed in his arm, and repeatedly he made himself let go of the talisman around his neck.

Then it was upon them—the final chamber, dank, dark, with only a single opening—the one in which they stood.

At the realization of what it was and what it meant, panic nearly overwhelmed him. "See?" he croaked. "What did I tell you?"

"What do you mean?" Trap asked, starting into the chamber.

Abramm bit back a shout of warning, since he could already see by the orblight that the chamber was empty. There was no threat, no ambush, no reason to stand here paralyzed with a terror that could only be described as irrational.

Realizing Abramm had not followed him, Meridon turned back halfway across the chamber. "Why aren't you coming?"

"I don't need to. I can see the room's empty from here." Even his voice shook. His gaze swept the rough rock walls, wondering if one of them was another illusion, behind which the shadowspawn he still sensed waited to leap upon them.

Meridon was staring at him as if he hadn't the faintest idea why Abramm had said what he'd said.

"What do you expect to find in there, anyway?" Abramm asked. "It's obviously time to turn around and go back, as I've been saying all along."

This seemed to confuse his friend even further. Then the light dawned. "The entrance is right there in the far wall. I guess you can't see it."

"You mean it's another illusion?"

"Yes. Come on. I'll help you through it."

But still Abramm could not move, the sense of threat rolling over him with powerful, mind-numbing force. His head had grown light, his limbs weak and jittery, and all he could think was to run, to flee, to get away. Oddly, it all seemed vaguely familiar.

Trap was frowning at him again. "Well?"

"There's something in there. Something terrible. I . . . I can't go in." The small part of him that was still rational cringed at the words, railing at him for being a fool and a coward besides, but it did no good.

"I do feel something, now that you mention it," Trap murmured thoughtfully. "But it's—oh. It's the griiswurm." He gestured upward, and Abramm saw that what he had imagined to be shadow pools between rock teeth were actually dark, tentacled blobs. More of them ranged along the wall ahead, forming a grotesque archway on the rock.

"They're there to ward the opening," Trap said. "Here. Put your hand on my shoulder, and I'll lead you through. Maybe that'll offset the warding."

Even so, it took all Abramm's willpower to forge onward. He clung to Trap's shoulder with grim determination as they crossed the chamber and finally plunged through the lardlike illusion into the darkness of night. And the tantalizing aroma of frying onions.

Instantly the fear receded to a more manageable level, and Abramm let out a silent breath of relief—cringing with embarrassment to think what a fool he'd been. There was nothing to do but put it aside, however, so he concentrated on getting his bearings instead.

They stood on the crypt's crumbling porch at the head of a narrow, steep-walled canyon whose pale walls were pocked with other tomb openings. From where they stood at its head, the canyon narrowed rapidly, its walls almost touching where they bent round to the right. There, an unseen campfire's bronze glow reflected off the sparkling sandstone walls and illumined the misty ceiling. A horse's sneeze and stamping carried with low voices on the cold, dry air. The unseen fire crackled energetically, its smoke scent mingling with that of the onions, stirring up hunger pangs that could only be ignored.

Wordlessly the two men picked their way around the ratweed clumps growing on the canyon floor and crept up to the bend. Within ten strides, the narrow passage widened dramatically, emptying into a broad wash where an Esurhite patrol had set up camp. Four of them stood near the fire, at half attention, shivering visibly. A fifth stirred the pan he had set over the small blaze and stared periodically into the darkness beyond the wash. A jumble of supplies lay close at hand—kettle, utensils, food- and waterbags.

The patrol's horses were tied to a rope strung between two huge thronetrees beyond the wash's edge. Abramm considered and abandoned the notion of sneaking around the camp's perimeter to the animals. The men did not look dazed enough, and the fire's blazing light did not leave sufficient friendly shadows.

He glanced upward, where the walls loomed even closer, maybe only three feet apart.

Three men strode into camp from the darkness, apparently having inspected the perimeter, and at the sight of one of them, Abramm nearly hissed with disbelief.

No rank-and-file soldier, the man was short and broad, his shaven head gleaming over a distinctive hawklike nose, his ears shimmering with gold honor rings. It was the Supreme Commander, Beltha'adi ul Manus himself.

As he approached, the soldiers who had been waiting snapped to full attention and saluted. Ignoring them, he spoke sharply to the flat-faced man following him, who barked an affirmative and also saluted. Beltha'adi stared hard at him for a moment, then glanced toward the cleft where Abramm and Trap hid in the shadows. Abramm froze, horrified at having been discovered so easily, then relaxing when, instead of coming after them, the Esurhite commander pivoted, stepped briskly to a shiny spot on the sand beside the fire—and vanished in a column of red sparkles.

Abramm blinked and resisted the urge to rub his eyes.

Trap tugged at his arm, beckoning back up the canyon. They retreated into the tomb they had just exited, moving to a point across the final chamber where Abramm could be free of the griiswurm's aura.

"What do you think?" the Terstan asked as an orblight flared to life.

"I'm not sure," Abramm replied. "That must've been one of his etherworld corridors. If we're not careful, we'll have a whole lot more than one patrol on our heels."

"I don't think they can come through that fast," Trap said. "Generating the power to operate them is supposed to be quite draining. They'd need a number of priests at the other end or would have to send some through to this end, which would take time. And energy. Then they'd have to send the men . . ." He shook his head. "If we do this right, we should be well out of reach before then."

"You have an idea?"

Trap sighed. "Not really."

"Well, I do."

Half an hour later Abramm hung fifteen feet off the ground, back and feet braced against opposing rock walls, cracked ribs protesting the position with a vengeance. His left hand was full of pebbles. Trap hung a little way below him, holding more of the same. The pebbles had been the hardest part of the plan—everything was either solid rock or soft sand. By the time they'd found enough to serve their purpose, dawn suffused the misty sky.

The camp lay below him, four of the soldiers now asleep, with the captain stretched out under the thronetree; two played at Bones by the fire, and the eighth stood a sleepy watch just below Abramm's perch, his dark lashes drooping over gleaming eyes, jerking open, only to droop again.

*I hope he's not too wool-headed to take his cue,* Abramm fretted. Glancing over his shoulder, he could see one of the orblights Trap had planted at the base of a rugged crevice cutting up the canyon wall, where stairstepping rock formations promised an escape route. It was an empty promise, ending farther up in ten feet of unscalable rock. The guards had undoubtedly seen that when they arrived, which explained why they had posted no one at the tunnel opening—that and the force of the griiswurm, which Trap said likely affected the guards as powerfully as it did Abramm.

Still, they might be tricked into forgetting what they knew. The kelistars had been Trap's idea.

Abramm looked down at his friend and nodded. Trap glanced back up the narrow ravine, and the first orblight floated up from behind its concealing bush. He tossed a few pebbles near the cavern opening.

The sentry gave no sign he had heard. Abramm waved for more pebbles, heard the answering rattle. The Esurhite jerked upright—

But it was only to keep himself from dozing off. Abramm frowned. *And they call* us *slug-headed!*

He motioned to Trap again and this time heard a distinct hiss that seemed, impossibly, to originate from the mouth of the cavern. "Go! Go!"

This was followed by a sizable rattle of pebbles—Trap must have thrown his entire handful.

The guard whirled, eyes wide. He gurgled a cry and hurried into the crack, drawing his sword as he passed beneath Abramm. His fellows leapt to their feet, the Bones cast aside, hands on their own blades. They looked inordinately frightened.

And then Abramm realized who they thought they were facing—not two weary, wounded, and weaponless northerners but the White Pretender and his Infidel, whose reputations surely surpassed actual skill.

The first man passed beneath Trap now as the others kicked their companions awake and followed. Another rush of pebbles, this time to put out the raft of kelistars Trap had earlier sent rising into the first guard's view. Hopefully the darkness and tension would make them think someone was moving into the cut.

And so it did. The first guard rushed forward. "They're getting away! They're climbing the wall!"

His companions in the wash raced to his aid, yelling for the others to circle around to the top and cut off their quarry's escape.

Sounds of frantic scrambling echoed off the stone walls, and as the officer himself hurried under Abramm, Abramm jumped into the wash. He landed on his feet and rolled with the momentum as Trap came swooping after him. As the Terstan rolled likewise and came upright, he conjured a huge orblight and set it before the ravine's narrow opening. Abramm hurled his own handful of pebbles onto the dark rim above them, just beyond where the others climbed in frantic haste. He received a volley of urgent cries in response.

Trap kicked wet sand over the fire as Abramm felt through the food bags beside it. A furious bellow erupted from the cut. Those within had discovered the wall of light. When they did not immediately burst through it, Abramm glanced at Trap, smiling. The light was harmless, stopping no one, but apparently they did not know that.

His hand closed on a sack that squished and gurgled. He snatched it up and found it tied to another of its kind. Hefting the pair over one shoulder, he found another full of hardtack and ran for the horses, where Trap had parted the rope with his Terstan light. Already he sat astride a tall bay and held a black by its halterlead.

Abramm stuffed the neck of the bread sack into his belt and leapt for the black's side, gripping ebony mane to pull himself astride. Trap threw the lead at him, and he wrestled the horse around. Orblights flashed into being all around them, popping and vanishing as stirred air carried them against the thronetrees, and so spooking the remaining horses that they ran off into the dawn.

The men who had climbed the bluff came sliding and stumbling back, a chaos of dark figures, gleaming steel, and curses. Abramm and Trap laid heels to their horse's flanks and thundered away into the shadow-steeped dawn, Esurhite shouts of outrage and frustration fading behind them.

They kept the horses at a steady pace but gave them their heads, and around midmorning they reached a paved road. When the animals stepped onto it as if it were familiar territory and trotted easily northward, the men pulled them to a stop.

"They're probably running for home," Abramm said.

"And home's got to be Xorofin," Trap agreed. "So we don't want to go this way."

"Unless we make for Ybal."

Trap squinted up the road. "Aye."

Abramm's horse tossed its head, pulling the rope lead through his hands. He let it slide, then took up the slack as he scanned the barren hills beyond the road to the east. Out there somewhere lay the SaHal. "We have no guide now," he said, the exhilaration raised by their escape falling suddenly flat. "No one to show us the secret way in or guarantee us acceptance among the Dorsaddi."

"No."

"And Beltha'adi expects us to go there."

"Aye."

Ybal was the sensible choice. He could find a boat and leave this land behind. But then the White Pretender would be dead. At Beltha'adi's hand. And all he'd done, all he'd risked, all he'd given up—would be for nothing. *She* would have died for nothing.

"We *are* wearing Dorsaddi robes," Trap said, seeming, as he often did, to read Abramm's mind. "And she said they'd be waiting for us, so they might not kill us outright."

"We're not Dorsaddi, though, and I think most of them believe we are. Remember how surprised those Undergrounders were when they saw us?"

Trap grimaced.

"And what happens when we can't reawaken that Heart Shettai was talking about? What happens when the great revival they are counting on us to start doesn't come to pass?"

Meridon shrugged. "Maybe it will."

Abramm glanced at him as the horse sidestepped and tossed its head again. A wave of prickles cascaded down his spine. "You want to go there, don't you?"

The Terstan stared thoughtfully at the low hills tumbling away beneath the mist. "I think it's where we're meant to go." He glanced aside at Abramm. "And I think Eidon will make us a way."

Abramm drew up the slack on the halterlead again, suddenly and profoundly uneasy. That strange sense of destiny had hold of him once more, that sense that he was being moved around by forces greater than himself, a pawn on the board of life. A pawn who could do nothing to stop being a pawn.

*"Go,"* she'd said to him, *"awaken the Heart."*

She had died to give him that opportunity. To throw it away now, even if he didn't have the first notion of how he would do as she asked, was surely betrayal of the highest order. And did he not have enough on his conscience already?

"Very well," he said softly, reining his reluctant horse around. "The SaHal it is."

# THE DELIVERER

## PART FOUR

CHAPTER

# 29

They kept the horses to a brisk pace, following the road through a ravine-riddled landscape dotted with gray-green sage and squat, black-trunked thronetrees. Except for the road itself, there was no sign of human habitation—only lizards, scrawny rabbits, and an occasional raven, flapping and soaring through the fringes of the misty ceiling.

In the absence of any immediate threat, Abramm became increasingly aware of his abused flesh. His shoulder was stiffening to the point where he could hardly move his arm, and a deep soreness webbed across his chest to merge with the throb over his heart, where an oozing scab had formed. With no adrenaline to override the pain, he felt his cracked ribs with every breath. And after more than two days with no real sleep, it soon took all his willpower just to stay on the horse.

Presently Trap gestured at the bags dangling from Abramm's waist. "Do any of those have food in them?"

Abramm handed over the sack of hardtack, but when Trap peered inside he snorted with disgust and drew out a fistful of dried, finger-long, green-and-black caterpillars. "Spima," he said, inspecting the morsel distastefully. "And they're not even fried."

"Is there nothing else?" Abramm took the bag back to look for himself. The spima's vinegary smell wafted from the opening, wrinkling his nose.

Some called them miracle worms, provided by Laevion at Beltha'adi's request back at the end of the first decade of his Wars of Unification. What crops had not been consumed or trampled by his soldiers had shriveled in an extended period of drought, producing a severe famine. Beltha'adi declared a realm-wide holy day, during which all would fast and bring offering to Laevion, goddess of life and plenty. Beltha'adi would and did seek her personally.

On the morning after, the realm was invaded by huge red moths that laid eggs in the thronetrees, protected by sacks of thick white silk. A month later the sacks burst open and millions of worms crawled out. They ate only the leaves of the thronetrees, their presence somehow accelerating refoliation so the trees were never really stripped bare, despite the worms' prodigious growth. Almost overnight they went from thumbnail-long slivers to stout, finger-sized worms. With nothing else to eat, the people fell upon them eagerly, and to this day the worms were regarded as both delicacy and staple, uniformly revered and happily consumed by all good servants of Khrell.

"Plagues, I hate these things," Trap said. He held one up as if in toast. "But, better than nothing. Thank you, Eidon, for your gracious provision." The insect crunched as he bit into it.

Abramm had never developed a taste for them, either, and only managed to down four by the time Trap had finished his first handful and took the bag back for a second one.

"I thought you hated them," Abramm said. "You're munching like a native."

"Purging spawn spore always does this to me." Trap crunched another worm. "Actually, they aren't so bad once you get going on them."

Abramm flashed him a doubtful glance.

Trap grinned, closed up the bag, and patted it. "I daresay you'll agree with me before this adventure is over."

"I'm hoping we can trade them for something better along the way."

Trap glanced pointedly at the expanse of deserted landscape sweeping around them beneath the ceiling of mist. "Who were you thinking of trading with? The ravens?"

"Way stations were never more than a day's ride apart on these old Ophiran highways."

"Aye, eight hundred years ago. Before the Cataclysm. Before the Wars of Unification. Before the Shadow came and the wind stopped and all the rivers dried up."

"There's bound to be some settlements left," Abramm insisted. Not all the springs would have dried up. And there were always cisterns.

"Well, I'm not sure it'd be a good idea to go blundering into one, even if we find it. If Beltha'adi's intelligence system is half as good as they say, word of our escape has surely preceded us."

"Not necessarily. He obviously wanted everyone to think we died in the Val'Orda, so he probably won't make this search public. Especially when he doesn't need men to find us."

They glanced uneasily at the sky, and Abramm half expected a dark vulturine shape to drop out of the mist right before his eyes.

He was right about the way stations. In the afternoon they came upon their first, catching the stench of it several moments before they topped a ridge and saw it nestled in the barren draw below. Three large, blockish buildings, broken and time ravaged, stood within the crumbling remains of a guard wall. Black fire rings scattered the semi-enclosed yard, and though the place looked deserted, smoke drifted from one of the chimneys.

They approached cautiously in the deep silence, feeling the touch of unseen eyes as in the distance a goat bleated.

Flanking the main gate, a pair of brightly colored prayer flags hung limply from sticks supported by cairns of red stone. Wreaths of onions encircled the sticks, warding away the staffid. In the yard, several patches of corn, squash, and more onions had been scratched out of the hardpan. This late in the year, with the harvest weeks over, the foliage was dry and pale, and at the far end, someone had begun to pull up the dead cornstalks. In a few months, once the annual rains refilled the cisterns and the ground had dried enough to work, they would plant anew.

As the two men passed through the gateway, the stench of rotting flesh overlaid the aroma of the latrine, drawing their gazes to a fly-enshrouded pile of fresh goat's legs and entrails lying beside the wall. A pair of ravens tore at the offal, while a lone chicken pecked the ground nearby. Somewhere out of sight in the draw below the station, more goats bleated, no doubt having been hurried away before the intruders could find them.

Fresh corn cakes and goat cheese were laid out on a low table in the main room of the building with the smoking chimney. The stone floor was swept, the shelves and jars free of dust, and the sleeping pallets rolled and stacked in the corner. A cornhusk doll sprawled beside them, and further on lay a tumble of small wooden blocks. And of course there were the ever-present swags of onions, guarding every opening.

The men looked longingly at the corn cakes but left them and moved on to the spring that erupted from the steep rocky hillside at the back of the compound. A massive thronetree, laden with white silk bags of spima eggs, stood guard over a ceramic pipe jutting from the red-brown rock. Water trickled from it into a square stone basin, which in turn fed a livestock trough. The trough held only a shallow layer of water now, though the thick green algae on its exposed inner sides showed it was usually full. The churned mud and crushed grass surrounding it confirmed what the offal and fire rings suggested—a large party of riders had recently passed through.

Necks crawling with the sense of being watched, the northerners watered their horses from the trough and refilled only one of their bags from the already depleted supply in the basin. Trusting there would be another station and another spring, they determined not to contribute to the hardships of the locals any more than they had to.

As they prepared to move out, Trap squatted by the tracks around the trough, thoughtfully fingering the jumble of grooves and ridges. Finally he straightened, frowning down the draw they would shortly be descending. "Two days ago at most," he said, wiping his hands on his trousers.

"Probably a division sent to block the boltholes at this end of the SaHal," Abramm said.

"Probably," Trap agreed with a grimace. With Beltha'adi's two Hundreds coming down from Andol to attack the north entrance at Jarnek, there'd have to be at least a small force sent south to round up any refugees. Abramm and Trap were supposed to have evaded it using Shettai's secret routes.

As they rode through one of the breeches in the guard wall, movement drew Abramm's eye up the barren hillside, where three shaggy-haired urchins watched them from atop a red-brown rock. He was close enough to see the whites of their eyes, stark against gaunt, dusty faces. Each wore a scrap of loincloth, their bone-thin limbs and hunger-swollen bellies revealed for all to see.

His gaze seemed to paralyze them, and they stared at him like deer caught in a hunter's torchlight. A sharp cry from across the draw jerked them free and sent them scurrying up the narrow ravine behind them.

The men rode on. At the bottom of the drainage, as they were about to round the end of a long ridge that would blot the station from view, Abramm glanced back and found a handful of raggedly clothed people standing near the guard wall. Even from a distance he could sense their fear and desperation, barely one step ahead of starvation.

The thought of the soldiers who had so recently passed through, eating their goats and drinking their water without a thought, ignited a smoldering anger in him. To those soldiers these people were worth less than some dogs. Fit only to serve and sacrifice for their betters, they would have been killed if they even so much as touched one of the Brogai. Even in the Dark Abode of death, they would exist only to be ruled by the lesser of the Chosen.

He remembered the arrogant claims of destiny and superiority, and part of him hoped he'd catch up to those soldiers, maybe teach them a lesson, exact a little justice—while another part observed wryly that it would be better if he did not, since fatigue seemed to have made him appallingly stupid. Just what sort of justice did he imagine two stiff, exhausted, weaponless men might exact from a group of at least twenty trained warriors who were well rested and thoroughly armed?

Daylight faded to darkness, forcing them to stop for fear of losing the road. Tying the horses to a thronetree, they collapsed on the sandy bed of the dry wadi that ran across their path. Trap muttered something about Eidon having to keep watch over them for tonight, and Abramm's last conscious thought was to hope that Eidon was up to the task.

He dreamt of Shettai, talking and laughing in a garden beyond a crystalline latticework aglow with a brilliant white light. Try as he might to peer through the slats, he could see nothing past the blinding light. Walking along the barrier yielded no end to it, and climbing it only brought him back to the bottom again and again. With frustration burning ever hotter in his breast, he finally hurled himself at the slats, hit them hard—

And woke up, surprised to find a raven tugging at the Terstan talisman he still wore round his neck.

It was gray daylight, but the bird was so close and its behavior so unexpected that for a moment he lay there and stared at it, sure he was still dreaming. When the creature put a splayed foot on his chest to brace itself and jerked at the chain again, both sensations were far too strong and vivid for a dream. In sudden affront, Abramm exploded off the ground, sweeping the would-be thief aside with an arm. Squawking indignation, the bird tumbled head over heels, and Trap sprang to his feet, groping for the weapon that should have been at his hip and turning frantically in search of the danger.

Recovering itself and still squawking, the raven flapped up into the thronetree across the ravine, ruffling its feathers and glaring down at them. In the foliage around it hopped a flock of sparrows, chattering and chirping. Abramm stood in the center of the wash, staring at them, hackles rising, while Trap picked up a rock and hurled it at the big bird, striking the shiny black breast. Cawing with renewed outrage, the creature tumbled wildly from its perch, then righted itself and flapped skyward. Another rock followed the first, then another, both missing their target. By then the bird had disappeared into the mist.

They stood motionless in the sand-bottomed wadi, waiting. Even the sparrows were silent. When the raven did not return, they exchanged a glance and, in unspoken accord, collected their bags, untied the horses from the tree, and set off again.

After breakfasting on spima washed down with niggardly sips of water, Abramm forced himself to work his bruised shoulder, circling it round and round, teeth gritted against the pain, until finally he could move it somewhat freely again. Then there was nothing to do but ride and think. And today he did not hurt so much that he could not think.

So much had happened in only two days he could hardly process it all, couldn't even remember it all clearly, the way it had whirled together. Despair and hope, agony and ecstasy, fulfillment and loss—his soul felt as bruised and battered as his body. It seemed like a nightmare. Hardly real. Hardly anything that could really have happened. That he should have survived the Broho, that he should be out here, free at last, riding toward whatever destiny held for him with the Dorsaddi. That she had loved him.

That above all else . . . she had loved him. The realization sparked a sense of wonder that was transmuted almost instantly to the gall of terrible loss. His throat constricted, his eyes teared up, and once again he found himself teetering at the edge of an emotional abyss. Then the wave of grief passed, and he regained himself, finding solace and distraction in a rising bitterness that eventually erupted into words.

"You ever been in love, Trap?"

He saw Meridon glance his way, though he kept his own gaze fixed upon the road. The Terstan's reply came slowly, reluctantly. "I have, my lord."

"Two years I loved her, longed for her. Finally I learn she shares my feelings, only to lose her before a day has even passed. Tell me . . . where is the good in that? Where is the *benefit*?"

Again Meridon was slow to answer. When it came, his voice was quiet. "She is with Eidon, Abramm. Her tears and pain replaced by perfect joy. Would you really want to call her back?"

Abramm's nape hairs stood up. Those words so closely echoed what he'd heard in that cliffside tunnel, he wondered briefly if he hadn't hallucinated after all. Maybe Trap had been the man he'd seen and heard. Perhaps somehow the power he'd used—

No. He remembered clearly that Trap had fallen unconscious by then, overwhelmed by the veren's poison. Trap hadn't even known Shettai was dead until later. It *had* been a hallucination.

But part of him wanted to believe those words so badly. So very badly. *"She is with Eidon . . . a place of perfect joy."*

He remembered the dream, the beautiful light, the singing, the way she had laughed and talked, the joy, warm and rich in her voice. Call her back from that?

"No," he whispered. Not if that were truly where she was.

"As for you," Trap went on, "well . . . you remain alive to choose."

Abramm flinched, the chills reaching now to the core of his being. *"And you, Abramm, son of Meren, remain alive to choose."* Exactly what that mysterious man had said to him. Exactly.

But it was a hallucination. And this . . . this was merely coincidence.

"I know what you're trying to do," he said sharply. "Confuse me. Play on my grief. Well, it won't work, so you may as well give it up."

Trap gave a weary sigh. "Do you truly believe I'm evil, Abramm?"

"Evil can masquerade as good. Moroq himself assumes the guise of a servant of Light when it suits him."

"And you think I am a servant of Moroq."

"I . . . I only know there was a time I was sure Saeral was good and true, and I was wrong. And all my life I've been warned how your kind deceive the unwary, twist the truth, cast your spells of coercion."

Trap looked pained. "So you think I'm trying to enspell you, then? After all this time, all we've been through? You really think I would do that, even if I could?"

"I don't know. I don't even know how to know." Abramm realized he was fingering the stone on his chest again and stopped. "If I can't trust what I see and hear and feel—"

"Then you go to the Words."

"The Words? The Words condemn you."

"Do they? Where?"

"Everywhere. The Words say Eidon is the perfect Light of Life. Righteous and holy, with no darkness in him at all. He's not going to let just anyone walk up and shake his hand. We must be cleansed, purified before—"

"And just how are we to do this?" Trap cut in. "You think soap and water will take care of it? Or throwing wooden sticks on a fire, or spending eight years adhering to a convoluted system of ordinances and restrictions? The Words say we're tainted, Abramm. Us and everything we do! Shadow cannot wipe away shadow!"

Abramm stared at him, startled by the passion in his voice. It was the first time Trap had ever spoken of this subject in any way but with cool, guarded objectivity.

The Terstan frowned, then turned his attention to the road, winding through the barren hills ahead of them. After a moment he spoke again, more carefully. "Why do you think Tersius had to die?"

"To make the Flames, of course."

"The Flames are a lie, created by the very darkness they claim to ward. But you're right about Eidon being perfect and that He can't ignore our failings. There *is* a price to be paid. It's just that Tersius is the only one who could pay it."

He fell silent, leaving Abramm to wrestle with his claims, which were all wrong—if only Abramm could find the words to explain it.

"So you're saying," he said finally, "that the most evil, vicious man in the world—Beltha'adi himself—could touch that stone and, if he wanted it, he'd be marked like all the rest of you? Carry the power of Eidon within him, as you claim to?"

" 'And Eidon said, I will *grant* you my light.' "

"Grant you so long as you've fulfilled the requirements."

"It doesn't say that. How about Amicus, midsector, line 40—'My Light is *freely* given. Whoever receives it will be my heirs'? Or the Illumination of St. Elspeth—'The light of Eidon is a *gift* to any who will receive it'? Or Salasan 1:20—'By his mercy we are made whole, not by our own deeds'?"

Abramm frowned. "You're taking all those out of context. If we had the books here, I could show you where you're wrong."

"A pity we don't have the books, then," Trap said, turning his gaze back to the road.

"What you're saying *can't* be right. It's . . . it just makes it all too easy."

"Yes. It does."

"Well, that's not right. It's not supposed to be—" A cold aura washed around him from behind, stopping his words as it stopped his horse, the mare's head coming up with a snort, her eyes rolling in alarm. Beside him Trap fought to control his own mount, the creature sidestepping, prancing, backing round into Abramm's horse. A brief, rhythmic hiss of wingbeats stirred the air and rustled the ratweed while the horses snorted and Abramm pulled the mare's nose almost to her neck to keep her from bolting. Part of him wanted to let her run, even as he knew they would never escape.

But the coldness faded without incident, the horses' frenzy waning with it, leaving them sweat-drenched and blowing as if from a hard run. The men on their backs exchanged a grim glance—the veren had found them and flown on by. Which could only mean it had more important tasks elsewhere.

Like aiding in the assault on the SaHal.

If Beltha'adi destroyed the Dorsaddi, the Deliverer would have no one to deliver.

# CHAPTER 30

They rode the rest of the day in silence, reaching another way station by midafternoon. This one was truly deserted, its spring long dried up. They passed it by without a word and stopped for the night leagues later.

Trap offered to take the first watch, and Abramm was weary enough that he did not argue. Not long after they had settled, however, he was jolted awake by the sight of Trap's right hand glowing eerily with the white light of his Terstan power, his grizzled face washed with its luminance. His eyes were closed, his features still with concentration, and for a moment the glow spread out from his hand, forming a saucer shape roughly the diameter of his forearm. Then it vanished, and Trap sighed as if he were disappointed.

"What are you doing?" Abramm asked, half suspecting him of trying some sort of persuasive demonstration to follow up their earlier conversation.

"Some of us are able to fashion a shield with the light," Meridon explained. "I thought it might come in handy if I could learn how."

Abramm couldn't begrudge him for trying. If they were attacked, they'd need all the help they could get. Abramm just didn't think they would be. At least, not by the veren.

---

They crossed the upper reaches of the Eranay Valley the next day. The road cut through the rumpled foothills of a great mountain whose dark slopes rose into the mist on their right. After centuries of drought, the river was dry, just another steep-walled channel cut into the gray-and-brown hills. An easy crossing today, but in a few more weeks it would be a raging torrent, rushing toward the vast network of cisterns and reservoirs waiting to be replenished downstream.

Beyond the river the road deteriorated further, its crumbling pavement often buried under sand or thick, dead grass. It was in such bad shape they worried they'd lost the route, until finally they crested a ridge and found the barren hillocks tumbling down to the lip of a vast, geologic cauldron, boiling with mist. A thin ribbon of road looped and twisted between them and the ruin of Sedouhn, crumbling at the cauldron's edge, the last of the Dorsaddi cities to fall.

They reached the city by midmorning and discovered that it supported its own complement of poverty-stricken settlers, carving out their living along its fringes. A small orchard, the pathetic patches of dead cornstalks and squash, the rock cairns with their onion wreaths and tattered prayer flags—all gave evidence of occupation, though they saw no one.

They rode through the slag-edged hole that was once the main gate and along an avenue of gutted buildings. Dark lines scored the pavement and ground amid deep blast pits. Arrowheads and weathered shafts by the hundreds lay in the sparse grass alongside rusting pieces of armor and decomposing bones.

The city spring, once delivered in an elegant, stone-walled pool, now bubbled up around broken and fallen blocks. Still, it was the most vigorous wellspring they'd yet encountered, and they filled all their bags, noting as they did the roil of tracks left in the drifted sand by the soldiers who had preceded them. Riding on, they passed through the inner wall, whose throne-wood gates had also felt the explosive powers of Broho magic. From there it was a straight shot to the final gates, which guarded egress into the SaHal itself. Remarkably intact, they stood at the end of a grisly gauntlet of throne-wood poles bearing the tattered skeletons of long-dead criminals.

All except the last four.

These sported fresh corpses, one pair mere hours dead. Though the four wore Dorsaddi robes, all were northerners—two blonds and two redheads. Their eyes had been put out, their hands cut off, their throats slit—but it was the red-fletched arrows protruding from their chests that had killed them.

Abramm was not aware of pulling his horse to a halt, but somehow he found himself stopped at the last post, staring up at the dead man's face.

From the Dorsaddi perspective, it must look a good deal like his own.

"Apparently Sheleft'Ai did not make a way for them," Trap said.

Abramm let out a long, low breath. They had known the Dorsaddi killed intruders, but seeing it in the flesh was more unnerving than he expected.

"At least we don't look as obviously northern as these fellows," Trap said. "I'll wager neither of the blonds had your eyes, either."

Abramm snorted. "You really think they'll let us get close enough to see my eyes?"

"At least we know they're still fighting."

Neither of them suggested turning back.

An iron grate and railing had been constructed immediately outside the slumping gate, extending over empty space to the narrow trail carved into the cliffside of the SaHal. When the horses refused to walk over it, the men had to dismount, cover the animals' eyes with their headcloths, and lead them across. From there, the road angled gently downward along the cliff, protected by a three-foot-high wall of Ophiran construction.

As they descended, the temperature plunged and the mist thickened, cutting visibility to a mere five strides. The wall stopped at the first switchback, and the trail deteriorated. Many of the paving stones were loose or missing. Deep ruts, exposed roots, and huge rectangular stones laid crossways to prevent erosion made the going rough. It probably helped that they could see nothing but mist. The dry, thick dust and scatterings of manure confirmed Trap's guess that the troop of Esurhites was at least a day ahead of them.

Time seemed to stand still as they rounded one switchback after another, steadily descending. The cliff walls loomed forbiddingly barren, home to only small grasses and occasional spiny cacti. Even when the switchbacks leveled off to a meandering, downsloping trail, the surrounding rock remained bare and dry.

Small crunches and crackles and whispers of movement sounded continuously around them, sounds Abramm repeatedly assured himself were just echoes of his and Trap's own passage. But with the mist making it impossible to confirm that, the back of his neck crawled again and again. Though there was a good chance the Dorsaddi had fallen to Beltha'adi's two-sided attack or were at least heavily occupied with fighting it off, he couldn't shake the feeling that they were out there, watching him. That at any moment a red-fletched arrow would zing out of the mist and bury itself in his back.

A more reasonable fear would be that they would round a bend in the rock and find themselves suddenly in the midst of the Esurhite patrol they knew had preceded them, but he could not shake the sense that it was Dorsaddi who watched them.

The road dropped onto a barren, rocky shelf, then into a narrow, red-walled canyon. Swarms of black- and gray-striped staffid disguised as rocks erupted to life before Trap's horse, scuttling off into the cracks in the rock around them. The clop and rustle of their passing echoed loudly off smooth vertical walls close enough to touch, and Abramm's feelings of claustrophobia mounted.

They found the first body at the canyon's end, sprawled facedown on the sand and attended by a pair of ravens. Clad in the gray tunic of the soldiers of the Black Moon, the man was weaponless, armorless, and bootless. Though his throat had been cut, it was the hole in his back that killed him—a bloody, torn-up mess, most likely the result of an arrow. The arrow itself was nowhere to be found.

Another body, similarly disposed, lay alongside the road farther up, the third in another excruciatingly narrow ravine, the horses forced to step over it. And the one after that.

In the mist it was difficult to judge distance or even time, but it seemed the Dorsaddi were giving their visitors lots of opportunity to watch and worry before they picked their next victim.

The fifth casualty lay at the point where the trail crossed a cactus-dotted shelf and dropped into a narrow canyon. "Well," Abramm said as they left the body behind, "it seems the Dorsaddi are everything their reputation claims them to be."

The Terstan glanced back at him, the grizzle on his jaw showing distinctly red, despite the dirt and lard that stained his skin. "Yet you'll note we're still alive."

"They're playing with us."

Trap cocked a brow. "Maybe they see we're weaponless, bedraggled, and riding obviously stolen horses. With no tack."

"We don't have the right coloring."

"We don't exactly look Esurhite, either." He turned to nudge his horse onward. "Maybe we're just enough of an enigma to stay their hands."

"And here I thought it was Eidon's doing."

"Oh, it *is*, my friend." Trap grinned back at him.

They emerged from the second cleft and started across a mist-bound flat. The trail climbed up over a rocky shelf, then descended around an old, dead thronetree, long since toppled on its side. It was the first sign of real vegetation they'd seen, and there was a crow-sized red bird hidden in the depths of its crown, obscured, but for its bright colors, by the gnarled tangle of dead branches.

As they rode past, Abramm's neck suddenly crawled with a fierce, sixth-sense knowledge of impending attack, and he whirled to find the bird—a small red heron?—launching itself out of the tree at him. Arena-bred instincts had him kicking his horse forward half a heartbeat before the realization that it was only a bird caught up with him. But as he knocked the creature aside with his free arm, something struck the other arm, jerking at his sleeve and pulling him off balance, even as his mount staggered and threw up her head with a snort. He glimpsed a red-fletched arrow bouncing on the stone beside her, and his alarm resurged with a vengeance. Moving with the momentum the arrow had imparted, he was sliding off the horse when she shuddered and collapsed with a groan, dead of the arrow in her heart. Crouched behind her now, Abramm frantically scanned the mist for signs of his assailants and wondered if the bird was coming back and why it had attacked at all. Then he saw it, lying where he'd knocked it, a third arrow buried in is breast. And it was not a heron, but a needle-beaked, long-necked feyna.

Which confused him more than ever.

Trap had wheeled his own mount back, still unaware they were under attack, when the Dorsaddi emerged from the mist, ghosts in salmon- and ochre-tinged robes, too numerous to count. They held longbows, raised and drawn, their gleaming broadheads all aimed at the northerners.

CHAPTER

# 31

They were seized and stripped of robes and tunics, the dragon brands on their arms and the holes in their ears seemingly something the Dorsaddi expected. They exclaimed over the talisman Abramm wore about his neck, however, and the golden shield on Trap's chest brought them to a standstill. They all had to examine it, fingering it as they exchanged soft urgent murmurs in oddly accented Tahg, but their interest did not stop them from binding both captives and loading them belly down across the backs of their horses.

Undignified and uncomfortable as the position was, Abramm counted it better than being shot and endured the subsequent passage of time stoically, trying not to think of what lay ahead. By the time they stopped, it was dark and his legs were so numb they wouldn't support him unaided. He had to lean dizzily against the horse that had borne him here until the blood flowed back into them. When he was recovered enough to walk again, he found himself in a narrow, steep-walled canyon, facing a huge-pillared edifice carved out of the red stone walls. A crowd of dark-faced, pale-robed Dorsaddi stood shoulder to shoulder around the newcomers, watching in ominous silence—until Trap straightened and his shieldmark flashed in the torchlight. Those nearest flinched back and began muttering among themselves, the tone angry and questioning all at once.

Hands still bound behind them, the prisoners were guided up the stairs and through the tall doorway into a massive torchlit chamber thick with smoke and packed with more hostile figures. Originally a natural formation, the chamber's floor had been paved with small square tiles of lapis lazuli and red agate. Two tiers of iron-railed balconies protruded from the walls above, their railings lined with silent, watching Dorsaddi.

The crowd on the floor parted before the new arrivals like water before a ship's bow. A good head taller than any of them, Abramm could easily see the dais at the chamber's far end, where a group of men waited. Two wore white turbans and white robes twined with purple-and-gold embroidery, gold medallions gleaming on their chests. The rest wore salmon- or ochre-tinted robes that were no different from any others, though Abramm figured one of them must be the Dorsaddi king, Shemm, Shettai's brother.

As Abramm approached and climbed the low stair to meet them, their hard, lean faces acquired detail. The white-turbaned men were clean-shaven, almond eyed, and grim lipped, and the medallions of each were different. One was a jeweled shield of solid gold with Tahg symbols engraved upon its face; the other was a glass sphere as big as a man's palm. Seeing them, Abramm understood why their captors had been so intrigued by Trap's shieldmark and his own Terstan orb.

The other men sported close-clipped black beards and dark hair pulled back into warrior's knots. Several wore the gold rings of fighting prowess up the sides of their ears, and one wore the wide gold neckband of royalty.

It was this one that drew Abramm's immediate attention, but not because of the gold band. Dark bushy brows met over the bridge of a long, strong nose, sheltering dark, almond-shaped eyes, his features a masculine image of Shettai's. The resemblance was so strong Abramm couldn't help but stare, a sudden catch in his throat. No question this was King Shemm.

He had no sooner reached that conclusion than he was jerked to a stop and shoved to his knees. Trap was forced down likewise as the patrol's leader slid the orb and it's chain over Abramm's head and stepped forward. He bowed deeply to the king, then handed him the talisman. Shemm glanced at it expressionlessly and passed it to one of the priests, who received it with a scowl. Slowly then, the king circled his prisoners, pausing to stroke the brands on their arms, to inspect the holes in their ears, finger the dust from their hair, and rub at the edges of Trap's shieldmark.

Finally he drew back and addressed the patrol leader. "How is it you bring them to us alive, Japheth?"

The man straightened. "I believe they may be the ones foretold, my Lord King."

"That is not for you to say!" snapped the priest who wore the shield medallion. A stout, thick-bodied man, he crackled with latent energy, a coiled spring ready to explode. "You know no outlander may violate the sanctity of the SaHal and live."

"We had them in our hands, Holy One," Japheth protested. "Three of us shot—none more than ten strides away—yet here he stands, unscathed."

An excited mutter spread out through the crowd, and the second priest, the one who wore the glass sphere, was staring at them with a sort of wondrous joy. "Sheleft'Ai made them a way," he said, turning to his cohort. "It truly is them, Mephid!"

"Bah!" Mephid slashed the air. "It was chance and no more. Save perhaps the delaying influence of wishful thinking."

"All three of them?" the second priest demanded. "At the same moment?"

"We treated these no differently than the others, Holy One," Japheth said.

"Aye, we shot the tall one's horse right out from under him!" one of the other men added.

Mephid was not convinced. "They are imposters!" He turned to the king. "More of Beltha'adi's tricks, Great One. I say kill them at once, and post their bodies with the others!"

"But, Mephid," said his fellow priest, "the others did not come with orb and shield. And that one's eyes—blue as Andolen silk, just like the Pretender's." He, too, turned to the king. "I say it is them, Great One, brought to us by Sheleft'Ai himself."

"The Pretender was lost in the warrens outside Xorofin!" Mephid exclaimed, glaring at his cohort. "Was that not how Chael reported it?"

They turned to one of the men standing at the back of the dais, and the king spoke. "Chael, is it so? Are these the men?"

Chael stepped forward, regarded them closely, then shrugged. "I cannot say. I saw them only from a distance."

"But you saw them go in." Mephid turned back to the king. "We all know no one comes out of the warrens alive."

"That is true, Holy One," Chael said. "But it is also true that no one can kill the Horror with a sword, yet the two I saw did."

"Nor stand against the Broho and live," the second priest said, "yet they did that as well."

Mephid slashed the air again. "Ast! You do not know that, Nahal! It is only a tale—and likely untrue."

King Shemm, who had watched all this without comment, now turned to his prisoners. For a long moment he studied them thoughtfully, wearing that same stony look Shettai had been so good at. Finally he spoke. "So who do *you* say you are?"

Abramm glanced at Trap and by unvoiced agreement assumed the role of spokesman. "I am Abramm Kalladorne, Prince of Kiriath, and this is my retainer, Captain Meridon of the Kiriathan Royal Guard."

The murmuring started up at once, as his words were passed back to the others and conclusions eagerly reached.

"We have been lately in the possession of one Katahn ul Manus, until we escaped the Games at Xorofin some days ago."

"You are the White Pretender, then?" Shemm's eyes seemed to bore right through his skull.

"I was."

The dark eyes darted to Trap. "And you the Infidel?"

"I was, Great One."

Shemm's gaze returned to Abramm—hard, sharp, strangely threatening. "Why did you come to us?"

*Here it is,* Abramm thought. *The moment you either do it or you don't.* He pulled back his shoulders and met the level gaze unflinching. "We were told we would find friends here—men who wish to throw off the evil strangling this land." He glanced at the men behind Shemm—the two priests and four attendants. "We were told you had need of someone to awaken the Heart of the SaHal."

Flint-hard eyes bored into him.

"You claim to be our Deliverer, then," Shemm said, in a voice as flat and devoid of emotion as any of Shettai's.

It was ridiculous. Abramm knew he was not their Deliverer. He knew there was not a blessed thing he could do here to help them re-ignite their Heart. He knew they would kill him when they learned that, but what else could he do? He had done all Shettai had bid him, and if he failed, if they killed him . . .

Heart pounding, he lifted his chin a fraction higher and pitched his voice loud so that it would carry through the hall. "Yes."

"You stand ready to prove that?"

"I do."

"Very well, then."

"Now, my lord?" Japheth turned to his king, gaping. "But it is past dark, and the Horror is aprowl, and—"

"If he is truly the one we seek, Japheth, the Horror cannot stop us. 'You will know him by his deeds, by the light with which he slays the Darkness.' " The king's dark eyes flicked to the priest, and one brow arched. "Is that not how it goes, Mephid?"

"It is, my king," Mephid growled.

"Then we shall let the Heart decide the truth. If he fails, we will kill them as we killed the others. Unless the Horror kills them first." He glanced at his attendants and the men sprang forward to lead the way through the crowd.

"He will need the orb, Great One." Trap's voice stopped the king and drew everyone's eye. The Terstan still knelt where he had been placed, and now, with the king frowning down at him, he elaborated. "The talisman you took from him. He will need it to awaken the Heart." He flicked a glance at Abramm, clearly urging him to take his cue.

Abramm frowned, annoyed at the Terstan's attempt at manipulation and reluctant to take back the orb now that he was freed of it. Did Meridon really think it might somehow ignite the Heart? And if it did, did Abramm want to be in the middle of it?

Or was it just the veren Trap was thinking of, and Abramm's need for some protection against it?

He was aware of the king's regard again, saw the questioning look in his eyes. The decision came all at once, riding that crazy, fatalistic bravado that had driven him from the moment he'd gotten here. Why not take the thing? What could it do now? He was going to die anyway. . . .

"He is right," Abramm said. "I had forgotten it was taken from me, but I will need it."

A moment the king considered, then he motioned for the priest to return the artifact. As the stone bounced once more against the scab on Abramm's bare breastbone, he flashed a sour look at the Terstan. As if this would change anything.

Emerging from the great hall, they traversed yet another canyon with numerous doors and openings carved into its salmon-hued walls. Iron brackets holding lighted torches had been fixed into the stone beside many of them, and often the doorways were blocked with beads or skin coverings.

Shortly they emerged from the canyon, the mist forming a woolen wall around them, reflecting back the torchlight and blocking view of anything beyond the radius of a few strides.

It seemed to Abramm that they progressed down a long promenade. An ancient pavement buckled and humped beneath his feet, and lines of gnarled, mostly dead olive trees loomed ghostlike in the mist beside them. Occasionally they stepped across deep, black-edged scores in the pavement or piles of rubble fallen across their path. In places the trees lay uprooted, their branches clawing at the men as they passed. Sometimes the mist shredded enough to reveal the doddering, age-stained remains of masonry walls jutting up from the rubble field. Sometimes the walls formed buildings with windows and railed balconies and frescoed doorways, only to fall away in rubble and blackened timbers and gaping craters awrithe with thousands of dark shapes skittering away from the torchlight.

Shadowspawn. Twisted things that watched from the mist and darkness. Staffid of all forms. Feyna. Griiswurm. He recognized right off the strong feeling of anxiety and aversion so peculiar to the griiswurm's aura, even spotted here and there the globular bodies and tentacled legs hugging the rocks and walls. Time and again, unseen horrors moaned and crackled and muttered around them, and once, from somewhere comfortingly distant, something roared. Or screamed. Or moaned. The sound reverberated off cliffs and mortared stone, making it impossible to pinpoint the direction from whence it came.

"I hope these people know what they're doing," Trap muttered beside him.

Abramm strained at the bonds on his wrists yet again, inwardly chafing with the helpless frustration of having his hands tied in the face of obvious danger. There had been no talk among the men since they'd left the hall, but now it seemed there was not even breath. All held either bow or sling, and all had eyes only for the torchlit mist around them.

They were well away from the canyon's protective embrace when the veren's familiar frigid aura enveloped them, stopping them en masse. Every gaze rushed skyward as arrows were nocked and stones slid into slings. Abramm stared at the wooly ceiling like everyone else, gooseflesh prickling his back and neck as he strained again at his bonds, about to burst with the need to be free.

But again the creature passed on without attacking, still just keeping an eye on them—or perhaps only waiting for the right moment. In any case, the aura faded, and the group released a collective sigh. The men who had gathered protectively around their king relaxed and started forward again.

Shortly they entered a wide plaza, its pale pavement buckled and scored by numerous trenches. At its midst stood a circular stone structure, double a man's height and shaped like a cone without its peak. It crawled with tentacled griiswurm and was encircled at the top by a lumpy iron railing from which three iron poles extended skyward. Once likely converging to a central point above the whole, now they were twisted and bent over the mound of stone and griiswurm. In fact, looking more closely, he realized the lumps on the railings were also griiswurm.

The Dorsaddi encircled it silently, and when all had assembled, Shemm ordered Abramm's bonds cut. He gestured to a fractured, half-buried stairway leading to the top of the pile. "The Heart is up there. Awaken it if you can."

Abramm's anxiety had grown so great he could hardly breathe, much less move, and he knew it wasn't just the aura of the griiswurm. The certainty of his death was hitting him hard now—and it terrified him.

He swallowed. "You must remove the spawn," he said, gesturing at the mound. "I cannot concentrate with them there."

As if concentration would change anything. *Yelaki!*

Shemm matched him frown for frown, suspicion burning in his eyes. He probably guessed it for the delaying tactic it was, but he waved his men to comply all the same. With spears and swords and arrows, they stabbed and pried loose all the larger spawn, casting them off the mound as others went round scooping them up and hurling them into the night.

Too soon the structure was cleared. Abramm stared up at the crumpled railing. That would make a good place for the veren to take him, wouldn't it? He swallowed grimly, feeling the eyes of the Dorsaddi upon him. Shemm still frowned—the priest, Mephid, was almost smiling, and Japheth looked puzzled.

*"Awaken the Heart,"* she'd said.

*Very well, my love. For you.*

He clambered up the ruined stairway and ducked under the railing that supported the ruined struts. It ringed a gaping crater some twenty feet in diameter. At its lowest point, half buried in rubble, lay a large crystalline sphere, roughly a forearm in diameter. The spore wriggling to life in his wrist and the sudden glow of the orb on his chest told him power dwelt in this place.

But how to awaken it, he still had no idea.

Grimly he walked the crater's circumference. Not much longer now and they'd see he didn't know what he was doing, realize he was indeed the imposter they had already accused him of being. Unless the veren came first.

Having circled the pit twice, there was nothing left but to step into it, and he did so, skidding down the stone scree to the bottom, hip-deep below its rim. There he spied a heavy, warped shield of bronze twisting out of the rubble and marked with the angular symbols of the Tahg.

> His light will protect us: the King of Light, the King's Light, the kings of Light, three and one. He is before us and with us and over us. Darkness shall not touch us, so long as we are in the Light.

He straightened with a chill. That was from the First Word. But what was it doing here? And rendered in the Tahg at that? The sense of destiny fell on him again, strong and compelling, a sense of being at the mercy of something—or Someone—far greater than himself, like a leaf caught in a windstorm.

He stepped over the shield, moved on to the pit's center, and squatted beside the reflective surface of the crystalline globe. This must be the Heart. It was slick as it looked but cool and dead to the touch. He stood again, imprisoned by twisted bars of metal stabbing up through the mist. A ring of hard-eyed Dorsaddi stared at him from below, the ruddy torchlight imbuing their still forms with a brooding malevolence.

*"Awaken the Heart,"* she'd said.

*I don't know how, my love. Curse me, but I don't know how!*

He stepped onto the buried globe, closed his eyes, and reached for the talisman on his chest, willing something to happen. The scar on his arm writhed furiously, and nausea swirled in his middle. Beyond that, nothing.

He let out his breath and looked at the stone in his hands. It gleamed softly, pale opalescent white against his dirty palms. That was all.

A soft word sounded behind him, followed by an ominous rustle. Then a loud cry split the night.

"Wait!"

He turned to see Trap scrambling up the mound, his bonds falling away in a cloud of smoke. Gaining the top, he turned, his body now between Abramm and the three archers who stood at Shemm's side with longbows drawn and aimed.

"Wait!" he cried again. "He does not know—"

"Now!" Shemm commanded.

CHAPTER

# 32

Light flared in a blazing corona around Trap's body just as the arrows released. Abramm saw them with unnerving clarity, floating slowly toward him while Trap fell backward in slow motion, still ablaze with white fire.

His left shoulder caught Abramm in the chest, though Abramm was himself already twisting down and away. He fell hard, on his left side, stones gouging his chest and shoulder, Trap slamming down on top of him.

Angry shouting rang out, followed by a clatter of arrows and bows and the thump and rattle of men climbing the mound. Trap shoved up off him and waved a score of clear white kelistars into existence as Abramm gasped back the air driven out of him in the fall. He started to press himself up when he saw the Heart flickering with the same white light as Trap's kelistars.

Astonishment drove him to his feet and back a few steps before he realized what he was doing, and he almost took an arrow in the arm for his incaution. He ducked back below the crater's lip, but before he could draw Trap's attention to the globe, the veren dropped out of the mist above them. It slammed into one of the rails and pushed off it, bending it farther into the pit, the metal squealing protest. Then it was gone in an icy wind, flapping skyward on powerful wings.

Breathlessly Abramm crawled up beside Trap to peer over the lip of the mound. The ring of bowmen had scattered. Shemm and his personal guard were already heading back toward the safety of the canyon walls. Others raced around the mound, all with arrows nocked and eyes cast heavenward.

With a shriek the veren plunged out of the mist again, pouncing on one of the king's protectors and leaping skyward, a headless body slumping to the ground in its wake. At that the Dorsaddi looked ready to bolt—a few did—but a good number of them had managed to hold steady and fire off some of their arrows. A handful still crouched around the mound, but even as Abramm noted them, they were up and chasing their fellows, taking their weapons with them.

"The spears," Abramm said, pointing. "They left some spears."

"Right." Trap was scrambling over the lip's edge in tandem with Abramm as the veren burst upon them yet again. Talons sliced Abramm's shoulder as he flung himself down the slope. Seizing the spear he had targeted, he rolled to his feet. Trap came up simultaneously beside him, and they stood back to back in the old arena stance, spears raised and ready. Torches scattered the cleared plaza, providing a sputtering light.

The creature swooped out of the darkness, coming at Abramm, arrows gleaming in its breast. He nearly impaled it before it veered away, slamming him with a wing and knocking him back into Trap.

"You have a plan?" Meridon asked as they regained their balance.

Abramm wanted to run for the safety of the canyons like the Dorsaddi were doing, but he knew that would only result in the eventual completion of their execution as imposters. Since he hadn't managed to ignite the Heart, they needed to do something else to prove their worth. "I think we'd better kill it," he said, watching the misty ceiling and settling into a ready stance. "How's that shield of yours coming?"

"Unreliable at best."

"Guess we'll have to do it hand to hand, then."

A flash of movement drew his eye, and he swung his spear in time to see a round, wet object hit the pavement and bounce. Guessing the ploy, he was already turning back, even as he sensed the massive body coming in from the opposite side. It swooped in too fast for him to get his spear on target. All he saw were gleaming talons reaching for his face, and he had to dive aside. He hit the ground rolling as white light flared somewhere past his field of vision. The creature squawked, a wing hit him, and the thing was gone again.

As he came to his feet Trap was rising as well, shaking his head. "I can't do it if I have to think about using the spear."

"Then you just shield and I'll spear."

It was back, bursting out of the mist, talons gleaming, huge wings spread out to swallow him. Abramm drove his spear into the expanse of black before him, helped by the beast's own momentum, which drove him back into the ground and ripped the spear from his hands. Then it was gone again, leaving a line of fire across his left shoulder. He could feel blood trickling down his chest and back as the scars on his wrist writhed with the new influx of poison.

Staggering upright, he glimpsed Trap gripping a broken spear shaft, then dove aside again as a heavy timber crashed to the pavement where he'd stood. Rolling away, he found another spear near the bottom of the mound and came up ready, but the veren had already landed, striding now toward Trap, its beak jabbing and stabbing.

Trap backed away, white faced, his right arm dangling oddly, his left held out, glowing with the white of his power, which the veren ignored as if it didn't exist. Abramm hefted the spear and ran forward, driving its iron head into the monster's back with all his strength. The creature screamed and whirled, slamming the spear's shaft painfully into Abramm's ribs. He dropped and scrambled away as the thing came at him, Dorsaddi arrows and his own first spear bobbing wildly in its breast. It beat him with its wings and stabbed at him with its beak, grabbed for him with its talons. Crabbing frantically away, he could not hope to move fast enough, but just as the thing loomed over him and he knew it was going to get him, a stone flew out of the darkness and struck it in the eye. It staggered, shook its head, and turned toward whoever had slung the stone.

Abramm rolled away, got his feet under him, and escaped, noting, as he did, a line of Dorsaddi watching from the mist's edge. As soon as he was clear, their arms came up in unison, slings twirling, then flapping with the release. A flight of stones shot through the night to batter the veren where it stood. Reeling anew, the creature screamed and leapt skyward into cover of cloud. The mist closed over it, and the sound of its wingbeats whispered into silence.

Panting, Abramm limped to Trap's side. The Terstan's right shoulder appeared to be dislocated, the arm useless, but there was no time to fix it now.

"Back to the mound!" Abramm said, grabbing up a third spear. No sooner had they started than a pair of large blocks fell from the sky, crashing onto the pavement in front of them. They whirled to face the veren as it swooped in from behind to attack them on foot. Trap made his fire again, and for the first time the thing flinched away. In the cover of that distraction, Abramm eluded the stabbing beak and drove a third spear into its body. A moment later the beak impaled his shoulder. He gasped with the shocking pain of it but did not let go, and then Trap was beside him, grabbing the spear with his good hand. White fire blared across Abramm's vision, blasting all else away.

Light rushed through his flesh, pain and purest pleasure, power and weakness, love and terrible loss. He saw a man, suspended between earth and sky against a cloud of dark, ravening hunger that seemed to be gathering itself to swallow him up. Terror loosened Abramm's hold on the spear, and he fell back, the vision lost.

He blinked, shook the spangles and blobs of darkness from his eyes, and saw Trap still hanging one-handed to the spear, both he and the veren enwrapped in the blaze of his power. The monster was thrashing and screaming, flinging its head madly, its beak thrust open, long red tongue fluttering. Convulsions wracked its body, and Trap could hold no longer. He dropped to the pavement and rolled away, coming up on his knees to watch as the creature's convulsions quieted to shudders and shivers, and then the last few twitches that gave way to stillness.

The Terstan backed away from it, gasping and sweat soaked and holding his useless arm as Abramm came up beside him. Abramm himself was already shivering in reaction to the spawn spore that streaked and spattered his arms and torso. Tens of tiny blisters had reared up where each drop of black blood touched him, tiny points of fire nearly lost in the pain now throbbing from the feyna scar in his wrist.

All around them Dorsaddi appeared out of the mist.

"You need to wash that stuff off," Trap croaked. He was himself completely untouched by the veren's blood, the wielding of his power having burned it away as effectively as one of his healing sessions.

"Aye. And you need your arm put back."

Meridon managed a half chuckle before his eyes caught on something past Abramm's shoulder and his brow creased. Abramm turned to find the king's party already upon them, gazes flicking from the dead veren to the two of them, their expressions very close to worship. Indeed, a moment later, the men surrounding the king—Japheth, the two priests, and all the others of his coterie—dropped slowly to their knees. At once the rest of the Dorsaddi followed suit, leaving King Shemm standing alone, leather sling dangling from one hand, longbow in the other. He stared at Trap with a stunned, fixed expression, his swarthy face pale, even in the torchlight. After a long moment he spoke:

"Truly you are the one foretold by the Prophet Eameth. The Deliverer who walks the road of death. . . . 'By him the Light will return to the people of the Shield, and by him will kings arise to slay the armies of Darkness.' "

And then Shemm, too, sank to his knees and bowed his head to the pavement. "Holy One, have mercy on us. We have been tricked so many times, suspicion has become our way of life. Any atonement you require we will make."

Around him his people pressed their heads to the ground in imitation.

Trap frowned. "I don't want your sacrifices," he said sharply. "I am only a man like the rest of you. Stand and face me."

At first Shemm did not move. Then, hesitantly, he raised his head and at length got to his feet. "You may be a man," the Dorsaddi said, "but you carry the fire of Sheleft'Ai."

"As can any one of you who asks."

Shemm frowned. "Your words dance the edge of blasphemy, Great One. How can we obtain the power of a god?"

Trap raised his hand and a small white orb appeared on it.

Abramm flinched—his mouth went dry and sour. *Fire and Torment! Not this. Anything but this!*

" 'I will grant you my Light by the blood of my Son,' " Trap quoted from the Second Word. " 'And it will dwell in your hearts and give you life. Reach out, therefore, and close your hand about it that you may live and that my power may become yours.' "

Torches hissed and sputtered in the breathless silence.

Shemm's dark glance flicked up to Trap's. Hesitantly he reached out and plucked the glowing sphere from the air. He turned it round and round in his fingertips, staring at it as if it held all the truths of life.

Abruptly his fingers wrapped around it, quenching its pale light. A rush of tingling rode the air, and as with Whazel, as with Shettai, a golden shield appeared on the Dorsaddi's hairy chest, glittering between the edges of his robe.

A susurration of astonishment arose from those around him, a rising murmur as word was passed to those who could not see.

Shemm stared at his now empty hand, then at his chest, and touched the shield with tentative fingers. He looked back up, his jaw slack beneath his cropped beard. "I . . . I . . . it is a miracle," he whispered.

"How may I receive this power?" Japheth asked, stepping forward, his yellow eyes pale in the ruddy light.

"And I?" the priest Mephid echoed.

"I as well," pleaded the other, Nahal.

Men and women crowded forward, jostling against Abramm, nudging him back out of their way.

Shemm looked to Meridon. "Will you conjure the little orbs for them?"

Meridon smiled. "You can conjure them yourself, my king. Merely remember and call them to life."

The Dorsaddi glanced at his fellows. Silence fell once more upon the gathering. Shemm's gaze left Trap and unfocused as he concentrated. Moments later a single white globe appeared, floating in the air above him. Others followed quickly, hovering over the group, tens of them, their soft white light reflecting off the wildly churning mists.

Out in the city somewhere, the roar-moan sounded again, more distant than before and almost mournful. None of the Dorsaddi seemed to notice.

Japheth reached up first; the others followed suit. Golden shields sprang into being right and left, glittering against flesh that moments earlier had been unmarked. Power crackled in the air, thick and heady, raising the hairs on Abramm's neck, the feyna scars writhing like liquid fire in his wrist.

He withdrew, trembling, an icy claw pulling at his gut. People surged forward around him, and more orbs bloomed overhead. He staggered free of the press to join the ring of those who watched in astonishment from the fringes, drew back even from them, until he found himself with the mound between him and the spectacle unfolding in the plaza.

Yet still that white light washed over him, close, as close as his own—

He looked down, saw the stone blazing against his breastbone, right where that golden shield would lie should he desire it. Suddenly panicked, he yanked it over his head and held it away from him with pounding heart. With his free hand he groped at his chest to be sure there was no shield.

What was happening? Why was it glowing like that? Was it the proximity to the others? It must be. *He* certainly wanted nothing to do with it! What he had just seen proved it was not of Eidon. That all those people could just . . . just *receive* it like that with no regard for their worth or righteousness. It was clearly evil.

He should throw it away now. The protection it offered him was not worth the risk.

And yet he did not move. Already it had him in its spell. How could something evil be so beautiful? How could it seem so right and true, so full of goodness and light and life? How could it pull at him like this, remind him so much of what blazed through that woven wall in his dreams, beyond which Shettai lived and laughed and talked . . . with Eidon?

Suddenly he realized that even after all that had happened, he still wanted to believe that Eidon lived, that he was good and true and gracious, that he was indeed the ruler of all, that he still held Abramm's life in his hands. For a moment he glimpsed that mysterious man with the scarred face and gentle eyes watching him, waiting for him to respond, to take the gift that was offered. . . .

His wrist wrenched hard, as if the worms of spore had suddenly expanded to twice their size. He realized then that he was touching the orb with his free hand, stroking the blazing surface with a finger, exactly as Whazel had done, exactly as Shettai had done. Cold horror blasted through him as he jerked it away.

*Get rid of this! Get rid of it now, before it enspells you even further!*

Without a second thought he slung the chain hard, the orb carving an arc of light across the darkness and vanishing.

He stared after it, shaking and panting, aghast at what he had almost done—and even so, fighting the irrational urge to run after it. Reeling from the waves of grinding pain that throbbed out of his left side, he swallowed down bile and fought to stay standing, his limbs wobbling like gelatin. He still hadn't washed off the veren's poison, and there was the wound the beast had dealt his shoulder, as well, festering already. He needed help, needed Trap, who was the last man on earth he wanted to see now.

Maybe if he just got away, just found a place to wash himself or maybe just to lie down for a time. . . .

He staggered around the mound, back among the Dorsaddi again, all of them jabbering excitedly. Golden shields glimmered on every chest, everywhere he looked.

Suddenly they all stopped talking and looked at him. He stared back through a haze of pain and confusion. Why were they staring at him like that? And why was there suddenly all this light? Surely it wasn't dawn already.

He saw the eyes of those nearest him widen, saw their faces pale and their mouths drop open as they stepped back, still staring, though not at him.

A horrible metallic shriek sounded behind him, and he turned to find the sun had somehow come to hover directly atop the mound. Flinging up an arm against the brilliance, he reeled away from it, as if it had struck him a physical blow.

"The Heart!" someone cried. "He has awakened the Heart!"

Abramm had one startled moment of understanding, followed by a new eruption of the poison in his body, and that was the last he saw.

# CHAPTER 33

The old Terstan's hand bit into Abramm's skinny arm, jerking him around. Though he was crippled and bent almost double, he still loomed over Abramm, blind eyes fixed upon him with unnerving accuracy. His gold shield glimmered on his chest, and the curd of an advanced case of the sarotis oozed over his lids and dribbled down seamed cheeks. He bent closer, shoving his face into Abramm's, the curd quivering, the sickly sweet stench of it making Abramm gag. "Answer me, boy!" he rasped.

But Abramm yelled and twisted free—

And found himself in a sandy arena, bathed in a white spotlight amidst a darkness filled with whispers. Zamath stepped out of the shadow before him, the red light of his amulet glinting off the sword in his hand. He cackled and bared his pointed teeth as he approached.

Abramm drew his own sword and dropped to ready position, eager to fight and confident of victory. But then Zamath turned into Beltha'adi, who laughed and mocked him. "You think that mark will save you! Fool! It has already killed you!"

Startled, Abramm looked down to find a gold shieldmark shining on his own chest, then blinked at the sudden obstruction in his eye. White curd plopped onto his hand, and when he felt, trembling, at his face, he found his eyes billowing with a wet, sticky, globular goo.

Beltha'adi laughed again and, Commanding him to immobility with a deep bellow, attacked. His sword flashed up through the darkness, then changed to an ax as it came down, chopping deep into Abramm's arm.

He awoke, gasping and shaking and sick to his stomach. Frantically he felt for his arm, found it whole and hale, though the scar at his wrist throbbed with a vengeance. Nor did he wear a Terstan's shield. It was only another dream.

He thought he'd had a lot of them recently, but he didn't remember waking up between them. Certainly he didn't remember waking up here.

He lay on a straw-filled pallet in a windowless chamber, clad only in soft cotton britches, his chest and feet bare beneath a scratchy woolen blanket. An oil lamp sputtered atop a low table near the pallet; its ruddy light danced off plastered walls and the pale folds of a curtained doorway beyond his feet. From outside came a metallic clinking and the murmur of voices. From an even greater distance, goats *maaa*ed.

*Where am I?*

Besides his wrist, his head and ribs ached, but he had no other pains, though he thought he should.

Frowning at the plastered ceiling, he groped past the dream images for real memories—the veren's death, the Dorsaddi's mass conversion, the rising of the Heart. . . .

Had that *really* happened?

He touched his temple, as if he might physically pull the memories from the fog in which they hid. He had been wounded, covered with poison, and the poison had made him sick. He remembered that. But there was something more. Something important, something even more disturbing and frightening.

The pulse of his blood throbbed in his ears as he lay staring at the mosaic of cracks and watermarks above him. Then, hesitantly this time, his hand slid again over the flat plane of his belly, across his chest, up to his throat. There was no chain, no magical stone. He really had thrown it away. After nearly making himself a Terstan.

Nausea swirled through him as his fingers went back to the hard flat bone over his heart, assuring himself once more that no golden shield lay there, assuring himself he really had escaped its power. But Khrell's Fire! He had come so very close.

He closed his eyes, shuddering with relief. No wonder he'd had that awful dream.

The door curtain stirred, and a boy stuck his head into the room, lamplight gleaming off the shieldmark on his chest. Even one so young as that could be changed! The boy blinked at him with dark, hard eyes whose inscrutability reminded him painfully of Shettai. Then he was gone, the curtains swaying in his wake.

Shettai. That last look on her face, of wonder and joy. *"It is so beautiful. . . ."*

And she, too, wore a shield.

He thought he knew, at least in part, what she had seen. And it *was* beautiful. And, saints help him, in spite of everything, in spite of all he knew and all he'd seen, part of him still wanted it.

"I have fallen to deception once already," he whispered to the ceiling. "How can I even think of doing it again?"

*Because it may not be deception this time,* a quiet voice in his mind responded.

For a moment he could not breathe, feeling poised at the brink of a terrible epiphany. *It can't be that easy. It can't.*

*What if it is?*

He swallowed. *What of the sarotis? You can't forget that.* The dream of the old man had held more of reality than imagination. He had met that horrid crone, had been caught by him, threatened by him, had seen that awful, stinking curd. Nor was the man the only one affected. *How could Eidon be in anything that causes such wretchedness and suffering?*

*Trap does not have the sarotis,* said the quiet mental voice.

*Not yet. But it is only a matter of time.*

*Perhaps. But how do you explain the rest of it, then? The protection? The penetration of the Shadow's illusions? The shield and the healing?*

*Deception! All deception.* It had to be.

His headache was growing worse, aggravated by the shifting kaleidoscope of his thoughts. He wanted to reach in and wrestle them to order, to demand they make sense of themselves, but the demanding only made his head hurt more.

He shut his eyes and gave up. Later, he told himself. When he was clearheaded it would make sense.

It was some time before he opened his eyes again and sat up. The room spun. Crossing his legs before him, he propped his elbows on his thighs, holding his head in his palms. His mouth tasted horrible, and he felt dirty and sticky. He speared fingers through his hair. Thick and oily, it hung past his shoulders in a tangled mass that would be a nightmare to comb. And this well-grown stubble on his jaw . . . How long had he been asleep?

"Ah, so you're finally back." A Dorsaddi youth entered carrying a tray of flatbread and tea. "And just in time, too."

He set the tray on the table beside Abramm's pallet, then rocked back on his heels, waving at the food. "I'll wager you're starving."

For the first time Abramm realized he was indeed. His stomach burbled as if on cue, and he frowned, still fingering the stubble. "How long was I out?"

"Four days. The fever broke last night."

"Four *days*?"

The other nodded. "In an hour, if you keep this down, you can have more."

"Four days," Abramm muttered again. A lot could happen in four days. Especially after . . . "What did you mean 'just in time'?" He reached for the flatbread.

The youth's chest swelled and Abramm noticed then how the slitted neckline of his tunic had been deepened and the flaps sewn back to reveal his Terstan shield. "With the Heart awakened," he said, "we mean to retake Jarnek and drive out the Army of the Black Moon!" He bowed. "I will tell the Deliverer you have awakened."

Alone again, Abramm crunched the hard bread, sluicing away its dryness with sips of tea as he thought. So that was the Heart, then. It really *had* happened. He pushed the memory away, shivering. And Jarnek? That was the northernmost Dorsaddi city on the main road through Hur, first to fall in the original conquest. The place Beltha'adi had sent those two Hundreds in preparation for his final invasion.

The Hundreds should have arrived nearly a week ago. Could the Dorsaddi possibly have held them back this long? And what did the awakening of the Heart have to do with it? Was it just a morale booster, or was it more?

He found a pale robe hanging on a peg beside the pallet and shrugged it on, then slipped through the curtained doorway. A short, vaulted corridor led to a spacious chamber plastered in a salmon hue and carpeted with an ancient Sorite rug. It was, Abramm realized at once, one of those rugs rarely seen anymore, woven with thread of gold and sturdy wool dyed with the rich carnelian that was derived solely from a worm native to Sori. A worm said to have gone extinct at least a century ago.

Low benches scattered the room beneath ornate hanging oil lamps, and one whole wall was an arcade of arched openings hung with wind chimes and sculptures of colored glass, glowing in the light of the sun outside.

Yes. The sun.

Abramm strode to the window in astonishment and stared at the valley that cradled ruined Hur. Blue sky arced in a glorious vault overhead; sunlight washed over the red-and-ochre cliffs encircling the city, bathing the gold-and-salmon stone of its broken buildings and reflecting off the pale pavement of its great plaza. The great orb stood above it all, blazing on its stanchions, a miniature sun in itself. Even from here it caught at him, its power singing through his soul, reminding him, inviting him—

He looked away, aghast that he could be so vulnerable, even without the stone on his breast. Truly he had worn it too long.

A herd of goats browsed along the near edge of the promenade that stretched away in front of him. Chickens scratched at weeds that had grown inexplicably green and vigorous. The vines along the walls, no more than thick bare stems last time he had seen them, now wore a mantle of vigorous, bright green growth, and the olive trees lining the promenade sported dense crowns of shiny new leaves. Birds chattered and fluttered in their branches.

"The spawn have all left," came a low, familiar voice from behind him. He turned as Trap stepped up to join him.

The Terstan was dressed in white—britches, tunic, and robe, the latter stitched with gold-and-green olive branches along its front edges. The tunic's neckline, of course, was slit and stitched to deliberately reveal his shield. His red hair was tied back in a warrior's knot, and his half-grown beard was already showing its curl.

Meridon did not look at him, his gaze on the view outside. "It rained all night and through the first morning after we came," he added. "Been clear ever since."

Abramm let his eyes be pulled back to that wonderful light outside, to the sharp lines and angles, the brilliant colors. "I thought the rainy season lasted a couple of weeks."

"It does. It's still some days off, in fact. This is the result of the Heart's aura, warding away the Shadow. I'm told it extends some three leagues in every direction."

Below them, the goats moved from clump to clump, their coats fancifully patterned in brown, black, and brilliant white. One of them wore a bell, which tinkled as it moved.

"I had forgotten how it was," Abramm murmured. "The trees look so green. And these rocks are almost red." Even the patchwork patterns of the goats' hides seemed alive and vibrant.

The Heart, blazing on its straightened stanchions, snagged his gaze again, stirring those dangerous longings. *Truly, I am enspelled,* he thought grimly, forcing his eyes away and his thoughts to other subjects. "The young man who woke me said something about attacking Jarnek?"

Trap nodded. "Shemm means to leave tomorrow, so we can strike just before the rains."

"I thought the rains stopped all chance of fighting."

"They do. If we can take Jarnek before they start, Beltha'adi won't be able to launch a counterstrike until they're over. By which time we should be well dug in."

Abramm cocked a questioning brow at him. "We?"

The Terstan grimaced. "Well, I *have* been rather involved in the planning."

"And hope for no less in the plan's execution, I'll wager."

"My first duty lies with you, my lord."

Abramm blinked, not understanding what he meant at first. "You mean your oath to Raynen?" He huffed and shook his head. "I think we're way beyond that, Trap."

Meridon stared stubbornly out the window. "An oath is an oath. And even the White Pretender needs someone to cover his back." The dark eyes came around to fix upon his.

"I'm not the White Pretender anymore," Abramm said with a scowl.

"You are in the minds of the Dorsaddi. And in the mind of Beltha'adi, too, I'd guess."

He had a point. So here it was—another choice. Another opportunity to step deeper into the affairs of these people who were not his own. His presence as the White Pretender would undoubtedly provide some motivation to them, even if he hadn't turned out to be the Deliverer. And he would surely unnerve the opposition, seeing as he was supposedly dead.

He snorted softly at the irony of that thought, for he had fully expected to *be* dead by now—his duty to the Dorsaddi prophecy discharged, his debt to Shettai paid. But nothing had turned out as he'd expected, least of all that he should find himself alive and faced with choosing to take yet another step along a road whose destination he could no longer even begin to fathom.

Part of him wanted to walk away. He'd come to the SaHal, as Shettai had asked. Surely that was enough. More than enough. Except . . . Even if he was not the Deliverer, he was still in her debt. He had been eager enough to take from her what by right belonged only to a husband. Should he not also be willing to accept a husband's responsibilities? If he'd taken her as his wife, would he not now be honor bound to stand with her people against their enemies?

He glanced at Trap. "Do you think there's any chance of prevailing?"

Meridon grinned. "Shemm's convinced of it. And I know Eidon will provide a way, if that is his will."

*Eidon.* With a shiver of annoyance, Abramm turned back to the window, deliberately keeping his eye away from the shining orb and fixing it upon the goats below him.

"My Lord Deliverer?" They both turned to find a man in the standard headcloth, ochre robe, slit-necked tunic, and breeches of the rank-and-file Dorsaddi approaching across the carpet. "Your pardon, sir," he said, stopping a few respectful strides away and nodding in the Dorsaddi version of a bow. "The arrows have been gathered, as you requested. Four thousand of them."

Abramm's eye snagged on the golden shield glimmering in the V of his tunic. Annoyed, he tore his gaze free and made himself look at the man's face, lean and swarthy, with a touch of gray in the short dark beard.

"See that they're distributed," Trap said. "Twenty to a man. What about the extra bowstrings? And the wax?"

"Still working on those, sir." The Dorsaddi hesitated, eyes flicking to Abramm and back to Meridon. "Sir, the Lord Commander sends his compliments and wishes to know if you'll be speaking to us tonight."

"My thanks, and tell him I will be."

"Very good, my lord."

Trap nodded a dismissal, and as the man vanished around the doorway across the room, Abramm glanced at him askance. " 'My Lord Deliverer'?"

The Terstan made a face. "I've tried to get them to stop, but they refuse. I suppose I should've been more forceful about it at the start, but I really didn't believe it would catch on like it has. It wasn't me that awakened the

Heart, after all—it was they themselves, accepting the Light into their flesh. Shemm says I'll never get them to stop now and might as well resign myself to it." His face reddened. "I guess I have, more or less, because I hardly notice it anymore. It certainly doesn't help that Shemm calls me that himself."

It was odd that Abramm should feel jealous at that. Odd and ridiculous and completely illogical that he would feel increasingly disappointed—even angry—as the realization dawned that he had been supplanted by his friend in the vaunted role of Dorsaddi Deliverer. He had never wanted the role in the first place, knew from the beginning that he was nothing more than a pretender. Yet now that the truth had come out, he found it surprisingly hard to swallow.

It was his cursed Kalladorne pride again—the bane of his existence as a Mataian novice. He had thought that the experience of slavery would have driven it out of him. But the last eighteen months of being the White Pretender had apparently resurrected it, for he found he did not at all like being relegated to the ignominious position of companion to the great Deliverer—even if Trap did refuse to claim the title.

He didn't much like seeing himself for an arrogant fool, either, however, caught up in petty considerations of rank and pecking order when there were much more important things to consider. And perhaps, given the things he had done recently, it was no more than he deserved.

So he swallowed his pride and his discomfort and said, "What's he like, this infamous Dorsaddi king?"

"Surprisingly humble—and sensible—for a Dorsaddi. But he *is* Dorsaddi, and their . . . um . . . self-confidence . . . can get a little overblown. Some were ready to ride on Jarnek the day after they received the shield." He paused. "Still, for all his pride, he does listen and sometimes even takes advice."

"You like him."

"I do. He's a good man and a strong leader. A lesser one could not have held this group together. Especially not now, with half of them bearing the shield and the other half not. It's been a real battle convincing them to let each other alone."

*So. There are others, then, who have refused.*

"I'm surprised," Abramm said aloud. "Seeing the king himself has it. You'd think his subjects would flock to imitate him."

"Dorsaddi are not big on flocking and imitating. Mephid, for example, thinks he ought to be king himself, or at least the true Deliverer. And in any case, you can't receive the shield unless you really want to know the One who gives it. It is your own desire that ignites its power. A man who doesn't want it sees only a plain, round pebble, completely ordinary and sometimes even faintly repellent. Picking it up would be like picking up a rock. Well, you know."

Abramm had turned his attention to the goats again, his middle suddenly tight and fluttery, his heart pounding. "And what," he asked, glad he managed to keep his voice neutral, "does a man who wants it see?"

"Ah, he sees it as it is—ablaze with light and life, filled with the presence of the One whose Light it is." He could feel Trap's eyes upon him now but ignored him, watching one of the goats, a little red one, as it leaped for the fork of one of the olive trees, scrambled briefly for a hold, then fell back.

"Some even claim they see a man—Tersius himself, perhaps. . . ." Trap's voice strangled into silence, and he stood staring at Abramm, his tension palpable.

Abramm felt as if his chest were wrapped tight with Dorsaddi thong, and he knew his face had gone dead white.

Trap's voice came softly, hardly more than a breath. "You almost took it that night, didn't you? *That's* why you threw it away. Because you nearly did it, and it scared the wits out of you."

Abramm's headache was back, as if little men pounded with tiny hammers along the inside of his skull. An image flashed through his mind—a man standing in the darkness, his marred features clear in their own light. Not Eidon, who could not be seen, but Tersius, who was both god and man and with whom men had once walked and laughed and lived. Who had not been consumed to make the Mataio's Flames, claimed Terstans, but lived on in the light of their magical orbs.

He shook his head, opened his mouth, closed it. Then he tried again, his voice barely more audible than Meridon's had been. "I left all that behind, Trap. Don't ask me to go back to it."

"You left a lie, and no one's asking you to go back to that."

Abramm shook his head. "It's not that easy. I *believed* in Saeral! With every fiber of my being I believed. And I was wrong." He drew a breath to still the trembling that had crept into his voice. "I don't ever want to be wrong like that again."

A breath of air blew through the window, and the chimes tinkled quietly. Outside, the goat made another leap, scrambled, and fell again. Another one, smaller, with white and black patches set against the red, came up to nuzzle it.

Trap exhaled softly. "You were a boy," he said finally. "And he set himself to deceive you—a master deceiver versus a ten-year-old. What chance did you have?"

"Still . . . I should have doubted."

"You did! Why do you think they never touched you in all that time of your novitiate? Because somewhere you doubted." He paused. "But things are different now. You know a great deal more about the world and evil . . . and truth. Certainly you know enough to choose."

He lifted a hand, and a tiny globe bloomed on his fingertip, blazing—*blazing*—at the corner of Abramm's vision.

Abramm rubbed his throbbing arm and refused to look at it, grinding his teeth with the effort of keeping his eyes away. After a moment it hardened and rolled down the Terstan's finger into his palm. He set it carefully on the sill, his eyes never leaving Abramm's face.

"I . . . I have to know it's Eidon this time," Abramm said. "No doubts. No questions."

"How can you not know, Abramm?" Trap waved a hand at the mist-free city with its glowing Heart and living trees and bright blue bowl of sky. "What more do you need?"

"Evil fights evil sometimes!" Abramm cried, dismayed by the desperation that rang in his voice. "How do I know it's not another trick? Just another lie dressed up in pretty clothes?"

"You know in your heart."

"I can't trust my heart."

The goat finally managed to make it up into the fork of the tree and was now straining toward the fresh green leaves, still out of reach. The others moved farther along the promenade, the bell on the lead animal clanking, the boys who were seeing to them practicing idly with their slings. Up the street a group of men laden with bundles emerged from one of the cliffside doorways and hurried away.

The breeze washed around Abramm again, warm and heavy with goat smell. The chimes tinkled. And after a time he said softly, "What of the sarotis, Trap? Do you just pretend it doesn't exist, or do you count it the price you must pay to stand on the side of good?"

The Terstan frowned. "The sarotis is caused by our own choosing."

"Who would choose such a thing?"

"Those who pretend it doesn't exist. Those who receive the gift, then turn away from it to follow their own path."

"But why would anyone, once he had the Light, refuse it if it really is good?"

"Because even when we have the Light, we still carry the Shadow. And the Shadow will always strain against the Light. When we let the Shadow have sway over us, when we indulge its desires and delusions consistently, ignoring the Light, refusing its entreaties—that's what eventually produces the curd and the madness. And any acquisition of spawn spore accelerates the process." He paused. "It's commonly believed that the sarotis will inevitably strike all those who wear the shield. But that is not so. It's merely another lie spread by the enemy. Far more people than you guess have worn the shield for years and have never shown a trace of curd. My father, for example, and others—people *you've* known all your life, in fact."

"Who are not here to prove this claim, I note."

Trap regarded him for a long, silent moment, then turned away, a look of frustration on his face.

"I want to believe you," Abramm said. "I really do. I just . . . I can't."

Meridon ran a finger along the sill in front of them. "Can't, my lord? Or won't?"

"If I could believe it was true, I'd do it in a moment. I would."

"Well, then, my friend, I suggest you ask yourself just what it is that's keeping you from believing. Because whatever it is, it lies in your own soul, not in the evidence before your eyes." He pushed back from the window. "I'd better go. I expect the king will call you this evening. In the meantime you get some rest."

"I feel fine."

"You are weaker than you know. And if . . ." He hesitated. "*Will* we be riding with them tomorrow, then?"

"Yes, of course."

Even if he said no, he had the feeling he would be pulled there anyway. A leaf in a windstorm. Carried along by forces quite beyond his ability to control or even understand. The question was . . . did anyone have hold of the windstorm?

# CHAPTER 34

"Do you ever wonder why you're alive?" Carissa asked, scratching the new staffid bite on her forearm and eyeing the salmon-and-ochre cliffs looming around them. She sat with Cooper at a wrought-iron table under an ancient, gnarled olive tree in one of Jarnek's outdoor restaurants. It was situated on the artificially constructed island standing at the point where two wide, currently dry wadis converged to become the one main channel. "I mean, do you ever think maybe there's no real purpose in it?"

"I think we're alive to serve Eidon," Cooper said.

"A stock Mataian response."

"If we keep the commands, we are blessed. If we don't, we—"

"Not good enough, Coop. These people do not serve Eidon, yet some of them are blessed."

He frowned at her.

"My brother wanted only to know and serve him—I have never known anyone more devoted to that cause. Yet what did it gain him?"

"He is surely reveling in the Garden of Light right now, my lady."

She snorted. "If there is such a thing. How do we know it doesn't all end at death?"

His frown deepened. "You certainly are being grim today."

She sighed deeply. "I feel as if my whole life has been nothing but one big blundering. Everything I touch turns to ash. Not one thing I have wanted have I received. Only pain and despair and failure. If Eidon really lives, what have I done to deserve that?"

"Nothing." He swallowed and looked up at the red cliffs, frowning more deeply than ever. "Nothing."

"Life isn't fair."

"No."

She let her gaze wander over the soldiers' tents pitched in the wadis to either side of them, the purple pennants of the Black Moon hanging limply from their standards. Most of the merchants whose booths would normally fill those dry washes had packed up and headed upland to beat the rains. Once the winds came and the clouds broke, all roads in or out would be transformed to churning rivers, and whoever was in Jarnek would be trapped for at least a month and maybe two.

The soldiers figured to be here that long, regardless.

Beyond them the terraced rock walls loomed under the mist, their curving organic lines merging gracefully with the sharper, more angular aspects of the villas built among them, even carved from the rock itself. Stairways and water channels wound between them, and she knew the cliffs themselves were riddled with narrow, mysterious canyons, laced with more channels and dams and cisterns, all part of the original builders' sophisticated hydrologic system. "Abramm would've loved this place."

"Aye, he would've."

"He'd have run you ragged and given Gillard fits."

Cooper snorted softly, and suddenly, beneath her veil, Carissa was weeping again. It often happened like this—a word, a thought, and all unexpected the grief took her.

Not long after that, Philip bounced up the stairs from the wadi, Newbold in tow, and hurried over to them, his eyes bright, face flushed with excitement. He had been wandering the city, listening to the gossip, and now he fairly overflowed with it—how the Dorsaddi Deliverer had come and awakened the Heart, how there was a hole in the mist over Hur, a good six leagues in diameter. "They say it's the White Pretender," he bubbled, "but I'm sure it's the Infidel!"

She listened halfheartedly, wishing he wasn't so wretchedly enthusiastic. Sometimes it rubbed her so raw she could hardly bear to be in his presence, and it took all her willpower not to snarl at him to shut up. "And why do you think that?" she asked.

"Because it's Terstan power. It has to be. Do you realize every time they've put out the flames in that Temple of Khrell, they've left behind the symbol of a Terstan shield?"

"The shield is a Dorsaddi symbol, too," Cooper said.

"Yes. I think there must be a connection."

Carissa felt a sudden rush of pity for him. He was so excited, so full of hope and confidence. How long before the curd started to fill his eyes and twist his bones? How long before the evil his parents had inflicted upon him moved into his mind and turned him mad? Life was *not* fair. No more for him than her. He just didn't know it yet.

She sighed.

"Milady, I have something for you." He had turned to her and was thrusting a small leather pouch into her hands, looking suddenly nervous and half embarrassed.

She fingered it open and dumped a pale gray pebble set on a gold chain into her palm. The setting was no more than a delicate gold claw holding the stone, which looked like an ordinary round river rock. Why would anyone want to put it into a setting and wear it around her neck? Worse, why would Philip think she might appreciate it?

He was watching her eagerly. "Do you like it?"

She stared at it in chagrin, glad again for the veil that hid her face. "Oh, well, yes, it's um—"

"Where did you get that?" Cooper demanded of the boy, as if he were unaware she had been speaking. "Did you steal it?"

"Of course not!"

"I thought you didn't have any money." The retainer's expression had gone stern and dark.

"I had some."

"Enough for a stone like that?" For some reason Cooper sounded incredulous.

Carissa looked at the stone again but could see no reason for Cooper to be so suspicious. It still looked like a common pebble, and she wondered now if the boy might have found it and merely had it set onto the necklace because he wanted to do something for her and it was all he could afford.

"I didn't steal it, Master Cooper," Philip said quietly.

"I'm sure you didn't, Philip," Carissa said before Cooper could reply. "And it was very sweet of you to think of me."

Philip turned to her in renewed eagerness. "It's to help ward the staffid. You were having so much trouble with them—"

"It wards staffid?" She picked up the chain and let the stone dangle before her, eyeing it with considerably more interest.

"So they say. And not just staffid, but other things, too. Evil spells and the like."

"Well, then, let me put it on at once!" she cried. "I wouldn't want to fall sway to any evil spells!" *At least it's not an onion!*

The staffid bites seemed to itch even more than usual as she fastened it around her neck, but it was worth it for the pleasure her actions clearly gave the boy. For a moment he looked ready to speak, but then he glanced again at Cooper and closed his mouth, the ghost of a frown creasing his brow.

"Ah," said Cooper. "Here comes Danarin. It's about time."

Carissa glanced toward the tents in the wadi below and saw the familiar form of their companion weaving his way among them, his dusky red tunic making subtle contrast with the military grays surrounding him.

Danarin had spent the afternoon in the south sector, visiting the gambling houses, hoping to resupply Carissa's depleted funds. She did not approve, but the trip here had cost so much in tolls and bribes, she'd had nothing left to pay the outrageous room fees demanded by local hostelers. If she didn't want to sleep in the wadi with the soldiers tonight, she had no choice but to rely upon Danarin's skills with the Bones and Dice and accept his charity.

His willingness to give it did not make acceptance easier. She trusted him no more now than in Qarkeshan, though her attraction to him continued unabated. He had, if anything, grown more handsome with their renewed association.

They had reached Jarnek solely because of him. At each checkpoint he'd contrived to get them through uninspected, playing the part of the young, wealthy Brogai lord. Though travelers all around were being forced to disrobe, the women escorted off to visit the commanding officers, no one ever lifted Carissa's veil or even contested his claims to immunity. She thought he looked far too pale of skin to pass for true Brogai, but no one else seemed able to see past the rings on his fingers and the gold round his neck.

She owed much to the Thilosian. It would be nice if she could feel unreservedly grateful.

Danarin bounded up the stairs and slid into the seat across from her, the gold threads woven throughout the fabric of his tunic gleaming and glimmering with his movement.

"Did you have a successful afternoon, Master Danarin?" Cooper asked dryly.

Danarin grinned and patted the bulging coin purse at his waist. "Indeed I did, Master Cooper." He flashed the grin at Carissa. "All soldiers' gold, my lady, have no fear."

She frowned at him, but as usual, her signs of disapproval had no impact. He merely smiled wider and dropped her a courtly nod. "I have also solved the problem of our night's lodging. My gaming partner was so pleased with our play that he has invited us to stay with him."

"I am not staying in another brothel," Carissa declared.

The Thilosian shook his head. "My lady, please. You know we had no choice."

"I'd rather sleep in the wadi with the soldiers."

"Well, fortunately, you'll not have to make that choice." He turned and pointed to one of the structures sprawling across the steep, terraced slopes overlooking the main wadi from the south. "That is his villa there, at the top of the face. He says you can see the amphitheater from his garden."

Her gaze went from the villa to the man. "You're serious?"

His grin widened. "I made him a lot of money today, and he's grateful. He all but insisted we come."

"All of us? Even Eber and Peri and the dog?" She glanced toward the two servants sitting with the baggage on a bench outside the restaurant's railed patio.

"It's one of the largest villas in Jarnek, my lady. The man has plenty of room. He's expecting us as we speak."

"Well, I suppose we mustn't disappoint him, then."

The villa's servants were indeed waiting to take their bags and wash their feet when they arrived, and the odor of roasting fowl ignited Carissa's hunger all at once. As they slipped into soft leather house slippers and their servants—plus Newbold—were ushered away to the appropriate area, their host strode in to welcome them. One of the wealthiest merchants in Jarnek, Ormah Fah'lon was middle-aged and balding, with a slight paunch and a dark goatee. Jewels glittered on his fingers and in his ears—ruby studs alongside the gold rings that betrayed a fighting past—and contrasted elegantly with his black knee-length tunic of fine wool.

He greeted Danarin warmly as Lord Iban, then turned to Carissa and seemed to start. His dark eyes flicked back to Danarin. "Your wife is *kaziym*?"

The servants had taken the outer mantle and full face-veil she was required to wear in public, leaving only the sheer half veil, which did little to hide her pale skin and blue eyes.

"Yes," Danarin said smoothly. "I bought her in Qarkeshan last year."

For a moment Fah'lon seemed inexplicably dismayed. Then the expression vanished, and once more he was warm and cordial. "Quite a prize it would seem, too."

It dawned on Carissa what they were talking about, and though Fah'lon went on to say something about his own wife unfortunately being absent, she hardly heard him past the outrage that rang in her ears. Wife? Danarin had told this man she was his *wife*? She glared at the Thilosian in a fury, not caring that her expression would be clear to their host as well. Wife? How dare he!

He ignored her, as usual, and said something about her beauty being balanced by a temperamental nature—which only raked her ire hotter. Then the men were turning away, moving down the tile-floored hall together, expecting Carissa to follow, as was the custom.

"And just what is *my* role in this little charade, I wonder?" Cooper murmured from just behind her.

She glanced back at him. "Chief retainer, it would seem, seeing as you didn't even warrant an introduction." She glared after the men as they disappeared through the doorway at the hall's end. "He will hear of this, mark me on it."

"I'm sure he will. Shall I stay here, then?" Cooper gestured around the spacious anteroom.

"That would probably be best."

Angry enough to spit, Carissa followed her "husband," promising herself that once they were out of Esurh, the relationship with Danarin would be severed, no matter how little money they had. Unless he irked her further. Then it would be severed tonight.

The spacious dining room, one long wall of which was an arcade of arched openings overlooking the city, held a low rectangular table flanked by the usual pillows. To Carissa's surprise, it was set for three—the men's places at one end, her own apparently at the other. Usually women ate separately, if not in different rooms, at least at different tables. This was a pleasing development, even if she was still a little too angry to appreciate it.

"I had not heard of the plague in Vedel," Fah'lon was remarking to Danarin as they settled onto the pillows. "This is of concern."

"I'm just grateful it has not reached Jarnek yet."

"Pray it never does! And that it does not reach Ybal, where my wife has gone. May the rains come quickly!"

As Carissa settled unremarked and apparently unnoticed, a gaggle of serving girls trooped in bearing platters of chicken, bowls of curried quail with rice, steamed onions and garlic, pickled baby beets, olive oil, flatbread, and grapes.

Carissa was served last and was feeling quite defiant when she refused to accept any of the onions. As she contemplated how she might eat without getting food all over her veil, Danarin came to her rescue.

"I noticed, Serr Fah'lon, that none of your women cover their faces."

Fah'lon shook his head. "We do not follow the Way of the Veil in this house. Nor any of the other dictates of Khrell. I hope this does not offend you."

"Not at all. We, too, serve other gods." Danarin paused. "I presume it will not offend you, then, if my wife—"

"Certainly not."

Danarin nodded at her, and she nearly forgave him the wife blunder, so pleased was she to dispense with the half veil. But as she dropped it from her face, Fah'lon's smiling interest gave way to a sharp, startled look, and he drew back in obvious surprise.

"Something troubles you, sir?" Danarin asked.

The man recovered his poise swiftly, the easy practiced smile returning to reassure. "Not at all. It is just . . ." He chuckled softly. "I guess all northerners tend to look alike to me. It's the blue eyes and the golden hair. They are so startling, it is all I see at first."

"Ah. Yes." Danarin's voice sounded strangely flat to her, odd somehow, like a courtier keeping his tone carefully neutral so as not to give himself away. But what could there be to give away here?

"You are wise to keep her covered. She is a prize indeed. And Kiriathan women are especially coveted these days, what with these cat-and-mouse games the Pretender is playing. The soldiers would love to take their frustration out on her."

"The Pretender?" Danarin drew back on his pillows, brows arched, a slight smile on his lips. "But he's dead, sir. I saw the body myself, impaled at the entry gate of Xorofin."

Ormah Fah'lon laughed. "How do you know for sure it was *his* body?"

"The man was obviously Kiriathan."

"So is your wife. We have no shortage of pale-haired slaves in the southland." He leaned forward to scoop rice and quail into his mouth. "The Pretender and his Infidel always performed painted and wigged," he said around the mouthful. "Few knew their real faces. The man you saw could have been anyone."

"Philip's insisted all along he got away," Carissa put in. "Remember?"

Both men turned to gape at her. Evidently the laxity with respect to the veil did not extend to conversation. With a frown of annoyance she returned her attention to her grapes, cursing anew this horrid land and its repressive culture.

"She is forward, this wife of yours," Fah'lon commented mildly, eyeing her with amusement.

"The northern blood," Danarin growled, frowning. "Sometimes she cannot help herself."

"And who is this Philip?" Fah'lon asked.

"One of our servants," Danarin said.

"Well, he is right." The Esurhite spooned onions into his mouth. "In truth both the Pretender and the Infidel escaped to the SaHal and re-ignited the Dorsaddi's sacred Heart. They say it has burned a hole six leagues wide in the mist over Hur and that the rains have come early there—gentle rains, not our usual deluges. It is rumored that the Dorsaddi have experienced some mighty religious revival and have even found their Deliverer." He paused, wine cup halfway to his lips. "Surely you've heard the stories."

"Wild tales, I thought. People laughed at them."

"The men in Jarnek are not laughing, friend. Nor is the great Beltha'adi." Fah'lon took a long draught from the cup, then set it down and wiped his mouth. "He was supposed to be sitting in Hur by now, counting his victories. Instead he's scrambling to replace the men he's already lost. Official count is less than a quarter of the two Hundreds he sent in, but the truth is closer to half. Another Hundred arrived two days ago—camped out there in the wadi—and he's working his priests near to death bringing in new men through the etherworld corridor in Khrell's temple. He is frantic to beat the rains." He chuckled softly. "And all the while the Pretender heckles him."

Danarin looked up from the chicken leg he was gnawing. "You really believe the Pretender is here in Jarnek?"

"Who do you think is orchestrating all these little raids, the wasp stinging the elephant? The Dorsaddi have brought the fight to Beltha'adi. Taunting him. Taunting his men. They appear, and the soldiers rush to meet them, only to have them vanish back into the canyons. Snipers pick off members of the patrols, so that many of the men are afraid of even leaving Jarnek. And despite the picket lines and the sentries—double the normal number—they still sneak into the city, burn the weapons stockpiles, steal the food, vandalize the temple itself, all right under the soldiers' noses without being seen, much less caught."

He laughed. "The best one was two nights ago when they diverted water from the fortress cistern into the main camp down there. Washed away half their gear and drenched everything. To say nothing of scaring the wits out of them. They thought the rains had come!" He shook his head, still chuckling. "It was a grand sight, let me tell you!"

Danarin was watching him intently now. "I can't imagine Beltha'adi would agree."

Fah'lon burst into a new round of chuckling. "No, I can't imagine he would."

Danarin returned to his chicken with studied casualness. "I had heard your sympathies did not lie with the ruling power, sir, but I did not expect you to be so blatant about it."

"My sympathies are well-known. I have expressed them to the Supreme Commander's face, in fact. Why do you think those soldiers are skulking in the street outside my house?" He leaned closer and spoke conspiratorially. "He believes I am in league with the Pretender himself and has my house watched in hopes of capturing him one day."

Danarin put down the bone he had gnawed clean and rinsed his fingers in the bowl provided. "And are you? In league with him?"

"Perhaps. Or perhaps I just enjoy the baiting." Fah'lon smiled. "If Beltha'adi's soldiers invade my home and turn up nothing, he'll have much to answer for among the local Brogai. And he has enough to worry about right now, without having to contend with them."

Danarin had nothing to say to this, and conversation took a new turn. Outside, the twilight deepened toward night, the lights of the soldiers' campfires burning like orange stars along the lines of the converging drainages. Crickets sang from the garden foliage and nighthawks called. Every now and then loud bursts of laughter arose from the camp out of sight immediately below them.

They had almost finished the final course—a jellied fruit mold with sweetened yogurt—when the laughter turned to a chorus of angry shouting, even as a yellow flickering danced across the facing cliffs. Fah'lon was on his feet and out on the terrace in an instant, Danarin on his heels. Carissa followed more slowly.

It was true they could see the amphitheater from Fah'lon's terrace, though it was some distance up the wadi. Its bench seats were carved into the curved wall of the canyon to form a half bowl that faced them almost directly, the wadi floor widening at that point to form the arena. Smooth, sandy, and bare, the expanse would have made a great place for the soldiers to set up their tents, though none had. At its midst someone had planted a heavy pole on which was impaled a huge black bird, headless, but still obviously a veren. Flames already burned its lower body, licking up around its chest, wherein was plunged a heavy stake topped with the large, stylized white diamond that had become the Pretender's insignia.

"See?" Fah'lon said with great amusement. "He lives. And while they're dealing with this, he'll probably steal into the temple and put out the flames again. Or loose the livestock and frighten them into a stampede. They did that last week, and I don't think the handlers have gotten them all back yet."

"Clever, perhaps," Danarin said, "but I don't see how you can ascribe it to one man, let alone identify him as the Pretender."

"I know King Shemm, and this is not his style."

"Still—"

"You would like to know . . . have I seen him? Have I talked to him?"

"Yes."

Fah'lon grinned. "So would Beltha'adi."

They watched while men tossed buckets of water at the burning veren, then pushed over the post to untie it. No livestock were apparently loosed, and if anything was happening at the temple—out of sight around the cliff wall—there was no sign of it.

Once the flames were out and things quieted down, Fah'lon led his guests back to the dining area, where they were just finishing the remains of their desserts when a servant hurried in. He whispered something into his master's ear that caused Fah'lon to nod.

As the servant departed, the merchant addressed his guests. "I fear some business has come up to which I must attend. If you'll excuse me?" Danarin nodded, but Fah'lon hesitated, his gaze flicking to Carissa, a slight crease forming between his brows. He almost turned away, then said, "The terrace and gardens are especially nice this time of year. I urge you to explore them at your leisure. It would, however, be wise to keep your lady covered." He smiled slightly. "As I said, the soldiers watch us always." Again he hesitated, as if he wanted to say more. Then his eyes flicked back to Danarin, and the hesitation vanished.

"Have a good evening," he said and strode briskly from the room.

CHAPTER

# 35

As Fah'lon's footsteps died away Danarin turned to Carissa with a smug expression. "It *is* the Pretender! And Fah'lon knows him—I'll bet my bag on it."

"We don't care about the Pretender," she said. "Why didn't you ask him about the Infidel?"

Danarin's dark brows arched. "I didn't think we cared about the Infidel, either."

"Philip does."

"I thought you were through with that. I thought you'd convinced him he had to let his brother find his own way home. For that matter, he probably has." He gestured generally around them. "This business is a Dorsaddi matter—of no concern to Meridon."

"Well, perhaps he's made it his concern. He has been exiled, after all. And the Dorsaddi did help rescue him."

"I still don't see how that concerns us. Frankly, I think we need to get out of here as soon as possible. This place is a powder keg waiting for a lit match."

From somewhere in the house came a singing bark, and she looked around, startled. "Was that Newbold?"

Before he could answer, a white-and-gold cat raced through the doorway and fled into the front anteroom. They heard another bay, then voices yelling.

Danarin shook his head. "I cannot believe you actually brought that dog with you."

"Without him we'd never have known Meridon was really the Infidel." Or that Abramm wasn't the Pretender.

A servant arrived bearing steaming cups of tea. After that they were left alone, listening to faint bangs and clatters from the kitchen and the murmur of voices, which finally faded to a deep, empty silence.

"Sounds like we're the only ones here," Carissa said presently, feeling increasingly uneasy.

"They're probably just done for the night," Danarin assured her. "How about we take a look at Fah'lon's garden?"

If anything, the sense of breathless expectation was stronger outside, though it may just have been the new mugginess that had lately crept into the air. It made the veil she'd redonned more uncomfortable than ever, and in a fit of petty defiance, she unfastened the face part and let it hang. They were alone in their host's private garden, for Haverall's sake! And anyway, it was too dark for some spying soldier to tell the color of her eyes.

Fah'lon's garden consisted of a series of walled terraces linked by short, wide stairways. Pots and planters held carefully pruned trees and shrubs and spilled over with sweet-scented flowers. Freestanding oil lamps lit the way. Here and there, stone benches stood around unlit braziers or small domed ovens.

The last terrace ended in a waist-high wall overlooking the camp in the wadi below. The acrid stench of burning dung tainted the air, unblunted by the flowers' sweetness. Behind an iron gate, a narrow stairway wound down through the rocks to what appeared to be a delivery area below. Beyond that, the slope tumbled toward the wadi, steeply on the right, less so on the left. Neighboring villas glowed amidst the rocks, and she could see figures walking back and forth from time to time in the lighted windows. If there were soldiers out there, she did not see them.

In the amphitheater across the way they'd removed the veren's carcass and added a ring of torches to illumine the sandy floor and ranks of empty bench seats. "Why doesn't anyone camp there?" she asked, gesturing toward it.

"It's reserved for the contest," Danarin said.

"Contest?"

"Rumor has it that Beltha'adi's challenged the Pretender to personal combat."

"You mean like the Pretender asked for in the Val'Orda?"

"Yes."

She frowned at him, noting uneasily that he had given the impression of having somewhat less knowledge—and interest—on this subject when speaking to Fah'lon.

"If the Pretender wins, Beltha'adi's promised to spare the Dorsaddi. If Beltha'adi wins, the Dorsaddi become his slaves." Danarin leaned his elbows on the top edge of the wall. "So far there's been no response. Unless that headless veren could be considered a response."

Carissa sniffed. "The Pretender would be stupid to face him now—if Fah'lon's right that the Dorsaddi already have the upper hand."

Danarin smiled that irritating, condescending smile. "Fah'lon's biased. What have these Dorsaddi wasps done that's of any real significance, after all? Once Beltha'adi has enough men and magic, they won't have a chance."

"So why issue the challenge?"

"To bait him. Every day the Pretender doesn't respond, he looks more the coward. And the Dorsaddi can't stand cowards. Moreover, it's to the Supreme Commander's advantage to resolve this as soon as possible. He has a war going in Andol, after all, and this is hardly helping."

"I suppose there are the rains to consider, too."

Danarin looked at her sidelong, a half smile on his face. "Indeed. I suspect both sides would like to wrap this up before then."

His gaze dropped to her chest, and his brows drew together. "Where did you get that?"

She looked down, saw the ugly stone of the staffid-warder gleaming against the dark folds of her gown. "Oh. Philip gave it to me this afternoon."

"His taste is . . . uh . . . unusual." The dark eyes flicked up to hers, watching her intently.

She shrugged and blushed. "He's only a boy. What would he know about fashion? I thought it was rather sweet of him. He said it was supposed to ward the staffid."

"It's ugly enough, I suppose. Does it work?"

"I haven't seen any since I put it on."

"Well, it hardly does you justice."

She snorted. "As if that matters when I must go about perpetually veiled and shrouded."

"It matters to me."

He turned fully to face her, his expression sober. The lamplight washed across the well-formed planes of his face, accented by the narrow, dark beard and those long lashes. She swallowed, finding it suddenly hard to breathe. Warmth spread over her chest and neck. And irritation, directed at both him and at herself for responding to him when it was the last thing she wished to do.

He smiled. "After all this time, you still do not trust me."

She lifted her chin. "No."

"Then I shall be forced to keep trying to win you. Will you accept a peace offering?" He withdrew a small bag from his pocket, opened it, and pulled out a slender choker. Tiny, threadlike swirls of silver arced delicately across air and space, an exquisite net for the stone it held, which was a work of art in itself. Dark at the center, almost brooding, it glowed with a sea-deep hue.

"It's beautiful," she breathed.

"It matches your eyes." He smiled. "When I saw it this afternoon, I knew I had to win it for you."

"You won this?"

He nodded. "Here, let me put it on you."

Laying the bag aside, he stepped toward her, then frowned. "Can I take this off first?" He lifted the chain holding Philip's staffid-warder. "I don't think they'll go together very well."

"Not very well, no," she acceded. "Here." Reaching up, she unfastened the chain herself, then stood as he reached both hands around the back of her neck. She felt his breath on her face and kept her eyes fixed on the potted tree behind him. Little thrills spread down her arms and back as his fingers worked in light flutters against her nape, and she was both relieved and disappointed when he stepped away, having done no more than put the choker on her.

He looked at it, satisfaction in his gaze. "Very nice."

She was struck with a sudden feeling of unease. Perhaps she should have refused. Would he think now that her acceptance bespoke the interest he so obviously hoped to cultivate?

A sudden shout echoed above, followed by heavy footfalls and a strange clinking, then more shouts. In the dining room, now well above them, the lights went out.

"What the plague?" Danarin ran for the stair. She hurried after him, confused, certain something awful had happened, not certain what. But midstair he stopped dead, and she ran into him even as he whirled to head back for the gate, pulling her after him. She said not a word, her heart hammering against her ribs. The only thing she could think was that the soldiers watching Fah'lon's house had finally launched their raid and that if they were to find her it could not end well.

Danarin yanked open the gate, iron hinges squealing frightfully, and they raced down the narrow path that had been carved into the stone. Smooth, sheer walls of sandstone hemmed them in closely. If they encountered any soldiers coming up, there would be no place to go.

Danarin stopped again, and again she rebounded off of him. He didn't seem to notice, staring at the sandstone wall, one hand trailing up it thoughtfully. Then with a glance back the way they'd come, he began to climb the gritty face. As soon as he was past her head she saw the hand- and footholes carved into the rock. He scrambled over the top, then leaned down to offer her a hand. She reached for the first handhole, realized she was still holding Philip's necklet, and hastily wound it several times around her sash before shoving the stone between sash and waist. Then she felt again for the hole and started up.

In moments he was pulling her over the rounded rock and into a small stone structure that seemed to be a covered cistern. They huddled breathlessly just inside the doorway, Carissa struggling to hear past her labored breathing.

"Stay here," Danarin whispered. He crawled back to the edge on his belly and peered down at the pathway they had just left.

She heard the footfalls first, then the voices and loud panting of the men who had come down through the garden. The footfalls stopped just at the place where they had climbed up the rock to the shack. She heard a quiet argument, a scuffle. A curse. A red light flared off the stone, and a chill shivered through her. For a long moment no one spoke. Then a sharp word echoed off the stone and they were moving again, some hurrying down the path, others climbing back up to the terraces.

She breathed a quiet sigh of relief, and shortly Danarin drew back to join her in the shack. Groups of men ran up and down the path several times. She heard more shouts, more clinks, the distressed cries of the servants they'd found. Did they have Cooper? Philip and the others? The thought made her ill. How would she ever get them back? Fah'lon had said if Beltha'adi raided his house and turned up nothing it could be very embarrassing for him politically, so perhaps he would be in a position to bargain. Perhaps Fah'lon would help. Perhaps . . .

But all she could think about was how much Philip looked like his brother, the infamous Infidel.

It felt as if they crouched there forever. Her bent legs went to sleep, and she even grew inured to having Danarin pressed against her side. Soldiers continued to run up and down the stair, flares of torchlight flickering off the rocks and fading. Once she heard someone yelling angrily, but the words were indistinct.

At last the sounds faded and darkness settled in, unbroken by any more passing torches. The silence had stretched on for some time when Danarin decided they could leave.

The delivery area at the bottom of the path smelled of animals and garbage, and was littered with barrels and refuse. It lay dark and silent, as did the villa above it. Keeping to the deepest shadows at the base of the rocks, they stole along the yard's edge to the unpaved cart road leading down and around the slope past the neighboring villa. Carissa was just starting to relax when a roll of gravel and the scuff of a boot preceded the advent of two dark figures looming up in the shadows around them. She squeaked in alarm as steel glinted in Danarin's hand.

"Easy, friend," came a familiar voice.

"Cooper?" Carissa whispered. Relief made her weak. She turned to the other figure. "Philip? Where are Eber and Peri?"

"Soldiers have them," Cooper said.

"I'd think they'd have you, too," Danarin said in a low voice. "That *was* you we heard up there when they first came in, wasn't it?"

"I wanted to warn you without drawing their attention to you," Cooper said. "Tried to draw them off a bit, but then I had to fight. They didn't expect that, so I got away. The others were down in the servants' sector and were caught by the men who came through the back door." He paused. "Even so, they didn't get very many."

"Well, that's good," Carissa said.

"No. I mean, I think some of the servants knew it was going to happen because most of them had already left. Around the time Fah'lon did, I think."

"How do you know he left?"

"I overheard the soldiers talking. They didn't get him."

"It was a setup!" Danarin cried softly, clearly annoyed. "I thought he was being helpful and friendly, and all the while he just wanted some bait for his trap." He muttered a curse under his breath.

"What trap?" Carissa asked.

"Remember what Fah'lon said about Beltha'adi wanting to catch him with the Pretender but having to be careful of the political ramifications? I think the Pretender was here tonight, most likely around the time Fah'lon left us. He probably led the soldiers here deliberately and then the two of them vanished, leaving only us for them to find and arrest when they invaded. I was supposed to howl my outrage and Beltha'adi was to be embarrassed again. Only we got away. Serves him right, I think."

Philip, it turned out, had escaped because he'd been out walking Newbold, embarrassed after the dog's outburst. He figured the soldiers had seen him but ignored him, since he wasn't who they were after. He paused at the end of his tale. "Did you say the White Pretender was *here*? Tonight?"

"I think there's a good chance of it," Danarin said.

"I never saw anyone," Cooper said. "Just the servant, and then Fah'lon hurrying away with him."

"So what do we do now?" Carissa asked.

Danarin sighed. "Find a place to hide, I think. Then I'll take a walk around and see what I can learn."

They continued down the cart path, moving quietly, fearful a guard might remain to surprise them. The neighboring villa loomed past the rocks below them, outer oil lamps casting warm salmon-colored pools in the darkness.

They had just left it comfortably behind when Newbold let out another of his spine-tingling bays and lunged at the end of the leash, dragging Philip behind him.

"He does that again and I'll cut his throat myself," Cooper growled.

The boy tugged on the leash, trying to haul him back, but the animal seemed to have his nose glued to the ground. His tail flipped back and forth frantically, and as he loosed another bay, Philip dropped to his knees and clamped both hands round the dog's muzzle to prevent further outbursts. But even with his mouth shut the hound hooted and yelped, more excited than Carissa had ever seen him.

"It's that cursed cat again," Cooper said.

"No." Philip faced them, a dark silhouette against the paler rock. "He doesn't chase cats. And he knows what we're after."

"He doesn't chase cats?" Carissa repeated.

"And there's a path here, you see?" Danarin said, pointing to a channel in the rock. "Heads straight up to the villa from the look of it. Someone coming down would have come right through here."

"And if the Pretender were here," Philip said, "my brother could have been with him."

"Well, that's not our concern!" Cooper hissed. "We aren't here to rescue him anymore, remember? And the last thing the lady needs is to get tangled up in some Dorsaddi uprising."

"If my brother is this close, Master Cooper," Philip said solemnly, "I'm going to find him."

"More like draw his enemies down upon him."

"They've all left, sir. If they hadn't, they'd be on us now."

"It's a fool's errand, boy."

"Nevertheless, I'm going."

"So am I," Carissa said firmly.

Cooper whirled to face her. "What?"

"If Captain Meridon is this close, I think it's worth trying to see him. I'd like to talk to him myself. He must know how Abramm died."

"This is madness! You don't even know for sure it *is* Meridon. And if it is, he's in neck-deep with the rebels, who aren't exactly friendly right now. If Beltha'adi's soldiers don't get you, the Dorsaddi surely will. You can't go. I forbid it."

"You are not in charge of this expedition, Master Cooper," Carissa said coldly.

"My lady, I will not let you do this."

"You have no choice in it, sir."

"Yes, Carissa, I do."

As the meaning of his words sank in, she stared up at him in shock.

"I'm afraid you are mistaken, sir," Danarin murmured, edging between them. "If the lady wishes to look for the Terstan, then she shall do so."

Tension crackled around them, and for a moment Carissa thought they would fight. In the end, Cooper backed down. "As you wish, my lady," he said tightly.

Carissa gestured at the dog. "Let him go, Philip. We'll see where he leads us. Just keep him quiet."

CHAPTER

# 36

As the northernmost of the Dorsaddi cities and gateway to the SaHal and lands beyond, Jarnek had once been a large and prosperous trading center. With the destruction of Hur and the enslavement of the Dorsaddi, it might have faded into obscurity except that Beltha'adi had decided to transform the existing temple of Sheleft'Ai to one honoring Khrell. That, plus the presence of numerous hot springs and baths, had kept the city alive.

But though new buildings of brick, sandstone, and even imported marble had arisen from the floor of the wide arriza at what was once its mouth, most of Jarnek still lay within the maze of narrow canyons south of that. The amphitheater, the treasury, the chieftain's palace, and the temple, all were carved from the sheer red-and-ochre rock walls, as were businesses, houses, storage chambers . . . and tombs.

Newbold had led them around the face of the terraced slope on which Fah'lon's villa perched, then down into the arriza, where the three dry wadis converged and the soldiers camped. Thankfully, they'd stayed well to the outer margins of that area, finally turning into one of the many canyons emptying into it.

Even in the dark they could feel the change, could feel the cold silence of the dead. The tombs at the canyon's mouth were large and well spaced, with elaborate facades carved from the rock—porticos, columns, narrow jutting roofs—and all were barred by locked iron gates. These eventually gave way to less ostentatious memorials and finally to mere holes in the walls. There were hundreds of these, at ground level and above, honeycombing the cliffs in ranks of dark, empty eyes. The stench of death wrapped them like a mantle, and the silence was crushing.

The dog snuffled back and forth, tail wagging, nose to the ground, dragging Philip behind him. He had stopped trying to bay some time ago—but that was a mixed blessing. If it meant they were not so likely to draw unwanted attention, it also meant the trail was starting to go cold.

Carissa was long past exhausted. It took all her concentration just to keep putting one foot ahead of the other; each time she stumbled she could hardly save herself from falling. And it seemed she kept hearing things in the darkness around them, ghostly sighings and whispers that could be the dead or Esurhite soldiers or, more likely, Dorsaddi sentinels. They would be watching, certainly, perhaps with arrows nocked. Even Carissa knew of the Dorsaddi reputation for shooting first and questioning later.

This was truly a foolish endeavor. Did she really think they would be able to walk into an encampment Beltha'adi's men had been seeking for days? Besides, it would be light soon, and then what would they do? Hide in the tombs? And for what?

The command to stop was on her tongue when Newbold dove left into one of the openings, dragging Philip after him. Danarin did not hesitate to follow, but Carissa stopped just outside the door. Cooper came up beside her. He didn't even have to say anything. She could feel his antagonism, could almost hear his thoughts—echoes of those she'd just entertained—which goaded her onward.

She stepped into perfect blackness, glad again for the half-veil, since even with it to filter the air, the sudden increase of the stench almost made her retch. It took a few moments to realize that her eyes were useless here. Newbold's excited panting and tiny whines filled the room, but she could see absolutely nothing.

"We need a light," Danarin said. "We're not going to get anywhere like this."

The need was granted at once. A fist-sized orb of harsh white light materialized on the tips of Philip's fingers, held chest high, swerving and jumping as Newbold pulled at the leash in his other hand. The orb cast eerie shadows up his face and seemed to emit a high, tooth-jarring whine. "Will this do?" he asked.

A chill crawled up Carissa's back. He was a Terstan, marked with evil. For two years she'd traveled with him, knowing it full well, but until this moment she had never seen the reality of it.

Beside her, Cooper gaped with open mouth. Danarin scowled, tight lipped, as if he, like Carissa, were gritting his teeth with revulsion, as if he, like her, wanted to snap at him to put it out at once. But he didn't, and neither did she, and so the youth turned and, lifting the orb ahead of him, let Newbold drag him down an aisle lined with ranks of carved-out niches that held the remains of the dead.

The aisle went on and on, finally spilling into a large, hewn chamber with two stone sarcophagi standing side by side at its midst, apparently the family patriarch and his wife. In the wall behind them were several panels of bas-relief, detailing the exploits of the couple's lives. Newbold went straight to the central panel, tail whipping back and forth, his whines interspersed now with half bays, choked off by the cloth muzzle.

"He's found something," Philip said, his light bouncing wildly with his efforts to hold on to the dog, who was now scratching at the door in between sniffing and trying to bay. Choked as they were, the sounds reverberated in the chamber with such intensity Carissa worried they would be heard by someone outside. If the Dorsaddi hadn't known they were here before, they surely did now.

"It must be a hidden doorway," Danarin said, hurrying to Philip's side.

"If it is," said Cooper, "it's no doubt barred from the inside." Newbold loosed a particularly piercing cry, and Cooper swore. "I told you to keep that beast quiet, boy!"

As if the words had somehow penetrated Newbold's one-track mind, he backed suddenly from the door and turned to face the aisle of corpses now behind them, exploding in a fury of choked-off cries. The rest of them turned to find themselves faced with five pale-robed figures, drawn steel gleaming in the stark light of Philip's orb. Five pairs of dark eyes glittered in dark, hard faces.

*We're going to die,* Carissa thought numbly. *Struck down before we can utter a word.*

Suddenly Philip was thrusting the leash into her hands and striding around the sarcophagi to meet them, carrying his orb with him.

"Please," he said in his rough Tahg. "We seek the Pretender—and the Infidel."

He stopped a few strides from the Dorsaddi, who had not moved, beyond lifting their swords a bit. They had slings and spears, as well. And there were more of them standing in the shadows back down the aisle.

Moments ticked by. Newbold had quieted his barking, exchanging it for low growls.

Then one of the Dorsaddi stepped forward, the movement sharp and explosive. He reached out with his sword and pulled aside the neck edge of Philip's tunic, revealing the golden shield burned into the boy's chest. For a long moment he stared at it, then stepped closer, the sword point still pressed to Philip's chest, and rubbed at the mark to be sure it was genuine.

"Why do you seek the Pretender and the Infidel?" he asked finally in a low, harsh voice, the Tahg oddly accented and almost too fast to follow.

"I believe . . . the Infidel is my brother."

The Dorsaddi eyed him sharply, then nodded and drew back, lowering the sword. He started toward Danarin.

"He is not marked," Philip said. "None of them are. But they are friends."

At the leader's sign, the other men spread into the room, briskly fanning out to relieve both Cooper and Danarin of their swords, then patting them down in search of other weapons. As one pulled a blade from Danarin's boot, another loomed up before Carissa, yanking back the veil and headcloth before she even realized what he intended.

Seeing her face and golden hair, he jerked back with an oath, eyes wide. The short, clipped, guttural words brought the other men's heads snapping around. For a moment five pairs of eyes and narrowed brows fixed upon her, followed by an exchange of glances she could not read. Then the leader nodded, and the man proceeded to pat her down as well, hard hands sliding brusquely over her body. He found the knife at once, slipped his hand through the slits in her gown to remove it, then continued down her legs, inside and out. She burned with embarrassment, choking on the gall of her utter helplessness and sickeningly aware of the fact that she walked a land where northerners held no station but slavery, and women even lower than that.

At the leader's command, the Dorsaddi closest to the panel now stepped to it and gave it two sharp raps. Something thumped behind it. Newbold backed against her leg, growling and half baying, shaking his head and trying to rub the muzzle off with a paw. She hauled up on the leash to stop him, and the panel scraped open, torch-bearing Dorsaddi spilling into the room.

Newbold went wild, lunging, straining, wriggling—frantic to get away. Then, before she could collect her wits and gain control of him, he somehow backed out of his leather collar and bolted for the open panel. Several of the men leaped to catch him and, failing that, raced after him in vain pursuit.

"Don't hurt him!" Philip yelled after them. "He belongs to the Infidel!"

But the Dorsaddi were already gone. From within the passage Newbold's songlike bay echoed from increasing distance, then chillingly turned into a series of yelps and ended.

*By the Flames! This is growing worse with every moment.* What had she been thinking to let Philip talk her into this? She should have known it would never work. Now Newbold was hurt, maybe dead, and they were caught and—

She closed her eyes and refused to think of that. Meridon was with them. Newbold had followed his scent down that tunnel. If it was true he had survived Xorofin and lived with the Dorsaddi, surely he would stop them before it came to that.

*What makes you think he has any authority over these men?* the insidious voice of her fear demanded. *What makes you think he'd even know? Or care? What—*

*Stop it.* Stop *it!*

She swallowed hard and made herself breathe deeply. Hysterics would serve nothing. Above all else she must be calm. If one of these canyon men did try to take her, perhaps opportunity for escape would present itself.

A harsh voice ordered the northerners forward into the dark passage, a warm, musty draft pressing against her face. The tunnel wound left and upward. From behind came a grating noise and then a *whump* as the panel was closed.

Shortly they entered a small, lamplit chamber, one wall lined with waist-high clay jars. There they were held under guard while most of the men disappeared into one of the corridors leading from the room. Moments later another man strode in, stopping abruptly at the sight of the captives. He wore a headcloth and beard, but Carissa recognized him at once, even as Newbold trotted up happily from behind—it was Meridon.

He stared at Philip in round-eyed astonishment, and the boy stared back, unmoving, both of them seemingly turned to rock. Then Philip gave a shout of joy and rushed into his brother's arms, gripping him fiercely, the two of them nearly the same height.

Carissa found her fear momentarily forgotten as a lump rose to her throat and tears stung her eyes, her joy for them bittersweet in the sudden, wrenching realization that there would be no such happy reunion for her.

Finally Meridon released his brother and stepped back, his glance falling upon Carissa. His brown eyes widened, and once more he went rigid, but this time his face turned slowly white. Mechanically he walked around Philip and stepped toward her, stopped. "Lady *Carissa*?"

His astonishment turned to dismay, then outright horror. "What are you doing here?" he whispered. "You can't be here. Not now."

She frowned, having expected a more positive reception. Swallowing the remnants of the lump in her throat, she lifted her chin. "We have come to bring you home—or away, in any case. Though our plans are somewhat in disarray at the moment. . . ." She trailed off, staring at him as if she might somehow see the truth in his face—that Abramm *was* dead and how he had died.

Meridon returned her stare, dumbstruck. Other men had followed him into the chamber during the reunion, but they had stopped just inside the opening and Carissa had ignored them. Now the Terstan turned slowly to look over his shoulder. After a moment she followed the direction of that gaze and found another northerner among them—the tallest of the lot. He was staring at her with the same horrified, thunderstruck expression as Meridon. He, too, wore a beard, thick, short, and dark gold in the lamplight. It gave him a fierce look, accentuating the hawkish cast of his nose, the dark, level brows, the intense blue eyes.

Familiarity smote her in a series of blows, harder and harder until recognition broke through the gates of her denial and pulled his name from her lips.

"Abramm?"

She was not aware that either of them had moved, but somehow he was before her, looming over her. How had he gotten so big?

Tears once more blurred her vision. "I thought you were dead," she said. "I thought—" Her voice failed. She flung her arms around him and buried her face in his chest, marveling at how hard he was, less a thing of flesh and blood than of steel and stone. The rough fabric of his robe pricked her cheek, and he smelled of sweat and dirt and horse. She hardly noticed, sobbing in earnest now, clinging to him as if he might dissolve beneath her grasp.

The storm passed, and they drew apart. Wiping away the tears, she peered up at him again. He had changed more than she would ever have thought possible. Yet he was obviously a Kalladorne. With the beard and that hawkish, imperious glare, his resemblance to their father was more pronounced than ever.

"What are you doing here, Riss?" He spoke the Kiriathan words with a strong Esurhite lilt, and even the timbre of his voice had changed—deeper, more resonant than she remembered it. The anger that sharpened his tone, however, was all too familiar. "Bad enough you were in Qarkeshan," he went on, "but Jarnek is on the verge of war."

"I know." She sighed deeply, feeling light-headed. "But there was plague in Vedel so we had to go around and . . . It is a very long story, Abr . . . er . . . I mean, Eld . . ." She stopped in uncertainty, her eyes flicking over him again, snagging on the sword scabbarded at his side, the dagger in his belt.

He scowled and dropped his hands from her shoulders, stepping back and half aside. "You were right the first time—it's Abramm. And that, too, is a long story." He scowled at Meridon.

Carissa stared at the aquiline profile—lean and strong, with a hardness to it Eldrin had lacked. She had gone so still she could hear her own breath. "You *were* the White Pretender!"

Her brother grimaced and shifted uncomfortably. For a moment she saw again the man who had strode so proudly into that awful arena, the ridiculous outfit utterly overshadowed by the regality and defiance of his manner. She saw again the white figure thrown by magic across the field, battered, bloodied, but staggering doggedly upright, inviting blow after blow until he had managed to shatter the arena gates and fashion a way of escape.

*"There is more steel in him than anyone credits him,"* Captain Kinlock had said to her. She did not think even Kinlock knew how right he was in that.

"Carissa, stop looking at me like that."

"I saw you fight at Xorofin, Abramm."

The grimace deepened. "Aye, well, I was very lucky. And we have other concerns—" He broke off, his brow furrowing. "*You* were in Xorofin?"

"After Katahn betrayed me and took you, I wanted to make it right—if I could. We've been following the Pretender ever since. . . ."

His expression was growing more and more aghast. "Are you out of your mind?"

"Well, I have Cooper with me. And some others. . . ."

Abramm's gaze shot to her traveling companions. He frowned and bent his head toward Cooper. "Is that *you* under all that, Master Cooper?"

"Aye, Your Highness." Cooper stepped forward, bowing deeply, his earring shining in the torchlight. As he straightened, she saw that his eyes were wide and fixed upon Abramm as if he were a ghost.

"And this is Philip, Captain Meridon's brother," Carissa said, gesturing to the youth and smiling ruefully. "We've shared a common goal."

Philip bowed, too, and murmured a respectful, "Your Highness."

Behind her one of the Dorsaddi muttered in the Tahg, "He really is a prince of Kiriath."

Abramm's gaze had gone on to Danarin, and Carissa's chest constricted. All the old suspicions roared back to life, rearing out of her memory like old Chelaya from her evil swamp. Suddenly everything he'd done in the last twenty-four hours took on new and sinister significance. Danarin had known of Fah'lon's leanings toward the Dorsaddi, had probably heard of his suspected dealings with the Pretender, as well. And he had seen Abramm in Xorofin when she had. Had he seen the truth that she had not? If Fah'lon had chosen Danarin to serve his hidden purposes, might not Danarin have also chosen Fah'lon for hidden reasons of his own? Danarin had been the one to insist they follow the trail tonight, all but threatening Cooper openly to do it.

*Fire and Torment!* Was it all just a ploy, all part of a plot to get himself down here face-to-face with the man he was sworn to kill? She wanted to shout and throw her body between them. But Abramm only stared at the man, a small crease etched between his dark brows, and Danarin did nothing but return the stare. She swept to her brother's side.

"This is Danarin," she said. "He has been our salvation—our guide and protector."

"Then you have my thanks, Danarin," Abramm said.

The Thilosian bowed. Unlike Cooper and Philip he did not seem overawed, merely cautious and respectful. "It has been my pleasure, Your Highness. And I am delighted that after all the lady has been through, her persistence has been rewarded."

"Mmm." Open suspicion colored Abramm's expression, and Carissa felt a profound relief. Evidently her brother's experiences had burned away his naïveté.

Her gaze returned to the sword hanging at his belt, its bronze hilt gleaming in the torchlight. The hand that rested upon it was still long of finger but callused and scarred. A strong hand. There was no concern in him, no bravado, only a quiet confidence and, riding that, a hint of deadly threat.

*The White Pretender,* she thought again. And laughed softly. Abramm glanced at her. "Something amuses you?"

"I was just imagining Uncle Simon's face if he could see you now. The White Pretender. He'd be speechless. And this . . ." She reached up to rub his beard and chuckled. "I wouldn't have thought you could even grow one. It makes you look quite fierce."

He cocked a dubious brow at her, the expression achingly familiar. Abruptly the laughter almost turned to weeping, and for a moment she wanted to fling her arms about his neck again, to bury her face in his shoulder and sob anew with relief and this crazy, giddy joy. But she controlled herself, remembering now that they had an audience.

Meridon, who had been eyeing her companions suspiciously, drifted up to Abramm's left side, an instinctive, almost unconscious move of protection. "We'd best get back, my lord."

Abramm's wry amusement gave way to a grimace. "He's right. I'm afraid we have no time for lengthy reunions. Come."

CHAPTER

# 37

Abramm led them along a narrow corridor to a large natural vault where the Dorsaddi had set up camp. Numerous brass oil pots held aloft on high poles shed their flickering light across the hundreds of men sleeping on the sandstone floor. Sentries walked among them and stood guard at the low, arched opening on the vault's far side, an outside entrance through which Carissa could just make out the stained, sheer face of an opposing cliff wall, ghostly in the growing light of day. Just inside it stretched a row of striped pavilions, the centermost of which was larger than the others and attended by a cadre of pale-robed guards. Horses shuffled and stamped in a shadowed far corner, the sharp odor of their manure mingling with that of sweat and dung smoke and fresh-baked flatbread. Everywhere she looked she saw piles of rope, longbows, arrows, spears, rocks—the accoutrements of war.

A compact, lean-faced Dorsaddi with strangely pale eyes and a striped headcloth met them as they entered. His expression did not change as he looked over the newcomers, though his gaze did hesitate on Carissa. Then he turned to Meridon and, with a nod toward Philip, asked in the Tahg, "This is indeed your brother, my Lord Deliverer?"

"It is, my Lord Commander," Meridon said. "And the Pretender's sister, as well. They have apparently come to rescue us from slavery."

The Lord Commander's stern face broke into a white flash of teeth. "A woman and a boy?" Grinning, he cocked his head at the two men. "I begin to be more certain we have underestimated your people's courage." The smile widened as he eyed Carissa again. "And perhaps their capacity for madness, as well."

"Who are those men?" Abramm asked, gesturing at the group by the main pavilion.

As quickly as the amusement had bloomed across the Dorsaddi's face it vanished, and he was all business again. "The warriors from Deir have arrived. I've sent the main body of them on to the southern plateau as you suggested." He paused. "They have heard of Beltha'adi's challenge, sir. Debouh is yammering to know when you mean to face him. *If* you mean to face him."

"That hasn't been decided yet," Meridon said before Abramm could respond, earning himself a sharp look from the latter.

The Lord Commander gave them both a calm nod. "Just so you know what's going on, my friends. Debouh is something of a hothead."

"Yes, Shemm's told us all about him," Abramm said dryly.

*Shemm?* Carissa thought. *He's on a first-name basis with the king of the Dorsaddi? Well, of course, he's the White Pretender.*

It still gave her goose bumps to think of it. For the first time in months she wanted to go home, to be there when everyone saw him, when they realized who and what he had become.

The White Pretender had turned to her and was speaking in Kiriathan again. ". . . take you to my quarters, such as they are." He gestured to the row of pavilions. "When I'm done talking to the king, I'll return and—"

"Absolutely not!" she interrupted. "You're not leaving my sight for at least a month. I'm going with you."

Muffled laughter rose up around them. The crease in his brow returned.

She waved a hand. "Oh, I know women aren't supposed to speak in public and all that. Believe me, I know! I promise not to say anything. Besides, you are no more Dorsaddi than I, so why must we abide by their silly rules?"

"Because the king is my friend, and I have no intention of insulting him," Abramm said firmly. "And because, frankly, this is none of your business."

She gaped at him.

"We'll decide what to do next when I'm done." He didn't wait for an answer, didn't seem to expect one, just turned and followed Meridon and his brother and the Lord Commander across the crowded floor to the royal pavilion.

It took her a moment to find her tongue. Spluttering outrage, she lurched after them, only to find a Dorsaddi blocking her path. She dodged around him, but another pulled her back. "I'm sorry, serra," he said in the Tahg, "but the Lord Pretender says you must come with us."

She would have struggled, but Danarin came up close on her off side. "Better, my lady, not to make a scene."

"But he has no right—"

"He is not your little brother anymore, ma'am. And I suspect in this place he has the right to treat you any way he likes."

The cold truth of his words quenched her resistance, if not her indignation. Teeth clenched, she let the Dorsaddi lead her to one of the side pavilions. A veil blocked off the sleeping area at the rear, and the front half was field-plain, furnished only with a worn, dusty, dark-patterned rug and a low table on which sat a flickering oil lamp.

Though Danarin followed her in, Cooper did not, standing as if on guard just outside the door. She glanced around the small space, then stepped back to the doorway, her irritation intensified by the realization that Philip had not come with her. That he, a mere boy, had been allowed to attend the meeting that was barred to her.

*By the Flames, I hate this land! These people are such narrow-minded barbarians. I cannot wait to be away and back to our home.*

"You gave him no real choice, my lady," Danarin said. "Challenging him like that in front of everyone."

She frowned at him, standing in the doorway beside her. "What are you talking about?"

"He is the White Pretender. Have you not seen the way the others look at him? Defer to him?"

She had not, being too busy looking at him herself. But now that she thought of it, she realized it was true. Moreover—

All at once she could hardly breathe. The White Pretender! The one who was supposed to face Beltha'adi in personal combat. Today, possibly.

Bright pinwheels spun at the edges of her vision as she gasped for air. "No," she murmured. "Oh, no . . ."

"My lady?" Danarin's voice came softly in her ear, and she realized that somehow she had come to lean upon his arm, her legs all wobbly beneath her.

She looked up at him. "He's going to face Beltha'adi. Isn't he?"

Danarin's handsome features hardened. "Meridon said it wasn't yet decided."

"Fah'lon said he had to do it. That if he didn't, everyone would call him coward and the Dorsaddi hearts would melt."

"Yes, he did say that. Here. Why don't you sit down?"

She let him help her to the floor, then leaned forward to drop her head into her hands as he settled across the table from her. "This can't be happening," she moaned. "It just can't be."

But it was typical of her luck, was it not? Typical of the cruelty of her life.

"Frankly, I don't understand it," Danarin said. "They're calling Meridon the Deliverer, so why would Abramm be the one to take the challenge? The prophecy says it's the Deliverer who's supposed to slay Beltha'adi."

"Perhaps that's what the discussion is about." She looked up with new hope. "And why Meridon said it hadn't been decided yet."

"Perhaps, but . . ."

"But what?"

He shook his head. "I don't know." He rubbed his nose and squinted out the doorway. Then his gaze came back to hers. "Have you noticed that most of these men are Terstan?"

"What?"

"They wear their tunics slit open so you can see the shields."

"I thought those were just Dorsaddi medallions—"

"They're not. I had heard rumors of this. That instead of wearing the shields as they have in the past, they were now actually branded with them. I didn't think it possible, but seeing as Meridon is apparently the Deliverer—I suspect what's happened is he's managed to convert most of them."

Nausea swirled under her heart. "You can't be serious!" And yet, as she sorted frantically through her memories, she feared he was right. Had not Philip said something about it himself?

Her pulse quickened. If Meridon had infected all the Dorsaddi, had he infected Abramm, too? Abramm had, after all, spent the last two years with the man, and in close company. It was obvious, watching them, that they shared a strong bond. And if Abramm had already been deceived once, was that not more reason to fear he might be again? There was that undeniably religious side of his nature, that fascination with things spiritual, that tendency to want to sacrifice himself for a higher good. She might not understand it, but she mustn't ignore it or underestimate its power.

The pinwheels were back. She laid a hand on the table to steady herself and made herself breathe deeply, the taste of bile bitter on her tongue.

Danarin laid a hand on her own. "No, my lady, it is not what you are thinking—Abramm is not one of them. Yet."

"He's not? How can you be sure?"

"He'd be showing it, like the others, if he were." He glanced down at his hand resting on hers and drew it away. "I suspect, however, they are pressuring him to change his mind."

"Then we must stop them!" She leapt to her feet.

He looked up at her. "How?"

She started for the door, turned back, wringing her hands. "I don't know. Something. We have to do something."

But what could she do when she wasn't even allowed to be part of the discussion?

Oh, that would be absolutely the end. To have come all this way, endured all she had endured, to see the miraculous change in him—the scrawny, fearful boy become the champion of legend—only to have him . . .

A vision of the old man of the hollow flashed in her head, his body bent, his eyes full of curd, his voice shrill with madness as he railed at the boys who came to tease him. It was replaced by her last memory of Raynen, raging about the sparrows, that line of curd already begun in his eyes. In a few years that could well be Abramm. And almost worse was the scorn he would receive from the nobles. The snickers behind his back, the snide remarks, the veiled contempt—scorn a hundred times worse than any he had yet received.

She swallowed another surge of bile and turned back to the door just as Abramm himself stepped through it, tight lipped and pale. It took only a glance for her to realize he was furious.

Danarin scrambled to his feet. "Your Highness," he murmured, bowing and quickly slipping from the tent.

Abramm let him go without comment, scowling at her as if he were only now remembering she was here and adding that inconvenience to the burden of his troubles. Her eyes flicked to the slit neckline of his tunic, and the sight of the bare, unmarked skin beneath it almost forced a moan of relief from her.

He looked down too, but at the bundle he carried in his hands—white satin, a froth of lace, a gleaming curl of white hair. Her relief bled away.

His scowl deepened and he stepped to the inner veil, casting the bundle onto the pallet beyond. "You shouldn't have come." He turned to face her, brows knit in a dark thundercloud.

"If I could've sailed out of Xorofin, believe me, I would've."

"I mean you should never have come at all. Everything you've done only makes things worse."

The accusation stung the more because she knew—horribly, unforgivably—that it was true. But what else could she have done? Guilt spawned frustration, and frustration, anger. "Well, I'm *sorry,* brother! Forgive me for the unconscionable folly of caring what happens to you!"

He stared at her stonily. "It's not a matter of caring. It's thinking you can do things you have no business doing." He turned away from her, paced a step to the veil, and turned back again. "What possible difference did you think you could make? Did you think to buy me back? Steal me away? A woman alone, with a boy and two retainers?"

"I had to try something."

"No, you didn't! Sometimes it's better just to accept there are things you cannot do. You should've left me to Eidon or the fates or whatever you want to call it and gone on with your life."

She snorted. "I had no life, Abramm."

"Of course you did! You had your husband—"

"I was a pariah in Balmark!" The words were out before she could stop them, but once started the rush of anguished truth was impossible to stop. "Relegated to serving as nanny," she shrilled, "to the bastard son of a husband who didn't care if I lived or died. What did I have to lose?"

He stared at her, his mouth half open, his brow furrowed. Pain flared across his face and was absorbed. He closed his mouth. "You left him?"

"Let's just say I was lost at sea." She turned her gaze aside, watching one of the sentries move among the ranks of sleeping men outside the tent.

He took to studying his hands and after a moment said, "Well, you can't stay here. I'm going to send you back to Hur. At least there—"

"No! I've not spent two years searching only to be parted from you now."

"Carissa, you can't—"

"Don't tell me what I can and cannot do. It's one thing out there—it's another in here."

"You have no idea what's going on here."

"Oh yes, I think I do." She hesitated, knowing she was about to tread on uncertain ground, then said quietly, "Let Meridon do it."

He went completely stiff, and though he did not look at her, she knew he understood exactly what she meant. More, she sensed this was not the first time the prospect had been put to him.

"*He's* the Deliverer," she whispered. "He should be the one to fight their battles. And in the costume who would know?"

"I . . . it's not that simple."

"Of course it is. You don't really believe they need *you* specifically, do you? They just need someone to wear the costume."

"But I have a chance of beating him." He was looking at her now. "If I left . . . it would be like running out on them."

"No. You would be . . . you would be saving me and returning home to help your own people. And Meridon is no slouch in the arena. Surely he has as much chance of defeating him as you."

When he did not speak, she pressed her point. "Abramm, think—think what you could do if you went home."

"Home? I've been exiled, Riss!"

"*Eldrin* has been exiled, not Abramm."

"But Raynen—"

"Hated what he did. It was eating him up. He only sent you away because of the hold Saeral had over you. And because Gillard pressured him, I think." She paused. "You were weak then, as well. But you are not now."

She had his attention, those startling blue eyes fixed upon her, the look on his face betraying the fact that he saw the possibilities. Encouraged, she leaned toward him and began to present her case in earnest.

CHAPTER

# 38

"He says he'll clear the south plateau of his men so our people can watch," Shemm said, nodding at the slope of rock before them. He lay on his belly at Abramm's side, the two of them cradled between sandstone hummocks, in broad daylight and in plain view of Beltha'adi's sentries posted less than a stone's throw away. The amphitheater lay below them, its carved stone benches ascending halfway up the far red wall, stopping at the point where the naturally sloping face grew vertical. This early in the afternoon, it stood empty. Later, that would not be the case.

The wall itself curved around in a bowl shape, facing southwest, making it the ideal location for the amphitheater. From their present position the two men could look down both sides of that wall, for the wadi turned sharply away from them at that point, curving back and around to the great temple, its carved-out columns and entryway façade flat in the misty light.

Abramm could not look at it without smiling. To have successfully baited the dragon in his den, not once but twice, made his heart warm with satisfaction. Even better had been the exploit with the veren last night. The chaos and dismay that spectacle had created made it well worth the trouble of hauling the body from Hur, and the scorch marks still stained the white pan of the amphitheater's floor. Even their ploy to get the soldiers to invade Fah'lon's villa had worked—though after that, nothing had turned out quite as planned. Fah'lon's noble guests, the bait for the trap, had escaped, leaving no one for the soldiers to arrest. And the gambit had brought Carissa back into Abramm's life, which had changed everything.

Grimacing, he returned his thoughts to the issue at hand. "He'll have men hidden in the temple," he said. "Ready to go. And in all the passages under the amphitheater. Probably in the treasury, as well."

The king turned his head slightly, dark eyes glittering at him from under the edge of his headcloth. "So we will do likewise on this side, eh?"

"So much as we are able." Abramm frowned at the opposite plateau where the dark figures of patrolling soldiers stood out against the pale sandstone and churning mist. The flanking force Shemm had sent out—at Abramm's suggestion—should be just about in place by now. It was a gamble sending them out, for it reduced the numbers they had to hold the plateau and launch any sort of offensive toward the Esurhites. But as long as they had their rear lines covered—Shemm had men guarding all the potential channels and passages by which Beltha'adi might seek to flank them—Abramm felt they had an adequate position.

"We'll be stretched pretty thin, though," he said.

"Very thin," Shemm agreed. "Japheth informed me this morning that, with the arrival of that latest Hundred your informant told us about, he will outnumber us two to one."

The informant was Katahn ul Manus, though only Abramm and Trap knew that. Claiming outrage over losing his valuable slaves, Katahn had joined Beltha'adi in Jarnek in a bid to retrieve them. In reality, he was playing a very dangerous game of deceit—one that had recalled to Abramm on more than one occasion the dire prophecy cast back in Vorta by Katahn's old priest, Master Peig. The one about losing everything.

"Maybe even three to one," Shemm added.

"Good," Abramm said. "You'll have more targets to shoot at."

The dark face came around to him again, flashing a grin. "You think like a Dorsaddi, my friend, not a northerner."

"You do not know many northerners, Great One."

Their eyes met, and the grins faded as Abramm's words evidently spawned the same thought in both of them. Abramm turned his attention back to the amphitheater. "If the Deliverer wins," he said, "it won't matter how many they have. Our man says most of them are already demoralized."

"Thanks largely to you, Pretender."

During the two weeks since they'd left Hur, Abramm had come to know the Dorsaddi king well. They'd hit it off at once, united by the common experience of being royalty, of having strikingly similar personalities, and, on Abramm's part, by the knowledge that this man was Shettai's brother—though they had never spoken of her.

Mostly they spoke of Jarnek and what they planned to do there upon arrival. In that, Abramm had displayed an affinity for strategy and tactics that had surprised him—if no one else. Shemm had sent out a call to arms to the other active Dorsaddi city of Deir, and while they waited for those forces to arrive, Abramm had counseled—and waged—a war of wit, harassing and bedeviling the enemy in his own camp in hopes of shaking morale.

It had worked. *The men are unnerved*, Katahn said in his last communication. *They know you are out there and their hearts are melting for fear of you. Now is the perfect time for the WP to come forward. If Beltha'adi even looks as if he might lose, they'll run if you launch a significant attack.*

Abramm hoped Katahn was right.

"I think we've seen enough," the king said. He eased back from the edge, careful to keep below the hummocks. A moment later Abramm followed. They withdrew to where Trap and Japheth waited, ready with a handful of others to spring up and shoot should the Esurhite sentries discover the royal spies in their midst. The group of them descended back into the narrow channel through which they'd emerged, where the sentries also wore Esurhite gray, though they were not Esurhite.

A growl of thunder rumbled in the distance.

"You're sure you will not stay?" the king asked as they walked down a narrow flight of roughly carved stairs. "You know how greatly I have valued your counsel. And your sword."

Abramm drew a deep breath. He wanted to stay. That was just it. He wanted to stay and to go with equal passion. When he had given the costume back to Shemm this morning, it had surprised him how much he wanted to wear it one more time, how strongly he coveted this fight. It was the White Pretender Beltha'adi was challenging, after all. And Abramm was the White Pretender, not Trap. Abramm carried the royal blood of Kiriath—he should be the one to represent his House.

Besides, if Beltha'adi was finally going to fight as himself, should not the Pretender do likewise?

And yet, even before Carissa had arrived, the others had been seeking to dissuade him. He was no match for the Broho of Brohos, they said, not unless he chose to take the star. Of course they would say that. They all wore the shieldmark and wanted everyone else to wear it, too. Mephid, in particular, had pressed him so fiercely he seemed on the verge of putting the talisman in Abramm's hand and forcing his fingers around it himself. They had nearly come to blows over it before Trap intervened.

"You cannot make a man take the star," he'd scolded.

"But the prophecy said three kings will slay the dragon's head," Mephid had countered. "He must take it."

Trap cocked a brow. "I thought you said the Deliverer was the one to kill him."

"All four are apparently involved."

"Mmm. Or else you've misinterpreted."

Mephid had scowled at him but had not argued.

"In any case, if he refuses it . . . well, this was known to Sheleft'Ai since the beginning and taken into account. He must not be the one your prophecy speaks of."

In point of fact, despite Mephid's attempt to drag in the prophecy of the kings, there was considerable evidence that Trap himself was the one. He was, after all, the Lord Deliverer. Indeed, there would have been no question of his going had Beltha'adi not specifically demanded that it be the Pretender who faced him.

And the Pretender had been more than willing to take up the challenge.

Until Carissa had shown up.

Now Abramm drew a deep breath and turned to face the king. "It has been my privilege to serve you, Great One, but I believe I have done all I can do here. You've made it clear enough that I am not your choice of champion, and truly you have no real need of my sword in the coming battle should it go as we hope—even if it doesn't, my hand would not be the one to turn the tide."

"And you do not wish your sister to be caught up in any of it. I understand that, friend. As I understand the call of *or'dai*."

*Or'dai*. Blood right. Vengeance. Justice. He had not given it a thought until Carissa had brought it up, made him see, suddenly and startlingly, that he could do it. That it was his right. That he could actually return to Kiriath and repay Gillard for his deeds. Face-to-face, sword to sword. The moment he had acknowledged it as a possible reality, the desire for it had boiled up, hot and driving, in his soul.

He need not die here. He need not be swept away by other people's concerns. He could seize the reins of his own life and go back, do what at the heart of things he wanted to do more than anything else in life. More, perhaps, than life itself.

The power of the need startled him, all hot rage and savage bloodlust.

"Yes," he said softly, hearing the passion shake in his voice.

"Go, then. If you move quickly, you should reach the rim before the rains. Sheleft'Ai guard you and keep you, and may you find at last the destiny he has for you."

"Thank you, my king."

Carissa was waiting at the opening to the cavern in which they'd set up camp, impatience tightening her lips. "Did you hear the thunder?" she asked as Shemm went on and Abramm drew up before her. "They say the rains may break before sundown."

"We should be well up on the rim by then."

"Yes, but . . . Abramm, I've been in the rains."

"Would you prefer to stay here?"

"Of course not." She turned to walk with him. "Did you ask him about Peri and Eber?"

"He said he'll send someone to free them."

"And pay them?"

"And pay them."

Cooper sat alone outside Abramm's tent, awaiting their return. He looked morose, staring blindly off into space, so that he didn't notice their approach until they were nearly upon him. Giving a start, he scrambled to his feet and sketched a hasty bow.

"Where's Danarin?" Carissa asked, looking around.

"I thought he was with you, my lady." Cooper flicked a glance at Abramm, then looked away, still nervous in his presence.

"Great," Carissa muttered. "Here we're finally ready to leave and he's off gambling." Scowling, she scanned the chamber, arms folded before her. "We should just go without him. It'd serve him right, and I'm not sure I want him with us anyway."

Abramm arched a brow at her. "Oh?"

"I don't trust him. I haven't since Qarkeshan."

"You think he'd betray us to Beltha'adi?"

Distaste flickered across her face. "No, he could have done that hundreds of times on the road from Xorofin. I just . . . He makes me uneasy, I guess."

"Aye, because he has eyes for her," Cooper said. "And he's a handsome devil, with no reluctance whatever in pursuing her, no matter that she's a noble lady and he a common sailor."

Abramm cocked a brow at his sister. She stared at the floor, red-faced.

Cooper said something mollifying, but Abramm didn't hear it, his attention snared by the man striding briskly along the line of tents in his direction. He'd half hoped he wouldn't have to confront Trap before he left, but clearly that was not to be.

The Terstan offered a nod of greeting to Carissa as he stopped in front of Abramm and looked up at him, his eyes keen and sharp. "Can we talk?"

Carissa laid a hand on Abramm's arm. "I'm sorry, Captain, but we really have no time to spare. Not if we're going to beat the rains."

Once Abramm might have used her intervention to avoid what he did not want to face. But he and Trap had gone through too much together for that, and anyway, her forwardness irritated him. He shook off her hand and stepped away with Meridon. "You go find your friend, Riss. This won't take long."

He walked off without waiting for her answer, Trap striding beside him. They paced along the remainder of the tent line, heading toward the horses picketed at the back of the cavern. For some time neither of them spoke.

"So that's it, then?" Meridon said presently. "You're really going to leave?"

"Yes."

"To go home."

Abramm glanced at him sidelong. "You want her caught in the middle of this?"

"Of course not."

"I don't want to die here, Trap. And I have a score to settle in Kiriath."

"A score." Disapproval soured his voice. It was a thing Abramm had never understood—Meridon's willingness to forgive those who had so deeply wronged him. His insistence that it had been Eidon who had brought them here, Eidon who would make it good.

They stopped at the edge of the picket line, standing on a small shelf of sandstone, a well of space separating them from anyone else. He could see the men out on the floor watching them surreptitiously, murmuring to each other—by now the word was surely out that he was leaving. He did not think they would understand.

Then again, considering the matter of or'dai, perhaps they would.

"And what of Saeral?"

The question cut into his thoughts, momentarily startling him. Then he snorted. "If I can stand against Broho, I can handle Saeral. Wasn't it you who was telling me how much more I know about good and evil now?"

"More, maybe, but not enough for that."

"Of course not," Abramm said dryly. "Nothing is ever enough with you, nor will it be until I wear your shield upon my chest."

Trap regarded him soberly. "Eidon is the only answer in this world, Abramm, and life is not about settling scores or being respected by people. It's about his power and his worth and what he did on that hill outside Xorofin. You must come to him as nothing. But you don't like that. You want it to be about *you*. *Your* sacrifices, *your* efforts to make yourself worthy." He paused, studying the horses without really seeing them. "It's pride, Abramm. That's why you won't believe."

"That's ridiculous."

"Is it? You've memorized more than half of the Holy Words. Go back through them, without the Mataian slant, and see if what I'm saying isn't true. Or are you afraid to put it to the test?"

Back up the row of tents, Abramm could see the wandering Danarin had finally returned—the group of them watched him and Trap as they talked. Carissa was wringing her hands, clearly distressed and apparently pouring out her woes to Danarin, who was frowning at him.

He turned back to the horses, pain and impatience rising together, and decision crystallized. "Carissa's right. If we don't leave now, we'll never beat the rains. I've got to go."

The disappointment in Trap's expression was wrenching to behold.

"I . . . I'm sorry," Abramm said, rushing on, as if hurrying would somehow ease the pain. "I hope someday you'll understand."

"I *pray* someday *you* will."

"Good luck with Beltha'adi."

He turned then, feeling wildly awkward, and hurried back to the others.

He saw Carissa's eyes fix upon his chest and realized then why she had been so quick to intervene, and the reason for her earlier distress—not because their time was running out, but because she was afraid he was going to give in to Trap's persuasions. The look of relief on her face when she did not find the shield she feared would have been comical were he not so torn himself. Despite all he had said, he couldn't shake the feeling that he was walking away from the only thing that would ever really matter in his life.

# CHAPTER

# 39

Carissa was beside herself with joy. For the first time since this whole wretched expedition began, something was actually going right. When Abramm had come back from talking with Meridon, tight lipped and scowling, it was all she could do not to crow aloud.

He led them off with a few clipped words, and for once she forgave him his incivility. She was willing to take a lot more if it meant saving him from having to face Beltha'adi or, worse, from having a golden shield burned into his chest. Now he was free to go home and become the great man he was meant to be. She could not wait to see the look on everyone's face, could not wait to see Gillard finally—*finally!*—receive his comeuppance. The White Pretender, a man who had faced down the monstrous Broho in the Val'Orda itself, would never be intimidated by the likes of Saeral. Or Rennalf of Balmark. He would be a loyal ally of Raynen, a valued advisor, and perhaps, eventually, king himself.

The thought spawned a little zing of warmth just under her heart. After all her twin had endured, it seemed a fitting end. Almost enough to make her believe there was some justice in the world after all.

For some time they descended a long, zigzagging stairway carved into the rock beside a series of dry catchment basins and crumbling cisterns. Russet cliffs flanked them closely on both sides, and the mist had dropped in from above with unusual density, reducing the world to a ten-foot pocket of visibility. Thus when the stairs ended in a sudden fifty-foot drop-off, it took her by surprise.

Apparently it took Abramm by surprise, as well. Until then he'd led them through a maze of canyons, channels, and stairways with the practiced ease of a native. Now suddenly he stopped, staring at the cliff beneath his feet as if it shouldn't be there. She drew up beside him, tugging at the folds of her gown where they had bunched uncomfortably beneath her sash. He turned back, his gaze flicking across the stairs, his face hard to read, even for her.

Uneasiness intruded on her joyful ruminations. It would be so easy to lose one's way in these convoluted canyons. With each looking very much like the next, how would you ever find your way back? And to be caught here when the rains came would mean almost certain death. A deadly fall, a flash flood, starvation . . .

Before she could dwell too much on those perils, he turned into a slit beside the stair's end as if he had never been in any doubt.

*False alarm*, she told herself.

Unfortunately, once the anxiety was sparked it didn't go away. The slit was dark; the cliff walls reaching high overhead bulged toward one another to blot out the misty sky. Though she had walked through numerous similar slits, this one suddenly made her feel trapped. Even with Danarin and Cooper right behind her, she kept shivering with the sense that someone was stalking them. What if Shemm had changed his mind? Had decided Abramm must play his Pretender role after all and sent men after him?

She tugged at the folds under her sash again and glanced over her shoulder. Neither of the men behind her seemed to share her uneasiness, both clearly caught up in their own thoughts. She was probably tormenting herself for nothing.

The slit dog-legged through the rock, narrowing to shoulder width and finally widening into a small grotto before spilling down into a curving, rubble-strewn basin that turned out to be another dead end. Abramm stopped there with an oath, scowling at the smooth concavity. Finally he turned back, muttering, "I must be more tired than I thought—"

Something about the way his head came up and that last word choked off made Carissa turn in alarm. Danarin stood facing them, but Cooper was nowhere in sight. Moreover, there was no sign of the slit they had just come through, only a sheer salmon-colored wall stained with black, rearing up into the mist at Danarin's back.

Which was not possible.

For a long moment they all stood there. Carissa stared at the wall and only gradually realized how odd it was that Danarin had not turned to see what had so obviously startled her and Abramm. When the oddness finally grew strong enough to direct her attention to the Thilosian himself, she realized the two men were staring at each other.

Danarin wore a faintly smug, almost victorious expression, and the amulet on his throat, which she had never noticed before, glowed with a faint red light.

The sudden crushing realization of disaster hit her at the same time her brother moved, his sword leaping to his hand as if he had conjured it there. It flashed in the gray light as he lunged toward the other man, who lurched aside in time to avoid the killing thrust, the point only snagging his shoulder.

As Danarin dodged up the basin's curved side, something cold clamped about Carissa's throat, the fierce pressure choking off her cry of alarm. She dropped to her knees, gasping and gurgling, clawing to free herself from whatever had her. Her fingers found only the necklet Danarin had given her on Ormah Fah'lon's terrace.

"Back off!" she heard Danarin say through the ringing in her ears. "I'll crush her windpipe before you take a step, so drop the blade."

White lights pinwheeled across her vision; the ringing became a roar. She tried to tell Abramm not to do it, but the world grew dark, and she began to fall. . . .

She came to lying on her side, air rasping like fire over her bruised throat. Her lungs craved it, demanded it, and at first she could do nothing but satisfy that demand. As her breathing eased closer to normal, she heard a voice from far off. "Kick . . . over here."

Metal clanked on rock, and something silvery flew across the ground in front of her. She watched Danarin stoop to pick up a sword and dagger. The sword he pitched away somewhere behind her, the metal ringing as it hit the rock.

"I see you have recognized my trifle," said Danarin as he slid the dagger left-handed into his own belt. A blossom of blood darkened his dusky red tunic at the right shoulder and he held that arm close to his middle. "I trust you have not forgotten how it feels to be Commanded?"

"I have not forgotten," Abramm replied grimly.

Carissa pushed herself upright to sit braced against the cool sandstone wall. Abramm stood at the midst of the basin against a backdrop of darkly striated rock. Every line of his body was taut, his hands flexed and ready, and though he was now unarmed, Danarin had not relaxed his vigilance.

"Don't think you can remove this one as easily as Meridon removed yours," Danarin went on.

He was speaking of the necklet, Carissa realized, cold and constricting around her throat.

"Who are you?" Abramm demanded, his voice as tight and strained as the rest of him.

Danarin chuckled. "You still do not recognize me, old friend?"

A cold breath of air shivered through the basin, and the Thilosian's face seemed to focus, as if it had been blurry before. Suddenly she cringed back against the wall, sick and light-headed with recognition.

Simultaneously, Abramm recoiled with a hiss. "Rhiad!"

*Is this a nightmare?* Carissa wondered. *A delusion? Did I fall and hit my head?*

Yet it *was* Rhiad, bearded, his pigtail shorter, but Rhiad all the same: head of the Order of St. Haverall, Saeral's right-hand man, and one of the most famous holy men in Springerlan, especially among the court ladies who had long lamented that his stunningly good looks were wasted in service to the Flames.

Shock paralyzed her as it apparently paralyzed her brother. Danarin—Rhiad—grinned back at them, cradling his injured arm to his waist. Memories scrolled through her head: the Thilosian staring after the White Pretender in the warrens beneath the arena at Xorofin, swooping down to rescue her at the city gates, offering aid, pushing them to follow Abramm's track, convincing her the Dorsaddi meant to harm him. . . .

Chagrin and horror welled up in her. And then shame. And anger.

"I knew I shouldn't have trusted you," she croaked. "Right from the start, I knew it."

Rhiad swung around, eyes wide as he looked down at her. Then he chuckled. "You should have listened to your instincts, my lady."

*Cooper!* Carissa remembered suddenly. *What has he done to you? Oh, plagues, what have I done? How could I have been so foolish?*

Misery gave the pain in her throat a knifelike twist.

"The High Father has been quite concerned about you, Eldrin," Rhiad said, turning back to Abramm. "I spoke with him earlier today. He is eagerly awaiting our return."

Abramm glanced around the basin, golden whiskers bristling at the corner of his jaw. His gaze flicked back to Rhiad, clearly questioning.

Rhiad smiled. "Surely after all the time you've spent down here you have heard of the mystical corridors that traverse the etherworld?" He gestured toward Abramm. "Look behind you."

Abramm glanced over his shoulder. A little less than three strides away, the air shimmered in a column of red, undulating threads. When he faced the Haverallan again, his cheeks were a pale, sickly gray.

Rhiad laughed. "Beltha'adi is not the only one who knows how to use them. We'll be back in Springerlan before an hour is passed. Soon now, after all this time and heartache, you will get to touch the Holy Flames."

"I'll die before I serve them," Abramm grated.

"Oh, I think not. You want too much to live. And the Father would never allow it, anyway. Your conversion will be slow and gentle this time. Although I do not think it will take that long." He smiled. "Deep down you want everything we have to offer."

"I want nothing you have to offer."

"No? My friend, you've spent two years in close company with that Terstan and still you are unmarked. It's obvious you don't want what *he* has to offer—and rightly so, since it'll only kill you. Besides. At home you are king now. . . ." He paused to let that sink in. "Yes, Raynen is dead. Threw himself off Graymeer's Point four months ago. The Crown would've gone to you, were you there to receive it. Now *Gillard* rules in your stead."

He pulled a leather pouch from his belt and tossed it at Abramm's feet. "There's a vial in there. I want you to drink its contents."

Abramm frowned at him.

Rhiad sighed, and the necklet cut into Carissa's throat, pain flaring across her world. She dug vainly at the collar, her throat crushed, her lungs once more on fire, the world again spinning wildly. A sharp distant word released the pressure, and when she had recovered enough to take notice again, Abramm was sniffing the vial's contents suspiciously. "Hockspur?" he asked. "But you already have your hold on me."

Rhiad chuckled. "You are the White Pretender, my friend. I've seen you fight. Besides, you'll need it to pass through the etherworld since you have no Guide to shield you. Drink."

"No!" Carissa cried, but it came out as one more gasp among many.

Abramm stared at the Haverallan, lifted the vial—

And upended it, dumping the contents onto the rock. Then he leapt for Carissa and grabbed at the necklet. Fire seared across her throat, and red light blazed up under her chin. She screamed and wrenched reflexively from his touch even as he jerked his hand back with a cry of his own.

Something white spun through the air between them and burst upon her brother's chest, spewing a cloud of lemon-colored smoke into his face. He staggered backward, hands to his eyes, coughing, gasping. Then he crumpled like an empty sack and lay still, the corridor's faint light shimmering behind him.

By then she was woozy herself, her mouth filled with a bitter taste, her eyes burning and watering. Through a wavering haze she saw Rhiad kneel at Abramm's side and withdraw a new vial from his robe. She was shaking, certain her throat had been cut. Tears trickled down her cheeks, and her breath came in ragged, wheezing sobs. A sharp pain burned at her waist—she must have fallen on a rock, though it felt like she had a live coal tied up under her belt.

But she had no time for hurts. She must do something.

Using his teeth to unstopper the vial, Rhiad pulled Abramm's head back, then had to use both hands, one to open her brother's mouth, the other to pour in the drug. As the vial tilted, she lurched up. But she was weaker than she anticipated and did not move quickly enough. The brown liquid streamed into Abramm's mouth.

Panic gave her strength. With a desperate cry she flung herself at Rhiad, bowling him over. Her fingers closed upon the hilt of Abramm's dagger, tucked into Rhiad's belt. She started to pull it free—

Then the vise closed upon her throat, swift and merciless. She lost the dagger and rolled away onto hands and knees. He started to rise. Ignoring the choking pressure at her throat, she drove into him, shoving him as hard as she could toward the shimmering column. He twisted backward, flailing for balance, and toppled half into it. The necklet's pressure eased at once, enough for her to lurch again and shove him the rest of the way, her hands burning—tingling with the proximity of the flickering shaft. A shrill whine pierced her ears, and the column flared bright red mingled with silver. Fire scraped over her nerves, a whirlwind of evil chitterings that sought to turn her inside out. Then a blinding white fire blasted it all into oblivion—sound, light, all of it. Even Rhiad.

All that remained was a dull, opalescent disk gleaming in the red sand.

Carissa staggered back, tripping over the weeds and the uneven rock, to fall on her bottom at Abramm's side. There, her fingers skittering helplessly over the collar she still wore, she gasped for breath and finally gave herself over to bitter weeping.

# CHAPTER 40

As soon as Abramm regained consciousness he began to vomit, and at first that necessity occupied all his thoughts. Once his stomach was emptied, however, and he had backed away from his mess to settle on the sandy slope a little distance below Carissa, he began to remember.

Rhiad had been here! Disguised as one of Carissa's retainers. But—how was that possible? And he was certainly not here now. Abramm scanned the bean-shaped basin, seeing clearly there was no way out of it—and that his only company was his sister.

She knelt beside him and pressed her water bag into his palm. The walls at her back shivered and shifted as if they were melting. He closed his eyes against the dizziness and drank, washing away the awful taste in his mouth.

Rhiad had been here, had sought to dull his will with hockspur and bring him back to Saeral. Or was it just a dream?

He opened his eyes and looked at Carissa, sitting now in front of him. Her face was pale, her eyes stained with the dark shadows of fatigue and fear, her neck red beneath the choker with its startling blue-green stone.

"He's gone," she said, and the raw hoarseness of her voice pulled another image from his tangled memory—Carissa gasping at his feet as she clawed at that choker and slowly turned blue. He had grabbed it, was driven off by a flash of searing heat, and remembered nothing more. Was it real, then? Was it not a dream but an actual event? But if Rhiad had been here, where was he now?

"I pushed him into the corridor," Carissa offered in that dry-leaves voice, turning to gesture up the sandy slope.

"Corridor?" His voice came out a low croak, hardly better than hers. And then he recalled that, too—the pillar of red mist that had set his arm afire and was to have taken him to Saeral.

"Into the etherworld," she said. "The disk is still over there. Does that mean he can come back?"

*Come back?* It was monstrously hard to make his mind work right, as if all his thoughts were drifting through fog.

She went back to look at the disk, pointing at it just in front of her feet. "I think it might be fading, but I'm not sure."

He stood shakily and went to see for himself. His arm twinged with the proximity, not so much with pain as with an awakened energy, an awareness, a drawing of like to like. Surely if Rhiad was able, he would have already returned. But maybe it didn't work like that.

In truth, he had no idea how it worked and finally admitted as much.

"Then we're trapped," she said, the fear she was struggling to contain raising the pitch of her poor, hoarse voice.

He turned from the disk to examine their prison and saw now that it had once been a cistern. Its ceiling had long ago collapsed in the large slabs of red rock that jutted up from the sand. The slit through which they entered might have fed it, or else was formed by other forces, possibly an earthquake. In any case, it was hidden to them now, concealed by Rhiad's magic, and though Abramm felt carefully over the portion of wall he suspected was not real, he could find no sign of it. He even tried throwing himself against the striated surface, hoping to break through the illusion as Trap had pulled him through in the tunnels outside Xorofin. To no avail. The image was as substantial as it was indiscernible from the reality, and all he did was hurt his shoulder.

At last he stopped trying and went to stand beside his sister, who had settled on the ground not far away to watch.

"So now what do we do?" she murmured.

He scanned the curving russet walls, the low, woolly ceiling. "I don't know."

Walking a circuit of their prison, probing his fingers along the walls produced no more than his attempts to find the entry slit, nor did it reveal to him any other means of escape. He returned to Carissa, seated at the basin's lower end, and sat beside her.

But only for a moment. Then he was up again, trying to climb the smooth face of the cistern where the walls curved over the least. That did not work, so he tried piling the sand higher against the wall in a likely spot. That, too, proved futile. In between he returned repeatedly to the place where he knew the slit to be, always finding nothing but solid rock, though he bruised his shoulder in the effort.

Finally, exhausted and boiling with frustration, he sank down beside Carissa again. Not to give up, he assured himself, only to rest while he thought of some other tack. In the day's uncharacteristic warmth, he had long since removed his outer robe and headcloth. Now sweat drenched his tunic and dribbled down his face as thunder rumbled in the distance, harbinger of the imminent rains. Once the skies opened, the channels in these rocks would roil with hundreds of small rivers and streamlets. It wouldn't take long for this cistern to fill. Perhaps the water would lift them enough to climb out.

But that supposed there would be a place to climb out *to,* where they wouldn't get washed away. That supposed it would not be churning so viciously with all the incoming streams they'd be unable to keep their heads afloat. It supposed . . . far too many variables to control.

The overwhelming sense of his own stupidity and helplessness held him in its teeth, wrenching his middle and filling his throat till he could hardly breathe. The mist and rock mocked him with their impenetrable, imperturbable faces. It seemed impossible that this could have happened—bizarre, unthinkable, and infuriatingly unfair. It made him want to shout and hit things. And when he thought that soon Trap would be facing Beltha'adi in Jarnek's amphitheater—if he wasn't already—he could hardly bear it. That was a battle Abramm should be fighting—a battle *he* had been brought here to fight. He was as sure of that as he was of anything in his life.

And he wondered now, with the cool clarity of hindsight, why he'd ever felt so compelled to leave. Yes, the rains would make travel impossible for another month, but what was a month after two years?

Beltha'adi had challenged *him*, not Trap.

All the hot rage he'd felt for Gillard, all the searing thirst for justice that had birthed the urgency to get back to Kiriath had somehow vanished. He was left empty and perplexed, as if the man who'd felt all that and let it dictate his choices was someone else entirely. He rubbed the ovoid scar on his wrist, feeling a slight twinge. Trap had explained the spore's function to him once. He'd not paid much attention because he'd counted it more of the man's Terstan babble. Now all he could recall was something about its ability to affect—even invade—the mind, churning up an inward mist of thoughts and passions so as to obscure any clear perception of the truth.

The truth that he'd had no business leaving. The truth that under all the talk and fierce lust for vengeance he'd simply been running away. Yes, part of him still desired that vengeance. And it appalled him to think of Carissa caught in the horrible, savage chaos that was almost certain to erupt in Jarnek this afternoon. But those were not the real reasons he left.

The real reason, the truth he had not wanted to see, was that on some deep level he'd known that if he did not flee now, he would very shortly be changed—profoundly and irrevocably. If he did not fill his mind with thoughts of vengeance and glory and obligation and run away, he would have to look squarely into the light of the Terstan star, into the credibility of the Terstan claims—

And perhaps into the face of his own pride.

*"You want it to be about you. Your sacrifice, your efforts to make yourself worthy."*

It was true. And yet it seemed with every decision he'd made, every action he took, he'd only made himself more unworthy. Almost as if he couldn't help himself, almost as if some part of him insisted upon showing him how weak and helpless he was. Now he was trapped like a fish in a bowl, every good thing he might have accomplished wrenched from his grasp. He couldn't deliver the Dorsaddi, couldn't deliver Carissa, couldn't deliver Kiriath—couldn't even deliver himself.

He dropped his head back against the wall and shut his eyes, letting the shame and self-contempt wash over him in wave after bitter wave. *How ironic,* he thought, *that I finally see the truth and it's too late.*

A strange sound penetrated his misery. He looked around, frowning, and when the sound repeated a moment later, he realized it was Carissa. She was sitting at his side, arms crossed on bent knees, forehead dropped on her arms, and she was weeping unrestrainedly. After a moment he laid a hand on her back. "It's okay, Riss," he murmured awkwardly. "We'll be okay."

The lie lay bitter on his tongue.

She shook her head. "No, we won't. You were right. I never should've come. Everything I've done, every way I've tried to help—it's just made more trouble for you! If not for me you wouldn't be here, and now you're going to die, and it's all my fault."

"Hey, no." He squeezed her shoulder. "You couldn't have known who he was."

"That's just it." She lifted her head, wiped her eyes with a trembling hand, and looked over her shoulder at him. Her face was swollen and blotched. "I never trusted him. It's just . . . I thought he was the king's man." Her mouth spasmed, and the tears welled again as she turned away from him. "I was so afraid for you."

"Afraid for me?"

She wiped her cheeks again. "That you'd . . . that they'd make you face Beltha'adi." Her voice trembled at first, then strengthened as she looked skyward at the churning mists. "Ormah Fah'lon said you'd have to do it. That even though the Esurhites were afraid, they wouldn't break rank unless you stood against him. And then . . . well, they were all Terstans, and I . . . I just wanted to get you away, free again. Free to choose your own life. And all I did was . . . oh, Abramm, I am so *sorry*."

He pulled her toward him and she came, letting herself be comforted in his arms. But her words echoed in his mind.

*"Choose your own life."*

Choose. He snorted inwardly. *Well, I guess I've chosen, haven't I?*

He wanted to tell her again that it was all right, but he couldn't. All he could do was squeeze her shoulder and smooth the golden ringlets that had come free of their tie.

*Oh, Eidon, I don't want to die!* The words burst up into his awareness, the wail of the terrified little boy who still dwelt within him. The boy who was suddenly facing the devastating fact that, after everything he had been through, he was going to die without Eidon, all because of his stupid pride. He would pay finally for his own folly with an eternity spent in—

He gritted his teeth and closed his eyes, forcing the thought away, shoving it back down where it came from, turning away from the images his mind seemed all too eager to supply.

Suddenly Carissa hissed and lurched away from him. "Oh, plagues!" she cried. "Cooper! What did he do to Cooper?" She moaned and held herself.

"He must be dead, or he'd be here now."

"He wouldn't be able to see through the illusion any more than we can."

She looked at him over her shoulder.

"He might even have gone for help," Abramm added.

"How? It'd be a miracle if he found the way back after that maze you led us through." She shook her head. "I wish now I'd let Rhiad take you. At least you'd be alive."

Agreement soared in Abramm's soul. Yes! Perhaps he would've found a way of escape. Perhaps he might have—

He snorted. "If not for you, he'd have pumped me full of hockspur and I'd be a mindless puppet. Is that any better than death?" It avoided an immediate entry into Torments, his treacherous mind supplied.

Carissa regarded him soberly for a time, then deflated and settled again beside him. After a few minutes she began to tug and pull at her sash, as if it were bothering her. Then she stopped and looked down, pulling away a charred strip of purple silk and something else—something that took his breath away and made him feel as if he'd walked smack into a stone wall. It was a Star of Life, shining in all its heart-catching glory, dangling from a golden chain that looked somewhat worse for wear. The setting was malformed, as if it had been melted, the nearest links twisted and flattened as if they too had been scorched.

She rolled the sphere between her fingers, its light spearing out between them, its power lancing into his heart. The spore on his arm burst alive, and with it came the familiar headache and nausea. But now, instead of distracting him, the spore's effects only served to affirm the truth of what they sought to hide. The power of the Terstan star was in direct opposition to that of the spore. And if the spore was of Moroq and Shadow and Evil—and it was—the Star of Life must be of Eidon.

He stared at it, transfixed, catapulted in a single moment from despair to hope. How could it be here? His mind reeled. She had pressured him to leave the Dorsaddi in part because she'd feared he'd convert to their religion. How could she be carrying the very facilitator of that conversion, dangling it tantalizingly in front of his face? Unless she didn't know.

"Where did you get that?" he asked.

His voice came out so tight and strained, she looked at him in surprise. Realizing immediately that if she had the least idea what this was, what it was doing to him, she might throw it out of the cistern before he could stop her, he forced himself to pull his eyes away from it and relax back against the wall.

"Philip gave it to me," she said finally, frowning at him with a ghost of suspicion creasing her brow. "Why?"

He shrugged with careful indifference. "Just curious. The Dorsaddi have a whole sect based around an orb like that."

That seemed to satisfy her. She turned that penetrating gaze back to the stone in her hand. "I think he bought it someplace in Jarnek, but I doubt he knew it was Dorsaddi."

*Not Dorsaddi,* Abramm thought wryly. *He must have made it for her, and she's wearing it unheeding.*

"It was supposed to protect me from evil," she said with a laugh.

"Maybe it did." He had his eyes closed now, had dropped his head back against the rock wall. The stone must have been what enabled her to fight the Command of the choker and to shove Rhiad into the etherworld.

More than that, he knew with a hot, breathtaking certainty that it was no coincidence she had it here now. No coincidence they had been brought here, cut off from everything else, walled away alone.

If he had doubted Eidon's hand in his life before, he did no longer.

After a long time he heard Carissa yawn beside him, counting his own heartbeats as he listened to her breathing slow and deepen, felt her relax in sleep against him. When he finally opened his eyes again, he was shaking and his arm hurt like wildfire.

*"You must come to him as nothing,"* Trap had said.

He stared at the stone, dangling at the end of the chain now twined between Carissa's limp fingers, its glow reflecting off the dirt-smudged fabric of her robe, sun-bright in this gloomy cistern.

He was, certainly, nothing. That had been proved over and over. Unworthy, wretched, flawed by an indomitable pride, well beyond hope of ever earning redemption.

He reached toward the dangling stone, extending a tentative finger to its surface. It tingled beneath his touch, and when he drew his finger away, the stone went with it, swelling, elongating, then pinching off to leave a second stone clinging to his fingertip. It balanced there a moment, then rolled, cool and hard and solid, into his palm. Staring into it, he saw something golden—

a shield?—fixed at its heart, and in that shield he sensed a presence powerful as a storm-tossed sea, yet gentle as the waves lapping around a child at play on shore. Not wrapping around him with confining tentacles as the rhu'ema did, seeking to trap and devour, but waiting patiently for him to come to it.

The man he had seen.

The man . . . Tersius?

His wrist pained him, sharply, insistently. The old protests shrieked with renewed vigor. *How can you think of doing this? You'll be marked for the rest of your life. Branded again, and worse, you'll carry a power that will cripple you and drive you mad.*

*Do you really want that?*

The question hung in his mind, and breathless silence pressed upon him. He heard the rush of his own pulse in his ears.

*I want . . . to know Eidon.*

*Through my Light will I shield and bless you.*

He had found a shield in this stone, and without it he was helpless against the Darkness—as all men were helpless, whether they chose to admit it or not.

He swallowed past the constriction in his throat.

*Through my Light will you stand against the Shadow.*

The orb lay on his palm, a perfect sphere of perfect Light.

*Through my Light you will know me . . .*

*I have hated you, Lord Eidon. Cursed you, fought you, forsaken you.*

*Yet I have not forsaken you, Abramm, son of Meren. Will you choose now? Will you take the life I offer you?*

Light flared, burning away the cistern's striated walls and sand and upthrust shards of stone. A man stood before him, dressed in white—Tersius. And somehow Eidon, too, separate yet incomprehensibly one. His face blazed like the sun, impossible to look at, impossible to look away from. His piercing eyes were blue as the vault of heaven, dark as the depths of the sea, bright as all the stars in the sky. They held all wisdom and power and looked into Abramm's very soul, seeing all that he was, all that he'd done—every last miserable failure in perfect, searing clarity.

Shuddering with awe and self-loathing, he fell to his knees. "My Lord!" he whispered. "I am not worthy."

*"No. But I have paid your debt."* Tersius held out a hand.

Abramm did not move. *"I have paid . . ."* Just as Trap had said. But . . . why?

Those dark, light eyes snared him. He saw again their wisdom and might and keen perception—and something more. Love.

His throat closed as he touched the reality of what that love had done and borne for him. In that moment he felt an echo of the shocking, searing pain of the Shadow's first touch, the excruciating agony of abandonment, the cold, soul-draining desolation of utter aloneness, where pain was the only reality—all undeserved, the debt another owed and should have paid.

*The debt I owed,* Abramm realized. Payment for all the resentment and selfishness and unbelief he had nurtured. For the defiance and the prideful delusion that he'd become a hero because of his own efforts. For all the affronts he'd committed and cultivated against the One who had made him, and loved him, and even now kept him alive. Affronts of graver insult than his small, wormish mind could even begin to grasp.

He shuddered again and dropped his head, choking on his own wretchedness. Shame burned in his heart, and he wanted to fling himself to the ground and crawl away.

*"Abramm, take my hand."* The voice was gentle, yet firm, drawing him back out of himself, drawing his eyes up to those of his Lord. *"I have paid your debt."*

Hesitantly, Abramm reached out.

Strong fingers wrapped around his own; gentle eyes smiled into his. He felt a rush of joy, and with it a golden fire surged into his palm, up his arm, into his heart. Clean and bright and achingly wonderful, it did not hurt save as deep, deep yearning finally fulfilled.

For the first time in his life he felt whole.

*"You wish to know me, my son. And so you shall."*

---

The light faded. Abramm still sat in the cistern, the red-and-ochre walls curving around him, Carissa breathing deeply at his side. He stared at his empty palm, then hesitantly fingered back the flaps on the neck slit of his tunic.

Glinting in the flesh over his heart lay a small golden shield.

# CHAPTER 41

He touched a tentative finger to the mark; it felt smooth and hard, slightly tender to the touch. As he rubbed it, Eidon's Light rippled through him—bright, clean, crystal tones that warmed his soul and recalled to mind that wonderful presence.

*Eidon.*

No question. No doubts, no cold queasiness. This was what he had sought for all his life.

Suddenly he saw the purpose in all that had happened to him. Not only in his having been delivered from Saeral's plans for possessing him—twice—but all the rest of it: the pain, the grief, the humiliation, and seeming desertions. It had taken no less to shake him loose of his pride, to clear away all the false notions to which he had clung so he could at last see the truth. It was all—and this was the supreme irony—an answer to prayer.

*Eidon, please! I want only to know you.*

*And so you shall.*

He stroked the mark again, wonder welling up within him. Had there been an altar at which he could worship, he would have flung himself before it in gratitude. But the altar, it seemed, lay in his soul now, a core of light and life he sensed would demand far more of him than the mere bending of the knee.

An answer to prayer, and much more.

Memories ran through his mind, incidents along every step of this journey he'd made—from the Holy Keep in Springerlan, to the galley ships of Katahn, to the Val'Orda, to this broken cistern deep in the Land of Shadow. He saw, as never before, the hand that had guided his path, protected and preserved him to this moment—not merely so he might know the Almighty, but so he might serve him as well.

He released a long, slow breath as conviction took hold of him.

The White Pretender was Eidon's creation, not Abramm's—a beacon of light and hope held out to a people who walked in darkness, inspiring those who longed for freedom and truth, reproaching those who exalted Khrell. From his first day in the Games, the Pretender had ridden the winds of destiny, slaying with ease the man who played the part of invincible Supreme Commander in symbolic affirmation of the dire prophecy that had been shrilled out before the match began.

Coincidence?

Even at the time he had sensed it was not. And though his defiance of Beltha'adi's claims of divine mandate had sprung more from anger and the pleasure he took in baiting the man than from any loyalty to Eidon, Eidon had used it, fulfilling purposes Abramm hadn't begun to understand.

Beltha'adi understood, though. Trap might be the Dorsaddi Deliverer, but the Pretender was the wasp that stung the emperor to madness, the person around whom the conflict turned. That was why he had to be slain, publicly if possible, and why Beltha'adi had asked for him rather than the Deliverer. If he learned the man he was to face today was not the one he wanted, it would be a great victory. The Pretender would be called a coward, proving by his flight the truth of Beltha'adi's claims of invincibility.

Chilled, he sat forward. *I have to go back.*

Immediately he was beset with memories of all the Terstans he'd seen die in the ring—broken, humiliated, tortured—and of Trap's assertion to Mephid only this morning that a man did not come to Eidon's power full able to use it. Even if Abramm took the star today, he'd said, he would in no way be prepared to face Beltha'adi's magic.

Yet the conviction remained. *I must go back and face him.*

But if he did, he would surely die.

The conviction only grew stronger.

But what of Carissa? He couldn't leave her here. She'd have to go with him.

The thought stopped. What was he thinking? Neither of them was going anywhere. *My Lord, if you truly do want me to go back, you're going to have to get me out of this cistern first.*

The answer came immediately, so startling, so unbelievably easy that he shouted with excitement and bounded to his feet. Disturbed by his sudden movement, Carissa stirred and moaned, but he had eyes only for the wall in front of him.

"What's happening?" Carissa's voice came low and gravelly behind him. "What's wrong?"

"I can see the slit," he cried, moving toward it. More precisely he saw where the wall shimmered and wobbled, betraying the illusion's presence. When he put a hand on it, it felt as solid as ever on first brush. Pressing harder, though, his fingers sank into it.

"You can?" His words had taken time to penetrate his sister's sleep-fog, but now excitement flooded her voice as she leaped up beside him. "Is it fading, then?"

She touched the wall, then turned to him, flushed and eager. Her eyes fell at once on the shieldmark, gleaming between the edges of his tunic. They fixed there, round and wide as the eager flush drained off into whiteness. "Holy Haverall!" she whispered. "What have you done?" Her eyes climbed to meet his own. "What have you *done*, Abramm?"

"What I should have done a long time ago."

She staggered back from him, then collapsed onto the sand before he could catch her, staring again at the mark on his chest and shaking her head. Tears glittered in her eyes. "How could you? How could you have done this?"

He crouched before her and seized her hands, but she jerked them away. "Riss, you don't understand. It's not at all as we've been taught. It really *is* the mark of Eidon."

She just kept staring at it, shaking her head as the tears rolled down her cheeks. "You've ruined everything."

"No, I haven't. This isn't like what it was with the Mataio. This is *truth*. It's what I've looked for all my life."

She didn't seem to be listening, or if she was, she didn't believe him. Words, he realized, were not going to reach her. Maybe actions would.

He stood and turned back to the wall. Trap had pulled him through two similar illusions outside Xorofin. Could he pull Carissa through this one now? He was new to this power. What if he lacked the strength or wit or whatever it took to get her through with him? What if he pulled her right into the stone? For that matter, what if he lacked the strength to get through all by himself, let alone with her?

He had to believe that wouldn't happen. But perhaps he ought to test it first.

He pushed his fingers into the rock again, drew them out, took a deep breath, and plunged forward. As before, it was just like walking through a screen of cold lard.

The slit stood empty and silent on the other side. As he suspected, the illusion worked both ways. Cooper wouldn't have known they were trapped or what had happened. But it looked like he'd gone back for help in any case. Abramm's sword, which Rhiad had earlier pitched away, gleamed in the shadow along the wall, and he stooped to pick it up. Then, with one more glance around, he pushed back into the cistern.

He expected Carissa to be suitably impressed by his seemingly miraculous feat and hopefully a little more receptive to the change in him. But she sat with knees drawn up, arms folded upon them, forehead braced on arms. She didn't appear to know he'd even left. Her shoulders heaved and her breath sobbed, and suddenly it annoyed him.

"Oh, stop," he snapped, sliding the blade back into its scabbard. "It's not as if I've died."

"It is as far as I'm concerned," she said to her lap.

"You know nothing about it. And everything you think you know is wrong."

Her head snapped up, her gaze glaring into his. "I *saw* the sarotis in Ray's eyes, Abramm. I saw his madness."

He grimaced, then said firmly, "The sarotis is not inevitable. Meridon's worn the shield nearly all his life, and there's no sarotis in his eyes. Nor is he mad."

"He's facing Beltha'adi in single combat."

"But not because he's mad. Now, come on. Let's get out of here." He held out a hand.

She stared at him, clearly confused.

"I told you," he said. "I can see the opening."

Her eyes flicked to the wall, which he knew had not changed in the slightest for her. They came back to him, her brow narrowing. When still she did not move he huffed his irritation and stepped toward her, hauling her to her feet.

"I'll pull you through," he said. "It'll feel strange for a moment, like you can't do it, but just bear with it and you'll be all right."

Before she had time to protest, he tightened his grip on her and strode through the illusion.

As they stepped into the slit, she uttered a small, tight "Oh" and nothing more. He let her go, and she turned to stare back at what to her would appear to be a solid wall. The look of astonished wonder on her face at least partially offset her earlier reproach, though he doubted it would change her attitude much. It hadn't changed his.

When they emerged from the slit where the cliff had forced them to leave the stairway, he nodded sourly. "I didn't think there was a cliff there."

She frowned at it. "That was an illusion, too?"

"He had to have some way to get us into that cistern." Abramm started up the stairs. A moment later he heard her follow.

"Isn't this the way we came?"

"Yes."

"But—shouldn't we be going the other way, then?"

"Cooper wouldn't have been able to see past the cliff," Abramm said. "He'd have gone back for help, and it's too late to beat the rains anyway."

She didn't argue with him anymore. It was work to climb the long, dog-legged flight of stairs, and neither of them had breath to waste on conversation. Likely they wouldn't have spoken anyway.

They had reached the top and were crossing over the rocky shoulder that separated one canyon from the next when a rushing roar rolled across the canyon-scored tablelands. The mists, so close earlier, seemed to have receded here, preparatory to the advent of the rains. Congealing into dark clouds that boiled low overhead, they flickered and rumbled with threat, and for a moment Abramm was sure that the threat was about to be realized.

But the horizon showed no sign of a downpour, and the blast of wind he was expecting never came. Instead the roar faded away to silence.

"What was that?" Carissa asked, coming up beside him.

He stared into the distance, and the urgency that had been gnawing at him increased twofold.

"I think it was a crowd," he said and set off in long, hurried strides. A high, thin squeal, faint in the distance, confirmed his suspicions. That would be the opening fanfare signaling the arrival of the contest's participants. There would be the usual ritual, Beltha'adi strutting around the ring, offering his obeisance to Khrell, boasting of his imminent success. He would be followed by the arrival of the Pretender, and shortly after that the fight would begin. In all probability, it would not last long.

He wanted to run full speed down the stairs angling before him, but Carissa would not be able to keep up with him, and he couldn't abandon her out here.

*Eidon, you know I am willing. Surely you won't allow me to get there too late.*

"Abramm, slow down! What is the matter with you?" Carissa's annoyance whined in her voice, grating at him further.

He started to answer when again he heard that odd squealing sound. Maybe it wasn't horns after all. That had sounded more like the bay of a hound and was coming from somewhere down in the canyon below. What would a hound be doing here? Had Beltha'adi conjured some new monstrous spawn to set loose in the canyons?

"I think that was Newbold," Carissa said behind him.

"Newbold?"

"Captain Meridon's hound. If Cooper did somehow reach Jarnek, it would make sense to send searchers out with the dog."

And then he saw them, scrambling around the sheer wall of a dam down below: the dog, brown against red, the youth following behind on the leash, Cooper behind him, and three Dorsaddi.

With a rush of wonder, Abramm hurried down to meet them.

As he closed the gap he saw that the boy was in a rage, his freckled face dark and clouded and, incongruously, streaked with tears. He did not notice Abramm and Carissa until he was almost upon them. Then, seeing them coming down, he let go Newbold's leash and stood where he was, panting up at them. And suddenly Abramm understood. Cooper must have come back with his story, and Trap, fearing he would die at Beltha'adi's hand, had ordered the boy to go out with the dog to find them. Philip would hate it, but it was the kind of thing Abramm could imagine Trap doing. It was the kind of thing he could imagine himself doing.

Carissa rushed around both him and Philip to fling herself sobbing into old Cooper's arms. About that time Philip saw the mark on Abramm's chest.

He frowned, uncertain, as he climbed the last few steps between them, but once he saw it clearly, saw it was indeed what he thought it was, his eyes widened, and like Carissa he stood and stared.

"I have to get back to Jarnek," Abramm said quietly. "And she can't keep up."

Philip nodded.

"I want you to take her round to the rear lines."

"But he's my brother—"

"He could have sent someone else after us, Philip. He sent you because he doesn't want you there." He paused, then nodded at Carissa, who was still sobbing in Cooper's arms. "Any more than I want *her* there."

Philip was frowning darkly. "You can't ask me to do this. Not when he's—"

"Fighting my fight. And if I get there in time, perhaps I can save him."

Philip blinked up at him, startled out of his protests. In the distance the roar started up again, and this time he heard another squeal that really was a blast of horns.

"Will you do it, then?"

"I . . ." The boy shut his mouth. After a moment he nodded.

Abramm hesitated. "I thank you for the gift you gave her. I pray she will find some comfort in it in the days to come."

He then spoke softly to the Dorsaddi, directing them to escort his sister and her party to the rear lines. Carissa had ceased weeping by then, and Philip had drawn her aside, ostensibly to learn from her what had happened. She stood with her back to Abramm, as if she could not bear to look at him. He wondered if she had any idea what he was going to do. If not, she was the only one who didn't. Cooper, who'd taken note of Abramm's new shield with only a start of surprise, had moved downhill away from the group once Carissa had released him. Now he waited there, eyeing Abramm speculatively. As the latter approached, the old retainer bowed. "Good luck, Your Highness."

"Thank you, Coop."

But then the man just stared at him, until finally Abramm was forced to push past him. There was something in the man's face or gaze that left Abramm discomfited. An intensity of regard that might be worship or something else entirely, neither of which he particularly welcomed.

Well, he had no time for that now, especially since he didn't think it likely he would ever see his old guardian again.

A lifetime seemed to pass before he reached the sentries at the rear flanks of the Dorsaddi force—now congregated along the cliffs and wadis south of the amphitheater to watch the match unfolding there. This close it was obvious the roar was of a crowd and not of rain and wind, though the clouds still boiled angrily overhead. Recognizing him from afar, the sentries immediately sent a runner to alert the king so that, by the time Abramm reached the crowd jamming the floor of the Wadi Juba, he was expected. The men, who could see nothing of the match itself and were only waiting to pour out of the wadi at the contest's end, greeted him fiercely, as if they had known all along he would return. Those nearest saw his shield right off, the word of his change sweeping the crowd like the first winds of storm, igniting a rumble of excitement.

They parted easily before him, many offering personal greetings and words of approval. Ahead, the amphitheater audience roared in waves, following the ebb and flow of the battle unfolding there. The sounds egged Abramm on, though he was deliberately controlling his pace so as to regain his breath before he entered the fray.

Rounding a bend, he finally saw the end of the wadi, where the two sheer red walls stood against the bright glow of unseen torches. He could see the ranks of gray-tunicked men seated on the curving benches of the amphitheater. Others clogged the cliff top above it and clung precariously to imperfections in the sheer rock between cliff top and the last row of real seats.

Closer to hand were the pale figures of the Dorsaddi, lining the near cliffs and also clinging to their sheer faces, some riding on others' shoulders to see past the crowd. From where Abramm stood, though, the ring itself remained blocked from view.

Thunder rumbled as the amphitheater audience burst into another savage cheer. Abramm gripped the hilt of his sword and quickened his pace despite his intentions otherwise.

Suddenly the crowd parted, and King Shemm himself stood in Abramm's path, forcing him to stop. The dark, shrewd eyes flicked at once to the shieldmark and back up to Abramm's face. A smile twitched at the hard lips; then that unreadable stone face descended.

"You truly mean to face him, then," the king said, as usual, getting right to the point.

"I do."

"Newly changed, you cannot prevail against him."

"Not in my own strength. But in that of Sheleft'Ai?" He smiled grimly. "Anything is possible."

"You have no costume."

"I'll fight like this. As I am. That should be proof enough." Shettai, he thought, would be pleased.

Shemm's expression never changed. "He will kill you, Pretender."

"No doubt he will."

For a long moment the Dorsaddi chieftain looked at him, staring deep into his eyes. Then he gave a single sharp nod and stepped back, gesturing to the lieutenant waiting at his elbow. "You'll need these."

The lieutenant stepped forward, three gold rings gleaming in the palm of his hand. Abramm stood very still as the tokens of his fighting rank were fastened back into his ear and his hair was retied into a proper warrior's knot.

"I need a dagger," he said when it was done, recalling that Rhiad had taken his.

Shemm slid his own free from its scabbard. Abramm took it with a nod, slid it into the empty sheath at his hip, then checked to see that his belt harness was securely fastened, that the blade released cleanly. By then every man in the canyon had become aware of his presence. The deep silence in the near periphery made the savage screams of the audience out in the Wadi Mudra seem all the more ominous.

Sudden movement rippled through the men around him, and the moment changed in an instant. Voices muttered urgently, their fear sharp and piercing. Finally the word reached Abramm and the king. "The Deliverer is down!"

He saw the alarm flare in Shemm's face and, for a moment, shared it himself. If Trap couldn't handle Beltha'adi, what chance did he himself have?

He pushed the fear away and reminded himself that victory would not lie in his own strength, but in Eidon's. He was here because Eidon had brought him here. He would go into that ring because it was where Eidon wanted him to go.

Lifting his chin, he said firmly, "He and I have fought together for nearly two years. We will fight together now."

He strode past Shemm and through the sea of Dorsaddi. Soon he had reached the mouth of the canyon and saw the great amphitheater beyond, ringed with torches as before. An archway of them stood on this side of the arena, the apparent entryway of the Pretender. Dorsaddi stood in that archway now, silent and tense as they watched the drama unfolding on the sand. Across from them, the gray-clad crowd on the stone benches had gone wild, screaming, leaping, and waving their swords in the air.

Abramm marched grimly forward, having to lay hands on the men in front of him to gain their attention and then their startled recognition as they moved aside. The Taleteller's eerily amplified voice boomed over the din, but the words were coming so rapidly and so excitedly it was impossible to pick out anything coherent.

Suddenly it choked off, even as the cavorting crowd across the arena stilled. A whisper of astonishment swept over it, drowned out by another growl of thunder. Then the Taleteller's voice echoed off the rock, each word clear in the silence. "This man is not the Pretender!"

The crowd erupted in a torrent of boos and hisses.

Abramm parted the last line of Dorsaddi standing directly under the archway. They gave way dazedly, their attention focused on the arena, where Trap was on his knees, bareheaded and reeling, his face pale and pinched as if he were sick. Burn marks reddened the side of his neck, and his white clothing was splotched with gray, as if it had mildewed. It was not dirt, for the sand on the arena floor was red. The front of his doublet was scorched and rent, and both his weapons glittered in the sand some distance away. The sword's blade appeared to be broken off a handspan from the grip, and the dagger's was a barely recognizable melt of metal. Beltha'adi loomed over him, elbana in hand, the Pretender's white curly wig dangling from its tip.

Now he flicked the wig aside and snapped the blade back, slashing through the charred lace to lay open the front of the doublet. Dead center of the already bleeding slash, the Terstan's golden shield glittered in the gray daylight for all to see. Snorting derision, Beltha'adi kicked him square in the chin with one booted foot, laying him out flat on his back against the red sand, where he rolled onto his side and made no effort to get up.

The crowd burst into excited shouting, and the Taleteller echoed them.

"It's the Infidel! The Infidel in the Pretender's costume! They have deceived us!"

The voice paused as the crowd went wild, a surge of sound thundering over the wadi. As it waned, the Taleteller continued. "Why would they do that, I ask you? But then, we all know, do we not?" It paused for dramatic effect, then shouted, "Because the Pretender knew he could not stand against the mighty power of the great Khrell's Chosen! And so he sent his Infidel, while he himself has no doubt fled back to his homeland, back to the land of the yelaki!"

"Yelaki!" the crowd took up the chant, screaming, waving their weapons now. "Yelaki! Yelaki!"

Abramm drew a deep breath, pulled both his weapons from their scabbards, and strode into the arena.

CHAPTER

# 42

He stopped ten strides from the gateway, and by then the crowd had gone silent again. All eyes were fixed upon him, dark faces over gray uniforms, over colorful tunics, over pale robes—but all of them male, all of them old enough to fight. They packed the tiered benches, clung to the cliff faces, peered in ranks from the rim, and filled the wadi itself, a sea of enemies whose combined gazes weighed on him with a pressure he had not experienced for a long time now. They were so quiet he could hear the hiss and sputter of the torches, the faint crackling of the flames in the belly of the great statue of Khrell brought over from the temple. A cadre of red-robed priests and dark-tunicked Broho stood guard at its base, holding off the common soldiers who thronged to either side.

The statue dwarfed them all. Its obsidian eyes, backlit by the belly flames, seemed eerily alive, and the open, smiling mouth, also lit by the internal fires, appeared to move and flex as if already laughing at his death. Though he had seen this idol—or ones like it—countless times, today it throbbed with a malevolent presence he had never before noticed. Today he realized it was not just stone and flame but something more. Something alive and calculating and knowing. . . .

An icy-footed worm of fear crawled up his spine.

He turned his gaze to the man who stood between him and the statue, the short, muscular figure of the Supreme Commander of the Black Moon, facing him now with a look of amusement on his dark features. He wore the black tunic of the Broho, the silver amulet shining brightly against his chest.

His shaven head gleamed, and the gold champion rings lining the margins of both ears flashed in silent affirmation of his skill. Over two hundred years of battle experience, they said. Enabled by the power of his god to be inhumanly fast, inhumanly accurate, inhumanly strong. Invincible, they said he was. Immortal.

The doubts Abramm had brushed off so easily back in the Wadi Juba returned in full force. Trap, bleeding and dusty, had managed to sit up and now gaped at him dully, barely holding himself conscious. Trap was experienced in the use of Eidon's Light. He was as strong and as fine a swordsman as Abramm had ever known. He was brave, confident, not easily rattled. Yet he was finished, overwhelmed by the same adversary Abramm now proposed to fight.

*Who am I to think I can do any better?*

He had reproved Carissa just this morning for trying to take on things she had no business taking on. Was he now doing the same? He had believed Eidon wanted him to come here. But what if he was wrong? Surely if Eidon were with him, he would not feel all these doubts.

With a sick, sinking feeling in the pit of his stomach, he grew convinced he'd made a horrible mistake. That it had never been Eidon's will at all but was only his own pride again.

And yet he was here. There would be no going back now. If there was a sea of Esurhites watching, so there was a sea of Dorsaddi watching at his back. He closed his eyes, blotting out the dark and supremely confident gaze of his adversary, and prayed. *If I have overstepped, my Lord, I beg forgiveness. You know my heart. I know I am not able to face him on my own, but I know that you are. I ask only that my death will be to your glory, not to your shame.*

He drew a deep breath, letting the doubts slide away, and opened his eyes.

"I have come," he said, and though he had spoken quietly, his voice blared over the crowd.

The dark eyes flicked down to Abramm's booted feet and up again, apparently ignoring the shield, though the look of amusement broadened almost into a smile. "And you are the *real* Pretender, then?"

Abramm straightened his spine a hair. "I am Abramm Kalladorne, son of Meren, prince of Kiriath, and I am no Pretender."

"Ahh." Beltha'adi glanced over his shoulder at the satin-cloaked box of VIPs on the first landing. "Is it really him this time, my cousin?" he asked.

Abramm saw Katahn then, sitting in the first row, flanked by his son Regar, who was almost unrecognizable with his shaven head and priestly garb. The Gamer looked up from the mark on Abramm's chest, favoring him with that typically ironic expression, one brow arched, a slight smile on his lips. "It is him, my lord."

His voice, too, was amplified, and there was in it a current of excitement that spoke to Abramm's soul, awakening in it a sudden flush of energy at the recollection that it *wasn't* just his own idea that brought him here. It was the notion that this moment had been prophesied; it was the realization that every event had been orchestrated to bring him here, even down to that Star of Life appearing in Carissa's hand when he had thought all was lost.

It really was Eidon's will.

As Katahn's last word died away, an excited murmur danced across the crowd. A puff of warm air ruffled the whiskers on Abramm's jaw, carrying with it the undeniable tang of rain. In the distance, thunder growled again. The heavens would open soon, ending all of this. But not yet.

Beltha'adi stepped back and addressed the guards standing near the box. "Move that piece of dung out of the ring and—"

"No!" Abramm cut in, bringing Beltha'adi's head around in surprise. "My people will see to him."

The dark eyes fastened upon him, speculating, still amused. "You have ever been a bold one, Pretender. But very well. It matters little to me, since in the end you will all be dead anyway."

Abramm turned to the Dorsaddi standing in the archway behind him and was surprised to find Shemm standing among them. Mephid and Japheth were already hurrying out to Meridon's side.

Once they had carried him away, Beltha'adi faced Abramm again, grinning ferociously. "So you send your second in to face me first, eh?" he said as he brought the elbana around to point directly at Abramm's chest. "An odd way for the Great Pretender to respond to a challenge."

"I'm surprised you think so, seeing as during all the months I challenged you, you had no trouble sending your seconds to face me." He brought up his own weapons, sword and dagger, and moved to the right, turning Beltha'adi's advance into a circle.

"I had other, more important matters to attend to," Beltha'adi said.

"As did I."

"Like the acquisition of that new decoration you wear?"

"That was one of them, yes."

"And you think now it will give you victory over me."

"I think that the power behind it will give me victory over you."

"The power of the dying god? Well, let us see, then."

The Broho attacked in a barrage of two-handed strokes that made up for their lack of variation by their savage speed. Abramm backstepped furiously, parrying every stroke handily, but was pressed twenty feet before he finally managed to tie up his adversary's blade and step in close to lunge with the dagger.

Its point tore the fabric of the Broho's tunic as he spun away, and they returned to circling. Again Beltha'adi launched a savage series of strokes, but Abramm was ready this time, choosing the moment, catching the elbana on his dagger as he stepped out of the line of attack and slashed at the Broho's open face with his sword.

He was aiming for the eye, hit the brow instead, only a tiny cut, but Beltha'adi lurched back with a curse. It wasn't from pain, but from the indignity of being the first one blooded—him who had expected not to be blooded at all.

They circled again. "You're good, Pretender," Beltha'adi grated, "but you're only flesh. And flesh isn't good enough to stand against a god."

Abramm kept his gaze fixed on Beltha'adi's. "No," he agreed. "It's not."

For the first time he saw something like uneasiness in the Supreme Commander's eyes, just a flicker, as of a thought formed and quickly squelched.

The long blade came at Abramm again in alternating diagonal sweeps. He blocked them with relative ease, despite the speed at which they came, wondering that the man still seemed to be playing with him. Again he fell into the rhythm, calculated his move, stepped out of the attack line and lunged, his sword driving for the unprotected armpit.

This time the move was expected. The elbana slid off the dagger to block, then whipped back from the offside in a counterattack. Abramm lurched back almost out of reach, the tip of the blade slicing his chest.

Beltha'adi followed him, lunging and slashing, and Abramm blocked him stroke for stroke, falling into that strange, misty-edged world where time both fled in an instant and came to a standstill, where he anticipated his opponent's moves before they happened and pain and fatigue held no sway. He had been here many times before and knew it always resulted in his best performance, knew in some back corner of his mind that he was performing well right now. No. Far more than well, better, perhaps than ever in his life. Nor had he ever felt stronger. It was as if fire burned in his veins, igniting his flesh with a power and precision he had never known before.

And when finally the Supreme Commander broke off to resume circling him, blade held out and ready, he saw that the uneasiness had returned to the other's eyes. It dawned on him, then, that perhaps this power in him was not a normal product of training and concentration and determination, was perhaps not his own at all.

"You are tired, Pretender," the Broho said, circling, his dark eyes boring into Abramm's. "Your arms are trembling. Your parries are weakening. You will not last much longer. . . ."

It was hard to concentrate on the words, hard to make them mean anything. And when finally Abramm managed it, they did not make sense. For he was not tired, nor did his arms tremble, and his parries were coming more swiftly and decisively than ever.

It was a distraction. He realized that the moment the elbana came back from a feint and cut into the side of his thigh, seeking to hamstring him, but he turned away in time.

He saw the Broho master swallow, saw the crease now etched between his eyes, lined with the blood from the cut on his brow as it mingled with rivulets of sweat. Other cuts marked the dark tunic, each of them glistening wetly. Abramm could hardly recall having made them, but in that moment, he realized he was winning.

The Esurhite was speaking again, his words coming breathlessly—something about a painful death. Abramm ignored him, falling back into the golden haze, seeing first the eyes, then the movements—peripherally, and yet focusing on each individually. It was as if his consciousness had expanded—he knew everything at once, so that no move, no trick could get by him. He lunged and swung and blocked and parried; he dodged and rolled and leaped and circled. And all the while the fire coursed through his veins, filling him with light and life and a glorious, exultant strength.

He wondered, finally, if perhaps he was dying and didn't know it. A brief glance down revealed his tunic reduced to blood-soaked tatters, yet still he felt no pain.

*His Light will be my strength. . . .*

*Lord Eidon, if you are indeed taking me, please, let me bring him with me.*

Beltha'adi sidestepped, looped free of Abramm's blade, and stepped back, circling, watching him warily. His eyes betrayed real concern . . . and something else. Something smug and knowing. A flicker, the barest flicker, a sense of something coming up behind, and Abramm turned just as the veren swooped upon him, his blade driving deep into its breast and the fire flooding out of him like a dam-burst.

The creature screamed as white light blasted the world away, its momentum carrying it hard into Abramm, bowling him to the ground and ripping his sword from his grasp as it plowed over him and was gone. Half-blinded, dagger still in hand, he scrambled to his feet, expecting to be attacked in this moment of weakness.

But the veren lay sprawled just past him on the sand, and beyond it the invincible Supreme Commander stood transfixed by surprise, staring gape-mouthed at the corpse. Slowly his eyes came up to meet Abramm's, and astonishment turned to fear. He shouted for his Broho to attack, but not one of the five beneath the statue moved. He shouted again, but still none responded. The five round-eyed faces gaped back at him, at the veren, and at Abramm, who, looking up, saw that his audience was no longer purely human. The men were still there, watching in silence, none moving more than the Broho. But hovering above them, slithering around them, dancing between them, were a myriad of amorphous shapes in a myriad of colors—red, blue, green, yellow, orange, purple, and every shade between. They quivered and pulsed and jittered, even sidled among the clouds overhead. Many of them hovered around the great idol, passing in and out of the eyes, the mouth, the belly, wrapping around it, reaching out and slithering back. There were more wrapped around each Broho and priest, some inside their bodies. One man glowed transparent with yellow light, another with red, their eyes flaring like bright coals.

They writhed and they whispered and they reached out to him. He heard their rasping, muttering voices, smelled the roasted-grain scent of their presence, felt the cold essence and the hatred—the utter and thorough black hatred for him and the Light he carried within him. If they could destroy him, they would do so in an instant, but the Light kept them back.

Rhu'ema.

He had never before seen one, but he knew that was what they were.

And he knew exactly what he was to do. As he started toward Beltha'adi, the latter let his sword drop, then threw back his shoulders and drew a deep breath. A veil of purple fire burst from his lips, riding the back of a deep, hoarse bellow. It slammed into Abramm with enough force to stagger him backward—but met a barrier of white light that absorbed it like water did flame.

He kept walking, and the Broho drew another breath, sent out a coil of black mist and then a jagged snake of red lightning. None got through the wall of white fire. Abramm drew up before the man, saw the fear in his eyes, the knowledge of imminent death and then denial fulminating into rage. Beltha'adi fairly glowed with the power of the creature within him, purple fire blazing in his eyes, out his nose and mouth, and through every rent in his flesh. The elbana lifted lazily, then swooped down. Abramm caught it with his dagger, drove it back and up, and grabbed its hilt with his free hand. As Beltha'adi released a hand to try to push him, Abramm tore the elbana away and slashed back with the dagger. He saw a shorter blade, pulled from a hidden sheath, coming at him low, but he ignored it, driving his own weapon deep into the Esurhite's chest.

The Light came upon him again, blasting up his arm and into the blade, into the body of the man impaled upon it. Purple fire flowed out of Beltha'adi's eyes and into the sky. Gasping and limp, the Supreme Commander of the Army of the Black Moon slid off the blade and slumped to the sand. A moment he knelt there in front of Abramm, looking gray and old and strangely puzzled. Then he toppled sideways to the ground—his mouth open, his eyes glazed and empty—and did not move again.

The power bled out of Abramm like water from a punctured drinking sack. His vision of the massed rhu'ema faded, and as it did he became aware of his body. Pain and weakness shuddered through him, and he staggered backward a few steps, dizzy and so sharply pain-sick he came to a stop and doubled over. His flesh seemed a roil of agony, and there was one place, a well of fire low in his side, he thought might be especially serious.

His knees were about to give way when he remembered where he was, what he was about. With hundreds of eyes watching him, and a battle in the making, he couldn't just collapse. Not yet, anyway. But for a moment he couldn't make himself straighten, either.

A few deep breaths, a gasped prayer, a resolute amassing of his will, and he wrenched himself upright.

He had killed Beltha'adi at the center of the arena and now stood between the corpse and the archway through which he'd originally entered, the Dorsaddi comfortingly at his back. The nobles in their box had risen to their feet and were staring at their fallen leader in undisguised horror. All but one.

Katahn met his gaze and nodded gravely, a gesture of salute. And more—there was undeniably something of awe in his look.

Abramm scanned the dumbstruck crowd, which even yet did not appear to have grasped the reality that their invincible leader was dead. Even the priests on guard by the idol stood stunned and motionless. And though the idol's stone grin had not changed, it somehow did not appear as pleased as it had earlier. Indeed, he could just make out the creatures he knew still swirled around it, could almost sense their outrage and the panicked frenzy of their activity.

It was time for the Dorsaddi to attack, while the enemy was still in shock. They should be rushing the field now, pouring out of the Wadi Juba, bellowing their war cries. But glancing over his shoulder, Abramm saw they were in shock themselves. Shemm still stood in the archway, Japheth and Mephid beside him, gaping as stupidly at the Supreme Commander's corpse as were the priests, almost as if they expected it to reanimate.

Perhaps they did.

Abramm jerked back around with an awful premonition. Beltha'adi lay unmoving, but the sense of energy around the idol had increased, and the clouds overhead were definitely darkening. Small flashes of color whirled around the great, laughing head. The priests began to chant, their mouths moving like puppets, their voices rising and falling in rhythm, gaining tempo and volume. He felt the power building, like a distant swarm of bees, setting his nape hairs on end.

The clouds boiled closer, flickering with a roil of inner light—red, blue, and purple. The air grew cold and heavy. Fear eeled into his soul, and though he lifted the dagger he still held and stepped toward his fallen foe, he knew without Eidon's power he could do nothing.

And Eidon's power, it seemed, was not forthcoming.

The mists dropped even closer, swallowing the rims of the cliffs, almost black save for the lights at their midst. Tension crackled in the thick air, and the idol flashed with scarlet light. A loud crack resounded across the sand as a gout of mingled color shot from the idol's ugly grin into the open mouth of the dead Supreme Commander.

The sound of bees mounted, a loud droning that momentarily resolved into voices screaming their triumph. Abramm shuddered, imagining the lights that must be out in that dark sea of startled faces. His heart was pounding double time, his knees quivered, and still the Light did not return to him.

On the sand before him, the corpse twitched, and the crowd gasped.

The corpse twitched again, then heaved a great, gasping breath and sat up. Red fire blazed in its eyes and out of its mouth and nose, danced with less intensity in the multifarious wounds, which were already closing. The fiery gaze came round to focus on Abramm, grinning in a red leer that was the image of the statue not twenty feet away.

And still Abramm was left with only flesh. He backed a step, trying to hold down panic and confusion. Surely Eidon would not have done all he had done only to abandon him now.

"I told you flesh was not enough to stand against a god." The mouth moved, but as with the priests, it seemed to be worked by an invisible puppeteer. The voice seemed to come from the clouds and the ground and the stands, echoing and bouncing around him. "Nor is the power of the worthless god you serve."

The thing lurched unnaturally to its feet, stepped stiffly toward him. He saw its chest swell as it drew breath to attack—

And two feathered arrows buried themselves in its heart, one from either side, both blazing with white Terstan fire.

The creature lurched onward another step, then halted, arms spread, mouth open. A great bellow tore out of it as the red light was suffused with white, and the thing fell to its knees. The arrows blazed whiter and whiter, the power spreading out from each shaft, flowing over the body, driving out the red, and finally flashing in a blaze of such blinding intensity Abramm had to turn away.

When he opened his eyes again, fighting to focus past the starbursts clouding his vision, he found nothing left of the Supreme Commander but a black, smoking smudge on the sand.

Across the arena, he picked out Katahn—Beltha'adi's own heir—standing with a longbow in the noble's box. Shemm stood armed likewise in the archway, the two of them in line with each other, the smoking hole between them.

Abramm lifted the bloody dagger, drawing their attention to himself. "Let all here know," he cried, "that there *is* a god in Esurh! And he will not be mocked!"

At his back, the Dorsaddi burst into a savage collective scream and raced en masse across the canyon floor after their enemies.

Then, almost as if they were generated by the passion of the Dorsaddi attack, the winds swooped down the wadi.

# CHAPTER

# 43

The carnage was swift and shocking, for the Esurhites owed much in Dorsaddi eyes and were granted no quarter. It was a tide of death to all in gray tunics, leaving them cleaved and bloodied on the benches and the sandy arena and up the Wadi Mudra to the main Esurhite camp on the arriza. Others died downstream and in the temple and the treasury and the chieftain's palace. As the clouds withdrew to their normal altitude, Abramm saw men fighting on the rim and knew that the flanking force Shemm had sent out was doing its job.

Abramm himself had grown alarmingly weak, and the wound in his side pained him so deeply it was hard to think of anything else. He had fallen to his knees—he did not remember when—and was having difficulty making himself get up again when Katahn found him.

Abramm peered at him in bleary surprise. "What are you doing here?"

"I can't very well go back with the Brogai, can I?"

"The Dorsaddi may kill you."

"I'll leave that to Sheleft'Ai." He hauled Abramm to his feet. "Can you walk?"

"I think so."

They headed back toward the Wadi Juba, the wind whipping steadily stronger against their backs. The torches had long since been uprooted and blown away, and now other things rolled and skittered by—barrels, palm fronds, saddle blankets, tenting. Sand pelted their cheeks and stung their eyes, and their hair was torn from the knots on their necks to lash about their faces.

Then, as the first spattering squall of rain dwindled away, a violent gust slammed into them, and a thunderous boom shook the ground. Struggling upright, they turned to find the statue of Khrell shattered to rubble on the amphitheater's tiered benches.

Dorsaddi raced by them, heading for shelter, many supporting wounded comrades. They shouted things as they went past, but their words were lost in the wind. Finally, though, one came to take Abramm from the other side, and with his aid they quickly reached one of the openings along the wadi floor.

A sizable crowd had already gathered in the vaulted chamber beyond, and once again all eyes turned Abramm's way. There was a moment of awkwardness—on their parts as they realized they'd run past the Pretender in their haste to escape the storm, and on his because he didn't like admitting he'd needed their help. Now, without the wind to contend with, he shook off the arm of the new man, and suddenly Shemm stood before him. He eyed Abramm with concern and Katahn with distrust, though it was clear he recognized him from their encounter in the amphitheater.

"This was our informant," Abramm said, stepping away from the Gamer. "Katahn ul Manus. Show him your mark, my friend."

Katahn unfastened his tunic and bared his chest.

"Your former master?" Shemm asked.

Abramm nodded. "*And* cousin and heir to the great Beltha'adi. Which, I guess, makes him king of the Esurhites now, if they'll have him." He flashed a half smile at Katahn.

Shemm regarded Beltha'adi's heir intently, seeming to see things Abramm could not fathom. Then he nodded once and said to Katahn, "I will take him now."

"I can walk," Abramm insisted, pushing away from them both.

They swallowed their protests as he reeled slightly, then took hold of himself and strode through the rapidly growing crowd. The men's compliments and congratulations embarrassed him, knowing how little he deserved them, but he received them graciously nonetheless. He spied Cooper's pale face among them, staring at him as if he were not human, but he was too tired—and hurting too much—to do more than nod at the man.

Yearning for the privacy to collapse, he shuffled on, spoke another thank you . . . and sensed sudden movement behind him. Instinct whirled him faster than thought. Jerking the short sword from Shemm's scabbard as he came around, he deflected the length of steel now plunging toward him. It missed his ribs but sliced his side, and he staggered back, dizzy from his efforts, as the man was seized from all sides. If Abramm hadn't called a halt, his assailant would have died on the spot.

Drawing a breath to steady his legs, Abramm straightened, gesturing with his sword that the man be brought forward. He came head down, and recognition penetrated slowly. "Cooper?"

The old guardian raised his face, misery in his eyes, and fell to his knees. "I swore an oath to King Raynen, my lord." His voice was rough and so wracked with emotion it was barely understandable. "To kill you if we found you. I don't believe he thought we would. *I* didn't." He paused, drew a deep breath that was nearly a sob. "Kill me now, my lord, and end this for me. I beg you."

Abramm stared down at him, leaning heavily on Shemm now, so shocked and benumbed by the betrayal he could hardly think. And yet he must. He must think, must resolve this now, must order the man executed for his crime. Mustn't he?

For the first time since Beltha'adi's death, Eidon's Light rippled through him, clearing his mind, sending strength back to his wavering knees. He recalled the sober, scarred face, the dark gentle eyes—and the cancelled debt of his own affronts, far greater than any Cooper might commit against him.

*I do not deserve even to live,* he thought, *yet here I stand with victory and honor and protections upon protection. How can I punish a man bound by an ill-made oath? An oath he could not have avoided making had he wanted to?*

Moreover, Cooper could not have picked a worse moment to attack or executed it more ineptly.

Abramm swallowed on a raw throat and was shocked to find what an inhuman rasp his voice had become. "I'll not kill you, Felmen Cooper. You were only carrying out what you were sworn to do." He swallowed again, mastered the tremor that had crept into his words, and pitched his voice to carry and convince. "You have failed, and but for my mercy you would never have another chance. I count that full satisfaction of honor's demands. Moreover, Raynen is dead, so the oath would no longer bind you in any case."

Cooper looked up at him, horrified astonishment now mingling with his shame. "Dead, my lord?"

"So I understand." His voice was growing steadily hoarser, and he was beginning to shiver. *If you don't wrap this up soon,* he told himself, *you'll be flat on your face before all of them.*

He spoke to the Dorsaddi at Cooper's side. "Stand him up."

On his feet, Cooper stared at the floor again, seeming lost and bewildered.

"You've shown your sense of loyalty, at least," Abramm said. "I would hope henceforth you direct it toward those who are your friends."

And that was definitely enough. He limped on toward the curtained archway not far ahead now.

"That makes *you* king, my lord," Cooper said in a low voice.

Abramm turned yet again. His old guardian was staring at him with wide eyes and pale face. That look of worship had returned, and there was nothing subtle about it.

Other faces stared at him in surprise, as well.

"The third king," someone muttered.

And at once the words whispered through the gathering. "Shemm . . . Katahn . . . Abramm . . . three kings."

Thus another prophecy is fulfilled, Abramm thought wryly. *I wonder what Trap will say to this.*

*Trap! Is he even alive?*

Cooper suddenly stepped toward him, startling his Dorsaddi guards. Before they could catch him, he flung himself at Abramm's feet. "You have bought my life, Sire. Whatever you ask, I will do; whatever I have, it is yours; whenever you call, I will come."

Abramm gulped, staring at him in astonishment, the ancient words of fealty registering slowly. Light's Grace! Was Cooper swearing allegiance to *him*?

Abramm shook his head. "We are not in Kiriath, Cooper. And I am not a king here. I am just a man like you. Although I value your loyalty and your friendship more than I can say."

He tried again to leave, but again Cooper stopped him. "Sire, the mark on your chest—they say it is free for the asking."

"For those who wish to know Eidon."

"If it is him you serve, then I wish to know him."

Startled, Abramm glanced at Shemm. "How do you. . . ?"

"You just think it."

And as easy as that, Cooper took the blazing orb from where it floated in the air, and the golden shield bloomed upon his chest. It was hard to tell who was more astonished, the giver or the recipient.

After that, it all caught up with Abramm, and he remembered very little, except that he finally did collapse, despite all his efforts not to. The pain returned tenfold, making him gasp and shudder, and someone found the cut deep in his side. He heard curses of surprise and anguish, shouts for aid, and after a time, even Carissa's voice, high-pitched with hysteria. Then it all faded away, and he heard only the incessant howling of the wind.

It was still howling when he awoke, accompanied now by the smack and spatter of rain. At first he couldn't figure out what it was, so long had it been since he'd heard it. He also had no idea where he was—some upper room along the Wadi Juba, perhaps. The arched window across the chamber revealed the canyon's familiar red face, veiled now in driving lines of rain. The wind blew away from the archway, fortunately, though heavy woolen curtains framed it in readiness should conditions change.

As his mind slowly churned back to awareness, his hand slid across his chest, fingers tracing over scabs and tender stitched-up slits until they came at last to the shieldmark glittering over his breastbone. A thrill of wonder swept him. It really had happened, then.

Sighing, he took closer note of his surroundings. He lay on a feather mattress dressed in silk sheets and accompanied by the usual excess of pillows. Sheer draperies descended from the ceiling above him, roped back to the wall. A brazier of coals stood nearby, and beyond that Carissa lay asleep on a mattress of her own.

He raised himself on his elbows to see her better, grunting with the pain it caused the wound in his side—the only one that had been bandaged. She looked haggard, and her face was lined with grief. Had she come to terms with what he was now? Or was that part of her grief?

Not wanting her to know he had been watching her, he slumped back into the bed, then gave a groan and a big yawn and rolled onto his side as if he had just awakened. She jerked upright. Her blue eyes fixed upon him, wide with surprise. Then she bolted from the room.

Not the reaction he had hoped for.

With a sigh he pushed himself back to a sitting position. After the first wave of dizziness settled and the worst of his discomfort had passed, he began to think about how he might get up. He was still sitting there when Trap came in, followed by Katahn, and for several moments it was smiles all around as they congratulated one another for surviving. Then his visitors settled on the floor beside his mattress and brought him up-to-date. He had been unconscious and fevered for nearly a week, thanks to the festering wound in his side. During that time the rain had continued to fall, the wadis had turned into raging torrents, and Jarnek was closed down. The Esurhite army had been decimated, those not slain by the Dorsaddi having been washed away in the floods. A few, Trap said, were no doubt being harbored by the citizens of Jarnek, but for the most part the threat was gone.

"And your son?" Abramm asked Katahn. "Do you know if he survived?"

The Gamer shrugged. "In truth, I pray he did not. Yes, I know he does not wear the shield. But Beltha'adi's death will leave a hole in the Brogai hierarchy, and my son . . ."

"Is heir to the position," Abramm said.

Katahn nodded.

For a moment they all sat in silence, contemplating the repercussions of that reality. Then Trap said, "Well, I've learned one thing these last two years, and that's that you never know when a man will change his mind about the truth." His glance darted to the shield on Abramm's chest, and his grin returned. "I've stared at that thing for five days now, and I still can't believe you actually did it. And these tales I've been hearing about your great face-off with Beltha'adi—"

"It wasn't *my* face-off," Abramm interrupted. "It was Eidon's. All I did was watch."

Trap cocked a brow as his gaze slid over Abramm's bared and battered torso. "I'd say you did a little more than watch."

"I have never seen a man fight like he did," Katahn said gravely.

"Nor I," came a new voice from the doorway. King Shemm stood in the arch, smiling at him. "It is good to see you awake, my friend."

The other two scrambled to their feet, but when Abramm started to do likewise Shemm waved him down. "As king of Kiriath, are you not my equal?"

"I am not the king of Kiriath, Great One," Abramm said. "Nor am I ever likely to be."

"I have heard differently." Shemm settled on a pillow, waving the other men back down beside him. He fixed his dark eyes upon Abramm. "We always thought the three kings would be Dorsaddi. But Sheleft'Ai proves time and again that he will not be constrained by our narrow ways of thinking." He paused, still studying Abramm, then returned to the conversation his arrival had interrupted. "My friend, you fought as if the hand of Sheleft'Ai was on you."

"It was," Abramm said firmly. "I would never have succeeded otherwise."

"I believe you. But . . ." Shemm turned to Trap. "Did you not say one newly changed could not use the power?"

Trap cocked a brow at them, then turned to Abramm. "Conjure us a kelistar, my friend."

"A kelistar?"

Trap lifted a hand, and the familiar palm-sized orb floated at his fingertips.

Abramm frowned, looking from one to the other of them. He tried thinking of it, as he had done to produce the Star of Life for Cooper, but nothing happened. Finally he shook his head and shrugged. "I give up. What do I do?"

"I don't understand," Shemm said.

Trap laughed softly. "As you just pointed out, my friend, Sheleft'Ai is not bound by our beliefs of what he can and cannot do, what he will and will not do. Generally it is true that one cannot use the power without knowledge and practice. But that does not mean he cannot use *us*—any time and any way he wishes. In fact, I think sometimes he enjoys using those we least expect him to."

" 'He uses the simple to shame the wise,' " Abramm quoted.

"Exactly." Trap grinned. "So don't let it go to your head. I daresay it'll be a long time before you experience anything like that again—if ever."

After that there was a great deal of catching up to do, each man with his own part of the story to relate. Of course, the others were all familiar with their side of things, but none knew just how Abramm had been turned in his headlong flight from truth. It was in the telling of that story that he realized Carissa had not returned.

Not until the next day, when he insisted he was sufficiently mended to be up and walking—and proceeded to prove it—did he see her again, seated by one of the windows of the upper gallery along the Wadi Juba. She was staring at the rain, a look of unutterable sorrow on her face. He started toward her, but the moment she saw him, she leaped up and fled.

Trap told him later that she'd kept rigidly to herself since her arrival, speaking to no one save the king, and that only because she had to. Her sole confidant was her retainer, Cooper, likely because she did not know he, too, wore a shield, since he had kept his conversion to himself and continued wearing his tunic laced up.

Over the next few days Abramm tried to catch up with her, but she always evaded him. Finally he summoned Cooper in frustration, and the old guardian only confirmed—miserably—what was already obvious.

"She hates the world right now, Sire. And you, I'm afraid, most of all."

"But if she would just talk to me, I—"

"She won't." A bitter smile quirked his lips. "She's a Kalladorne, m'lord. And you know how stubborn *they* are."

Trap also counseled patience, and so Abramm let her alone. Fortunately he had much to occupy him. Being the hero of Jarnek—however reluctant—he found himself drawn into Dorsaddi life and culture as if they were his own. There was much to be done in preparation for consolidating their conquest of Jarnek once the rains stopped, and he had as much of a knack for directing large and complicated projects as for guerrilla maneuverings. His advice was constantly sought, his opinion solicited, his company courted. And when he wasn't busy with planning, he was practicing with sword or sling or longbow, or attending Trap's lectures on how to live in the power of Eidon's Light, or helping translate Katahn's copy of the Second Word into the Tahg.

He saw Carissa only now and then, and he tried to assure her by manner alone that he was open to her approach, but she was well and truly a Kalladorne when it came to stubbornness, and she did not seek him out.

Six weeks after the rains started, the clouds rolled away, leaving a vault of blue sky arcing over a land laced with streamlets and waterfalls. As the floodwaters receded, Jarnek opened its doors and the people emerged, reveling in the fresh air and glorious light.

Abramm was hard at sword practice with Trap one morning when he noticed Carissa standing at the back of the ring of spectators that always gathered to watch them. As usual, he pretended not to notice and finished the workout as if nothing had changed. Afterward, wiping away the sweat as he mingled with the onlookers, he made his way casually in her direction. For once she held her ground, looking up at him expressionlessly when he stopped in front of her. Her face had grown thinner, older looking.

"You are very good, brother," she said softly.

"Thank you."

"Maybe as good as Gillard." Her eyes caught on his mark and flinched away.

Someone whistled low to him, and when he looked, Trap tossed him a linen tunic.

"But of course, you don't really care, do you?" she said as he shrugged into it.

"Care?"

"About Gillard."

He pulled the tunic down around his hips. "No. I guess I don't."

Her lips made a moue of distaste, and she studied the room behind him, letting the silence stretch out uncomfortably. Finally she drew a breath and said firmly, "I've come to say good-bye."

"Good-bye?"

"The roads opened yesterday. I leave in half an hour."

"I see." He wiped his face again where new sweat had beaded, stealing sidelong glimpses of her. "Where will you go?"

"Thilos, I think."

"And then?"

"I don't know yet." She stared across the empty room and fiddled absently with the rings on her fingers.

"You don't have to do this," he murmured.

"Yes. I do." She stilled her hands and let them fall to her sides. "I don't belong here."

"You could."

"I don't *want* to! I hate this place. I hate the land, the culture, the people . . ."

"These people have been nothing but kind to you since the day you arrived."

"Only because they hope one day to convert me! I can feel it in their eyes, the way they look at me."

"Carissa, half of them don't even wear shields."

She folded her arms and frowned at the floor. Then shrugged. "It's what you want, though, isn't it? For me to join you?"

He couldn't deny it.

"Well, I can't, Abramm." And now, finally, she met his gaze. "And because of that there's a huge wall grown up between us. A big, bright, golden wall shaped like a shield. A wall I will never break through!" She fell silent. Then wiped her eyes and looked away. "I feel like I've lost you as surely as if you'd died."

"Carissa, you haven't lost me at all. Nothing has changed."

"Everything has changed! It's all you talk about. It's all you think about. It's all you live for."

"That's not true."

"Then, come home with me."

He frowned at her.

"See? You're enslaved as surely as you ever were."

There was nothing he could say to that, and finally he sighed. "What would be the purpose of my going? Gillard is king now, and he'll not give that up without a fight. Not to me. People would die, and for what? I have no desire to rule. I am happy here."

She looked at him long and hard, then turned away and wrapped her arms about herself. "Well, I am not. I don't belong here, and I don't believe you do, either, but it's plain you're never going to see that. So I am going. Good-bye, Abramm."

And before he could say another word, she walked away.

He and Trap went up to the cliff top to watch her leave, the camels snaking alongside the stream, now gleaming in the wash at the base of the cliffs. The sky was very blue, the sun so bright they had to squint, and a hot breeze ruffled their headcloths and beards.

"You were like her once," Trap said presently. "Not so long ago it seems to me."

"But she doesn't even want to listen."

"Did you?"

"More than her, surely."

"Less, I'd say."

The head of the caravan was nearly across the arizza now. He could still pick out his sister, swathed from head to toe in gray and covered by a blue shade with gold fringe. Cooper rode behind her, wrapped in pale Dorsaddi russet, oathbound, as he'd been nearly all his adult life, to keep her safe.

Abramm loosed a long, regretful sigh. "I shouldn't have let her go."

"She must make her choice before him just as you have, my friend. And you must give her the freedom to do so."

"But—"

"Do you think he will pursue her with any less vigor than he did you?"

*No. Of course not.* Squinting out across the arizza, Abramm watched the caravan move into the narrow opening of the wadi that would lead them up out of the SaHal.

"It's frustrating, isn't it?" he said after a time. "Knowing the truth but being helpless to make others see it."

"Yes." Hand raised to shield his eyes, Trap, too, watched as the last of the camels disappeared. Then he turned to Abramm with an ironic smile. "Sometimes, though, they surprise you in the end."